# DRAGONFLY

## ALSO BY SYLVIA KELSO

*Amberlight*
*Riversend*
*Source*

# DRAGONFLY

## SYLVIA KELSO

WILDSIDE PRESS

## Dedication

*In memory of my parents*

## Acknowledgements

*Many more thanks to the ever-patient Carla Coupe, a model among editors, and to Chris Howard for matching patience over the cover art.*

Published by Wildside Press LLC.
www.wildsidepress.com

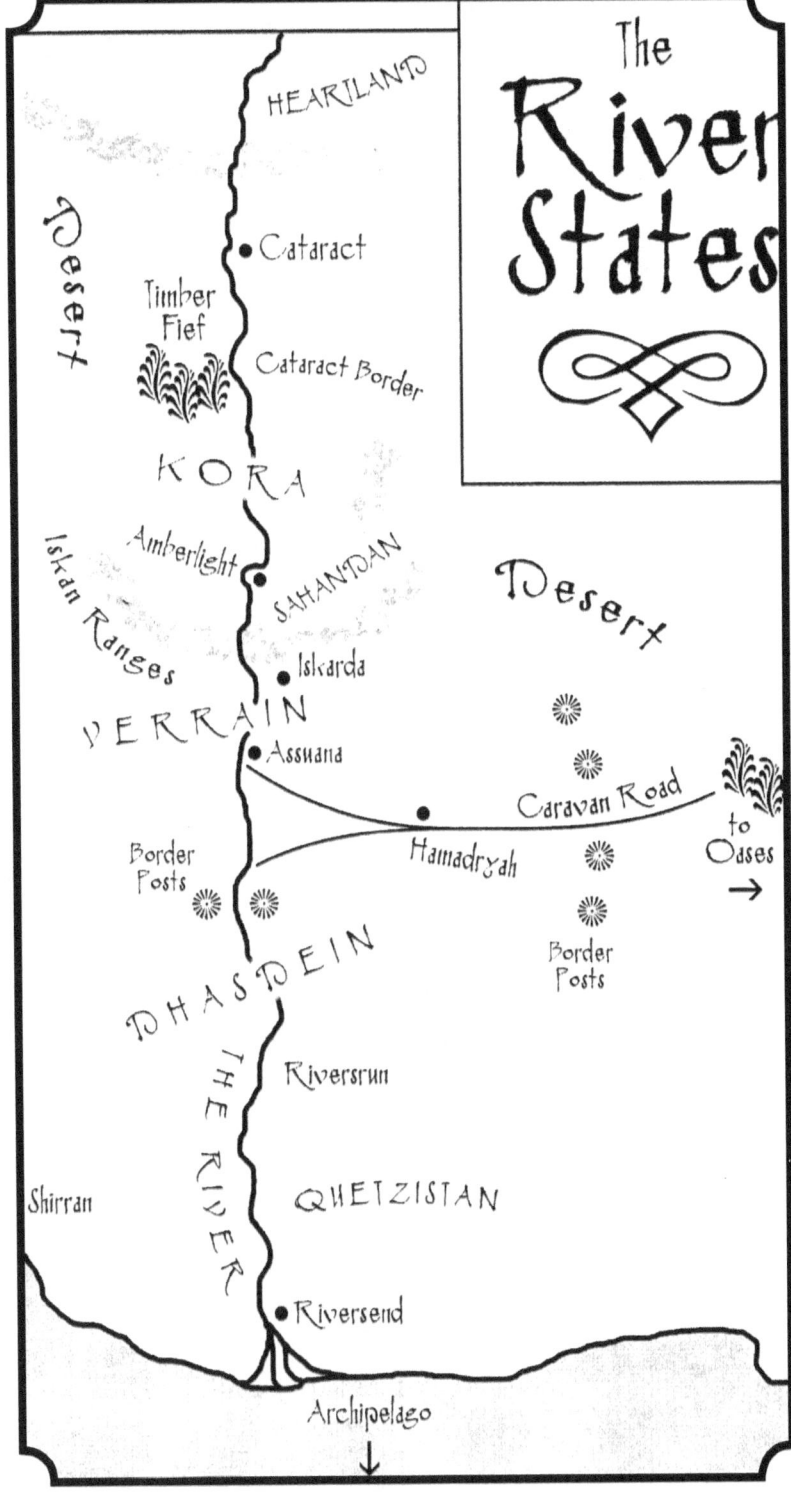

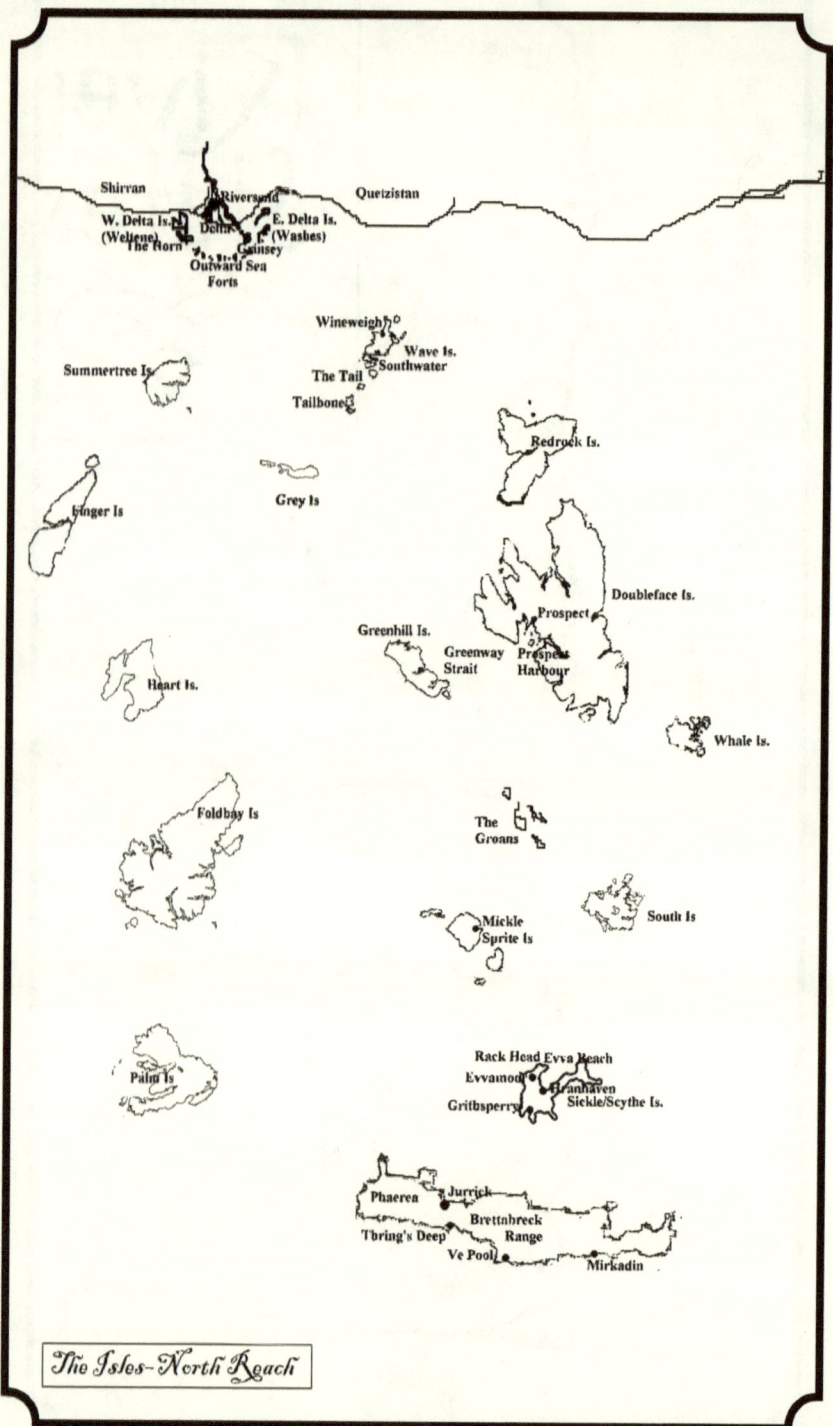

Shirran

Riversend

Quetzistan

W. Delta Is.
(Weltene)
The Horn
Delta
Gunsey
E. Delta Is.
(Washes)

Outward Sea
Forts

Wineweigh

Wave Is.
Southwater

Summertree Is

The Tail

Tailbone

Redrock Is.

Finger Is

Grey Is

Doubleface Is.

Prospect

Greenhill Is.

Greenway
Strait

Prospect
Harbour

Heart Is.

Whale Is.

Foldbay Is

The
Groans

Mickle
Sprite Is

South Is

Palm Is

Rack Head Evva Beach

Evvamod

Branhaven

Gritbsperry

Sickle/Scythe Is.

Jurrick

Phaerea

Brettabreck
Range

Thring's Deep

Ve Pool

Mirkadin

*The Isles–North Reach*

Inganess

Terrace Is

Eithay

Rostack Is

Fleshes

Yinstey

Mulen

Sandouin Is

Skall Is

Gildair

Hellir
Straits

Cuwen Is

Hamair Is

Burayn

Muirwick

Muickhond Cape

Hostack Cape

The Strand

Fursvar

Suli

Furshead

Rangar

Hivell
Straits

Hivell Is.

Hvalwrast
Reach

Haugar Cape

Sticklefing Cape

Hringstenn

Handelond

Kaastria Is

Bakki Cape

Kaldr Is

The Isles- South Reach

# CHAPTER I

His nickname is woven through my life's oldest memories. Yet when the crown prince of Dhasdein first crossed our path in the flesh, by human time I was already twelve years old.

I say human time, though Two grows impatient with such words as "years" and "human," especially where we are concerned. Small wonder, since my mother estimates Two's memory runs for seven centuries and more, back to the founding of the oldest House of Amberlight. But I need human terms to measure space and interval, to divide Two's memories from those of my own flesh and blood. And even before we could speak aloud, the recollections of this flesh involve that name.

It comes first in a rare snippet from within my cradle: my mother's quick, slightly burred Uphill Amberlight accent, its vibrations familiar from the womb. ". . . more to a prince than that?" My father Alkhes' plosive consonants, clinching home the broad Quetzistani "a":

"Prince? The man's a blighted dragonfly!"

When I was old enough to place the word, Two gave me an image to match: insects like jewelled daggerettes darting, hovering above water, glittering scarlet, glistening lapis lazuli, and the gauze shimmer of their wings. So for our first five years in human time, Dhasdein to me remained some fabulous insect empire, ruled by the most glorious flying creatures of them all.

I tried to explain that to my father Sarth, when in human time I was just three. Learning to speak, my word-hoard already a prodigy, though Two understood far more than I. So she had pushed us into the council room after that mirror-signal came: double urgent, passed up from the River at Marbleport, triggering a full council, Telluir House and Iskarda village both.

The council-room latch was beyond my reach, but Zuri, Trouble-head and hence perpetually belated, was the last person in. I ducked between her shin and the swinging door and she grunted as she mis-stepped clear of me. Catching the back of my smock, she grunted again as Two sparked at her, however mildly. Then she scanned the table, scooped up and dropped me in my father Sarth's lap, growling, "Take care of this."

Twisting in his arm, trampling for balance on his thigh's familiar warm solidity, I got upright enough to see over the table edge.

At its head my mother was just ready to speak: high-boned Amberlight nose leveled, brandy-brown eyes narrowed, rampant curls escaping a Crafter's single plait. Opposite us sat my father Alkhes, that wing of silky black hair such an anomaly among the brown, crinkle-curly heads of native Amberlight, but his green and brown gear a match for the cloth under my feet. Like the enduring, so-slight tension that spoke from them both, warning, troublecrew: alert, war, danger. Off-duty or not.

Troublecrew extraordinary, Zuri slid in beside Sarth. Under the table, their knees brushed. I knew they were both part of my mother's consort, if I could not yet understand more. He must have passed some eye-message, though, because my father Alkhes rolled his own eyes half-up. *Let be.* And turned his attention, as my mother drew open the signalers' scroll and began to read.

Two can reclaim her words intact. I scanned reactions, which I was just learning to decode. Next down-table were the Craft-heads and specialists: I read uncertainty there, impatience over postponed work. Beyond them sat the village folk: Zdana, the Mother's Ear. The village Head, Darthis.

Zdana was mute. Darthis, monumental as a boulder, sat stiff enough to emulate one. My father Sarth's knee was rigid under my foot, my father Alkhes' stillness had tightened till my belly squirmed. Through them all ran a deeper thread of what I recognise now as fear. Familiar fear.

My mother let the scroll run shut. I looked to the twin bastions of Iatha and Hanni, posted at her elbows. House-steward and Head's aide. I still classified them by look and smell: Iatha's salt-grizzled plait and raw cheekbones, Hanni's prim expression and scent of records and ink. But it was Hayras, the shapers' Craft-head, who grumbled, "They never learn."

I could already interpret Zuri's suppressed twitch as an irritable, *What did you expect?* Crisp with her own irritation, Iatha finished the familiar exchange.

"It's Dhasdein."

Hanni tightened her lips. My mother nudged the scroll with a fingertip.

"The Empire's respect for allies, affirmed. Patience, certainly required, the cause understood. But surely, for imperial convenience, we could fulfil our promise—could offer just one small prophecy? After three whole years?"

The whole table growled. Exasperation, protectiveness, wrath. My father Alkhes fairly spat the verbal version. "She's too young!"

The rest exploded then. Outrage, details, suggestions cracked together like burning sticks while with her council craft my mother let them burn the upset out. Until my father Sarth spoke, that pure Tower accent and effortless projection overriding everyone.

"Signed by the Empress?"

Everybody stopped. The eyes all turned. Surprise, spinning sharply to respect.

I had seen my mother's tiny, almost wry smile before, as I would see it over and over again after. The salute of a duellist, to a master in the art.

She said, "Signed by the crown prince."

The uproar burst again. Sentence shards slapped over me, bearing atop them Ahio the shaper's outraged bawl. "—make *him* her hatchet-man!"

A couple of people laughed. My father Alkhes did not. And before my father Sarth spoke, his belly muscles had clenched in a way I already recognised.

"The Crown Prince Therkon was famed as a wastrel and a libertine. In his father's day, shrewd camouflage. His mother weighs him better. Nor does she fear to give that worth its use."

The pause this time was sharp as fear. Ahio, scarred and inured to risk from a lifetime of working qherrique, finally spelt the menace out.

"So the Empress passes him her message. Both messages. This time, word from the hatchet-swinger. Next time, phalanx troops?"

Even my father Sarth twitched. My mother held Ahio's stare, and answered distinctly as chisel strokes on a block.

"Unless we find a way to hold them off."

Zuri stiffened. Iatha glared. In her outrage Ahio actually spat as far as the brazier.

"What, run like a pack of Craftless hill-rats? Bow and scrape to that primping dragonfly!"

The uproar burst again and this time I did not heed. My three year old human brain fought Two for domination, clawed back the memory of my father Alkhes' words above my cradle, Two's image—I tugged my father Sarth's arm to bring his ear down and spluttered into it, "Wings?"

"What, dearling?" He did lean closer, his arm curving tight in a way Two would suffer from no-one else. "Wings? What wings?"

"He. Him."—"Crown prince" was too much for my tongue, but the image had reached Two now and it excited us both. Projections shot through my head, humans walking on two ordinary feet, then humans with wings spread behind them, the brilliant gauze of the air-borne insect, vibrating, expanding, huge—"He have wings?"

"He—Therkon?" He was too surprised to use the title, even though he caught my drift. "No, he—Chaeris, why do you ask?"

My father Sarth had been the Mother's Ear: a man, yet the Mother's chosen hearer, speaker for the reborn qherrique, core of all our lives. No-one else would draw so swiftly to the matter's heart. But before I could wrestle the rest into words my mother's voice clove its own way through the noise.

"S'hurre . . ." Craft-folk. An honorary title, since half the council had no Craft at all. "In whosever name, Dhasdein has sent their usual question. And we have nothing but the usual reply. Prophecies were promised the River, yes. But we have planted the seed that once spoke to us. If it grows, it no longer replies. And," she glanced once at me, swiftly, but the love in that look was edged and deadly as a sword, "the other voice, that *may* give answers, will do so in its proper time."

Then her eyes flicked sidelong. "Sarth," she said, "I'll need some—polite—threat."

\* \* \* \*

It chagrins Two excessively that, without unearthing that letter from the archives, we cannot tell what they actually wrote. Two can retrieve anything in that seven-hundred year span before my birth, but once I began to live—Two claims it was in the womb, somewhere during my ninth month—we can recall only what has happened, or been recounted, before my own eyes and ears.

We did see the next message arrive, first of anyone in Iskarda. At five years old in human time, I could read mirror-signal flashes, and after that Two could no longer suffer second or third-hand information. In my sixth winter, we asked to join the signal watch.

"I *have* a fur jacket, like they do." I spread both arms to display the thickness of sheephide, the wolf-fur hood trim. Our current pride and joy. My father Sarth had made it that autumn. "We'll be as warm as the others. And I can read the signals, Ma, you know I can, we can! We need to have the news first. We need to know!"

My mother's eyes turned to Iatha, silent behind me in the House-head's bedroom door. Over my head I read the half-laugh, half-dismay, the exchange of meaning fleet with years of shared experience. "Oh, burn it!" she said.

Iatha stepped over the threshold. She rarely entered this room, where I had cornered my mother with her boots not yet laced, amid the tangle of bed quilts, the dense mix of her and my fathers' body-scents that spelt most deeply, Home. But before she spoke my father Alkhes appeared from the jungle of coat and clothes-stands at the bed-end, and said abruptly, "Call a meet with Derinno." The signal-roster Head. He glanced at me, sharper than a blade. "If Chaeris can read the signals—so."

My mother's brows flew up and down again. I could almost catch the smothered maternal protests, the stern acceptance of a future woman's right. The knowledge, passed yet again between them, that the usual children's rules did not, must not apply to me. And then the slight, wicked warning of a parry stroke.

"And if she proves herself? Who wards her on watch? It's no load to put on signallers."

He tossed his head back. Black silk flew in a way I had known since my eyes would focus. "I'll do it," he said.

So we were out on the mountain-side in the wake of the last snowfall, my father Alkhes yet again stealing time from his own troublecrew round to shepherd us to the watch-station, its broad-based stone cairn and platform spatched with snow-melt, all four of us muffled to the eyebrows against the skinning-knife wind that swept round the quarry-gate. We were staring into the mist and snow-mud dappled lowland distance when the next mirror began to blink. Two must have decoded it even faster than Latsa, the actual signaller.

"Courier on road. Sealed message scroll." Then the coded sequence that meant: Dhasdein.

I saw the courier ride up, too, equally muffled on her sweating mule. And disappear round the quarry corner, while we stormed and cried and pleaded, and my father Alkhes stood at the platform ladder-head, repeating evenly, "You are on watch. You cannot leave, for whatever matter. You chose this work. This is your duty, Chaeris."

Two was sparking white at my fingertips, we had to know the message, I may have screamed that before we leapt at him. We both see that moment yet: the grey scrim of snow and mud and mist and my father against it, immoveable as a quarry block. Black hair flying, black eyes unwavering. He knew what we were. He knew what might happen. And whatever befell, he would not move.

So I heard the message only hours later, third-hand, fourth-hand, after the watch finally drew to a close. And I would need records to tell what excuse or threat they found to ward off Dhasdein that time, too. Because that was my week on roster, and again, we were on watch when the council met.

\* \* \* \*

In my seventh year the message again came up from Marbleport, this time bringing its own imperial courier. I saw him pass, jewels and parade armour flashing, on his tall bay horse. At the plough-handles Ahio's daughter Fira snorted, "Freighted the poxy beast upRiver with him, just to make a show!" Before she caught me with one foot across the furrow. "Get back and stir that team, Chaeris!"

Like me, she was doing her duty in the spring fields, but I knew better than to argue. Like her mother, she was by Craft a shaper. Forget tantrums. She would not have been impressed by sparks from naked qherrique.

I saw the horse in the House stable, though all Two's pleas and imprecations could not bring me within the rider's range. "No," my mother answered flatly, when we besought her outside the council-room. "You don't go near him." And called Ahio and Verrith, veteran troublecrew, to see her veto fulfilled.

We did glimpse the message satchel, gaudy with diplomatic seals of passage: from the closest downRiver border post with Verrain, from the further border post with Shirran, and even, Hanni eventually told me, from southernmost Mel'eth. And we garnered a snatch of conversation, my mother and Iatha striding into the communal kitchen. Shia, Head's cook even in Amberlight, had exercised her magic to keep yet another over-due dinner palatable.

"Tez thinks not," Iatha had grunted. My mother, staring straight ahead as she did in crisis-thought, grunted too.

"Tanekhet's uncertain. So's Asaskian."

Tez was my half-sister. House-heir, in charge down at Marble-port, our bridgehead for the marble on whose sale Iskarda lived. Tanekhet and Asaskian were part of her consort, as I had known since I was three. But for all my coaxing, neither my mother nor my fathers, nor Iatha, would let slip the uncertainty's source.

* * * *

In my tenth year I saw neither message nor messenger. Like all House and village girls, by then I had worked with the plough-teams and the slingshots to protect sown seeds and ripening grain, had harvested plums and helped brew beer, and gathered roses for Midsummer festival. I had been taken hunting to learn the hills, and practiced painting tally-marks on a quarry block, and as a House child I would be tested, one day, for Craft. But though I still stood signal-watch, my new prenticeship was a gulf away from them all.

"Not a place for children, no." A very small meeting, that one, just my mother, my fathers, Zuri, and me. "But Alkhes and I," my father Sarth, using his blankest council-voice, "think it would be for the best."

My mother's eyes flew from one to the other and back. "Chae-ris?" The end of the word rose. "In the troublecrew?"

"Only to learn," my father Alkhes said. "Yet."

My mother stared. And bit her lip.

"The other children . . ."

"Chaeris is already a hand taller, Tellurith." My father Sarth said it without expression. He did not have to add, *Chaeris has never truly been one of them. Even before this.*

My mother looked at him in turn. Not a House-Head's look. A woman's, at a trusted intimate proposing a change she has nei-ther foreseen nor likes. A mother's, finding her daughter ready to take another, momentous step beyond the baby, the infant, that was hers most of all. To her, not so much an advance to maturity as another degree of loss.

She turned to Zuri. Between them, too, questions seldom needed words.

And Zuri looked back with her rain-grey, rain-cold trouble-crew eyes and said, "We can ward Chaeris anywhere in Iskarda. Possibly we could do it outside. But the best guards can fail. Bet-ter if she learns to ward herself."

Almost invisibly, my mother flinched. All of us knew what Two and I were, not only to her or to my fathers, but to the House, to Iskarda. To the River and its restive states, Verrain, Cataract, Amberlight. To that fire below the horizon, the brooding presence of Dhasdein.

Even I could have voiced the addendum. We all knew what it would mean, if some raider, some kidnapper, managed to find me alone.

"Chaeris has wards." My mother spoke slowly, again voicing what we all knew.

Zuri returned, unflinching, "Not wards she can trust."

*Two and I are trying to be good! We haven't had accidents this last twelvemonth! There's no call for people to look at us the way they do!*

I had no chance to shout any of it. My mother and Zuri had locked eyes as on a practice floor. Then she shot at Zuri, "You think you can train her? Troublecrew? My troublecrew—!"

"We think we can train her," my father Sarth said. "Alkhes and I."

My mother whipped round. A cutting, shaming revelation, that even she doubted our control so deeply she would count me and Two a risk to her troublecrew, not the other way round. Her expression now made me want to hide under the council table as I had done in toddlerhood.

My father Sarth stood up. "I think," he said softly, in that pure Tower accent, "that if anyone in Iskarda could meet Chaeris on the fighting-floor, and trust her and Two to keep control—even in losing—it would be us." He glanced at my father Alkhes. And then he turned to me.

"So, daughter. What do *you* think?"

There had been a great deal to assimilate, not all palatable. But now I had to swallow: at the prior pains, at this newer, fearful joy. "We—yes, Da. We would like to train with you. To learn to— manage ourselves. And we would never—never—do you harm."

None of us needed to mention the lawless past when, however unintentionally, that had not been so.

* * * *

The new roster brought risks and chances at which, in hindsight, I quail as my mother and Zuri must have. But beside troublecrew war-work, tactics, weapons, the more perilous fighting hand-to-hand, came the extra dimension: learning to bring our impulses, that my father Sarth said might go right back to the Amberlight qherrique, under more than haphazard control.

So we were on the practice floor, deep in a loose-form hand-to-hand bout, when Zuri's second blew past what was ordinarily the dining-room door, calling, "Hanni! Where's the Head? Signal just sighted. From Dhasdein!"

I missed a check. My father Sarth pulled the blow that would have sent me head over heels. We stuck as if the instructor had called time, frozen in mid-move. As in a bout, his eyes held mine, but I saw their expression change.

Then, as coolly, as evenly, as my father Alkhes atop the signal-platform, he said, "Take stance, Chaeris."

Two rose in frenzy behind my eyes: *It's a message, it's news, it's vital, we must know!* I thrust the panic down like another assailant. We were prenticed, admitted where no other child and almost no adult could go. More than that, we were trusted: to have learnt that lesson from the signal-station. Not to need it again.

I said, "Guard," and pushed Two from my awareness, as I could do only in the furious intensity of fighting hand-to-hand.

Later, I heard the message contents, no more than a variation on the other velvet demands. At three, at five, at ten years in human time, they had been the same. But in my twelfth human year, everything changed.

* * * *

"I have to go." My mother had Iatha by both hands, halted just outside the council-room. Her unheard-of exit in mid-meeting had brought Two and me out right on their heels. "Errisal wouldn't—Errisal would never ask—! Not for us. Not till the absolute last—Yath, you know—!"

Iatha produced her dour, wordless grunt. They seldom used names, let alone touched. Superfluous, when they had been closer than sisters since before the fall of Amberlight.

"I wouldn't leave for anything else!"

The tone brought Two hackling toward sparks. Iatha glanced inside, where the messenger still sat puffing on a chair. A copper-dark Heartlander, sweating in his sailor's clothes. He had run with the summons, physically, all the way from the River, uphill to Iskarda.

"They pulled double-oar down from Cataract—it came post through the Heartlands—" she actually wrung Iatha's hands. "It left Forest-landing a whole moon past." She almost hurled Iatha's hands away and took four charging paces down the passageway. "We'll be longer getting that far, and who knows what's happened since? Yath, it's *Thilliansar*!"

"Ah." Iatha growled it in her throat. "The Source."

My mother whirled to speak, and stopped. Her eye had caught me and I knew already that neither she nor Iatha would let slip more. The Source, the River's head, lay somewhere beyond the Heartlands, and somewhere up there was a mystery to do with my mother's beloved partner, Errisal. Her image fascinated Two, because they were like mirror pictures, down to the speech, the mannerisms, the walk. I tried to look harmless and incurious, lest my mother banish me altogether. But my feelings must have been plain as hers.

She yanked in another huge breath and opened her mouth as if to dive underwater. Let it out, and came to take me in her arms.

"Dearling. Chaeris. It will be all right."

She stopped with a jerk and behind her I saw my father Alkhes stop too, mid-stride halfway up the passage, with an armful of travelling gear.

"Iatha will be here. And Eria's been village Head two years now. Duitho will lead the troublecrew—you know Duitho, you've trained with her. Tez will come from Marbleport. Your cousins will be here—"

She broke off in mid-breath. We looked in each other's eyes. Then she shut hers a moment, and leant her forehead against mine.

"Yes. Both your fathers have to come with me. And Zuri. And Varris, too. She's Alkhes' laf. You know what that means." Two had told me long since. A Heartland warrior, pledged to an older, honoured, worshipped fighter, and pledged to more than war. Varris would not stay behind and live.

"And . . . the others, yes. Not Azo, this time," veteran trouble-crew, she would stay to bolster Duitho, "but Ahio and Keraz and Quiran and the ship-women from Marbleport. I—we'll need them all. Everyone who's been—who knows the River that far."

In case, Two translated far too fast and knowledgeably for comfort, of losses on the way. A better chance some might still reach wherever it was, to offer what help the remnant had left.

"Ah, dearling, it cleaves me to leave you too." She folded me more than tight. I felt the sob heave in her own breast. "The first time we've ever—and for such a cause—and for however long—"

I hugged her back with tears burning my throat. When my eyes lifted my father Sarth had come to stand by my father Alkhes. In both their faces I read, clearer than in my mother's smothered voice, the true depth of this farewell.

We had not parted in my life's length. As soon expect the sun not to rise next day. I opened my mouth to bawl like a truly human twelve year old, *You can't leave me!* And Two spoke instead.

"*We have to go with you. We have to see.*"

My mother pulled her head back, more in consternation than surprise.

"Oh! No, no—" She caught herself. And me as well, tightly in her arms. "*No*, Chaeris, dearling, I know you and Two want to learn things, have to learn things, but—"

"*We must go! It's the Source!*"

"I know, I know what it means to Two, but no! The road—Mother shield us, it's too far, too dangerous. And we're known, remembered, if anyone realised who you were . . ."

I had never seen my mother panic in my life. But my father Sarth was there already, his arm drawing us both in, that deep voice saying, over-quietly, "Chaeris, you know who—and what—you are."

And I did know. I had been twelve years learning what I had felt, however unclearly, that day in my cradle when I first heard the name Dragonfly.

"Da." I leaned against him and tried to swallow the tears. Tried to behave as that voice asked of me. As a woman. As a woman of more than Craft. As the cynosure of Iskarda, and the hope of the River. And the blood, the all-enduring, ever-enduring blood of Amberlight.

"I know it's r-risky. It's just that Two . . ."

"We will come back." He spoke so quietly, it was more than statement, or even promise. "When we do, everything we know, we will tell you. Or show you. Everything."

I understood what he meant. And that he understood what it meant to us. For Two, above all.

I looked up the now shortening way to his face, those statue's bones, the perfectly set topaz eyes. Amberlight breeds beauties, women or men, but my father Sarth had been notable, even in Amberlight. I sniffled, because I could not help myself, then reached out to lightly tug the end of the troublecrew braid, bronze-dark highlit with copper, and the occasional thread of silver now, falling over his breast.

His hand covered mine. "Troth-word, yes." We had used the touch that way before I could walk. And from somewhere, for me, he found a smile.

"Oh, Da . . ."

I think we all wept a little then, the four of us with our arms round each other, there in the middle of the passageway. Before they had to hurry off, with more than usual Head or troublecrew's haste, to haul out their old travelling gear and begin assembling provisions and plans.

And not two days after, I stood by Iatha in the market-place, and worked to bite the tears down, to keep a seemly face, that would become the centre-post of Iskarda, as we waved goodbye. As we watched them ride away.

* * * *

"It has, of course, been just a matter of time."

Tez's oldest partner turned the latest parchment on the council-table with one delicately fastidious fingernail. Both Two and I knew, now, the serpent and thunderbolt blazon on that broken seal.

"To be sure," Iatha snapped. "Just a matter of time. But why in the Mother's name did it have to happen now?"

Without raising his head, Tanekhet lifted his eyes to her. Forest-green eyes, half-hooded, detached and ironic as they had been in the length of Two's memories, as well as mine.

"One would hardly suspect Therkon—or the Empress—of lacking intelligence."

"Of course they know how often you clean your fingernails!" Iatha slammed a palm down so hard the winecups jumped. "But to come so blighted pat: Tellurith barely gone a three-quarter-moon . . . Mother aid us, after *that* message, they'll be upRiver of Amberlight already, and what hope have we of warning her, let alone bringing back—"

She stopped short. Her eyes slitted. When she spoke, it came out softer than a hiss.

"Do you mean—?"

Tanekhet held up both palms, acerbically calm. "If you people could avoid jumping to conclusions quite so fast . . ."

Tez leant forward in my mother's chair and said across him, "You mean, that Dhasdein didn't just have good enough intelligence to write so soon? Or to know my mother would leave? Or when? You think they engineered the summons?" A dagger pause. "Or its cause?"

Iatha literally snarled. Tez looked at Tanekhet as my mother had used to look at Sarth. Near, dear, and for wisdom an unfailing resource.

Tanekhet shut his hand over the parchment. The seconds trickled like coins falling in a balance pan. I forgot the ache in human memory that at every corner still listened for my father Sarth, that looked at every voice for my mother or my father Alkhes to charge through the outer doorway, dusted with snow or marble-grime. I forgot even the pang of watching Tez assume her post as Regent, not half a moon ago, installing her whole consort and their three children in our big, empty house.

Two was trying to run projections, pulling memories of Tanekhet in similar situations, when his judgement had decided nations' fates, recollections that he had once been Suzerain of Riversrun, the Imperial heart-province. Not simply Tez's partner, my foster-father, but the real master of Dhasdein.

"No." He let the word out on a long, judicious breath. "It is not—plausible—that Dhasdein, even at its height, could—arrange matters—anywhere—upstream from Cataract."

And, Two had told me, he had been chief intelligencer at Dhasdein's height. If anyone could say that with confidence, it would be Tanekhet.

I said, "So they just have very good intelligence."

We had been admitted to councils in my eleventh human year, after troublecrew training proved itself. Until this year, I had rarely ventured to speak. Now Iatha gave me her accustomed snort. Tanekhet did me the honour not to smile as to an outsider or a child. His other partner Asaskian said, "And a cutter's eye."

Meaning, as good a sense for the critical moment as a cutter would once have had, to establish rapport, and then lay blade to a mother-face of the qherrique.

Tanekhet sat back, not bothering to smooth his sleeve after the minimal shrug that retorted, *Yes.*

"It is certainly the optimal moment. Tellurith and her consort, down to the estimable Zuri, gone beyond recall. A new, if not, ah, lesser, party just installed at Iskarda."

"You mean," Tez said without heat, "an untried Heir."

Tanekhet inclined his own head. He would not demean her, either, with pretty lies.

"And," Asaskian said, "Chaeris is twelve years old."

So long as I remember Asaskian has been the unchallenged beauty of Iskarda. Slender as a palm tree, beautiful in face and feature as her cloud of waving bronze hair, elegant in demeanour as an old Amberlight House-head. When she lost an arm in the Dhasdein raid, it did not spoil her looks. Or her wits.

"She's only *twelve!*" Iatha cried.

Nobody bothered to reply. Twelve years was already a very long time to stave off an empire seeking such a promise's fulfilment. As

Tanekhet said, the end of Dhasdein's patience had been only a matter of time.

"What in the Mother's name do they think she can tell them? 'Rith told me. I've *seen* it. Even the seed couldn't say straight out, This will happen, or that! Do they imagine she'll be any better, blight and blast their eyes!"

The lift of Tanekhet's brow supplied the retort. They don't have to imagine, and they don't care. If it's never been done before, if it damages the vessel, the oracle, what matter? They only want results.

"As this says." He did not have to touch the parchment again. Or modulate the faint acidity in his voice. "The crown prince expects to land in Marbleport by second quarter of next moon. He is leading an embassy, for which he wishes safe conduct to Iskarda, where he hopes to 'consult'." The curl of his lip highlit the euphemism. "For an 'embassy' he will naturally bring an escort. Five or six pentarchies of phalanx troops."

Iatha spurted profanity like an over-boiled pot. Tez looked down the table and said, "Duitho, how many troublecrew do you have?"

Duitho's cheekbones still bore the faintest hint of a blush. Nobody need do more than lament Zuri's absence to drive home its consequence: a young, untried Trouble-head, left, perforce, in the hope she need only keep a watching brief in Iskarda.

"Azo's here," she said. "And Verrith."

Tez had been Amberlight Navy. In crisis she still sounded inscrutable as an officer.

"And?"

Duitho's neck stiffened. "With me—five more."

"And no light-guns."

Duitho was troublecrew. She did not bite her lip, still less burst out, *None of the younger crew have light-guns, those came from Amberlight, they're dedicated to one person. We can't—yet—make any more!*

Seven troublecrew and a village or so, a couple of Crafters with cutters they used to quarry marble. Against two or three hundred heavy-armed phalanx troops.

"*We can do,*" Two said, "*what you did before.*"

Tanekhet's eyes whipped round. He had known me before I left the womb, he had heard Two speak as soon as I could manage words. He knew the speaker now.

"'Before'?" Then Tez's brows snapped up. She has my father Sarth's blood, sure enough.

"Diplomacy? A delaying dance? Legal points? There's nothing illegal about a signed, sealed ally sending an embassy to Iskarda."

"Diplomacy?" Iatha shot at me. "What *about* diplomacy, Chaeris?"

"For an embassy, we can make rules too."

"What rules? How many times they piss on the road up—!"

Tanekhet actually laughed. It broke from him in a quick spontaneous spill as soft and husky and infinitely flexible as his Dhasdein courtier's voice.

"The escort." His eyes danced at me, young as a boy's in his lined but still finely modelled face. "We make rules about how many soldiers our 'holy' environs will admit."

Iatha checked in mid-word, her own brows flying up. "But will they heed?"

"For an embassy?" Tanekhet was laughing inwardly. "By the rules of diplomacy, they must."

Iatha's snort was more than eloquent. They had the power. What would enforce rules but their choice?

Asaskian said it out, in her cool, soft voice, "And if they don't?"

Tez watched Tanekhet ponder. In matters of Dhasdein, he almost always had the final word. Two remembered, with some detail, consequences of the few times he had not.

"It is officially an embassy," Tanekhet said slowly. "When he can, Therkon still prefers glove to fist. He will not care for Dhasdein's reputation, should he discard protocol *quite* so soon."

Tez's left brow went up. Like my mother, she wore her hair in a Crafter's plait. Loose ends tendrilled round her face, but there was nothing soft about the set of her jaw.

"So, arrange a Note? From Amberlight?"

Tanekhet nodded. "Dhasdein is no longer its previous force. No Archipelago galleys or Imperial marines. No wine-excise from Shirran or slave caravans from Mel'eth. Nor levied troops. If Amberlight made representations, on the sanctity of an ally . . ."

Iatha drew an audible breath. "You think, even now, Amberlight's strong enough?"

Tez and Tanekhet calculated together. Two was calculating as well, with plenty of information even up to the war when the city fell, but little for the last twelve years. Just before Two exploded, Tez said, "They have last summer's galleys. And five more on the slips. Enough to hold the River." She meant, stop downRiver trade. "There's Verrain. And Cataract."

"The one owing independence to Amberlight," Tanekhet murmured, "the other remembering Zuri, as Regent. I think, if Amberlight called . . ."

Keshaq said, "Verrain would come."

Tanekhet's third lover seldom spoke in council. He was exotic in an Iskardan council-room as Tanekhet himself, bronze-black, eagle-nosed, flamboyantly beautiful. High Quetzistani blood, but with a past whose acquaintance with a very different Verrain spoke in his look.

Tanekhet smiled at him as he smiled at no-one else. "Yes," he said. "We could be sure of Nathyx."

"And Cataract would send." Iatha turned it over, sure as Keshaq. "So with Cataract and Verrain behind it?"

"In that case, yes, Dhasdein might think twice about defying Amberlight."

"So do we warn them beforehand? Have them back the Note?"

"Do we think Therkon will wait for a Note?" Asaskian's mouth suddenly pinched. She remembered too, her face said. The speed, and the lack of scruple, with which Dhasdein could apply force.

Iatha's hand clenched on the worn pine boards. She had lost a husband last time Dhasdein came in force to Iskarda.

Tanekhet's eyes weighed them both. Then he said, quite gently, "Therkon is not his father. Nor is the Empress."

Iatha sighed, letting hands, shoulders relax, and Two ran past me a collage of other times Iatha had moved so: accepting the advice of the expert. Preparing, on one man's word, and he an Outlander, to hazard Iskarda. And so much more than Iskarda.

"So we send a quiet word to prime the Amberlight Assembly, and another to Nathyx in Assuana. And a signal to Cataract."

Eria sat at the far table end beside Duitho, quieter than Keshaq. As my mother said, she had been village Head two years, but in more than looks she resembled her mother. And like Darthis, she had a way of scuttling plans almost made.

"How if Therkon *doesn't* listen? If he already hasn't listened? If he arrives tomorrow? With all his phalanx troops?"

Asaskian looked startled, Iatha taken aback. She never had been able to handle Darthis. But Tez answered coolly as a Navy officer.

"Then we do what we'd do in any last resort. Send Chaeris into the mountains with the trouble-crew and some trappers, and let Therkon do his worst."

* * * *

I took Two's recall of Dhasdein's worst to bed with me, and the memories did more than trouble my sleep. I rose heavy-eyed and twitchy, to bungle half my workout with Ashar, the latest troublecrew second. Duitho, my previous sparring partner, was in the hills, checking tracks and setting sentry posts.

Going back inside, I braced myself for the usual onslaught: the consort's eldest daughter was barely three years my junior, but my differences, let alone being troublecrew, always brought them round me like flies. It was a shock to find the inner corridor quite deserted. Run to earth among her records, Hanni eventually told me they had begun to pack.

"Tomorrow," she said, abstracted among lists and notes, "Asaskian's taking the three of them to Amberlight."

It was one more crack in the new normality than I could bear. Duitho was still out. Tez was immured in the council-room with Iatha and the day's first batch of mirror signals. Hurrying down the front steps I encountered Tanekhet and Keshaq, fresh from their own training bout.

"Tanekhet!" Foster-father or not, he had stopped me calling him "father" years ago, and given my father Sarth's memories, I could understand why. "Tanekhet, what's happening? Are you leaving us?"

"My dear." I was shaken enough to make him reach out, though he had learnt before I was conceived not to lay hands, uninvited, on anything to do with qherrique.

"Be easy, Chaeris." It was real concern. Sprung from affection, if not love. "Asaskian is going, yes, to Amberlight. To manage our concerns there." He meant, to ensure the Assembly backed us over the Note. "And to be on hand should events demand an, ah, more immediate response."

A front line, then. Or an outpost. Two's glosses flew through my head, with more unnerving connections in their wake. "But taking Darr? Saarieq? Aretho? If it's to be dangerous—!"

It would take more than one flustered girl, even such a girl as I, to panic Tanekhet. He gave me what I had heard Tez call his Suzerain look.

"Asaskian goes to manage affairs. Your cousins," we all called them that, though in truth only Tez's girl Saarieq was my blood-kin, and a convoluted blood-tie at that. "Your cousins are going, because we cannot afford to offer hostages."

I gulped while Two's explanations tore through everything else. Hostages. Beloved levers to force obedience to an enemy. Far more vulnerable to capture in a village like Iskarda than in a city like Amberlight. Even under direct attack.

Tanekhet held my eyes and kept that steely fidelity to truth. "You will never fall into hostile hands, Chaeris."

No, I would be up the mountain, with trouble-crew to fight for me and trappers to hide me. Unlike my cousins, I would never come in risk. While in Iskarda . . .

"No, my dear." He did take hold of me that time. Lightly as a practiced lover, a feather clasp around my wrist. "Tez and Keshaq and I—and the people—will be perfectly safe."

"But how can you be sure? Two showed me, when they came before. Tanekhet—!"

"Nothing like that will happen now."

"How can you say that . . ."

"Because Therkon remembers last time. Because whatever we may do, he will see it never happens again."

I stared into those forest-pool eyes and saw a certainty whose basis was beyond Two's scope. But Tanekhet had never pandered to my age or my status or my fidgets. What he said was his best shape of the truth.

"If he brings all those men—?"

"He will not bring all those men."

"Oh. Then . . . Oh. You sent a Note?"

"We sent a Note." This smile was real amusement, quick and glancing as forest water caught by passing sun. "Saying with great politeness that the Head's daughter Chaeris is still very young, and must not have her home disturbed. Iskarda's council has just ruled that any embassy be limited to the envoy and an escort of six troops."

I stared like a witless boy while Two and I both tried to run the implications at once. "So they know you know why they'll come.

And they know you won't let the escort in. And—what happens now?"

"I should expect Therkon, in a gentlemanly way, to dispute. Point out the distance, the risk of Mel'ethi bandits, perhaps. He will not be so crass as to remind me of his value, as crown prince."

It was exactly like haggling in a market, I realised: a contention of strategies with compromise as its aim. "So what do we say next?"

"We repeat, the Head's daughter is young, and further, shy. Should she be alarmed in any way, any embassy will have wasted its time."

"Shy? Oh, I am not!" He grinned along with me. He too knew it was an utter lie. But all the same . . . "Isn't that rather, rather—"

"Uncompromising?" He had followed very close on my thought. "At some point, one must draw the final line."

"So he'll know, if they try to push things—?"

"Six men or six hundred. If they push things, you will simply not be here."

I let Two run the scenarios, and they almost came up clean. "Do you think you can bring him down to just six men?"

He chuckled softly and lifted a hand in a fencer's salute. "Twenty, perhaps."

Still a far cry from five or six hundred. I let myself breathe out. "And—it's all going to take time, isn't it? Like before? Our Note's just gone. It has to go clean to Riversend. And then his has to come back. And then ours has to go downRiver again. Mother aid us. He said, here, second quarter next moon, but our Note will hardly be there!"

Tanekhet nodded. "It is always worth the effort," he murmured, "to buy time."

It all seemed far less intimidating, under his dry, long-schooled view. Only one question remained.

"So if it's all so safe, and so far off anyhow: why send Darr away? And Saarieq?"

"Ah." He gave me another quick, flicking smile. "It is not wise to tempt an opponent—even, in this case, an opponent like Therkon—beyond enticements he can resist."

He changed a look with Keshaq that spoke volumes neither Two nor I could read. But the other question had already leapt into my head, the worst question of all.

"But if—if he knows all that, and he comes anyway . . . Then what will I do?"

The smile vanished. After a moment he said, "If he comes despite all that, we will call on Dhe and the Mother. And act as They command."

\* \* \* \*

Which meant, in plain speech, that in the last resort he himself had no idea.

I could not put my trust in gods I had never met. The projected time-span was far more comforting. Second spring moon Therkon proposed to arrive. Errisal's message had come down on the heels of the last winter flood, my mother and her consort would have the spring drop to help them upRiver. The River-fall would quicken voyages both ways, but the best speed Two could estimate for a double-bank galley would still not get messages between Dhasdein's capital and Marbleport in less than a moon and a quarter each way. If the haggling went as Tanekhet seemed to expect, it could be mid-summer before the departure, let alone arrival, of the embassy itself.

By then, as Tanekhet hinted, anything might happen. A wrangle over the tolls, and the River closed to Therkon by Verrain. An insurrection in Dhasdein's provinces of Quetzistan or Riversrun, some diplomatic intervention engineered by Asaskian in Amberlight. Even, I used to dream in the night-watches, that my mother would be back, the trouble upRiver already dissolved, all of them here again, making us safe.

In the meantime, working out with Ashar or Duitho, standing signal-watch, trying to draw comfort from the company of Tez and Tanekhet, I tried to tell myself that the Notes were still passing. At the least, we still had time.

We all reckoned without Therkon. He had written first from Riversend, but he followed his letter upRiver. His second Note was written from Deyiko, on the Dhasdein border, where he was negotiating River tolls with Verrain and Shirran and Mel'eth. The two former Dhasdein provinces were now independent, scandalously grasping states, but Therkon evidently did not expect problems with them. He accepted our conditions for an embassy, and looked to reach Iskarda, with his six man escort, on the second-last day in the third quarter of the moon.

"This moon! Blight and blast the man, that's not eight days ahead!"

Iatha actually sounded alarmed. Tez was scowling, Keshaq a perfect thundercloud. Even Tanekhet had grown unwontedly, visibly tense.

"I thought you said the Notes would stop him. I thought you said—!"

"My lady Iatha, I am not qherrique."

Tanekhet's return anticipated even Tez's defence. Flat and hard as a blow from a quarterstaff. All the eyes flicked, uncontrollably, to me.

"Neither," Tanekhet finished coldly, "in the earth, or in the flesh."

Now I could feel them trying not to look at me. Two was more than hackling. Two was charged to spark.

It came out in a husk, my throat was so dry. "Then do I—must I try—is it time—"

"No!" Iatha and Verrith yelled it almost in chorus. Iatha shouted, "Not with Tellurith away!"—"Not for Therkon!" Verrith bawled.

"But aren't I supposed, one day, to be—"

Iatha leant across the table and gripped my hand in her gnarled paw and Two never made a spark.

"Dearling," she said harshly, "nobody knows what you are supposed to be, beyond yourself. That's all your mother wants for you. To grow up, and make your own choice in the matter. In your own time."

I stared around. They had always found me strange, they had learnt to be wary with me, some might have feared me, once. Nothing showed but honest outrage now. And concern, strong as my fathers'. And protectiveness.

"I think . . ."

"*I* think," Iatha growled, "you're a twelve-year-old girl, and you'll stay that way. Whatever or whoever says otherwise."

"But he's coming! He's still coming! After everything we tried. When he gets here, what am I supposed to do?"

"Leave that," snapped Iatha, "to us."

Over her, Tez said in her Navy voice, "No."

She ran her eyes around the table. The echo of my father Sarth marked her profile, but my mother filled her voice.

"This time," she said, "I think the choice is for Chaeris."

I half-saw Iatha bend like a drawn bow; I did hear Duitho's gulp. The center of my vision was Tez, leaning forward on an elbow, almost casually, it looked.

"Chaeris," she said levelly, "do you know what Dhasdein wants?"

I stared into her narrow golden-flecked eyes whose shape spoke neither my mother nor Sarth. Her own mother, I knew, had been a Navy captain. There were times I felt that presence still.

"An oracle?" I hazarded.

"A prophecy. Yes. Do you know what that means?"

"A question. And an answer. About—what's going to be?"

"The future, yes. Do you know, when Dhasdein has sought one, why Iskarda has kept saying, No?"

I bit my lip to master the humiliation. "I thought—I was too young?"

Iatha growled in her throat. Still holding my eyes, Tez shook her head.

"Did you ever wonder why *we* never asked? For ourselves?"

The answer was the same. Mutely, I could only shake my head.

"Have you thought what would happen? If someone did ask? And you, *or* Two replied?"

"You mean—if it was right?"

Tez gave one silent nod. Two's calculations were already running, memories, projections, extrapolations flaring like qherrique charges through my head. It was Two who replied.

"*A true forecast would bring the River here. Wanting answers too.*"

Iatha's neck relaxed, and stiffened again. Tez sat back, with a look like a Navy gunner through her sights.

"Have you thought what that would mean, for you? For Iskarda?"

Two thought for me. All the River coming, as it had once to Amberlight. Embassies and rulers and nobles and this time everyone down to common folk, as they had not done to Amberlight. But Amberlight was a city, with people and arms and defended space, rules and the means to enforce them, to ensure the city could never be conquered, coerced, bribed. Or besieged night and day with petitioners, its own lands and places invaded, its life simply swamped. Whereas Iskarda . . .

"No!"

Tez nodded, sharp and curt. "Iskarda's a village. We have our folk and our ways and room for ourselves. We couldn't even handle a year's worth of single pilgrims, we have nowhere to lodge them. And if we began building such a place—if we tried to provide the rest—"

"It would be like a Riversend temple, only, only worse. Houses and markets and horse-fairs, food at robber's price. And people living off the, the petitioners, and bribes, and—"

My tongue locked. Even Two had not seen what I saw then.

Quite quietly, Tez said, "Yes. Without an escort, you'd never step outside again. Never go to the quarry. Visit the village. Work out. You'd lose your life." She took a long breath. "You'd never be—human—again."

The silence went down and down and down as if she had taken the cover off a pit. In that hush I looked into the depths, and met what I had always known. It took Two to reply.

*"Are we human now?"*

Tez's very features seemed to change. I saw that she knew what I had born, from the children no less than the adults, even in Iskarda: the stares, the whispers, the near harassment, from those never sure who or what you were, and given far too much cause, in the early days, not to try finding out. A margin-dweller, a mystery, unintelligible and incalculable. At best, a strange, alien sort of hope.

Then she said fiercely, "Yes, you *are* human! Even if we have to say, *Human, too*. But you know now what Iatha means. Your, our mother said it to me, once. 'Everybody knows what she is. Nobody knows who she is. But if she has to carry a Head's load, or worse things, it won't be until she must'."

I was swallowing tears, desperately. The nadir of unwomanliness, to break down in the council-room.

Tez fanned both hands on the table-top. "You are twelve years old, in human time. But you have Two's memories. And all you've learned. So I think it's time for you to choose, now: do you want to hear Dhasdein's question, or not?"

I could only gulp, caught between pit and pit. If I said, Yes, and failed? If I really was too young? If I never had the gift at all?

"You will be Craft one day," Tez added almost casually, "in any case. You have your mother's blood. And my father's, and that goes back to the best ears in Hafas House." She meant, those best able to establish rapport with qherrique.

So it would not matter if I tried to be an oracle and failed. I could still learn to use a cutter, or a light-gun, one day. It might almost, in the long run, be better for Iskarda.

What if I tried, and it worked?

My hands were in my hair, tugging at the bushy tail that might one day be a plait. "I don't want Iskarda to be like that!"

"No." Tez's voice was very quiet.

"But I can't—I don't *know*!"

"Can you ask?"

And now the whole room was holding its breath.

*Can you ask*, she had said, casually as ever, that ultimate question, only ever answered by a House-head in Amberlight. Make rapport with the qherrique, work it, with shaper or cutter, a Crafter could do that. But only a Head could ask for guidance, for an oracle, and get a reply.

"Two can tell you, and us, anything from the past." Infinitesimally, Tez's eyes narrowed. "Has Two ever, uh, spoken, about the future to you?"

I struggled to express what Two did, finding only the past's answer, my own mother's reply to the Dhasdein scribes about the nature of qherrique: your words do not work, do not work, do not work.

Two answered for us both.

"*We must know what we see.*"

"Everything you can learn, you want to know, yes. From last season's block tally to the names of the Dhasdein dynasties." I could not tell which of us Tez addressed. "But next season's tally: can you estimate that?"

"*We speak what we know!*"

"Ruand," Iatha used the Head's formal title so sharply even I jumped, and Tez lifted both hands swiftly and sat back. Oddly enough, she did not seem displeased. I could feel my muscles shaking, about to spasm, as they would sometimes when Two sparked the worst, my belly beginning to quake. But Tez simply nodded to me. Or to us both.

"Two doesn't want to consider the future, and you've never tried. You don't even know if you should ask. Will you leave it then, in our hands? To give that message to Therkon? Rather than speak yourself?"

Two's agitation eased. I nodded, grateful I did not yet have to manage words. It was Eria, at the table end, who asked the unsettling question yet again.

"And if Therkon won't leave it at that?"

Tez looked at her, then at me, and said, "Then we consult with Chaeris."

"And if—"

"That," Tez said evenly, "will be in the Work-mother's hand."

The cutter's invocation. It used to be a common prayer. It was also the House-head's sealing phrase: *I have spoken. The debate is closed.*

# CHAPTER II

Question how we would, neither Two nor I could get any more out of Tez. Cornered, Tanekhet would give me a courtier's answer and slide away. Iatha knew less than I: it all deepened my apprehension as the last quarter moon slid by, till Two was sparking at the least alarm.

I also had a demonstration, in small, of a true prophecy's effect. Therkon was bringing six guards, a personal servant, a cook and a chamberlain, and the fuss over what to feed them, where to lodge them, who would fettle their mules and do their washing, went the length of Iskarda.

With Asaskian and the children gone our own house had the most spare room, but though the most secure, it would also put them closest to me. Eventually, it took the whole council's decision to billet them at the Market inn. From there they might stray into the village, or elude our troublecrew, but they were on the outer environs of the House. As for food . . . by the last day, I could have consigned Therkon's fads and preferences to the River bottom along with everything else.

Nor did I see them arrive. I was forbidden so much as to peek from an upper window, let alone, perish the thought, stroll by like some nameless worker in the street. Instead Azo took me up past the village cistern to the high valleys where the hares had begun to breed, and we hunted there all day.

It was nearly dusk when we came home, the time when, usually, I love Iskarda most. Spring, the trees full of pristine new green, the irises in sheltered spots flowering creamy gold or horizon blue, the air redolent with growing grain. Iskarda's single street full of homing workers and hunters and men fetching the last wood, sunset steeping the high, gabled wooden house-fronts in dusty gold. And beyond, the great tapestry of the River's prospect, faded and blurring under immanent night.

That evening the street's feel had Two jittering before we reached the market-place. Everybody for once wanted to talk at if not with me, gossip or opine about the arrival, orate, worry, exhort. It took Azo, dour, stolid, silently interposing a wall-solid shoulder, to get me in our gates without a check.

With my cousins there, Darr would have raced up in the passageway to babble everything I did want to know, what time they came, what they looked like, what was happening at the Market, under the stress of housing a crown prince. I could almost hear his high-octave squeal, "And you should've heard what he said about the baker's rolls!"

As it was, I had only Iatha's grumble of, "The usual speeches. Tez offered 'em hot water and a night to recuperate before the yapping starts."

The reception, I knew, had been in the market square, Tez and Eria together. In our kitchen, Shia had heard the prince had been courteous if travel-stained, after bucketing on muleback the fifty miles up from Marbleport. Duitho and Ashar were already up the village on patrol.

"And tomorrow," Iatha added flatly, "you're out at daylight. Before it starts."

Before the council meeting, she meant. The house was on edge too, a fine underlying tension I could neither escape nor ignore. Having failed to pump Iatha on what Therkon actually looked like, I let them push me out of the kitchen conclave when my yawns grew noticeable, and went almost willingly to bed.

* * * *

Azo did rouse me at dawn: I could tell from her even rarer than usual words that she was no happier in exile than I. We prowled the higher hills, going gradually blind to the spring revelations of new beasts and the onset of familiar flowers, and by a little after noon we were both at rebellion point. Azo made the merest demurral, when I said, "Let's go back to the look-out. I want to see the qherrique."

The women of Iskarda have used the place time out of mind, in formal ceremonies for the Mother, for trysting, or just to be alone. Inevitable that the House should propose it first, when the time came to establish our seed, the tangible legacy of Amberlight. And the qherrique had been as willing as we.

We clambered to the closest crest above the village, right to the brink where the bastion of creamy grey rock thrust from its cluster of low-growing, pure white snow-helliens. Azo made one circuit, a bare formality, and settled on a backside-polished boulder. I stood a moment at her back, while we stared out through greenish silver leaves over the River's green and silver prospect, and down, in a hawk's vista, onto the street of Iskarda.

Neither of us had to say that they should have eaten by now. The Market workers would be soothing frayed nerves after another meal's success—or debacle. Tez and Tanekhet would be back in council. And so would the embassy. Surely, at this hour, we could go home?

"I'm hungry," I said.

Azo did not answer, but the line of her neck agreed.

"Could you get something, do you think? Even if it's at the Market." I giggled a little, too tired and bored and stressed to help it. "One of his majesty's rejected rolls?"

Azo gave me an eye-corner, but I knew she was trying not to snort. She said, "You'd be alone."

"What would get me up here? What *can* get me up here? Especially," I stood back a pace, "if I'm with the qherrique."

I withdrew another step. Azo eyed me dourly. Then she growled, "So stay there," and got up herself.

I walked dutifully back to the secret bay among the rocks. Tiny hyacinths had always grown there, purple-blue, so my father Sarth once claimed, as the depths of a sunlit sea. Around them thin mountain grass swayed and jounced in the wind, and through the helliens' dancing shadow, at a boulder's foot, I saw the qherrique.

When they planted it, the year I was born, it was no larger than the pearl it had once seemed. Now my father Alkhes called it the size of a Dhasdein phalanx shield, a man's armlength in diameter, rising at the boulder foot, a mushroom rock, an oysterless pearl, a gleaming, convex, mist-grey curve. A presence. Two had already acknowledged it.

And the seed was beginning to glow.

In the old days, coming to the mother-face, the cutters would sing. Crafters preparing to work the cut slabs would sing too, the merest troublecrew waking a light-gun would hum. I alone had no need, though sometimes I liked to. But as the seed would never, had never stung me, so when I came, it always knew.

The light welled up in the boulder-shade, softened by high sun but purer than moonlight and as clear. Here, if nowhere else on earth, I was not unusual, my greeting not uncertain. Here I was known and welcomed by my own.

I walked up, as even my mother or my father Sarth would hesitate now to do, and laid my hand on the breathing stone.

How long I—we—stood there I have no idea. Very often when we touched I would lose track of time. Nor can I put into words what thoughts, or feelings, or whatever they cannot be called, that we exchanged. Like the exchange itself, its matter is not something that fits in human terms.

But eventually, as if reluctant as I was, the glow began to fade. I sighed, finding muscle and bone and earth underfoot again. Then I took my hand away and stepped back a pace. There was no need to say farewell.

The outer world re-assembled: swaying grass, tick-tack of hellien leaves, a little sigh of air through the balmy spring afternoon. Sunlight ricocheted among the rocks, shadow dappled the hyacinths and the flank of the qherrique. In a year or two, my mother said, we could take the next step. Someone would bring a cutter, in the moon-dark and her own cycle's dark, and make the covenanted approach. Take the first, almost miniature slab, this time with a truly complete assent.

And sometime after that we would have new light-guns and cutters and shapers, and once again, all the tools of Amberlight.

I lifted my hand once more, as I always did, in acknowledgement of the pact: and stopped.

Someone was coming through the rocks.

Not Azo. I knew that instantly. The foot was light, but not troublecrew's stealthy, almost soundless tread. And not a woman. It was slightly too measured, the pace a little too long. A man.

Our men could come here now. Some did, those who found rapport with the qherrique, who would follow a Craft one day. But this was a stranger. I knew as if I saw it, hearing that careful, just not quite hesitant footfall among the stones.

I turned about as troublecrew would and stood four-square, Two roused and hackling, before the qherrique.

At first I thought it was Keshaq. The black-bronze hair was as straight and silky, drawn back from temple and forehead with beauty's carelessness, the features were as exotic, the long coffee-dark eyes, the high brow and flaring sweep of nose. He was as tall and narrow-built, his muscle carried in haunch and chest rather than width, and he moved with the same unconscious, bone-deep bearing of birth and rank.

But Keshaq never sported a knee-length tunic of some flame-orange, almost diaphanous, double-thread silk, over narrow cotton trousers of glistening leaf-green. Or a shirt whose embroidery would beggar temples, just in the narrow band the tunic revealed. Rings did not glitter on Keshaq's long, beautiful hands, nor did he pull back his hair with jewelled pins, and secure it in a thillian clip.

I stood like a lump of rock. My nascent troublecrew reflexes could not get past, Sweet Work-mother! How did he get up here *alone*?

He navigated the last rock-step. Looked up. Stopped.

For a moment I saw some dark, beautiful deer, elegant and cautious, picking its way through a dangerous wood. And then a deer that had thought itself, just this once, unpursued. For one blissful moment, free.

Then, just noticeably, he drew himself up. He was the foreigner, the interloper, and he knew it. My body language must have been shouting, *Stop, Stand back, Beware. You have no business here.* His eyes met mine, cool and steady, the armour complete now. Even at a disadvantage, he would be composed.

After another moment he said, not quite tentatively, "Damis."

It is the old Amberlight word, title, courtesy, to greet an unwed maid.

My lips parted and my breath caught. Mother aid, what should I call *him*? But Two already knew.

"Your Highness," I said.

He did not start. He was a crown prince, after all, trained and inured to almost anything. But for half a flash the eyes did widen, in more than surprise.

Then I realised where Two had got the title. Iskarda would say, *Sir,* Amberlight, *My lord.* "Highness" was a Dhasdeini usage. Straight from Tanekhet.

When he spoke it came with his rank's authority. He said, "You know the Riversrun Suzerain."

Oh, Mother! I nearly cried. He was as fast in the wits as my fathers, he already had a first-class clue, he need only look behind me to guess the rest. The one person he was not supposed to encounter in Iskarda. The one person I should never, ever have met.

Without knowing it I took a step back. I forgot to be troublecrew, I put my hands out as Two had suddenly ordered, not to protect but to take shelter, to protect myself.

He saw past me then. His eyes did open, almost white-ringed in that dark flamboyant face. He said, "You're the one. The oracle."

Two answered before I could stop it. *"And you are the Dragonfly."*

* * * *

For all his birth and schooling it caught him unawares. His eyes flicked downward, over his clothes, perhaps. Then he let out a little involuntary laugh.

"So some call me," he said.

"But what," I had the weirdest sense Two was actually quoting, using others' words as happened under stress, "are you doing here?"

His chin lifted a little. Again his eyes went past me, this time by intent. After a moment he said, "I wanted to see the qherrique."

With a touch of longing, and a stronger touch of defiance, that told us both what he understood. No need to reply aloud: he was a stranger. And a man. Strange men do not, are not permitted, to approach the qherrique.

The next question was reflex. "Where are your troublecrew?" I asked.

He actually shifted weight a fraction, the sort of move that would have been a shuffle in anyone else. "Ah. Well . . ."

"You gave them the slip." I was too surprised for outrage. "You didn't leave them outside the rocks. You never brought them at all!"

"And where, pray, are yours?"

The unaccustomed Iskardan frankness might have stung him, or perhaps the return was pure instinct. I could feel the color rise, though, on my face.

"Azo's just gone to the village. I'm perfectly safe!"

His eyes went past me again and the expression became something I understood. Recognition, wonder, a rising hint of awe. And then wistfulness, for a marvel he would never share.

"It does talk to men. Sometimes." I stopped. To go on would only be telling him what he already knew. Even to remind him how little freedom he must have left.

"But," I said again, "how did you get up here?"

His eyes went down and up. He knew what I meant. Then he ducked his head a half-fraction and a hand brushed his jaw.

"The, ah—the salad. There was so much oil." Less off-balance, he would never have committed such a solecism as to criticise his hosts' food. "I had to postpone the meeting . . . They had leave to wait."

To leave him alone. To let his notoriously sensitive stomach settle. It was not just gossip or exaggeration, and down in Iskarda the Market workers would be chagrined to their souls.

But he did not know that. Therkon, crown prince of Dhasdein, the Empress's hatchet man. Staring at me in defiance that this time shielded embarrassment, or maybe, something more.

A flash of Two's memory played past me. Therkon the crown prince, the cipher, the nonentity, extinguished in his father's shadow. Perhaps, belittled by his father as well as the rest.

"I'm sorry." It was out before I thought. "They were all so worried, but they didn't know what was safe—" My father Alkhes' audacity rescued me. "Our intelligencers aren't as good as yours."

He nearly gave a little gasp. Surprise, affront? Our eyes met and locked while the rest of the understanding passed between us. Going both ways.

Then his stance loosened, his eyes' focus widened, and the long mouth eased. I had a moment's image of that dark, beautiful deer, temporarily at bay. At length, with the hunters' passing, lowering its head, safe now to turn away.

"I found a back-stair." Now he spoke with a soft, flexible quiet that had nothing in common with Tanekhet's mannered calm. "You should not blame them. They thought I'd have to lie down an hour and more."

"So you came out."

His eyes tracked round again, this time with a different wistfulness. "The qherrique: it was a reason. I thought—it seemed—quite wonderful, that somewhere, along the River, you could be quite alone."

The choice of verb said it all. Where he *could* have been alone, for a crown prince of Dhasdein the ultimate luxury. But I had been here first.

"I'm—"

The little gesture was purely imperial: *apologies are unnecessary. Other gifts have cancelled them.* His eyes came back to me, this time frankly curious.

"I thought," he said, "you were only twelve."

"I grew." I had become accustomed early to winnowing curiosities at a glance. Some were comfortably innocent. More were wary, some hostile, the worst, both invasive and prurient. To this one Two and I responded as easily as grass to the sun. "My mother thinks Two helped. Because of the River. You know?"

Because of the impatient waiting world. Because of Dhasdein.

He inclined his head a little. Admission, acknowledgement. But it was candid wonder in his voice. "You look, sixteen, seventeen."

"My father is tall . . ." The wave was upon me, it was shoot it or overturn. "My father Sarth. You know?"

He nodded solemnly. His eyes were still fixed on me. I reassayed that attention, and still found no taint of prurience. No hint of adult-to-child patronage either. I might have been his own age.

I took my own bracing breath. "You know I have two fathers, I suppose."

After a minute, he said, "I heard."

The pause spoke our common knowledge. Of course he had heard, just as he had known where to find the qherrique. Dhasdein intelligence.

"It—sometimes people feel confused. Sometimes, they—they—"

He moved a fraction, almost as if to put out a hand. "People always talk," he said, "about the unusual. Or," with a wry little turn of the voice, "the notable."

As they had talked about him. For the length of his life, with reason or not.

"Yes. Well, I suppose I am—notable. But, my fathers. It isn't just my mother's consort. They are supposed to be my fathers in, in—"

He did move this time, his face suddenly alive with more than interest. "They tell the story," he said. "When you were born, you had two shadows. Both your fathers' faces. I always thought it was something to do with—" He gestured to the qherrique. But there was no wariness in that movement, no revulsion. If he saw me as a specimen, and there had been Dhasdeini scribes, I knew, who would have liked nothing better than to dissect me, to him I was a live specimen: a thinking, feeling being.

"Yes," I said gratefully, relaxing into the speed of his understanding, so like my fathers' own. "My mother says that. If it could choose to be—reborn—with a human—" I looked to be sure he understood all I meant—"it could choose to have two fathers as well."

He had understood. His eyes went once to the qherrique and back, and then the momentary sadness passed. "But when you were born," he said softly, "your mother was so pleased."

"Yes." I could almost smile this time, remembering with Two's memories as well as his. "So I don't really care if I have one blood-father or two, and if anyone else wants to worry about it, they can."

He had been watching me closely all the time. Whatever he read from that last sentence, his eyes narrowed a little. Then he said abruptly, "You don't look like them. Any of them. Your father Alkhes," it came without a stumble, "his hair is much blacker, and his skin is white. You have the Amberlight skin, but your hair is straight. And your father Sarth's is lighter. Yours is like—black coffee. With lights of gold. You don't have your mother's nose, either. When you move or speak, sometimes I can see all three of them. Just the turn of a phrase. Or the shape of your cheekbone at a certain angle. But that is not you. In the end, you are someone else. I don't know who that someone is, but it is not them. Even the sum of them is not you."

Nobody in Iskarda, not even my mother, had ever seen so far into my heart. I stood with a feeling of enlargement, of surprised recognition, of a gratitude close to joy. Such as a riddle, given life, might feel at being finally fathomed. Rightly known.

He gave me a diffident little smile and another gesture, this time pure Dhasdein: *I have over-stepped, and been presumptuous. Pardon me.*

"Tell me, if you will, about your fathers? Your mother's consort? Was that not part of her, her plans for change?"

It was a deflection, a mannerly ward for my feelings. Old news, too. Yet despite the newly restrained manner, he sounded genuinely interested. And still, despite the subject, without prurience.

"You mean," I said, "the plan to end marriage? As it was in Amberlight?"

The corners of that long, usually governed mouth winced a little, but he nodded.

"No more men's towers? No more—losing—firstborn sons? And men, as well as women, able to marry or, or have more partners, as they wish?"

The spark of interest had brightened. "Has it worked?"

"Not really." I could not help echoing my mother's disgust. "There aren't towers, or any more sons lost. But even the young women just want to share one man between two or three of them, or marry a man and keep a partner, but not allow him one. Except my sister Tez's consort, it's all just like before!"

He was laughing. Openly, shaken clean out of manners and wariness and composure, a soft but lung-deep burst of laughter that warmed me like spring rain.

"Ah, damis, seen from Dhasdein, all of that is change!"

He caught himself, and managed the sketch of a bow. "Forgive me. I only meant . . ."

"*It is unimportant,*" Two said.

He heard the difference instantly. His eyes went wide and my own heart cringed. Now he knows how different I really am. Now he'll be put off, or shocked.

Or worse, I would not let my heart say, afraid.

I put my own chin up and stood waiting to meet my fate.

His eyes flicked once to the qherrique and back. He drew a sharp little breath. Then he said, "Who was that?"

Not, What. Who. Suddenly my quaking heart swelled with more than relief.

"That was Two," I said.

"Two?" Then his whole face lit. "The qherrique? It, you—she? can talk as well?"

"Two. Just Two." I could have laughed aloud from simple happiness. "He, she, it, doesn't work. Say, She, if you want. Two, because we are two. And Too, as well as me."

He actually took a step forward, his eyes shining, still with that candid curiosity welcome as a companion's touch. "And Two? Is Two the qherrique?"

"We think so," I said.

"That is—that is most wonderful." I could have opened like a flower, at the focus of that warmth. "Tell me, has she—" suddenly he waved his hands in a sort of frustration, trying to look past me and at me at once—"Two, how do I talk to you? Or do I talk to, to," he visibly drew the name back, "to Chaeris?"

"You talk to me," I said. "Two is me. Or I'm her. When Two wants, she'll say things I miss."

"Oh." He could get worlds in a syllable. Comprehension, eagerness, excitement far beyond simple interest. "Tell me then, Two—no, Chaeris. When did you first know—Two—was there?"

"As soon as I began knowing." I could not remember a time otherwise. "She was there before that, of course. I just wasn't old enough to tell."

His eyes told me he was envisioning a life with no possible chance of solitude. And its more amazing obverse, a companionship one would never want to lose.

"And," he visibly struggled over questions' choice. "How does it work? Do you feel Two, like an arm, or an eye, or is there one place where—she—stays?"

Questions posed since I could string words together, as my close kin or our own physicians tried to fathom the enigma in their midst. I had no time to consider how readily the answers came for him.

"It seems more like something we, I, carry in the blood. Everywhere and nowhere. What I feel, Two feels. What I see, Two sees. Two just has memories, lots more memories. All the memories, like this seed had." I did not have to reach out to the qherrique behind me. "Everything it, they, we brought from Amberlight."

His face opened in pure amazement. Almost faintly, he said, "All?"

He had seen the seed, Two remembered, when my mother came back from the Source. He too understood what it would mean, to call on Two's resources, and see back to the beginning of Amberlight. To the moment when a human first bespoke qherrique.

This time when his gaze returned to me it held longing doubled, tripled. More than longing. Unfulfillable, unkillable desire.

Two flashed an image past me and as suddenly I understood. My mother with my father Sarth, somewhere in outdoor dark. My mother saying, with wonder in her own voice, "You're a philosopher, Sarth." Adding, softly, "That means, you don't need to believe things, you need to know."

And Therkon was a philosopher too. Just as for Two and me, his instinct was to learn things. That, not embarrassment, had unlocked his shield at this encounter's very first. The pure acquisition of new knowledge gave him joy, the need was a hunger in his heart.

But unlike my father, he was a crown prince of Dhasdein.

I saw the deer again, dark and beautiful, and turning, always turning, in the confines of a net.

"I could show you," I said.

"Two will do it." I actually took a step forward, when he blinked. "For some people, we can transmit. Like my mother, with the seed, for Tanekhet." I bit down hard on, *I want you to be one of them.* "Just let me try."

Carried away by his desire, the philosopher had already answered, *Yes.* He actually lifted a hand before the crown prince caught up. And after him, the man.

The way his stance, his eyes changed, was a southerly down my back. I bit hard to cover the tremble in my lip.

He had seen. His own face replied. He made me a grave half-bow, philosopher and prince at once. "Lady Chaeris, there is nothing I should like better. For myself."

Cold reality was returning, priorities first. "Your troublecrew wouldn't like it," I said.

He went to say, Yes, and then, caught by truth, No. Then he said, diffident but determined, "Lady Chaeris, I am a stranger. And you know I have heard . . . how . . . how Two . . ."

"Oh, Mother. That was long ago. Two knows better now. Two only sparks when we're really upset, or stressed, or—it would be all right!"

He did pause. Then he said, more diffidently, "They told me— the first time. Your own father. Alkhes saw you on the cliff here. Almost over the cliff. He ran and caught you and the—and Two— his arm was useless for three days."

"We were young then! Just learning to move! The old qherrique was anchored, even the seed they just carried about. But I, we can walk, Two was so excited—" In his face wonder fought with doubt, but not hard enough. "We just wanted to measure the drop! We were going to climb down, far enough to guess. My father didn't understand, he was terrified, and he . . ."

I had to stop. The image of my father's shock, the pain, the way he had carried his arm in that sling, was graven too deep. I hung my head in our common shame, struggling to suppress the tears.

He had taken his own quick forward step. Stopped. Silence again, stretching painfully, wider and colder, as the companionship ebbed away. I had imagined him more than a philosopher. And after all, he was no different to anyone else.

I did hear him draw in his breath. And the change in his voice as he said, "Lady Chaeris?"

I looked up. The light had left his face, but the philosopher remained. Sober now, with all the ruler's wariness, and the man's simple caution. Steeling himself, however knowledge and commonsense protested, not to be afraid.

He said, "I—we—could try."

His face told me what mine had said. He produced a little smile. Half shy, half impudent. The man, pleased to have pleased me. The philosopher, cocking his thumb at rules.

I reached my hand out. In a moment, his came to my touch.

\* \* \* \*

When I opened my fingers it was the philosopher who looked back at me, dazzled and delighted, and still distant as a man finding himself in love. Like his, my eyes still held the pale, distant winter sky, the Amberlight hillside vacant of Houses or citadel: the face of Amanazar.

It must have been another thirty heartbeats before he realized I had not let go.

He looked down quickly at our hands. His eyes flashed up with all the other reflexes jerked awake and I shut my fingers as lightly as I could and said, "Two would like a favor. If you please."

The old childhood phrase half-disarmed him. His fingers relaxed a little. Then the prince inclined his head, an unconditional, imperial assent.

I said, "Two wants to learn you." I held on at the twitch of his wrist. "There's never been anyone from Dhasdein here. All we know of it is, is second-hand. We, I, just thought . . ."

He had been startled, far enough to show the struggle of shock and some form of amusement, and very imperial affront. *You want*, the arch of his chin demanded, *to learn Dhasdein from me?*

"Well, after all, you are the Prince!"

The affront dissolved in an almost helpless laugh. "Ah, my lady." Then he became somebody quite new, a practiced, more than practiced courtier. "Such a petitioner, who could refuse?"

He smiled into my eyes with such blatant charm I almost recoiled. In the pause he glanced swiftly over a shoulder, head cocked. Listening. All prince again, seeking what we both ought to have expected. Voices, troublecrew challenges, thud of feet. Gauging, from their absence, how much longer we might stretch this magic interlude.

Before he turned back to me and asked gravely, "What must I do?"

"Uh. Ah—could you, um, sit down?"

He did splutter then. But he also disposed himself with grace's brevity on the nearest handy rock. The sun had come further toward afternoon. The inclining light flashed across his eyes, far darker than the usual Amberlight bronze or brown, the silky sheen and the flare of jewels in his hair. Raising his brows in something that was not quite regal hauteur, he looked expectantly in my face.

One stride had me so close he suppressed a recoil: Two was rapaciously eager for so much wealth. But it was an echo of memory, something unexplained about Zuri and Sarth, that sent my hands first to his hair's thillian clip.

The pin came out and I drew it carefully clear. We were eye to eye now, and I read the flicker of expressions, doubt, a certain alarm, something that, in an Outland woman, Two would have called modesty flouted, if not outraged. He kept still, deliberately, as I palmed the clip and two-handed, began to spread out his hair.

Undone, it was longer than I had thought, almost down to the end of his shoulderblades. But it was the texture that fascinated us, as silky but far lighter than my father Sarth's, with no sign of his slight curl. It hung over my fingers in skein upon skein, slipping, slithering, darkly glistening as some fragile net.

Therkon had grown still. When I looked up, he was watching me, as fascinated as Two.

I came a little closer, so my upright thigh crossed close to his. With the back of my free hand I did as Two wanted. I smoothed my knuckles very lightly down his cheek.

He almost jumped. I did hear his breathing jerk but I was all but swallowed in Two's response, greedy as qherrique feeding on heat. His skin was smooth, with an underlying roughness I had felt before, on my fathers' faces, a shaven man's hint of beard. But the bones, the bones of that bold jaw and cheek were entirely different.

I drew my knuckles right down his jawbone to the chin, and up. He quivered all over, as a truly tuned string does when its neighbour is struck. I let the pads of my fingertips slip over his temple, the bridge of that arrogant nose, back to the startlingly delicate framework of his ear. Over his forehead, Two absorbing every detail and dimension as water melts into sand. Along an eyebrow, then with a finger under his chin, tilting his eyes to mine.

His tension was part incipient affront, part something else. His breath had quickened, his eyes dilated. When I looked into their depths the oak-water irises had almost vanished. It was darkness, entire and absolute, that looked back.

Two knew that look, if I did not. Our thighs brushed and he gave one quick jerk. Then Two leant over and touched his mouth with mine.

His breath met mine in an uncontrollable gasp and his hands instinctively went to grasp my hips. In the same moment he tried to let go, to pull away, and Two made an imperative noise and clamped my own hands over his.

Whatever he or I might have wanted, Two gave us no choice. She slid my tongue along his lips, making him half-gasp again before his own responses cut in.

His hands firmed under mine. His mouth opened, he straightened up and tilted his head to reach closer, and his tongue came to answer my own.

Practice, I can recognise now. And skill, atop a fine native talent for love. Or at least, for dalliance. Attentive, too, to his partner's desires, anything but hungry, a man who has always had his fill of both. Two was cascading memories past us, Two was a fire in the blood, urging me on, Two understood and wanted what would happen next and suddenly among the flow of unknown bodies a flash shaped my mother and my fathers, naked together in a moonlit glen—

I tore my mouth away and stumbled back. Without words I screamed, *Stop!*

Two's contact snapped. I was alone with myself amid mundane dirt and rock.

Elsewhere I could not look. I clung to the refusal while, slowly, the dance of my blood calmed, while I made the lowering discovery that my body alone could be as lawless as Two. My heart steadied, finally. Unconsciously I wiped a hand across my mouth.

Then, at last, I had to face the man I had touched.

He was looking as bewildered and shaken as I felt, with a fine touch, atop the confusion, of wounded, truly imperial pride. But he regained his balance far faster than I.

Silently he stood up, raised both hands and scooped his hair back. Held out a hand, as silently imperative. I gave him the clip.

He fastened it home. His every muscle spoke pure affront. In a moment, as silently, as thoroughly outraged as his body-speech proclaimed, he would turn and go.

"It wasn't you!" I burst out. "It was something Two did. I—I didn't expect—"

I stopped, feeling the flush rise as it too often did. Looked away, unable to help myself. I had been abashed often enough by Two's memories. I had never been led so far astray.

There was a chasm of a pause. Then, icily calm, his voice enquired, "Did you learn enough?"

I had ado not to close my eyes in pure misery. He had been so understanding, so alight with such a welcome, more than a friend's interest. And I could not even explain.

It was Two who said, *"We are ashamed."*

My very bones felt Therkon freeze.

*"We are of age,"* Two said. *"This year."*

He had to know what that meant. A woman's moon-phases. I wanted to sink in the dirt and wriggle away. I grabbed for control and Two flatly refused.

*"We wished to know what it is, how it is, between women and men."* Two seldom used, or could not often achieve inflection, but urgency surfaced now. Almost passion, it felt. *"We wished to know, for ourselves."*

*Let me do it,* I was yelling, *stop, don't make it even worse!*

*"But we—I—did not know the way. We—"* a sudden break, sharp as glass. *"I apologise."*

Two had never said such a thing in my life. I had never heard Two use the pronoun "I."

The pause built, and built, and teetered on the brink of impossibilities. I have to breathe, I was thinking, or I will die . . .

It was Therkon who let his breath out, a quick audible chuff. Then his boots moved beside the rock.

"My lady."

He stopped, and began again.

"My ladies." I could understand the falter. Two and I would strain even a crown prince's store of protocol. "I think I also am ashamed. Shall we," it was formal but not icy, "shall we call that a mistake? And—begin again?"

*"Begin?"* Two yanked my head up and he put both hands before him with genuine haste however convincing the laugh.

"In the River-lord's name, not like that!"

"I only meant," he amended, as I stared at him, "perhaps we might, uh, begin to talk again?"

*While we can*, expanded his look, quiet, composed now, too aware of the time ticking inexorably with every click of a hellien leaf.

"Yes." I could feel my own face light, I was almost silly with relief. "Yes, we could do that, oh, I'm sorry, that was something, I can't tell you, but I never meant—"

*Forgotten*, answered that gesture, elegant as everything else. Now he even managed a faint, wry half-smile. "Though I must say, my lady, I never expected to be so, so taken in my own net."

Not the deer, turning and turning in those distant, silken chains. But though I caught his sense, the irony of the investigator investigated, what took precedence was my own shame.

"It was my—our fault," I said to the rock. "Two, I, we worry so much. They're all going to rely on us. They'll ask what to do—and we have to know everything, how can we even forecast a flood height, if we don't have all the possible facts? And men and women, the, the sex thing, it's so important. If I miss one small thing, I'm so afraid I won't—we won't—we'll say something, and it—it will be wrong . . ."

The words dwindled. I kept my eyes down, wanting now to creep entirely away. The helliens tick-tacked suddenly, in the wakening breeze. Inside the rocks it felt like the egg of the world. Absolute, unbreathing hush.

Then Therkon hitched himself back onto the boulder, moving over to make room, and said, more than gently, "My lady. Will you sit down?"

\* \* \* \*

Gauche as ten-year-old boy, I sat. I feared to move any further, and he kept silent until all my awareness narrowed on his faint scent, his breathing, the sense of his presence, so tormentingly close.

He murmured, "I think I know what you mean."

I was too ashamed to look up. But I felt the way he, too, braced himself.

"I." His hands moved, locking one over the other wrist. "I carry a burden as well."

I did not have to ask. I had seen the philosopher, the desires he could not fulfil.

"Dhasdein. I have seen Dhasdein come from a great empire to," the gesture finished, *to a shadow of itself*. "I am not sure that was not my fault. But it has set me . . . in debt, to what is left."

I looked up then. He nodded a fraction, as if I had spoken aloud.

"I was trained and raised . . . as you were. Though I was to be," a wry expression, "a prince. An," the inflection was past irony, "heir-breeder. A figurehead. A fledgling 'emperor'." He flicked a hand. "Once, I could avoid that path. For safety, I had to play the fool, the spendthrift." Another, very conscious pause. "The lover. Only to survive."

"*Antastes*," Two said.

His arm tensed, but he did not flinch. In a moment he said, "My father. Yes."

Then he looked round to me and raised his chin. "Now, I have another part. My mother—the Empress—depends on me." He read my face and his mouth corners turned down. "What do they say? The imperial hatchet man?"

"You aren't like that!"

It was out before I could help myself. He eyed me sidelong, and the ruefulness deepened, hardening into something else.

"Oh, yes," he said quite quietly. "Be sure, my lady. If I must be, I can." Now his whole face was cold and inhumanly beautiful, merciless as the veritable axe.

"There is," he finished softly, "more than enough blood on my hands."

I looked down and tried to quell Two's memories of Dhasdein's descent on Iskarda. Tried not to think what future this warning might predict. But irresistibly, invincibly, both Two and I drew back the other memories. The deer. The eager, inquiring philosopher.

Greatly daring, I reached out for his hand. And after one tiny hesitation he gave it to me.

I took it palm down, but he turned it upward in my grasp. I opened out the fingers, long and slender and dark against my milk-coffee Iskardan skin. The nails were beautifully shaped and perfectly manicured.

I said, "Your hands are beautiful."

He took the meaning. His fingers twitched once and relaxed. "Useless," he answered ruefully. "Not like your fathers'." A quick pain crossed his face. "Or Tanekhet's."

I had noticed my foster-father's hands when I was four in human time. They had the same shape, graceful and elegant, but the skin was rough, the palms calloused, and on one hand nails had been torn away, leaving gnarled scars. I had asked, *What did that?* And for the first time we were denied knowledge. His consorts, my own fathers, even my mother's face had closed. Then, abruptly, they had spoken of something else.

So I asked again now, uncertain of the response. "What happened to his?"

His mouth clipped tight and thin and he averted his face. "He was tortured," he said to his sleeve. And then, muffled, "I tortured him."

"You—!"

"I gave the orders. He—he planned it." That long, too-feeling mouth twisted. "In our own ways, we betrayed each other." The note changed. "As well as Dhasdein."

Both of us understood that inflection. *Don't, if you care for me, ask any more.*

After a moment I smoothed my fingertips across the elegantly shaped, polished shields of nail. Then I said, "For a crown prince, for an emperor, I think these will do."

"You think?" It was almost a laugh. The fingers curled involuntarily over mine, and I felt the rings.

The thunderbolt and serpent had been carved on the big bloodstone over his first knuckle. An imperial signet. We knew that instantly. The other, on his wedding finger, was a simple hoop of gold. Set with three seed-sized, matched, magnificent blue-white thillians.

"What's this?" I asked.

He was quiet a moment. Then he said, "It belongs to the crown prince. A betrothal ring."

My heart seemed to fall mysteriously under the arc of my breastbone. "To whom?"

He looked up sharply and it was mostly surprise. "To Dhasdein."

"Oh."

That time earth itself fell under me, as if air had opened in the solid ground. Of course, he had said it already. The deer turned and turned before me, in the net it could not, would not let itself try to break. Dhasdein. The rule of empire, the weight of empire. The crown prince's responsibility.

I shut my hand on the suddenly illusive warmth of his fingers, as if a ghost would slip between us and all in a moment drift him away.

"My lady?"

I looked up, and it was the philosopher, or just the man, who looked back. Quiet, gentle, concerned for me. As if we were of the same common, companion flesh and blood.

Then the concern became a slight, conscious constraint. I read the signs of an unwelcome but pressing decision and waited for him to release his hands. However courteously, to move back.

He said, "My lady Chaeris, if you understand all that . . . then you know why I am here."

Two did not have to tell me. I said, and it sounded hollow too, "For Dhasdein."

"Yes." He bent his head a little, but he did not look away. "And I know you are young. And you need knowledge still. And I would not wish—now—to press you." He hesitated. When he went on, it was open stress. "If I might just—"

Then he jerked his head up like a genuine deer and I heard the frantic, panting voices, the thump of multiple feet among the rocks.

# CHAPTER III

"It wasn't my *fault*!"

I had never felt so near the threat of an actual whipping before. I fully expected confinement on bread and water until the whole embassy was back in Riversend. No-one had resolved the confusion turning my world and my stomach upside down, but eventually the uproar bouncing off the council-room walls drove me to bawl like a true twelve-year old.

With Iatha's jaw still half-down I exploited the equally shocking hush.

"I didn't intend it. I didn't expect it. I didn't want it! If you have to blame someone, blame his troublecrew. *I* didn't let him get up there! It isn't my fault and it isn't Azo's either. She only did what I asked!"

Azo's shoulder hunch contradicted that. I would have pressed on anyway. Had not Iatha, after one glance at Tanekhet, suddenly gathered herself up and let out a foundered-pack-mule sigh.

"Yes. We're counting chip-falls here. We should plotting the next cut."

To lead the shift of a debate was always Iatha's prerogative. I knew better than to answer. Tez had words assembling, but it was Eria who spoke.

"Let us first find the root of this."

Tanekhet's head swung quickly. Until now he had been noticeably quiet. Eria ignored him, looking only at me.

"Chaeris, will you tell us: why?"

I could not help a thoroughly unmannerly, "Why, what?"

"We know why you were there. And why you were alone. And how he came there. But why did you stay?"

It was the one thing even I had not thought to ask. I stammered, "I don't—the rocks. I couldn't have got past . . ."

Eria's stare was inscrutable as Darthis' had been, and as unwavering. "But he would have let you by: if you had asked."

It was true. My heart admitted it. He had never been anything but mannerly. He would have let me by. If I had asked.

Tanekhet sat up slightly but so suddenly and after such long immobility that the whole council looked. He caught my eyes and pinioned me with that intense green stare.

"Chaeris, favour me. Think carefully. And however," a rueful little smile, "however odd, however trivial—however embarrassing it seems—tell us. The truth."

I stared in earnest. Two was flinging questions and extrapolations broadside and finding nothing pertinent. "The truth about?"

"The reason you stayed," he answered softly. "In your own heart."

Only Tanekhet could bring out something like that in full council without sounding either fulsome or over-dramatic. But his face told me the question's weight.

I looked at Eria. Her stillness said she had not only followed, but agreed.

"When I said, I didn't need troublecrew." They had had it all out of me, word and almost look. Except for the kiss. The mere thought of that still heated my ears. "When I said that, he looked at the qherrique again. And he said, 'I see.'"

It did seem trivial. It was embarrassing. Meeting Tanekhet's eyes, I tried neither to falter nor to blush. "And—I was sorry for him."

Nobody had to bellow, you felt sorry for the crown prince? Dhasdein's hatchet-man? The one man on the River who could, with a word, crack Iskarda like a nut?

It was Tez who dropped the next words like a fall of silk. "Chaeris, did you feel, at any moment, that the choice was not wholly yours?"

"What?"

Their faces told me she had taken Eria and Tanekhet's thought right into the gold. Tez just watched me, unblinking. Then she said, "Ask Two how the old Heads felt, when the qherrique spoke."

Eria twitched. Hayras sat up. But Two was already running the memories, the moments when, over and over, House-heads of Amberlight had turned to the oracle only they could use.

Two left me to answer. I looked back into Tez's waiting gaze and silently shook my head.

Iatha's hands relaxed. Tanekhet said decisively, "That does not prove anything."

At the stares a hint of steel slid into his voice, "S'hurre, if this meeting was intended, the paths could have been laid long since."

Iatha's expression made him turn a hand out and close it into a fist. "Come, you remember for yourselves. When Tellurith chose to save Alkhes, it was after a message, yes. But how many chances had already matched to bring the two of them together, at that time, at that place? To allow that choice?

"And what," he went on, "brought these two together, now?"

"Dhasdein troublecrew," Tez looked wickedly ironic at Iatha's expression, "losing their crown prince? Too much oil in a salad-dressing? Chaeris getting hungry up the hill?"

"Two people led," Tanekhet answered softly, "by a chain of pebble-falls. Despite everything we expected. Despite everything we could do."

There was a fathomless hush. I heard myself say stupidly, "It was meant to happen? But then—who arranged it? And why?"

Tanekhet swung but it was Tez whose sharp gesture forestalled Iatha, and preceded a dagger-point stare at me.

"I think, Chaeris, this time, you could try to answer that. You know where to ask."

Ask Two. And it was not about the future. It was an extrapolation, pure and simple, from what had already happened. What we already knew.

But it was the first time anyone had asked us to do the thing in earnest. To play the oracle.

My hand was suddenly trembling as the air seemed to tremble, shaking-tense. I turned myself inward, and for the first time, formally, consciously, I asked.

Two's extrapolation, that ran always on the margin of my awareness, accelerated past coherent images. The inner and outer worlds became one unbroken blur, then disintegrated into frenziedly roiling white.

The council room came back as if I had opened a door. Two said, and it seemed to echo inside my skull, *"There is reason to say, intent. If not arrangement. But not ours."*

We had answered. We had not panicked. We had not failed. I sat panting, my hands clenching and opening, my heart slowing in more than pure relief.

Tanekhet smiled at me and leant over to touch the back of my hand that was damp with sweat. Softly, he said, "Good girl."

* * * *

I had no time to savour the achievement. As always in Iskarda, in Amberlight, the council was already two paces beyond the crisis point. Iatha was saying sharply, "If that's so, then it has to be—" the jerk of her head indicated the hill behind us. She meant the seed, I realised. "Blight and blast it, we're back in Amberlight!"

Discussion burst. They had dismissed us, that newly shocking chance of Two's complicity dwarfed by the greater alarm: that we were back with the old ways of qherrique, unheralded, incalculable influence, and now with not one but two unhuman players in the game.

"The Mother aid us," groaned Eria, clutching her head. "How do we deal with *this*?"

"We shoot the narrows as they come." Tez spoke decisively enough to hush them all. "S'hurre, Two did not say there *was* intent. We still don't know if things were 'arranged,' before. The seed couldn't tell us. Even Sarth's stopped trying to work it out. And another thought. It took a certain mass to fire a Navy lightgun. If it took all the thirteen motherlodes in Amberlight to—perhaps—arrange things, earlier: then can our qherrique do it now?"

The startled expressions said how few of them had considered such practicalities, but Hayras and Charras had already turned to me. "Chaeris," Charras burst out, "if it was intended, can you figure, Why?"

Tez stopped in mid-breath. The whole group had focused. And my pulse was already leaping, my stomach turning, Two at the cusp of explosion or fright.

"*There is no basis—we need more facts!*"

Tez slammed the table and snapped, "Charras, enough!"

Charras was already trying to apologise, to retract her head like a turtle's neck. I half-saw Tez whip her eyes around to draw the others' attention from me.

"*Why* is currently as unanswerable as, *If*. We would be wasting time to ask. As for what we do now," the smile was bleakly ironic. "Has the initiative not already passed?"

Almost as fast as Two, she had made the projections and drawn the conclusions from that meeting up the hill. Iskarda's moves had all been preventive, defensive. It was the other player who had led events, by whatever means, whosoever intent.

"S'hurre, use your wits." She snapped it when the fresh uproar reached shouting point. "We tried to shield Chaeris and we failed. We cannot expel a perfectly legal embassy for a mischance neither they nor we could prevent. We cannot break off negotiations. We do not know enough to take any other path." She curled her lip and tossed it among them like a Dhasdeini fire-bomb.

"At this point, we can only wait upon Dhasdein."

\* \* \* \*

Even in my own little room behind my mother's quarters, I did not sleep well that night. The dark swarmed with speculations too wide-reaching and nebulous to finalise, too disquieting to ignore. What if chances *had* been manipulated, what if it really was by our qherrique, and above all, to what end? And repeatedly, ousting every other concern: now, what would Therkon do?

It did not help that, with both my workout and mirror-signal watch cancelled, I came bleary-eyed into the kitchen just as his Note arrived.

"Mother blast the man!" Iatha clutched her morning coffee, eyes blearier than mine. "He could give us time to eat!"

"He knows better." Tez was already dressed, neat as a Navy officer. "He has the initiative. Why would he let it go?" She broke the seal and spread the parchment summarily on the kitchen table, among the night-watch's dirty plates.

Tanekhet came wandering in, hair on end, in an elegant but untidily fastened robe. "Tez, must we all rise before the forsaken cockerels . . .?" The rest snapped off. He took three strides to her shoulder and picked up the scroll.

After what seemed an aeon he raised his brows, once more the courtier, and let it run shut. "No doubt," the tone made it faintly condescending, "he had the chamberlain scribbling drafts all night."

Tez gave one little splutter and suddenly drew his hand against her cheek. "You," she said, with more than amusement, "you never change."

"I daresay not, my dear." He glanced down at her, brows slightly raised. "It always seemed to amaze Dhanissa, too."

The look between them suddenly sparkled with memory, with amusement brilliant as a jeweled knife. Then Tanekhet swept a glance round the rest of us, all jittering in our seats.

"Predictably," he said, "the crown prince requests a consultation. With the council of Telluir House. And since they have already met without untoward consequence, with my lady Chaeris."

He let the scroll drop gently beside the butter pot. "Why this has to be conveyed before breakfast . . . You will excuse me, Ruand. I must attempt to dress."

Iatha got her wits together before he vanished. "Wait! What do we, what are we going to say?"

Tanekhet looked back in delicately bored astonishment. "My dear Steward. What can we say, but, Yes?"

* * * *

"He's so casual," I marveled, when chance put me beside Tez in the exodus. "Like it's nothing to bother about."

Tez gave me a not quite amused look. "He's had a lot of experience."

"I don't," I confessed, "feel half as bad now." And she did look wryly amused. "The worse it is," she said, "the better he can make it feel."

Not a comforting thought to take into the council room before second watch. Full morning light blazed on the undecorated walls, the plain wooden table, the motley chairs and stools, making me both conscious and slightly ashamed. Therkon must have a dozen council chambers, Two's memory held gorgeously appointed Riversend palace halls. How he would despise this!

We lined one table side, leaving the other for the embassy. Tez took the centre, Tanekhet at her left elbow, Iatha at her right, with me sandwiched between Iatha and Duitho. And Azo, and Keshaq, standing close behind Tez, as if they were not merely troublecrew but bodyguards. A very unsubtle warning, I thought it. Till I heard Tanekhet murmur as he passed Keshaq, "Not even for me?" And Keshaq retort, tight-lipped. "*For* you. Never, at a table with *him*."

Two was still refusing to show me more than Therkon had hinted about that connection, when the embassy arrived.

Therkon came in amid a thicket of burly six-foot troublecrew, all lowering and pressing close as round a captured criminal. I had thought to be embarrassed, seeing him again. Instead my heart turned over to the image of a trapped and fallen deer, entangled beyond rescue in the nets.

Then the shoulders parted, and as Therkon emerged, his Trouble-head gave him a white-hot warning stare. And Therkon dropped his head a quarter-inch and gave it back.

I did not have to reconstruct a night of fulmination and recrimination worse than ours, or a close pass to troublecrew mutiny. Nor, catching the side-wash of that look, did I doubt who had prevailed.

We all rose. Someone drew out Therkon's chair. The chamberlain, by the quill, rolls and slate, materialized at his left elbow, and the Trouble-head smouldered up to Therkon's right. He ran one glance along our faces and his eyes met mine.

One brief glance, and in such a situation, naturally masked. But the acknowledgement was more than politician's relief.

I sat down with my stomach settled, and about my heart an insidiously rising warmth.

The chamberlain and Iatha exchanged openings. I absorbed Therkon meanwhile. That dark dramatic profile, the elegant sweep of hair, in a topaz and ruby clip this time; a ring on the other hand as well, even a bracelet, chased gold and topaz, on the wrist. A golden-red tunic whose full, open-ended sleeves stopped just short of impediment. I had not noticed the trousers, but it dawned on me, with a shock of near delight, that whether for pride or provocation, he had dressed to look the Dragonfly.

"Ruand." He had already inclined his head to Tez. "My ladies." His eye met Tanekhet's for one electric second and the hair crisped on my neck. Then Therkon went on, impassive now as Tanekhet himself.

"I have come to make a proposal," he said. "And to ask a favor—a very great favor—of Telluir House."

Two was in turmoil. I clenched my hands on the nether table-rim. *No matter if he asks for a prophecy, if he demands, if he threatens*, I ordered. *You are not to spark.*

The stillness said the others shared my dread. Only Tez, with matching calm, nodded Therkon on.

He lifted his head a little, the tilt of a listening deer. Then he said, "What news has Telluir House of the Archipelago?"

Tanekhet's expression measured the audacity: to request a meeting we could not refuse, to announce himself as seeking a favour, and then presume to exploit our intelligence. Not simply of the River: of the remote, unknown, countless islands that stretched away into the ocean south and west of Riversend.

Tez did not answer that we had very little word and less concern. Or add that these were lands once half-ruled by Dhasdein, still barriered beyond their own borders, complicit with us in an event Dhasdein at least might not wish to recall. Surely, their news should come from him?

She did raise her brows and return mildly, "Is there something Iskarda should know?"

Therkon turned a hand out. Light flashed on the new ring. A big hazian, glowing red as a coal in its nest of thillians.

"Ruand, you know we still trade overseas. The islands need our fine goods. Cloth. Weapons. Sometimes, grain. And," he shifted a shoulder, "we will pay a good deal for their wine."

Tez did not have to nod. We all knew wine had been a prime import when Dhasdein ruled the Archipelago, if at an exorbitant excise rate.

"With peace, the trade has grown."

None of us let an eyebrow climb. Let Dhasdein save face with the euphemism of "peace" for what had been successful rebellion and independence for the Archipelago.

Tez answered blandly, "They still see Wave Island red, sometimes, in Amberlight."

Therkon nodded. Then he rubbed a finger up from the inner point of his eyebrows and said, "Something is wrong."

"With the trade?"

"The trade, and more." He set both palms on the table and the chamberlain's expression told me this admission had been a major battle-point. "There are pirates in the islands, yes. There were always pirates. We take measures, frequently. Escort the traders. Raid a nest, sometimes." The shrug filled in: a chronic problem to which we apply ongoing remedies, because the trade makes it worthwhile.

Tez was extrapolating too. "They've suddenly increased? The whole trade's at threat?"

"They have increased, yes. The trade is . . . I would not yet say, entirely at threat."

Tez waited. The Dhasdeini Trouble-head's scowl was close to pain.

"But we are losing ships," Therkon said softly, "in the open sea, before they ever reach the islands. Far more than we ever lost before."

"Storms?"

"There are always storms. These are huge, unexpected storms. And one season, yes, would not be unusual. This has been year after year."

This time Tez's eyebrows did rise. "How many years?"

Therkon looked her straight in the eye. "Five."

I twitched, unable to help it. Five years was anomalous out of measure. No wonder they had come, no wonder they had accepted any condition for the embassy, no wonder they had kept trying and trying . . .

My palms began to sweat. But nobody, yet, had looked at me. Tez and Therkon were still eye to eye, and his face warned, *There is more.*

In a moment Tez said, "Go on."

Therkon's fingers shut. The Dhasdein signet glittered, one broad flash of light like a moving spear.

"Now, Dhasdein is getting refugees. Ship-loads, boat-loads of refugees. Not from pirates. From the islands. The Archipelago itself."

Iatha moved, decisively. Tez glanced aside, smoothly passing the initiative.

"Factions?" Iatha said. "Some kind of civil war?"

The Archipelago galleys and their marines had been a power for Dhasdein. Small doubt the struggle would be ferocious if they fought internally.

Iatha's glower added, *If you want help from us, we expect truth from you.* Therkon only nodded, a frank acknowledgement. And said, "We do not know."

"But surely these people talk—!"

"Not to us."

"They ask for shelter," he went on, when Iatha stared. "Asylum. They offer whatever they have. Gold, family gods, sometimes a child. They are islanders, not ship-folk. They will tell us the place they left. Why they left? No."

"*There is a pattern,*" Two had it out before I could stop her, "*in the places? The names?*"

All the Dhasdeinis understood where that went. For the chamberlain and Trouble-head shock battled consternation and the bone-deep impulse to secrecy. Therkon looked at me with frank relief.

"There is a pattern—my lady Chaeris. Yes."

He knew who had spoken, but he would not betray Two. He gave his Trouble-head one last quelling stare and turned back to me.

"A good many names we do not know. They are South Reach islands, a long way from where Dhasdein ever went. The Archipelago is huge?" Two and I nodded understanding. That dark double-wave of eyebrow contracted in a frown.

"The pattern of names we do know says: whatever expelled these people is moving." His mouth set. "And it is coming this way."

\* \* \* \*

With the moments of impact past, the other Dhasdeinis seemed almost relieved. For them, the worst was over. All the secrets had been bared; now, perhaps, there might be some recompense. They looked openly and hopefully at me.

The consternation our side had been kept to a minimum. I did feel Iatha move beside me, the spring-taut tension in Duitho, but they both knew better than to touch me outright. And Tez was still holding Therkon's eyes.

"So," she said, "Dhasdein has come to Iskarda."

"For an oracle, yes." Therkon hit it straight into the open. "But not to ask what we should do."

Tez actually stared. Reckless beyond even these new limits, Therkon looked at me and said, "Lady Chaeris, if you will hear us. If you will look on our behalf. We would ask only, Do you know—have you any idea? What this thing is?"

He had not unmasked Two, but his direction was clear. Not the future, the past. Not the cloudy terror of forecasting without information, but a straightforward search of the already known. Two's memories.

With every other caution lost, I had just wits to choose words myself. I said, "Let me think."

The withdrawal, the blur, the white hiatus was easier this time. I slid back into the council room with Iatha wringing tense beside me. I could see, in the Trouble-head's face across from me, the mingling of revulsion and rapacity, and fear.

And frank and clear and nothing further from repulsed, the anxiety in Therkon's eyes.

As our looks met he did relax a fraction, signaled by his rings' little ripple of light. Then he dipped his head, very nearly a reverence. And waited, with real courtesy, for me to speak.

I said, "We have no records of such a thing."

Two had let me reply. Given the Trouble-head's expression, a relief. And no sort of assistance with the actual question. I did not have to read that from Therkon's face.

*"We need more information,"* Two said.

Tez's head snapped round and she said crisply, "Chaeris, if you don't know enough already—"

I forestalled Two with an effort. We did not need to shake the Dhasdeini underlings any further with mentions of "we."

"I have information about the River, up to and beyond Cataract. I have information about the past. Back to the founding of Amberlight." I could feel Iatha flinch as if I had ripped a bandage off. But if Therkon had not told them, they would find out soon enough. "I have information about Dhasdein—mostly second-hand—" I did not dare look at Therkon in case his lips should twitch. "But almost nothing about the Archipelago."

Several people started to yell at once and Tez bawled, "S'hurre!" in a battle voice. In the instant's hush Therkon spoke.

"This comes appositely to my favour, Ruand."

Tez wheeled on him, past masking her own wits. "Chaeris is going nowhere. Least of all Dhasdein!"

Everyone else, excepting Tanekhet, was shocked mute. The hiatus went on and on while both of them glared till I wondered the very air did not spark. Then Tez let out a long silent breath. And Therkon brought his chin down half a notch and said quite quietly, "My lady Tez. Do you have a choice?"

The others yelled then, all at once. Tez let them shout as my mother might have, heedless of the Dhasdeinis, heedless of all but the need to ride out their own shock. I had no time for them either. My stomach was turning over, little white flashes had begun to cross my eyes, I could feel myself start to pant. *No,* I shouted desperately, *no, not now: let them talk, let them talk, it's not going to do any good—it won't help anyone if you blow up!*

Two was not listening. The paroxysm built and built and in final desperation I slammed one hand on the table myself.

The spark cracked like a thunderbolt. The stench rose like flame. Ten, fifteen people shocked voiceless, the room areek with charring wood. Me with one hand in the air, and under it, a black, smoking patch wider than my palm across the tabletop.

Two screamed, *"We must go! We have to go! No givens, no working points, no projections—no patterns—Iskarda, Dhasdein, the River, islands, islands-islands-islands . . . .! No facts, no facts, no FACTS!"*

* * * *

Someone had me, lightly but firmly, by the wrist. Instinct and experience made me flinch, but that grip out-dated conscious memory: Caitha, senior House physician. A touch known from the day that she delivered me.

"Pulse within limits," her brisk physician's voice said. "No other damage. A short rest, perhaps a cup of verrian tea. Hanni, would you see to that?" Her fingers brushed the back of my neck. "Chaeris, do you feel ready to sit up?"

*Not in the least,* I wanted to squawk. Not to meet all those faces, the familiar ones saying how I had disappointed them, the unfamiliar ones full of revulsion, contempt, fear. And he . . .

I squeezed my eyes shut. Two was repentantly invisible. But I remained a woman, my mother's daughter. A scion of Telluir House. The blood of Amberlight.

I opened my eyes, composed my face like plaster setting, and levered my cheek off the tabletop.

And they were all gone, except Tez, now slipping into the chair Caitha had used, beside me.

And beyond her, Therkon.

I should think all of the air went out of me on one winded squeak. He did stretch his hand out instinctively, but Tez made one quick motion and he drew back.

Tez did not touch me, either. I feared a blistering rebuke. But her question was not for me.

"Are you so sure," she said, "of your favor now?"

I looked sidelong in time to catch Therkon's face. Not the philosopher, but the prince, the sovereign who had subdued minions with a glower.

Before he turned his attention, a yet more quelling retort, to me.

"Lady Chaeris, I should perhaps have asked you to begin with. But I have no desire to estrange you from your folk. They have rightful claims on you. They have raised and protected you, and it is small wonder they would meet my request with—distress."

In his own way, as masterly a handler of devastating euphemisms as Tanekhet. I felt Tez bristle, but she did not speak.

Unlike her, I was past diplomatic finesse. "What request?" I said.

He looked straight up at me, those bronze-black eyes closer than they had been the moment before we kissed, irises darker than their deep fringe of lash. The beauty was devastating as the force of the intent.

"That you come to Dhasdein," he said.

Tez had extrapolated it. I was past reasoning. Two was mute. I said blankly, "What?"

"Lady Chaeris." He did pause, for whosoever sake. "This will be to Dhasdein's vantage, I openly confess. We need you. I begin to see we need you desperately. This with the Archipelago is, is beyond our experience. You may not have information yet. But to have you at hand, as newer word does come in . . . to have your advice, if patterns begin to shape . . . We would not ask you to consider the future—"

Tez cut in brutally, "Not yet."

Therkon offered her one slicing glance. "But perhaps, if you are ever to look ahead, it is this information that will complete the pattern. Where better to gather it, than in Dhasdein?"

And he knew the one and only lure to bring Two out of that skulk. New facts. On an area so scantily covered, on the further question whose pressure I could already feel like a yoke over my neck. Dhasdein, perhaps the Archipelago itself, was in some serious danger. Could I deny them the possibility that one day, we might try a projection of the future with facts enough to make it work?

"Your pretext is also your rebuttal," Tez said, flat and harsh. "If Chaeris goes to help protect Dhasdein, she is in the same peril as Dhasdein."

"My lady Tez, *Dhasdein* is not in peril yet! That is precisely what I am trying to prevent—"

He stopped, with a flare of nostrils that left their rims dead white. Tez's silence, ironic, walled, said he had not helped his case.

"Let us consider then," Therkon resumed, this time with a definite sting of silk, "the case of Iskarda. Ours are not the only intelligencers here. What will you say, when word that our embassy was received, that we asked questions and had answers, reaches Verrain? And Amberlight? And Cataract?"

Tez might have turned the blow. I could not help but flinch. He glanced at me, and the concern was almost clear of political taint.

"You know," he said very softly, past me. "You cannot have failed to predict it. And it will not just be the Assembly and the rulers that come."

Tez's shoulders moved. Therkon nodded, and said what she would not.

"You lack the resources to shield the lady Chaeris, in Iskarda."

"We have them," Tez ripped back, "in Amberlight."

Therkon's jaw clamped. Then he said, "What will you tell their Assembly, when some crisis arrives and they vote for an oracle?"

Tez more than glared. I knew the Amberlight assembly, the people's rule, was hers and my mother's pride and delight. And Two's memories showed me too often how it could be flawed.

"And how will Chaeris fare, if your slumfolk riot in Riversend?"

"If you think we would risk her beyond the palace—"

"Since when have palace guards been incorruptible?"

"Dhasdein is not Verrain—!"

"And Dhasdein is half the River nearer the Archipelago."

For a second more Therkon held her stare, while the fire in those eyes spoke all the crown prince's offense, exasperation, wrath. Then he sat back, turned both hands out, and slightly bowed his head.

"Very well." For the first time, he sounded openly tired. "We are an embassy, not a bandit raid. We will accept your judgement. Take what precautions you choose."

*For the time,* he did not add, *when the peril approaching Dhasdein comes upRiver to you.* But the menace was there, in the way he extricated himself, slowly as an old man, from the chair.

Tez watched him with a face of solid flint. I tried to emulate her, but I was seeing the deer with hounds on its trail, flagging, denied sanctuary. Turning mutely away. And Two was watching a cornucopia of knowledge drawn from between our very hands.

"I want to go!" It burst out of me like a broken water-pipe. Two cried for me, "*We must go to Dhasdein!*"

"Chaeris—!"

"Tez, he's right! We don't have the facts and we can't get them here. I can't even project accurately for today because for half the River, we don't know! And as for this thing in the Archipelago—" I overshouted her—"It's coming this way! There's no reason it won't reach Dhasdein like the refugees did! Are we going to sit here and let other people get destroyed for us, when we could have helped, when we might have saved us all!"

The last sentence made her jerk as if I had hit her on a burn. Her mouth opened and I yelled again. "And if we ever are to know the future, it will have to be for the River as well as us!"

Beyond the table Therkon had paused, but he had the wit not to attempt anything more. He simply waited, almost as completely effacing himself as was possible for a dragonfly, while Tez glared up at me, and I glared back.

Until she said flatly, "This is a matter for the House."

\* \* \* \*

When the door closed behind Therkon I covered my own anxiety with affront. "You were very hard on him, weren't you? He was only trying to do his best. For Dhasdein. Maybe for the River as well."

She had got up, but she paused and gave me a look where exasperation and pity mixed. "And Therkon has been playing imperial councils like a lyre since he tied up his hair. Do you think he found it hard to play a twelve-year-old girl? Even one like you?"

"He didn't play—!"

She gave one horse-like snort. "He *played* that last scene like a Delta tragedy queen. Sooo meek. Sooo quiet. Sooo lost and wistful—soooo—"

"He couldn't have played Two!"

"Blight and blast it, Chaeris, of course he could! Ten minutes with you would tell him Two's weak spot and where else did he aim? Information! Facts!"

*It wasn't like that,* I wanted to yell. *It isn't like that!* Up the hill he had been the philosopher, he just wanted to know. And he saw how it upset us not to have the information. *He knows why we want it. He wasn't just using us!*

Infuriatingly, stupidly, my eyes blurred. The best riposte I could manage was, "He wouldn't do that!"

She stopped stock still and stared at me, eyes narrowing as if back behind a gun. Then she rubbed a palm over her face and said almost gently, "Chaeris, he'll do whatever helps his people, however he feels about the tools. I know he will. Because I'm a Head, like he is. It's what I do myself."

\* \* \* \*

The council argued the matter, if argument is the apposite word, for the next two days. At times I thought it would come to weapon-holes in the walls. The first day I waited with fuming impatience, sure of the way within myself. But as I came down the passage almost at daybreak the second day, I heard the voices in my mother's room.

It was Tez who spoke, with irony and wryness atop hardly submerged stress. "Last time, I wanted to save the River, and it was you saying, *Put us first.*"

The door's hinge-crack gave me her back view, cross-legged on the great old bed. In a moment Tanekhet came round the bed end, a view of his chin, a half-buttoned shirt.

Tez said, "And now, what *do* you say?"

His fingers stopped. Then he answered, too neutral, "This is a matter for Telluir House."

"You think you aren't Telluir? After all this time?" Her voice firmed. "*I* say you are of the House. And I am Ruand. I also say, give me your opinion now."

He tucked his chin down to give her that under-the-brows look. "It will not please the House."

Tez sat up with a jerk. A pillow flew on the floor. "You want to let her go?"

His expression said it all: she was Ruand. She had the final say. To dispute was a waste of time.

"She's too young!"

"Chaeris is twelve." Tanekhet's voice was neutral again. "But Chaeris is not alone."

"No, Two's with her. In her. Who knows how? Mother aid us, a twelve year old girl and a seven hundred year old—something. What will Dhasdein make of that? What if they try to 'study' her? If they call her a freak? A monstrosity?" Suddenly her voice quivered. "I couldn't bear her to be—"

He moved then, coming to her side. She laid her head against him and he slid an arm around her, one hand touching her hair. "She would hardly go outside the palace—"

"The palace! I've been there, too. How will she fare, in that serpents' paradise? Intrigue, factions . . . And the Empress. Not to mention Therkon himself!"

When Tanekhet did not reply she buried her face deeper, the words muffled in his chest.

"He'll twist her round his finger. He did it here, just the other day. She's never met a man who—she's twelve. She's never been out of Iskarda!"

"Two will be there . . ."

"What does Two know? She only remembers decisions. She's never made them herself."

In profile, his own brows had set. He said evenly, "She will have escorts. Troublecrew. I thought, perhaps Azo and Verrith?"

"Azo *and*—?" Tez's head came up. I could read the dismay. The two stalwarts Zuri would have relied on to uphold her new inexperienced Trouble-head.

Tanekhet too paused before he spoke.

"She must have someone. And would either, this time, go alone?"

"No. No." The qherrique had enrolled Azo to seek the Source, without her partner, a pairing made in Amberlight. "No. They'd never do that again."

Tanekhet let the silence ask for him, Is there any other choice?

"No," Tez said flatly. "It must be both. But . . ."

"But?"

"O Mother's aid, they're good, but they've never been to Dhasdein. And there's only two of them."

"Surely, two like that? And Chaeris is practically trouble crew now?"

One hand jerked. "If Therkon lured her somewhere—forbade them to come. Some secret cursed place. He only has to mention information, Two will follow him anywhere!"

Like me, I felt Two wince.

Tez's face was still buried. There was more than an ache in her voice. "If I wasn't Head. If I could just go with her. Myself."

Perhaps unconsciously his face smoothed. He ran a finger over her plait. "You were troublecrew once, yes, for Tellurith. Between the pair of you, you plagued me for weeks."

She produced a watery half-laugh, half-sniff. Then her shoulders clenched. "But it's Dhasdein this time. What are we to do if they keep her there? If they held her there? If she couldn't even get a message out! Oh, Mother aid me." Her hands came up over her own ears. "If anything happened to her . . . what would I say to Tellurith?"

My own heart was bumping unevenly in my throat. Not least at the look on Tanekhet's face.

At last he put a finger under her chin and lifted her head. "My heart," he said, softly, somberly, "if I read this aright, Chaeris will go, whatever we do."

Tez started back. He let her move, but held her gaze.

"They have already met. Despite all we did. If that was intended, then, we must expect, so is this. And if we refuse to let her go this time—what lever will come next?"

Even in profile, Tez was going pale. "You mean, next time they will use force?"

"I mean, next time, it may not be Dhasdein."

Tez froze where she sat. Then she moistened her lips. "This—intent. This—purpose. Whatever it is?"

Tanekhet produced the tiniest of shrugs. And said the next words with a surgeon's lethal delicacy.

"Or whatever it is, in the Archipelago."

I tried to make my wits work. To remember to breathe. All my self seemed to be beyond that door-slit, where they were still face to face in the silent, listening room.

Then Tez turned her head away. Gathered a crumple of linen and let it drop. When she spoke, there was an echo of Therkon in her almost lifeless voice.

"Then this time, too, you're right. We," a bitter little laugh, "*have* no choice. We have to let her go."

# CHAPTER IV

I heard it all again as the House laboured its way to Tez's conclusion, while their spelling out of perils and mischances sharpened the pangs of dread already goring me. To leave Iskarda. To abandon everyone who cared for me, all that had been my life, with no certainty of ever seeing it again. Without even my mother's knowledge, with only Azo and Verrith as shield, to thrust myself headlong upon the charity of strangers. And those strangers Dhasdein.

Two added worse threats, a storm on the River, a sortie from Mel'eth or Shirran to ambush Therkon's galley. A sudden breach with Verrain, and the entire scheme stillborn? The thought of betrayal in Dhasdein brought me near enough panic, but that spectre nearly finished me.

Under it all boiled our own peculiar stress: that we had to go, whatever the dangers, whatever the loss. That the urgency, whatever its source, was imperative. We could not afford to wait a single day.

With heroic effort I managed not to shout all that at everyone who rehearsed the general laments in council, or poured them out on me. I even managed not to let Two spark more than a time or two. But at the last, only one choice could be made.

Therkon agreed to a full formal meeting without the slightest demur. He even accepted the banishment of all other Dhasdeinis. Though he must have been fretting worse than I, he came into the council room more devastatingly elegant than ever, in a flame-gold brocaded over-tunic and driven-snow white shirt, no ornament but his two rings, settling just a little too quietly into a seat.

In equally courteous silence he waited out almost the entire Iskardan jeremiad of threat and lament. But when Iatha reached bluster about harm to me, and very unsubtle reminders of Dhasdein's past behavior, he thrust out a hand with a jerk that drew every eye to the charred patch on the tabletop.

"Do you think, my ladies, that we have not learnt our lesson?" The Dhasdeini clip on his final consonants was very clear. "Or if we did forget the past, after that reminder, that anyone in all Dhasdein would dare lay hands on the bearer of qherrique?"

Iatha snorted at him with her worst belligerence.

"What guarantee is that, against the chances of the River and war? An arrow out of Shirran, a Mel'ethi bandit. Or just another storm—"

Therkon stood up with a jerk that overthrew his chair. "Madam," the courtesy came like a slingshot, "I will be the lady Chaeris' surety." He tossed his head back. His eyes burned. "If harm comes to her, I will answer for it with my life."

The air seemed to ring behind his voice, adding everything he had not said: *I, no mere man but Dhasdein's crown prince, the Empire's shield and hope.* Sealing this pledge with the promise of his own flesh and blood. Speaking, beyond question, from the truth of his own heart.

I had to drop my eyes like the merest bashful boy. My throat was swelling with something that was not grief, even though my eyes had misted almost to tears.

Iatha had sat back, though her silence was not abashed. Her eyes narrowed. It was Tez who answered, coolly as a flung bucket of water, "Telluir accepts your pledge."

Yet again their eyes locked. After another aeon, Therkon let his chin down, and made Tez a bow of most imperial courtesy. "Dhasdein thanks Iskarda, my lady. For its trust. Above all, for its gift." He did not bother with vows and protestations of how Dhasdein would treasure it. "Have I your leave to prepare, now? Whenever you set our departure, we have no time to waste."

* * * *

Dhasdeini troublecrew swamped him a step beyond the door. Duitho slid out after them, while with belated laments the council began to disperse. Azo and Verrith closed on Tez: a first-hand briefing, no doubt, on Dhasdein. Iatha and Hanni went last, together, as they had been so long. But between me and Tez, Tanekhet had remained.

He was watching the door, and something in his eyes spoke amusement, and memory, but an affectionate, almost admiring memory, as of a man recalling a child who is now, in both senses, well grown. I saw Keshaq read it too, for he did not wait as usual. As he moved off with his version of the sinuous troublecrew tread, I slid to Tanekhet's elbow myself.

He smiled at me, despite the tiredness he was showing like the rest. "Well, my dear, you will certainly have the best possible shield."

"Yes." Pride, and something else, kept shutting my throat on anything more. "Tanekhet? I wanted to ask: that ring he wears?"

"The signet?" He looked faintly surprised. "Reputed to be his father's own? Left in the palace, when Antastes went?"

Two knew "went" did not mean the usual sense of "died," even for an emperor. I brushed that aside. "Not the signet. The other one. The triple thillians."

"The betrothal ring?" The remnants of smile vanished. "Wedding him to Dhasdein?"

"He said that." *Do not*, I threatened Two, *do not you dare let me blush.* "But is that what it really means? He's plighted to the Empire? He can't marry anyone else?"

The hint of constraint vanished too. "No, my dear, certainly not. Therkon," he gave his fingers a more than eloquent twirl, "has not been niggardly with his, er, favours. But he will as certainly marry. The Empire will, in time, need another heir."

*An heir-breeder*, said that soft, momentarily bitter voice in my memory.

"Oh. Of course." Let Two's insatiable curiosity, I prayed the Mother, also be credited with this. "But—who?"

"I mean, who's he likely to marry?" I expanded in a hurry to Tanekhet's incipient astonishment. "A, a, is there anyone in mind?"

"I should think, several." He had made the ordinary assumption. He was his calm, incisive self again. "I doubt, at the moment, I could give you actual names. But some great family's daughter, out of Riversrun, certainly. Not, I should think, Quetzistan. Not this time."

"Oh." Two wanted to ask, why not Quetzistan? I had more pressing parameters. "But still, someone from Dhasdein?"

Tanekhet's brows went up. "Do you see Therkon consenting to marry a Verraini merchant's get? With not even a Family to boast?" The great Families of Verrain had vanished, Two had told me, massacred in revolution twelve and more years ago. "Or an Amberlight Assembly delegate?" His mouth curled. "Let alone some tribal scion out of Cataract?"

My own mouth went on speaking, it seemed, without my consent.

"And not—not—"

Tanekhet's brows went to his hairline. Then he leant over and took both my hands without even a hesitation and Two let him hold them as his eyes held mine.

"Chaeris. My dear. My very dear." It was love, as well as pity in his voice. "Therkon would need to thank the River-lord on his knees, daily, did he ever have the chance. But no. Not a princess. Not an outland princess. Even one like you."

My throat had entirely shut. My lips could only shape a pathetic, ineffectual, *No?*

Tanekhet tightened his fingers a little. "Dearling, I know." He had never called me that before. "He is extremely beautiful. And gallant. And no-one would blame you, after that—avowal—if you thought he perhaps feels more than kindness. But, my little one . . . you are twelve years old."

I kept my eyes on the table rim and locked, *He said I looked seventeen!* In my throat.

"And he," Tanekhet was saying softly, almost reluctantly, "he has had his choice of the Empire's great ladies, these twenty years." He put a hand suddenly under my chin and made me look at him as he had with Tez. "Dearling, listen. Remember that, in Dhasdein. The crown prince is a great lover: not least because, when he loves, he does it with his heart. His whole heart. But they do not call him Dragonfly only for his clothes."

I tried to keep my lips shut, hearing that voice here in this very room. *I will answer for her with my life.*

"Ward yourself," Tanekhet was saying even more softly, but with a note of urgency. "Should the inclination ever take him, do not let him sunder yours."

He was in more than deadly earnest. I tried to look obedient, and not to gulp. Or break into tears. But I did find words, after all.

"Not even to marry?"

"Chaeris . . ." It was almost open pain.

"If I said—the one I wanted? The only one?"

He shook his head sharply, once. "Oh, my little one. Can you stop and think a moment? Just a moment? I can believe you feel so. That it seems so. But have you heard what I said? About Dhasdein?"

Two spoke, finding words where I could not. "*No outland empress.*"

"In Dhasdein, no." Tanekhet was past tact himself. "But that's not all. Picture for yourself, what would happen here, if you married him."

I pictured, Two pictured, and both our senses reeled.

"Ah, my dear." Tanekhet did not have to expand. "It's not possible, no. Not for you."

Not for my mother's only daughter, the River's oracle, the king-post of Iskarda, the child of my fathers and the heir of Amberlight. Not to leave her home-place. Not to enter the heartland of the oldest opponent, if not enemy. To blight Iskarda's hopes and future, and become an empress of Dhasdein.

And if it were possible, memory burst on me like a thunder-clap, would he ever ask? After Two made it so clear she wanted him as much as I did? And the way she did it?

Light as a moth's touch, with his little finger Tanekhet wiped beneath my eyes. He did not say, *Cheer up. It's for the best. Eventually, you will forget.* He did not say, *Iskarda will be grateful, even if they never know. Iskarda will live by your sacrifice.*

No more did he give me any kind of vilely sanctimonious praise. Touching my cheek once, he asked, gently matter-of-fact, "Has anyone thought, yet, to begin packing your clothes?"

* * * *

The House farewelled us as we had farewelled my mother, in Iskarda's market-place. I could hardly see, let alone speak, in the maelstrom of loss, forebodings, simple fear, and almost as frantic an excitement. To be leaving Iskarda. To get on a mule, and go beyond the quarry, to ride even past the first mirror-signal post, to see, for ourselves, Marbleport. And beyond that, the length of the River, at last.

Two has full memory of the House farewells. I do recall Tez's hug and double kiss. The quiet of her voice, so at odds with the stoniness of her face. And after her, last of the House, Tanekhet.

Who also kissed me like a kinsman, on each cheek, and alone thought past the House's concerns, to say with his faint, acid, nobleman's smile, "Now, my dear, gather knowledge like a bee in a clover-patch. Fill yourself to the limit, at last."

My own heart lifted. I kissed him back, which I could do now face to face. "Thank you," was all I could manage, but I daresay my expression was gloss enough. He gave me his full smile, that almost no-one saw except Tez. Let go my hands, and turned, the smile fading, to the one behind me. Therkon himself.

I felt the tension spring between them again. Therkon's face was a mask to match. But then he took an abrupt step closer, swung his shoulder to block the House folk off, and said with urgent, with open longing, "Tanekhet?"

Tanekhet's motion of withdrawal, of rising hostility, checked.

"I have wanted to say, for so long," Therkon was speaking quickly, near fumbling, almost under his breath. The voice of a much younger man. "I could never tell you. Before. But I never intended, I never wanted . . ." He held Tanekhet's eyes even as his hand clenched. "I would never have wanted—Deyiko."

That look untangled puzzles at a glance, even as it added dimensions I had never dreamt. Something at Deyiko had hurt Tanekhet, in a way Keshaq had never forgiven. *Tortured him*, I heard Therkon's own voice saying amid the boulders. And Tanekhet had never forgiven either. But to Therkon, Tanekhet had been more than Dhasdein's Suzerain, a great noble, a traitor. Tanekhet had been at the core of his own life. A cherished presence, lost, but never resigned.

*Answer him,* I was saying silently, my own teeth clenched. He was crown prince in earnest now, Dhasdein's Heir, Dhasdein's hatchet man. But whatever prize he took from Iskarda, this could leave him burdened with a shame, a guilt, a loss no-one else could ease.

Tanekhet had lowered his lids. It was the Suzerain's look, hooded, inscrutable. I saw Therkon's hope fade. But then Tanekhet's eyes rose. He sighed a little. Then he said, quite gently for Tanekhet, "Given the situation—what could either of us do?"

Therkon's every muscle seemed to spring in relief. His hands rose and he caught them back. He too, I saw, knew Tanekhet well enough not to attempt an embrace. But those eyes' radiance promised some fitting recompense.

Aloud, this time audible to everyone, he said, "I give you my word. I will take care of her."

Tanekhet looked him full in the face. And suddenly smiled as he had to me, and gripped Therkon's shoulder with his scarred right hand and said, "Dear boy." Meaning it. "I know you will."

\* \* \* \*

That exchange lingered, in the little space left from the exigencies of the mule's gait, not to mention my galled behind, from recording every visible detail of the hills and road and way stations before Marbleport. It lingered even when the flower-strewn, spring-green hills opened on a white scatter of houses, the arm of quay, and the endless steel-grey distance, ripples of current flawing its mirror sheen, that announced the River itself.

Thankfully, there were no more personal farewells. We lodged in Marbleport's biggest inn, with me shielded now behind Azo and Verrith's barricade. I had only to record the town and its folk, try to blot out the consternation at our news, and absorb the sum of Therkon's state: the two hundred phalanx troops of his real escort, paraded between the warehouses, and the two Imperial galleys and troop-transport that would carry us all to Dhasdein.

The galleys were what they call fives, the new, larger sort that had replaced three oarbanks with five men to each of sixty oars. As they rowed us out Two and I snatched details, the dark-varnished, clinker-laid side, massive oarhafts flattened along her flanks, the deadly ripple over the submerged reef of ram. And, when I finally conquered the rope ladder, the stern-deck with tiller and steering oars, the flap of Imperial ensign at her prow, serpent and thunderbolt black on unbroken white. All else vanished in Two's frenzied calculation of logistics for quartering, feeding and supplying over a thousand water-borne men.

I was inured to scarlet by then: the phalanx officers ashore flaunted their cloaks, the entire escort wore crimson kilts. Therkon himself had appeared that morning in the scarlet cloak and kilt of a high Dhasdeini officer. Only his troublecrew and mine kept their camouflage colors, almost lost amid the field of poppies on the galley's deck. But Two was focussed on the vistas ahead.

Azo just blocked our sortie to the rowing benches in the waist, the foredeck beyond, horrifically overcrowded now with Therkon's escort. But before Two noticed the hen-coop superstructure that would house officers and guests, the timing piper struck up. The rowing-officer shouted. The oarblades rose, slid, and dipped. The air reverberated to three hundred men's hissing grunts, the River revolved suddenly, and Marbleport slid away backward under huge banks of snow and charcoal mid-spring clouds.

After that I had no time to remember, let alone miss Iskarda. Forget the galley: here was the River, and worse, the Riverside. Slipping by us, two banks of it, every moment leaving more unscanned, unknown—we could not have been a mile downstream before Two was yelling at Azo, "Too fast, too fast! Make them stop! Make them slow!"

We were still on the stern-deck. An outer perimeter of Dhasdeini troublecrew surrounded us. Therkon and his phalanx commander had withdrawn to the cabin, but the captain himself was by the steersman, resplendent in more scarlet this and that, recoiling at Two's shouts with scandalized disbelief.

"Miss—madam—lady—You, tell her we're under way. We've landfall to make, we can't stop—!"

Azo retorted stonily, "Tell her yourself." Two, already frantic at what we had missed, fairly bellowed in his face, "I say, Wait!"

He thought I was a madwoman, and in Two's frenzy, he was near right. She might well have had us lay hands on the steering oars, but of a sudden troublecrew parted, the captain fell back., and ducking out to me came Therkon himself.

"My lady Chaeris?"

"Your Highness." I nearly sobbed with relief. Then I got as close as I could without actually grabbing his arm and went tiptoe to hiss in his ear, "It's Two, we can't see everything, it's going too fast, can we just stop?"

The memory of that charred spot on the table was in his face. He began one sentence to me. Swung on his heel and addressed the captain instead.

"Have them back water and move inshore, if you please."

I missed the details of royal confusion aboard both galleys, before the transport ran on, while they edged aside from the main current and lay to, almost in bowshot of the shore. Therkon had ushered me right back under the elegant lift of the stern fan. Now he turned to face me at the rail.

"Lady Chaeris," he said softly, "how much of the River does Two already know?"

"I don't—I'm not sure—" But Two was already answering him. "Oh. This is Amberlight land."

"And seen before?" He watched me, almost without expression. Except, in his eye, a gleam that spoke, not the prince handling a difficult situation, but the ever-curious philosopher.

"Oh. Yes." The memories were unreeling now. I took a great breath of relief. "Yes, we, Two does know it. Not this time of year, but yes, she remembers—"

"Then do you think, we might make do with, ah, matching memories, every mile or so?" He smiled suddenly. "The galley, you can inspect when we lie to this evening. And if such matching proves enough, then I think, by tomorrow morning, we will reach Verrain."

"Verrain?" Two's lust got into my own voice. "Can we see *that*?"

"As much as we can, my lady. But, may I mention? I have been three weeks out of Dhasdein." He made a diffident little gesture. "By now the Empire will need many decisions, many answers." He moved a hand toward the cabin door. "I can deal with some as we travel, but . . ."

"But?"

"But," more diffidently, "we have had no news from Riversend, or the Archipelago, for more than, ah, one of your moons. Shirran and Mel'eth are not friendly. It would help, till we come into Riversrun, if we could, ah, make all possible haste."

*A Shirran arrow*, I heard Iatha saying. *A Mel'ethi bandit.* Therkon's eyes, steady but worried, added the rest: no news might not be good news. The Empire would have need of him.

I bit my lip. But even Two could be brought to some sense of restraint.

"I suppose," I said, "we could have another look. Coming back."

His smile spoke relief, understanding. Equal bravado. He bent his head to me gravely. "Thank you," he said, "Lady Chaeris."

Then he turned about and used his imperial voice. "The lady Chaeris may bring us an oracle, but to do so, she must gather knowledge. All the knowledge she can find. Whatever help she seeks in that, we will give."

\* \* \* \*

Which meant, added the captain's glower, that even if she demanded such lunacy as lying to on a good current in open water, Therkon would obey.

But the day was better, after that. Even if Two had to check the Riverside every mile or so, even if Therkon, or Two's own fuss, had put a circle around us wider than a plague sign would make. Even the looks, gone past wary to alarmed or belligerent or openly repulsed, could be borne. Because that night I would see over the galley. And tomorrow, we would shoot the narrows through the Iskan ranges, into Verrain.

For now, there was the River, somber grey, murky green, sapphire and celadon in patches of abrupt spring sun, and passing craft to learn: Verraini or Dhasdeini freighters, their differing rigs and figureheads, sweeping by under full sail or labouring on the oar. Local craft with a pair of sweeps and a protesting cow amidships, or a sideful of waiting nets. And the enormous breadth of sky over-arching them all.

For the narrows Two matched my mother's memories. Zig and zag of rusty red granite cliffs, the River curling into tumultuous white, flights of grey-blue thin-leaved trees on each bluff, sudden magical prospects between. Green and gold in distant sunlight, patches and patterns of unfamiliar crops, framed by mountain edges against a background of celestial blue . . . until the last gap opened into the vast quilt of tilled fields and crowded villages, the spectrum of clothes and castes, the veining roads and paths and alleys full of ox-carts, horse-carts, palanquins, bright military flags, the rising boil of dust that was Verrain.

Two had me in the bows by then, almost hanging over the ram. I hardly noticed the unfortunate troops trying to stack themselves three and four deep against the break of the foredeck. Nor, though it was their territory. did the sailors dare approach. I never heard the light, even tread that did come, till he leant his elbows beside mine over the topside rail.

"Azo," I burst out without bothering to turn, "there aren't any Families so there can't be estates, so whose are those soldiers? There, those are cavalry, aren't they, but they don't have camels—Oh."

"Division-mayors," said Therkon, in his soft philosopher's voice. His eye-corners creased. "Verrain's Land-chief has made districts and wards and shires of the estates, and given each its Assembly delegate. They are forbidden to gather wealth as the Families did. But they all wish to display—pomp."

"An Assembly like Amberlight?" This was so new Two left me no time to feel constrained.

"Except for a nation, rather than just a city. Yes."

The countryside faded as questions boiled up. I grabbed the topmost. "And does it work?"

"It seems so. At any rate, after some twelve years, the Land-chief still leads Verrain."

Assembly delegates, fuss and faction, the most cumbrous imaginable form of government. And the freest, another voice cut sharply across Two's recollections of the new Amberlight. Giving the highest possible number of the people some voice.

"Could you do it in Dhasdein?"

The query was instantaneous, kindled from Two's flash of the Families, the iron pyramid which had supported the Verrain president, the great estates, so few owning so much of everything, the entire economy reliant on slaves. And then of the great nobles and kinglets whose rule persisted in what of Dhasdein's empire remained.

His eyes jerked round to me. Then he took one elbow from the rail and turned physically, body language speaking his attention's depth.

"Is that what you would have me do?"

He had both hands up before I could draw breath. "No, no, my lady Chaeris. I do not wish you to, to calculate what would happen, or even to ask if it could . . . I beg your pardon. I spoke without thought." He ruffled a hand swiftly over his hair. The long mouth twisted in a way I was coming to know. "In Verrain, there was a revolution. The Families, who had endured time out of mind, were obliterated. Wiped out, overnight. We did not have such a—house-clearing—in Dhasdein."

*You lost whole provinces*, I bit off on my tongue. Two was already extrapolating the rest.

*"Then you could not cast the nobles out?"*

He met my eyes and turned his hands out. He knew who had asked. "To change so much? The cost would be enormous. In time. In warfare, and other struggles. In lives."

*"Especially,"* Two said, *"now."*

Therkon glanced quickly behind us. He did not have to say, *You mean, too risky, with this threat of the Archipelago?* He did nod. Then he bit his lip, and swung abruptly away. And then back to me.

"My lady Chaeris—ah, I swore I would not do this. But if I only knew—" He clenched his hands on the broad span of rail and let go. The Dhasdein signet sparked fittingly to the sun. "If you could tell me, with what you do know. If you could just guess—"

My mouth went dry, my heart jumped up in my throat. He wanted a prediction. An oracle. He was going to do exactly as Tez had warned.

I could make a fuss. Alert troublecrew: Azo and Verrith were right at my back, they would have heard, they would be tense to intervene. I could have the decision taken from my hands, as it had been in the rocks, when he was on this same gambit's brink.

But he was Therkon. The philosopher who had understood, and perhaps been affronted, but never affrighted by us. The crown prince who had pledged to protect us with his life.

I got out, in a near whisper, "What would you ask?"

His head flew up and his eyes went wide. Then he actually hit the heel of his hand on the rail. "Ah, my lady, forgive me. If it were not for Dhasdein—if I did not have to ask—" I heard Tez, a week and a hundred miles behind: *It's what I do myself.* "But." A quick, hissing breath. "With what you know now, give me your best estimate. Can I advance, at this point, against whatever is in the Archipelago? And safely leave Mel'eth and Shirran in my rear?"

However inferior our intelligencers, Iskarda gathered the Riverword: we had no alternative. And Two had followed the reports since I was old enough to understand words. The white whirl enveloped me before I had time to realize Two would assent.

The whirl faded. "*We know Mel'eth and Shirran's resources,*" Two said. "*We lack full figures for Dhasdein. If you took twenty galleys to the Archipelago, what reserve troops could you raise, at need, in Riversrun?*"

Therkon's jaw very nearly dislocated. Then he shot one look across the deck, where I did not have to look to know his Trouble-head was out of earshot. Braced himself, and began, in complete candour, as crown prince of Dhasdein, to reply.

I wish, I found myself thinking, as he concluded, that I could pass this on to Duitho. But of course, I never could. Yet another trial for an oracle. Conflicting confidantes.

"*We lack information for the Archipelago,*" Two said. "*That is a constant. But with what we know now, an expedition would be feasible. The risk behind would be less than that of delaying to meet the risk in front.*"

"How much less—!" Therkon stopped himself in mid-breath. "Oh, my lady, forgive me again. I have my answer. It's enough. More than enough."

"*How much less,*" Two said precisely, "*we cannot more exactly calculate, till we see Dhasdein.*"

"Oh—!" The smile came then, genuine, wondering, devastating. The grateful emperor. The marveling philosopher.

Gravely, but without hesitation, he reached out and took up my right hand. Neither of us wondered that Two never thought to spark.

"Lady Chaeris, you already have my lasting gratitude." He bent his head and drew my hand higher to set a kiss, light, exquisitely graceful, on its back. "Tell me now, is there anything you wish? Any small recompense I can make?"

He was smiling across our fingers. The crown prince, the House-head, who had used his tool and found its worth high, and given me courteous gratitude. The philosopher who had watched Two in action, this time for himself.

The man, I wanted to think, who might also have the tiniest scrap of affection for me.

As for recompense: I swallowed Two's most unedifying suggestions and ordered, *Shut up. I don't understand the half of that, and you shan't make me blush!*

"Well. When we come to Assuana. If we don't stop, can we at least slow down?"

He burst out laughing, that spontaneous deep but soft spurt of amusement I had heard among the rocks. "For you, my lady, we will lie over for the night. And if you wish to go into the market next morning, right into the market, not simply the piers, there will be an escort, yes." The sparkle suddenly sharpened. "Would you wish to go further? Perhaps, to meet Nathyx?"

"No, no, please." What if Nathyx wanted questions answered too? "I know about him. At least, enough." I could have done with more, given Keshaq and Tanekhet's occasional remarks, but not at that risk.

"No?" Therkon cocked his head. For a moment it was the dark, beautiful deer again, now stepping freely into some sunlit space. "Something else?"

Two responded, and my breath stopped. But they were puzzles we had never been able to solve. And Therkon, of all people, must know.

"Will you," I took my courage in both hands, "answer two questions for me?"

The flicker of ruler's wariness was hardly there before it had gone. "I would hardly have the right to refuse," a little smile that took the sting out, "were I so inclined." He turned out his ringless hand, leaning sidelong on the rail now: *Ask.*

I drew a deep breath and said, "Why does Keshaq—look so much like you?"

\* \* \* \*

For an instant I was facing not merely the emperor, but the imperial hatchet man. Then that graven menace softened. The crown prince rubbed a finger once between his eyebrows and answered soberly, almost reluctantly, "Because—Keshaq—is high Quetzistani blood."

Two assayed all possible implications in a flash and gained nothing. He read that, and rubbed his brows again.

"And the Empress. She is Quetzistani."

High Quetzistani, it went without saying. Full Quetzistani, I realized. So her looks must have been handed on. So he looked like Keshaq, or Keshaq looked like him, because—

"We are not kin." Now the gravity was deepening to sombreness. "The Empress' clan is the Jhuir. Since—before her marriage—they have led Quetzistan."

Even at twelve I knew enough about people to let him go on in his own time.

He looked down the River, and said the rest to the verdantly springing crops of Verrain.

"Do you know what it means? Keshaq?"

"*Thirsty*," Two said.

"Thirsty, yes. And so, also, Unappeased."

I bit my tongue on Two's, *Unappeased for what?*

"His clan," said Therkon, still to the Riverside, "was Ku*o. Once, they led Quetzistan. Before—the Empress wed."

Not, 'my mother.' The Empress. Implications, correlations, related information were flying past Two and me now like a stream of lightning sparks. Old Amberlight intelligence of a change of rule in Quetzistan, a clan coup, more than clan work, intervention, help, provocation from Dhasdein, an upheaval, a bloodbath, and the suspicions of past Trouble-heads, firm however unproven, of the instigator.

I put out both hands and grasped the rail myself. The River seemed to heave and shudder ahead of me. Faintly, I heard myself say, "Tanekhet?"

Therkon very nearly jumped. I did hear his smothered gasp. Then the deliberate steadiness with which he answered, "He engineered the, the rising, yes. For the emperor's marriage. To," the steadiness faltered, "make Dhasdein safe."

Replaced the dominant Quetzistani clan, Two's ruthless recollections filled out, welded its substitute to the Empire. Removed, excised the opposition. Down to its very roots.

What had that meant to Keshaq? Loss of kinsfolk, more than certainly. And for himself?

*Slavery*, Two answered brutally. And would not go on.

"He," my throat was dry, "doesn't forget."

Therkon gave a great sigh and turned to lean side by side with me, a sag in his shoulders that had nothing to do with emperors. "No. Keshaq does not forget."

No wonder he had brought troublecrew to Iskarda, no wonder they had been all but mutinous when he slid off by himself. "You should never have gone off alone! If he'd known—if you'd met—!"

Therkon dropped his head and said to the rail, "I am safe. However he and Tanekhet 'arranged' it. He has forsworn revenge."

I waited. He said it bitterly, to the River beneath us. "But like him, I cannot forget."

That their blood was kind if not actual kin, and Keshaq's once as high as Therkon's own would be, in Quetzistan. That their matched heritage spoke in their faces, and he could have met Keshaq's fate. And Keshaq's amnesty, like his own blood-guilt, Therkon could not forget.

"It wasn't your fault!"

He lifted his head and attempted a smile. "My lady." More softly, "My partisan. No, it was not my fault. But it is there."

"But you like, you liked Tanekhet!"

This time the head came up in a jerk. Then intimidation yielded to a twisted little smile.

"My lady. Forgive me again. I forget how much you do know." Or Two knows, he did not have to supplement. "Yes, I cared for—I still do care for Tanekhet. I was born in Dhasdein. I thought myself Dhasdeini, most of my life. And he, as a boy he was my model. My steering star. I tried to copy everything he did." The long mouth did twist. "I thought, if I could manage that in small things, I could also manage the way he—ruled the Court."

In that second my own heart affirmed that every rumor about the way the old emperor despised his heir had been true. My hand went out before I could help it, and one of us put it over his ringed fingers on the rail.

"You did manage," I said.

His fingers jumped, but he did not pull away. It was I who did that, feeling the blush burn out to my very ears. "I'm sorry. I never meant—"

To touch him again, uninvited. Without the pretext, let alone the grace, with which he had touched me. To invoke those moments in the rocks when we touched him before.

He did reach out as he had once in our council room, before Tez's look warned him off. "My lady, it was I who never should have burdened you with old injustice. Old," wryly, his brows quirked, "foolishness. Not at all fit for," I literally saw him reach, *for a twelve-year-old girl*, and jib. He looked up and smiled at me, however ruefully, without constraint.

"That is foolish too, is it not? When you already know so much." Then he moved a shoulder and put it behind him as firmly as a Head's gavel coming down. "Tell me, what else did you wish to ask?"

"Oh." If the first question resurrected ogres, this might level walls. But he was waiting. To hedge off now would be almost as great a slight as might the question itself.

"Did Dhasdein," I looked him full in that dark, arresting eye, "arrange to make my mother leave?"

"What—?!"

He caught himself before both troublecrews could leap. Rearranged his body, made every muscle signal, *False alarm.* Smiled at me, as glassily false as the posture, with the hatchet man's glitter in his eye. "My lady, what do you mean?"

I faced the River in my turn. "They thought, in Iskarda, when your message about the embassy came. That it was so soon after my mother went. That it was so . . . convenient." I knew he would fill in the sense as fast as Iatha herself. "Iatha said: was it more than good intelligence? Did you—Dhasdein—not just know she'd gone? Did—was it—arranged?"

And the other echo sprang back to me, Two's own answer about our meeting in the rocks. I nearly banged the rail myself and cursed. Blight and blast it, maybe it had been arranged. But not by Dhasdein!

It was too late. The words were out. I stared at the River where a covey of Verrain sampans had just eluded more than my cursory glance, and waited to meet a Dhasdeini massacre of my own.

"My lady."

He said it through his teeth. The effect is rare but quite unmistakable. The rest came in the emperor's voice, with all the weight of an emperor's affront.

"No."

Impossible to doubt, as futile to seek more. Beyond forgiveness to apologise. I said it to the deck, in the smallest voice I had achieved since toddler-hood. "Thank you."

I heard him gasp. Splutter as he had in the rocks. Struggle, no doubt, with assorted imperial outrages, and suddenly laugh, the true laugh, smothered almost as fast as the splutter before he wheeled back to the rail and addressed the River, voice still quaking with subterranean wrath and erupting mirth.

"Not at all."

Then his hand touched my elbow as he went on in almost normal tones and loud enough for troublecrew's hearing, "Does Two remember that town? Now it's harbour for the whole North district of Verrain."

\* \* \* \*

We did stop at Assuana, and I had ample time to explore the market, from its junk-and-jewel-box quays to the length of the main market-place: Therkon's stomach rebelled at something in the day's breakfast, and his cook threw a royal tantrum, doubtless fuelled by enforced silence in Iskarda. When the mainmast stopped reverberating, the captains had been reduced to mute compliance. We would lie to till the provisions had been changed for something fit to feed the crown prince, and till the crown prince himself could comfortably travel again.

"It was nothing to do with Iskarda." On the stern deck, when we finally got under way, Therkon was almost shamefaced. "Nor your provisions." He looked down and consciously kept a hand from touching his midriff, above the splendour of a phalanx officer's palm-wide, bronze-studded, serpent-buckle belt. "Simply my cantankerous, wretched . . ."

"And that's not your fault either."

I got a flash of direct glance and smile, a sun-glint through the gloom of chagrin and undoubted embarrassment. I might have had time to recall Tanekhet's warning, but Two had other concerns.

"Do they know why?"

Therkon snorted softly. "Do you think no-one has asked?"

And what would be the point of repeating doubtless stressful examinations, pointless catechisms? *Think*, I ordered Two in exasperation. *Run some inferences, first.*

"No particular food, then?"

The troublecrew had backed off a little, even Azo and Verrith. The look he gave me was untrammeled surprise. And then, a dawn-glimmer of hope.

"No particular food, no."

*And?* I demanded of Two in rising irritation. *Can't you see what you're doing?* He thought—he hoped—we could solve it. Produce an oracle. Make a true diagnosis, cure him. *And do you have the facts for that?*

"*Let me,*" said Two, "*think about it. At least until Dhasdein.*"

Let *me?* I did not have time to question or expostulate. The glimmer of hope had become full morning. Crown prince and philosopher said with truest gratitude, "My lady, you are too kind."

*Remember*, I threatened us both when he had disappeared back to the hencoop, *Tanekhet's warning*. Be wary, control yourself. Don't let those instants of devastating open feeling wash your defenses right away.

* * * *

It was another two days downRiver before I belatedly thought to ask, "Why didn't Nathyx want to see me?"

"Ah." We were back on the stern deck, in what was becoming routine: Therkon's mid-morning break from his labours in what, at evening, would become his quarters, his troublecrew's quarters, and Azo and Verrith's and my room. The cook had produced the now usual white milled poppyseed roll. Therkon leant on the Riverside rail—troublecrew flatly forbade him the bank-side—while closer midships, I sat on an incongruous formal chair.

When he did not go on, Two extrapolated. "*You prevented him?*"

"Ouch," said Therkon, and shifted his shoulders. "No, not, ah, prevented . . ."

"A bargain, then?"

"The Nine-limbed Adversary . . . no." I could complete the formula, from overhearing sailors: The Adversary fly away with whatever vexed the speaker. In this case, our wits.

"Well." He gave me that slightly too-charming smile. "There was a, a bargain of sorts, yes." As he looked in my face something made him suddenly put his chin up. The smile disappeared.

"I had to tell him where I was going, and—who—I hoped to bring downRiver. And, yes, pledge that I would at least ask you to see him. When we came back."

He knew what he had done. He did not need to glance aside at Azo or Verrith. But he did hold my eyes, and there might have been shame, or a shame-faced plea for forgiveness, but what I read there was a different plea. For understanding. For acceptance of a ruler's necessities, drawn from how much he had already shown me, honestly, openly, of his life.

"And does that pledge cover us," I said at last, "past Deyiko?"

He relaxed suddenly on the rail with a smile that made me clutch Tanekhet's warning like a tree-trunk in a flood.

"My lady. Yes. Nathyx is not the sort to dabble in treachery, but the agreement does cover us across the border. Both into, and then out of, Deyiko."

Where Nathyx kept his word, so we passed from the relative safety of Verrain to the questionable Shirran borderlands: and dropped the transport, along with a hundred troops.

"A balance," Therkon explained wryly. "Less defense, but considerably more speed. And better manoeuvring, if trouble came."

Two watched them go with a different regret. Only then did I realize how sequestered I had been, locked in a double ring of troublecrew. I had talked to Therkon. I knew the name of his cook, Tuor, his Trouble-head, Deoren, his phalanx-troop commander, Euchan, but except for Tuor I had hardly exchanged a word with them. As for the actual troops . . .

"Two wanted to learn some soldiers," I said regretfully, as the Dhasdein-side quays slid behind. "Now all those are gone. And we never seem to get near these, anyway." At which Therkon spluttered aloud.

"Euchan's threatened them," he said, becoming extremely straight-faced, "with castration and decimation if one gets in spearlength. Let alone has you trip over his feet."

"Oh." Then the too familiar awareness of difference, avoidance, hidden repulsion changed. "You mean that's why they all herd up on the foredeck whenever I go down there? Why didn't you tell me? The poor things are crowded enough as it is!"

From his expression, the comfort of phalanx rankers was their leaders' last concern. But he took instant advantage. "Then, my lady Chaeris, will you do them as well as me a favor? Will you stay off the foredeck, until we reach Riversrun?"

* * * *

Two had my three parents' memories of the River through the old territories of Dhasdein: so it was easier than I had thought, to watch from astern as the land grew both emptier and more fertile, to match recalled names with the little Riverside towns as the low rolling hills swelled into fawn and muted spring green under drifting clouds of sheep, masked by the River fringe of mighty red-barked helliens. Quetzistan to the left, Shirran to the right, looked little different.

Therkon did not have to tell me the Quetzistani sheep-herders were almost nomad and scorned farming, while hidden up the largely empty roads, along the many small tributaries, lay the vineyards that provided Shirran's chief income. Nor did he have to explain why the troops now stood watch in a triple rota, one group armed on deck, one below, one relieving at the oars. Or why we never hove to except at some Quetzistani quay, or what the tension was that wrapped both galleys in a silent thundercloud.

But Shirran let us pass. In twelve back-breaking runs we reached Narmin, the Mel'ethi border-post.

Without surprise I found Therkon had made agreements here as well: the galleys paid a toll, and there was a customs officer, but it was all done on the Quetzistani bank. Next morning we embarked on the shortest leg of the trip, between Shirran and Riversrun.

Mel'eth stretches far into the west, down to the ocean beyond Riversrun's border, but its River frontage is relatively narrow. We had one momentary scare, when a cedar raft coming downRiver all the way from Cataract mistook its heading and nearly fouled the second galley's anchor in the dusk, but otherwise, Mel'eth was quiet. Five days saw us to Serythir, once the Riversrun boundary, now the first true border-fort of Dhasdein.

We arrived late on a muggy mid-spring afternoon, with a release of tension visible as the sun-play on great silvery heaps of drifting cloud. As the galleys worked in to anchor by the solid stone quay, carefully beyond bowshot from the watch-bastions, the troops on shift were actually joking while they rowed.

Therkon on the stern-deck was smiling too. Until we saw the rowing boat put out.

A fair-sized boat with two pairs of rowers and by the scarlet and flash of precious metal, a dignitary rather than a steersman astern. Not waiting to traverse the quay afoot. Headed at racing speed for our galley, whose ensign marked the crown prince's craft.

Therkon grimaced, but not in surprise. "Excuse me, my lady Chaeris. It will be news, of some sort."

He did not have to add that news delivered by such a messenger, at such a pace, was usually bad.

The boat came alongside. The dignitary teetered up the ladder: scanned the deck, fixed Therkon, and burst out, "Your Highness, we must speak! Instantly!"

They were half an hour in the hencoop, with Deoren's crophaired Dhasdeinis lowering progressively darker about the door. When they emerged, I felt no surprise that Therkon was giving orders and the rowers had been summoned, the sailors already gathered forrard to weigh anchor, before the messenger's boat cast off.

In galley terms perhaps a third of a watch's light remained. Two proposed a hamlet called Gratha as night-stop, no more than ten miles downstream. What could send them off for such a small gain, after a long wearying day? I tried not to chew my fingernails as Therkon went down his roster of officer-briefings. Until at last, in the first mellowed glow of sunset, he crossed the deck to me.

Two said, *"Word from the Archipelago?"*

Therkon nearly recoiled. Caught himself, and managed a clipped fragment of smile. "I do forget." The smile snuffed. "Not the Archipelago. Yet. There has been a storm."

I did not need Two for this. "In the ocean? This side the Archipelago? Your ships?"

"Five of them. Five first-class, deep-laden freighters. Travelling together, carrying silk and inlaid furniture and fine-tempered weapons. And grain." The long mouth set into iron. "A couple of sailors were blown to Greenhill on the lid of a dower chest. A refugee boat brought them home."

Another voyage then, back to Dhasdein, atop the original excursion, and the ship-wreck's span. "How far is Greenhill . . . How long ago?"

His eyes closed solidly with mine. "The storm came when I was traveling upRiver. In Verrain."

"In . . ." Then Two turned the world to roiling white.

Reality came back. Two was saying, *"That is too soon."*

Therkon said, "What?"

*"If there was influence, it was not ours. Or from Iskarda. If there was intent, the interval precludes a sure forecast. Sheer wantonness."*

Therkon almost wailed, "What?"

"I'm sorry," I gabbled, shutting Two up with a snap. "Two means, we didn't arrange it, and neither did the seed, the Iskardan qherrique. And if it was arranged, to stop you finding me, or bringing me downRiver, then it was done too early to be sure it would be needed. So it was pure—wantonness."

"Arranged? To stop me? Not to bring you? *Arranged?*"

"They talked about it in Iskarda." Of course, his head had to be reeling as ours had then. "That when we met, in the rocks, it was just too big a coincidence. Too many pebble falls, Tanekhet said. And it was the same when my mother and Alkhes first met, and, and maybe that was—arranged. And—"

"The River-lord save me." Therkon hardly ever blasphemed. But his brains were catching up all the same. "They thought you," his eyes added, *either of you,* "might have done it? Or, or the seed?"

"Two said, it wasn't us, but it *could* have been arranged. Tez said, if my mother was meant to meet my father, it must have taken all the motherlodes of Amberlight to fix it. And maybe our seed was, is—too small."

Therkon's voice failed altogether. Then he took a two-handed grip on the rail below the stern fan, and swallowed. "Lady—my lady Chaeris, will you answer me truthfully? Is there—could there be—some other qherrique?"

It was a question all Iskarda had asked long since. "So far as we know—no."

Therkon looked as dazed as a man just hit on the head. But there was no daze inside.

"Then was it, could it have been, uh, arranged by—something else?"

Two said, *"The probabilities of such an event at that moment being chance are too low to be plausible. There are too few facts to fix a source."*

Therkon actually gulped. But his wits had been more than spurred awake. "Then *something* could have arranged it. Tried to stop you coming downRiver. So you *are* important. We do need you in Dhasdein."

The flare of hope snuffed in its moment of birth.

"But was it arranged," he was suddenly overcool, "to stop you coming? Or to be sure you came?"

"Oh." This was a level of suspicion worthy of Iatha. "You mean, was it meant to be a, a bait?"

His eyes did not waver. "For Dhasdein, yes."

My flesh had chilled. My hair was creeping upright. Whatever forecasts of disaster I had learnt in Iskarda dwindled to insignificance. Never, before, had I expected this to touch me personally. Never had I been physically, immediately, afraid for myself.

I swallowed too, and knew I did not need to spell out the answer's second part.

"Two doesn't know."

A quick evening breeze washed over the stern-deck and bore away the smell of tar and water-worn wood and sweating, apprehensive men. The timing pipe rose into earshot, a tune I had heard them use to move quarry blocks at home. Oars, planks, rigging, creaked in time or counterpoint. I sat on my silly formal chair like the most ordinary twelve-year-old, and watched Therkon think. Revolve, extrapolate, construct decisions that would shape my life.

His attention came back to me. He was suddenly very still.

Then he said, too evenly for reading, "Tell me the truth, my lady Chaeris. Do you wish to go back?"

*Can I?* I knew my eyes asked, with shock, with alarm, with instinctive hope. And his answered, dark as the weathered galley-planks and as unwavering. *You can. I will take you. If you really want.*

"Oh . . ."

I said it stupidly, mind riven by twin visions: turn the galley about, back upRiver, disembark at Marbleport. Fifty miles up the range, and Iskarda. Tez, Iatha, all the others. Home.

Away from risk, and peril, and Dhasdein. And the future. The unknown.

Stupidly enough, what tipped the scales was a trivium: the thought of working our way back through the gauntlet of Mel'eth and Shirran, with men who had rowed their hearts out to bring me this far. And what they would feel, if I bade them turn around, and run the risks twice over. Row me back again.

"My lady." Therkon suddenly had both my hands, sitting on his heels before me like the veriest cabin boy. "My lady, if you wish it, you have my word. No-one will blame you." Sometimes his understanding was so sharp it cut. "You can go."

That magnanimity dropped the last straw on the load. "Oh," I said again, and heard the sob rise like panic. "I can't. I can't! It would just be for me, it wouldn't fix anything and Dhasdein would still be stuck, and whatever it is could really happen, and it might get Iskarda as well!"

I clenched his hands like a life-rope and fought desperately not to disgrace Iskarda before strangers, not to weep like a chicken-heart at the first true threat of battle. To deal with it as would my mother, and Tez, and Iatha, and all the women of my kin.

The tear-veil faded. Finger by finger, I unlocked my hands, and had time to notice the imprint his rings had left on Therkon's own fingers, before I looked in those shadow-deep eyes and got out, almost composedly, "Thank you. But no. I should—I will stay."

The reward was in that expression, in the instant when he very nearly kissed my hands. My pulse was still quaky and I had time to rehearse Tanekhet's warning, twice over, before I reached the outer world in time to catch the end of the crown prince's commands.

". . . double-speed at every second oar-relief. And sail till after sunset. My lady Chaeris has chosen to go on with us. Now we can, we must, make best speed to Riversend."

# CHAPTER V

'Best speed' worked until the third day out of Serythir: then the rain began.

They were scuds at first, quick passing showers. Then came squalls, sudden boisterous clouts of wind that made the galleys lurch like an unbalanced horse. By midday our speed had halved, both clouds and rain had thickened to solidity, and the wind, though still gusty, had settled its bearing. UpRiver.

"Spring snap," Azo said, as we unearthed our wet-weather cloaks. She did not have to add that it would blow from the south, cold as very winter, and rain with it, maybe the best part of a week. She glanced forrard over the troops huddled under half-rigged tent-flies, the streaming rowers. "We'll stay inside."

Amid all the off-watch officers and Therkon's entire suite, imperial affairs conducted in earshot, and the brazier his body-servant insisted on keeping alight, we survived till mid-afternoon. Then I demanded we reclaim the stern-deck. The captain rigged an awning, which did little more than rattle, but our cloaks kept us dry, and a workout now and then kept us warm.

Though the hencoop was soon crowded daylong with drenched, exhausted rowers, Deoren had flatly refused to let Therkon outside at all. Nevertheless he escaped the third day, and scrambled under our awning with his own version of midday bread and cheese.

"It's a pity you've had such a poor view of Riversrun, my lady Chaeris," he said, politely setting me innermost along the hencoop wall. "This weather is most inconsiderate."

I took my eyes from the shivering but deeply impressed steersmen fixated on Verrith, wiping her knives after a last throw into the hencoop wall, and heard Azo strangle her rare, true, belly-laugh. I was too busy battling Two's explosion of, *Unseasonal, dangerous, not factorable in our data*! to manage more than a gasp and a, "Yes. Yes, it has been a—a—disappointment—" And let his bright sidelong glance assume all the rest.

"We must hope," the quirk of a smile acknowledged it all, "things improve for your first view of Riversend."

I swallowed the panic along with the questions. After all, he knew no more than we about the possibilities of intent or delay, and their reasons, or the records of past springs that could retort, *This is not outside the usual*. And I was Tellurith's daughter. A woman of Iskarda. If he could handle it urbanely, so could I.

I said politely, "I hope so. Yes."

* * * *

Perhaps the River-lord heard him, for the wind eased just above the Gates, the huge gorge down which the River falls past the guard citadels in a long chute of white-frothed water, torn round bulwarked islets where, in war, they would fasten the enormous blockade chains, designed to prevent downRiver attack on Riversend. I knew Azo and Verrith were thinking with me that if worst came to absolute worst, they might hinder attack coming upRiver too.

Then the pale sealight's threshold widened and we swept past a convoy of upward-labouring freighters into the Delta's brief immensity of reeds and labyrinthine waterways and the mirror-shimmer of endless water under open sky. Before it narrowed into the stone-paved banks and fetid by-canals of outer Riversend.

From Two's memories, almost nothing had changed. First slums, then factories, then the factory owners' quarter, the seats of the great merchant guilds, then abruptly divergent neighbours: the nobles' city estates, ashore, and the boat-city afloat. Refuge of the entirely homeless. Probably, I thought, resort of Archipelago refugees.

On the thought Therkon said beside me, "We do try to help them. The Archipelago folk, at least."

"Yes," I said at last, my breath easing. "I mean—I think you would."

He had caught the slight involuntary stress on "you." He inclined his head gravely. The somber expression matched his splendidest garb yet. The over-tunic was actually cloth of gold, an opulently brocaded almost blackish purple, the narrow Dhasdein trousers were true black, some kind of handkerchief-soft suede, and even through the River's spectrum of odors I caught a hint of scent: something subtle, almost crisp enough to call bitter, but every tang of it proclaiming, Expense.

He must have caught my sniff. The smile flickered. "One must do one's best," he murmured, "for the Empress."

"The Empress! You're going to the Empress? Tonight!"

Under the cloud, the light was already waning toward dusk. Starting back from the rail, I saw torches kindle along the crest of a wall that met the left River bank. Bringing his profile out in chiseled shadow against what I already knew were the lights of the Imperial quarter, as he murmured, "I think, she expects us both."

The best I could manage was a gulp.

Unlike my parents, we disembarked at the emperor's private wharf. In full dark the quayside blazed with cressets and hand-borne torches, light flashing off burnished armour, flapping purple cloaks. An Imperial guard dekarchy, complete with full-face helmets and twelve-feet high pikes, restraint for a seething mass of dark but lavish silk and brocade and velvet getting heedlessly wet in the drizzle's glitter. Palace officialdom.

At the gangplank foot Therkon was engulfed. The uproar smothered the dekarch's bellow, the salute-crash of grounded pikes, but after a precarious moment, as we tried at once to find our land-legs and keep our feet, I found the whole mass was oozing backward down the quay. Therkon must simply have kept moving, bearing officials along.

Suddenly the press opened, the Imperials materialized on our heels, Deoren's men had fanned out ahead, and Therkon himself was at my side, saying mildly, "My lady Chaeris, we go this way."

Marble, bronze, gold, glass, exquisitely tended, exquisitely alien plants, frivolous follies, towering facades, bedizened porticoes slid past, above immaculate paving flags. Rainbow garb and fusillades of perfume announced courtiers sallying for the night. My parents had seen it by day, but Two identified the occasional landmark. Frequently enough to stay calm until Therkon lifted his voice to include Azo and Verrith, who would be getting tenser by the second as the River fell behind.

"First we find the lady Chaeris' lodging. Then we will seek audience of the Empress."

Next day revealed the 'lodging' as an Imperial palace suite with an inner court, an outer door and guard niche, complete with guard, and fittings as you would expect. Kitchen, bedrooms, private bathroom, dressing room, meeting room . . . Feeling positively bilious, I left Azo to check defenses, which eased Verrith, at least. We took an extra moment of defiance to unearth our most decent shirts.

My mother's memory gauged the Empress' audience-room as small and informal, in Dhasdeini terms. Beyond the filigreed bronze door, the floor was for once not marble but a riot of entwining rose, ochre, umber, muted blue: priceless Quetzistani rugs. The chaste cream plaster ceiling had been coffered with bronze rosettes, the grey-blue marble fireplace bore a delicate bas-relief of lilies and leafy hunting spears. From a gilded cedar chair before it rose the Empress.

As my father Sarth remembered, she could have met him eye to eye. A living tower in a cascade of celadon-green brocade Quetzistani robes, she had a chaplet of pearls to confine the multiple braids of thick black desert hair. And a face whose features I already knew far too well.

Therkon made the Dhasdeini noble's greeting: palms to forehead and lips, a bow to the waist. Deoren, the only escort permitted past the door, went prostrate. Verrith and I stood dourly upright, inclining heads, and trying not to feel like beggars in our plain brown Iskardan coats.

Naturally she had looked to Therkon first. She held out her right hand, the emperor's favour sign. He took two paces and bent with all his courtier's grace to kiss the Dhasdeini signet on her own forefinger. As he straightened she smiled in pleasure as well as open relief and said, "Back safe."

She sounded like him too, in tone, in timbre, though without the Dhasdeini consonant clip. From her face, I know he smiled.

She took his other hand a moment. Whatever passed between them was the warmth of kinfolks' flesh and blood. And kin well-loved.

Then she released his hands and as she looked past him her eyebrows rose, before her smile turned dazzling. She said, "Tellurith's child."

Therkon turned, but she was already bearing down on me. "Ah, you are her child indeed." She took my shoulders and surprised Two beyond demur as she turned me like a veritable child to the gold and bronze extravaganza of the nearest triple-flame lamp. Her hand traced down my cheek, and she actually laughed in silent delight.

"Her brows, her bones, her look. Oh, it *is* Tellurith. And so tall, already. Like your father." Her hand slid over a shoulder to touch my hair. "Like both of them."

The hand came back. Both hands cupped my face.

"I bid you welcome," she said. "Most welcome, Chaeris of Iskarda."

\* \* \* \*

Were you determined to be curmudgeonly, it might have been read as a political, a ruler's relief: a desperately needed, thoroughly dangerous pawn gambled for, won, and at last to hand. Fresh from the River and the weather and the night, and the fear that had underlain it all, it was only the welcome that I felt.

I stammered something, and managed to bend my head a little further. She laughed softly—she very seldom laughed out—and let me go. Then the mirth snuffed like a candle and she looked deep into my eyes.

"Do you think you can help us?"

It was the voice of the Empress. The weight of the whole Empire was upon her, the weight that even Therkon did not bear. And she had the imperial power.

I gulped and without thought my lips opened. Two said, "*However we can.*"

Her eyes went wide: long, long eyes, accentuated even beyond her son's impact by the outlining kohl. Her head actually went back a little, and my heart sank out the bottom of my chest.

Then the stare changed, and I knew whence Therkon had inherited his philosopher.

"It's true." She almost whispered, but not in fear. "You *are* two." Suddenly I felt what Two had felt, an echo, a resonance. It had not been mere chance, a guess or a blood-gift. Once she had known, had handled, had been sib to qherrique for herself.

Two said, "*You were Jhuir priestess.*"

I could almost hear Therkon's, *Owww*. I flinched and tried to grab control. Two ignored me. So did the Empress.

Quite simply, she answered, "Yes."

Two put my hand out. I had to reach up quite a way, and I could almost hear the entire audience hiss in consternation, but my fingers brushed her cheek. Two said, *"One day, perhaps, again."*

For an instant she was her son, a philosopher promised knowledge's ultimate gift. For another she was as Two remembered the Amberlight Heads, with that gift reft away. And then, she was the empress.

Straightening to full height, those eyes gripping me like a vice. Just not managing to suppress the urgency, the need, and to ask with a vestige of composure, "Is that a, an oracle?"

*What in the Mother's name*, I raged at Two, *are you thinking? We have no certainty, we have no right to make promises like that! So she was Jhuir priestess and handled the clan statuette—you did this to Therkon! Are you crazy, to torment her as well?*

Two said to the Empress, "It is 'perhaps'."

She had in truth been a priestess. She unlocked the riddle in a breath. It was not disappointment that flared in that narrow dramatic face: it was hope, struck as from flint into a sudden smile.

"Oh," she said, and it became admiration. "Perhaps the truth. Perhaps one day. Perhaps an oracle. Yes?"

Two answered gravely, *"Perhaps."*

She caught her breath on a laugh. Then, slowly, she drew back. But it is, I tell Two now, purely imagination that she seemed to grow taller as she moved. As if we had released not merely flesh and blood, but the spirit within her. Now, like a woken eagle, she was readying to fly.

Then she drew the wings in, smiled at me rather than Two, and said with the warmth of a pleased hostess, "Tomorrow, you will come with Therkon, to the council? To hear what news we have, and tell us what you think. But for now, you would rather go with your watcher, yes? And sup, and quietly to bed?"

\* \* \* \*

The sun was out next morning, with a wind brisk enough for both to reach our court. As a gust rattled the breakfast-room tapestries, Azo squinted out the inner door, whose opening had so discomposed the servants, up past the sentry on the roofline to where broken streams of cloud skated across a teary blue sky.

"Easterly," she said.

So the snap was over. Wishing earnestly for something fit to wear at what would doubtless be a full imperial council, I said, "Then we needn't take our cloaks?"

Azo gave me an eye-corner. A shaken head.

"But it's going to be fine—!"

"And it can turn like That!" Verrith snapped her fingers. Her look at Azo added the rest. Assassins or ambushes can defeat the wariest troublecrew. Without armour, the last hope of protection was the thick, oiled goat's-wool of an Iskardan wet-weather cloak.

"He said, we'd never go outside the palace—"

Azo gave me one look.

"Well, at least we could walk round inside. Two's never seen the half of it."

"Council," answered Verrith flatly. "Going there, you'll see enough."

Meanwhile, they decided, Azo and I would use the courtyard for first workout. We had circled twice on the damp flags, gingerly aware of tall bystanding earthen pots of iris and hyacinth, when Azo suddenly signaled, *Break*.

Verrith had vanished to the outer door. Azo's hand dived inside her shirt. I had no time to exclaim, *Really, a light-gun, in the Imperial palace?* The knock had become a messenger, already striding through the breakfast room.

Therkon himself, in narrow black Dhasdeini trousers and a shirt whose cuffs flashed pristine white against the indigo of a silk-wool coat. Official's parade dress, I reckoned. A thillian clip flared in that matching swathe of hair as he gave a beckoning nod to Verrith, and they both stepped out to us.

"Lady Chaeris." The inclined head was normal, but all his other body language signaled haste. Or, as his eyes caught a new burst of sunshine, some kind of excitement as well.

"I hope you've been comfortable? The beds," a demure look, "were not too soft? The food? Very good. My lady, there is news. From the Seaward forts. At the Delta mouth. The wind's brought in flotsam. Something, this time, the Sea-watch cannot fathom. An urgent signal, this morning. Direct to me."

"Something?" Two had nearly rushed me off on the spot. "From the Archipelago?" He was nodding sharply. "Wreckage? No, more than wreckage, people?"

"Survivors. The signal says nothing else. Either it's beyond their guess, or—"

Or it was not beyond their guess, and they knew it was too sensitive to risk. Even in the heartlands of Dhasdein.

"Oh . . . They can't bring it here?"

"Unsafe to move."

Wreckage could be moved. Whole people could be moved. But if the flotsam was a survivor, or a survivor's knowledge, or simply that survivor's state—Two's calculations flared white across my eyes and already the rest seemed a long since given.

"You have to go out there?" Another knife-quick nod. "Now, this morning? And you want me to come too?"

With a visible effort he checked his own haste. Turned his head to Verrith, then Azo.

"S'hurre," he said carefully. Troublecrew are not Crafters in the full sense, but the respect's intent was clear. "S'hurre, I know we said, Not outside the palace. And this is only the first day in Riversend. But, if we did go—could you ward the lady Chaeris?"

Azo's look was more than clear. Ward her? Nobody can guarantee safety anywhere, and you ask us to do so in a strange city, on some sort of excursion into the very mouth of peril, the verge of the open sea? Her neck muscles flexed for the head-shake and Two overrode us both.

"*We must go. New word, from the Archipelago, an eye-witness—We MUST!*"

Without intent both my hands flew out and by equal reflex Therkon and Azo jumped away from me. But as I half stumbled forward Verrith bellowed, "Chaeris!"

The voice of troublecrew. My teachers in their trade. The women who had taught me not merely how to master Two, but the tenets of Amberlight.

"I'm sorry," I panted. I had to wring my hands together, whatever the risk. "Sorry—sorry—but, Verrith—we have to go!"

The silence fell like rock with nothing in it but my breath. Therkon was standing rigid as Azo. Verrith came close up to me, eyes fixed on my face.

"Do you know this," she said, "Chaeris?"

Her eyes gripped mine, coffee-brown slitted Amberlight eyes, darker than the fuzz of hairs along her grizzled Crafter's plait. *Be sure*, those eyes said. *We will go, if you say so. Risk us all. But you are hazarding far more than our three lives, if you say, Yes.*

I swallowed what felt like half my heart: but the answer was there. Not Two's panic now. Not reason and logic either. Inexplicable, undeniable, it came to me as oracles had come to the Heads of Amberlight, from somewhere between qherrique and my own heart.

I said, "Yes."

* * * *

Deoren was even unhappier than Azo. He and Therkon had a full-scale set-to right in our doorway, Deoren arguing in an ever more frantic undertone about the council, the weather, the risk, the uncertainty, the double uncertainty—the glance he flung past the desperately wooden-faced sentry told me he meant, The chance your so-precious tool is meant to turn on you—Therkon growing more and more hatchet-like, until that last protest cleared the blade.

"You," the sentry jumped a foot in the air, "send to the guardroom for an escort. You," to Deoren's shoulder-man, "inform Lord Erren that the council is postponed. *You*," right in Deoren's face, "take whoever you want down the slips and ready that Nikonian."

He wheeled on us three mesmerized spectators. "My lady Chaeris, allow me to trust in your troublecrew. We will inform the Empress. And then," it was pure hatchet, "we will go."

Deoren actually threw his hands in the air. Therkon stormed off down the passageway with Azo scouring to reach the lead and me and Verrith bobbing in his wake.

I daresay news could travel the palace even faster than Therkon walked, for when we coursed up to yet another filigreed bronze door, the two Imperials on guard lowered their pikes in salute, and the door opened as readily as before. But this time, it opened on the Empress.

She wore plain, or at least pure white robes, with half a fore-arm's wealth of gold, and gold beads knotted in her hair. Doubtless workaday gear, for an empress. The startled look and outthrust hands were another matter.

"Therkon—!" And then, as the officials behind her made them-selves distant. "What is it now?"

He bowed briefly over her hand. He explained, even faster than before. "I have no idea what's there," he added. "Or for how long." The change in her eyes said she understood: how long a desper-ately injured man might live. "I'll take the new patrol-ship. She's in trial so she'll be ready, she's fitted for marines. The weather's fair. I can be out before tide-turn. Back before dark."

He was straightening, voice and body together declaring, *I'm going now.* For a chink of a second her face was that of a mother, of all too-anxious kin left behind. Then she sealed it up.

"Take the Nikonian, yes. You have authority for the dock? You can catch the ebb? The council can wait. But, Therkon: use your own guards. Not marines."

"It will hardly need—" She gave him a look. "Majesty. As you command."

He bent for her hand. As he moved she looked past him and saw us.

"Therkon!" Her hand jerked back, he jerked upright. "What is this? You can't think—"

"Majesty, a most crucial choice. The lady Chaeris may see, know, recognize something we do not. We can't take the chance of—"

"We cannot take this chance! Tellurith's girl? Not a day in Ri-versend, Tellurith's girl, *and* you, on the self-same ship?"

Shock stabbed me like a veritable knife. Of course she was right. No matter that I was Tellurith's daughter, and for some reason precious in myself. I was also the new hope of Dhasdein's, of the River's defense.

And Therkon was its other half. And the cost, the chance of some unexpected but successful assault, attack, ambush taking us both . . .

The world wobbled and returned in a thunderclap from a tide of whirling white. Two said, *"Empress, we must go."*

At my back I felt even Azo twitch.

*"This information, from this source, at this time, cannot be lost."* Now it was even, steady, the voice of completed deduction. Of an oracle. *"Any other dangers dwindle in comparison. To miss this chance may be fatal. To your enterprise. To Dhasdein. To the River as a whole."*

The Empress did suppress a gasp.

*"You asked our help. We pledged to give it. In whatever way we can."*

Her lips opened. A lesser woman would have burst out with the predictable protests and equivocations and demands for some other alternative. Dhasdein's empress only closed her lips again. And presently, quite steadily, asked, "This is your best advice?"

"Empress, yes."

She looked at me then as a Ruand, testing the tool she had to hand. Trying with all her might to gauge its truth. To guess if its capacity would equal the test.

Then her hands sank and she drew herself up.

"Take the guards," she told Therkon. "Take weapons." The slight emphasis told me she meant Therkon to do so himself. "Take—"

She stopped. Already, she had remembered the tide. Even listing precautions would be delay.

"Chaeris." She stepped clean through the guards and put her hands, again, either side my face. "My—lady. Fare well. Fare very well. We accept your help. We wish you, as soon—as soon as may be—" The emphasis was more than admonition, "safely back."

I had time to touch her hands with my own, and stammer something, before she turned to Therkon, almost at my side.

"Prince." He kissed both her hands this time. "Go with our good will. Our . . ." The words tailed off. As he bent before her she slipped a hand lightly over the curve of his hair, infinitely light and quick, infinite tenderness. The rest was just audible. "Dhe see you blessed."

A Dhasdeini would invoke the River-lord. But Dhe is the old upRiver goddess, the Mother of Verrain and Quetzistan. Kin to our own Mother, in Iskarda.

"Manya," he answered, almost under his breath. I know now it means Birth-mother, in Quetzistani. He bent his head to her. The smile, brilliant, heart-breaking, said all the rest.

I am so grateful, now, that he could leave her that.

* * * *

The Nikonian was berthed across River, in what they called the Army quarter. We tramped down between Dhasdeini trouble-crew and a whole file of Imperial guards, to board an Imperial runabout, for want of a better word, and Two near twisted my head off trying to watch the hire-gigs and fast-sculling messenger shallops, the big municipal galley ferries, the familiar freighters in ballast or load. And sharp in the bright, gusty morning, the forest of naked masts and slapping white pennons above the naval stores and building slips.

Dhasdein army docks had foiled even old Amberlight's intelligencers. Two nearly went berserk as the runabout skated up a regular street of a canal between pillared galley stables, into a stone-lined basin redolent of pitch and tar and steam-heated wood. I was still swiveling left and right in almost tearful haste as we moored.

Deoren had sent his minions, if he defied orders for himself. The basin's Ruand was on the wharf in person. And the Nikonian was ready to launch.

On the slip she seemed ungainly as a beached duck, baring the ample pitch-blackened draught below what, afloat, would be a low, sleek, carvel-built side. But her topsides were varnished bright, her bows bore in red and white the lucky seeing eye, and below the elegant breast of her plumed figurehead thrust a small but saw-toothed ram. Afloat, bobbing, dancing on the restless water, she looked, after the fives, like some bright little fighting cock.

Two almost had me off the gang-plank trying to see the oar arrangements: she was double-banked, a type we had never met before. But the oarsmen were already thundering to their places, the Imperial guards had halved, with more than acrid protest, and ten filled the marines' places forward, behind the leather fighting screens. Therkon and I and our troublecrew had been herded onto the stern deck, where the captain was bawling a spate of over-anxious commands. Deoren's vehement efforts to get Therkon into an officer's cloak were cut short as the flute struck up, the prow came round, and she headed for the basin gate.

Two and I were still trying frantically to record every possible detail as her head swung downRiver, and I was looking back to Riversend.

Nearest lay the great spread of the River itself, sparking blue in the sun, traced in countless foaming tracks of white. Brown or blue or scarlet hulls spattered it, sails bulging white or blue or brown, the striding legs of oar banks one, two, five, ten, fifteen-strong. And the scent, heady as the wind, of deep water, tidal water, tar and cordage and ships.

Behind that the city's variegated battlement stretched from eye to eye's edge, blending back into a huge mosaic of towers, spires, front upon serried building-front, wharves, quays, vistas down receding streets. Mightier, you would swear, than any threat could fell.

The Imperial quarter's sea-wall had dwindled to a distant dark, where strollers beaded like upright ants, when at last Two or I sighed, and shifted hands on the stern rail, and reclaimed the nearer world.

The Nikonian had set her sail, as two-bankers can do running. It is the virtue of their design. The immaculate white square boomed and bulged to the wind's thumps, the serpent and thunderbolt a reverse shadow on its breast. The bow was ducking and slashing into what had become a moderate swell, and up forrard, I thought, the guards would already be getting wet.

Beside me the captain was holding forth to Therkon, all anxiety gone. "See that, y'Highness? Never a one of y'cumbersome old fives'd do that. Wind's round flat nor'east and she's lying to it near as a gull!"

Therkon answered something civilly enthused. He had given in to Deoren and wrapped the big scarlet cloak round him, and the bite of wind under my hood told me he had been wise. Already, I realized, we were almost out of shore-sight. All round us spread corrugating, brightly glinting muddily-blue water, restive as a half-mastered horse.

At my other side I felt rather than saw Azo cock her head, was aware, like her, of clouds streaming across the bitterly pure blue sky. The look on her face made me edge closer, and under cover of another seamanly rapture, mutter, "What is it?"

For a moment I thought she would not reply. But when I silently insisted, she answered me troublecrew style, from a mouth-corner.

"Wind's working nor'east."

"He said so." After the downRiver trip, a ship no longer felt peculiar. But the Nikonian was no five, and this was no steady River current. We were bouncing like a veritable fighting cock, and the acres of water made me uneasy too. "It seems to be all right?"

Her lips tightened. Then she suddenly shrugged. "He's Dhasdeini. It's his water. Should know what he's doing." But her gaze went back, as if unable to leave it, to the eye of the wind, and a little chill slid down the back of my own neck.

North-east, in old Amberlight water-lore, is the bad luck quarter. The wind that blows athwart the River current, and given force enough, can drive any ship, as onto a lee shore, onto an unwelcoming bank.

I bit my lip. Then I said, "Well, there's no bank out here to run into." Azo, water-skilled as most old Amberlighters, almost shuddered at the landlubber's phrase. "And he said we'd be back before dark."

Therkon himself hulled that first comforting premise a bare five minutes later, coming to show me the channel buoys to either hand, twisting an angular serpent's course among what, he assured me, were sand-bars and shoals dangerous, even at high tide, to ships of sufficient draught. "But have no concern, lady Chaeris. *Aspis* is shallow draught, and weatherly. They have already taken her right out to sea. And her captain knows the Mouth like the back of his own hand."

For all my own nerves I could tell that he was abstracted. Unsmiling except when he remembered to. Even while he spoke, his eyes kept turning forward, past the curve of the sail's edge to the white-sharp line of horizon sky.

\* \* \* \*

Despite a busy wind on our quarter and the ebb behind us, I had a near headache before black specks nicked the horizon, swelled to a string of net corks, and turned from silhouette to the dour grey of Delta stone. A long, long chain of fortification, sections of boom and palisade replacing land-borne breastworks between the blocks of fort wall, lookout towers perched high above the battlements, staring out to sea.

A natural reef had bowed out one side of the main channel. The Empire had extended it with countless loads of fill into a mole fit to support the forts, light-houses, slips and ramps for patrol vessels, quarters for the Sea-watch. Even as Two made my head swim with calculations of the incalculable amounts of old building debris and quarries' waste, I was thinking that Dhasdein could hardly have made clearer its view of the Archipelago.

We exchanged ensign signals with a couple of small galleys patrolling the channel, then *Aspis* headed for the right-hand fort. A cluster of glinting metal and flapping scarlet had already formed above the narrow water gate. A portcullis rose slowly. *Aspis* eased under, still bouncing slightly, and up against the even narrower quay.

We clambered up stairs for the formal presentations: first Therkon and the fort commander, then, to my embarrassment, "The lady Chaeris of Iskarda," Therkon announced formally. "A valued ally of Dhasdein." I cringed in sudden fear he would announce what as well as who I was, but he added firmly, "An observer with lore we may not know."

The fort commander was a weathered slab of a man with a face like rough-carved cedar. I only realized how anxious he had been when he bowed and said, "The lady Chaeris is most welcome," with a fervour far past courtesy.

He had stowed his sea-trove in the infirmary, up on the middle floor. Out of the sea-brume, he informed us, tramping up another broad flight of hewn stone stairs, but not so high the wind could chill, or fumes blow from the great oil-burning lantern, reflected in huge double mirrors, that marked the channel by night. "Here we are, Your Highness. In here."

They had left windows, tall lancets full of sunlight from shore and seaward, and plastered the walls. It looked white and clean, but safe, with no taint of ill-health, only a strong scent of lavender. "Burn it for soul's ease," muttered the fort healer, half-embarrassed but anxious as his commander. He did not have to add aloud, *Not much else we can do.*

The bed had been drawn close under the outer windows, as if they hoped the patient might catch a breath of native air. The shape looked hardly larger than a child's. The profile on the pillows said otherwise.

Our first Archipelagan. Two and I could only stare. Coppery skin, through the grey of sickness or privation, gaunt over fine bones, with something like the Shirran fold of skin above the eyes. Carefully tidied, loosely plaited black hair. Hardly a face to stand out, anywhere along the River. Even for what the healer had read from the skin shade, the flaccid mouth.

". . . boat grounded on the Horn. Right up past North Shoal. Fair swell running. Storms, maybe, out there." The fort-commander was muttering too. "*Insis* saw them go in, but too far away. Pulled two others out after. Ribs stove in, one went there on deck. T'other'd broke his head." He had died here later, for all their efforts, added the tone.

"I'd not have troubled you, sir. Except, this one talks."

Therkon murmured something. The officer's heavier voice took him up.

"Off and on, yes. No. Not to us."

Two's recall glossed that with a rush, Therkon himself in our council room: *the refugees won't say what drives them out.* But if this one were half-conscious, in fever or delirium, that stricture might not hold.

Therkon said quite clearly, "You've kept a record?"

"Kept a watch. Would keep a record, sir. If we could understand what she says."

She. Not merely the slightness of privation or the shrinking of mortal injury, but the physique of a woman beneath. What had she been doing on a boat so off course, so damaged or driven, as to ground on a Delta shoal? Whence had she come, with family, among accustomed crew, or in flight with strangers, to a thoroughly unfamiliar sea?

The silence behind me broke. The fort-commander said, too evenly, "The best we could think, sir—even if *you* can't understand it—was, you ought to know."

Still with the hint of final recourse that said, because Therkon was in truth leaned upon and trusted beyond reason, he might have some solution, if all else failed.

Therkon did not reply.

It was a dozen breaths before I understood. I all but spun around. They were all looking at me: Therkon, the Imperials' officer, Deoren and his shoulder-man, Azo and Verrith, the fort-commander and his entourage. All the eyes asking the same. *Can you do it, if we can't? You are the truly last resort. Can you help us, if not her?*

My mouth was dry. It took a moment before it would work. I said, "I can try."

\* \* \* \*

I saw Therkon's jaw relax. But he waited, making no suggestions, giving me command. Until I looked at the healer, and had recourse to Two myself.

"*What was the boat?*"

I suppressed a blink, but the fort-commander answered at once, clearly getting the point.

"Fishing boat, once. Out of Wave. Trawler, then made over for line-work."

"*Not their own?*" Wave Island, Two's scanty memories told me, was too close for the language to be unfamiliar. He nodded in acknowledgement.

"*Old? Unseaworthy?*" Two was learning naval terms as fast as I.

"Old, yes. They'll sell 'em, the worthless ones, to refugees." He had seen more than one, added the tone. "No telling, though, if it was unfit first, or got that way."

"*There was a storm?*"

"Nothing here but a southerly buster. Could have been a lot worse, out there."

Out there. On the open sea, this side Wave Island. Or the un-known seas beyond.

A little chill went up my neck. I said, "How often does she speak?"

If they could not understand her, it was hardly likely they could have any intelligible record. We would have to wait for her next words, whenever they came.

The healer's twitch out-paced his words. "She talked a lot in the night. Moved around, very agitated. We got some soup down her." An apologetic look. "But she's not been happy, not under-standing us. And . . . we've no women here."

I had no time to tender his own anxiety. "She's quieter now?"

His head went down. It was barely audible. "Hardly moved. These last two hours."

I looked at Azo, whose eyes spoke the conclusion back. She was sinking, and probably sinking fast. The faintest of chances I could follow anything she said, but we might already be too late.

I looked at Therkon. He, after all, was in command. He would bear the weight of the choice.

I said, "Can we wake her up?"

His eyes told me he understood: if we wanted even a chance at information, we would have to harass a woman almost certainly dying. A woman driven from home, no telling how far or how long ago or at what cost, but long enough to have lost her own vessel, and with it, perhaps, her possessions, her kin. And solely for our own needs, we would disturb her final hours.

He turned to the healer and said, "Would she wake?"

The healer understood too. He forebore to protest as any heal-er should. Just pursed his lips and answered, eyes downcast. "We could try."

Therkon shut his eyes a moment. I saw the human behind the crown prince, not merely begging forgiveness for what the prince must do, but feeling with the victim. And then, forming feature by feature, the hatchet man.

Then he said, wholly without expression, "Try."

They brought warm bricks and pillows, and, incongruous in a military fort, a vial of smelling salts. They propped her up, gently as a baby, and settled the bricks under her feet. Then I drew as close as I could before her, and the healer, crouching on the bed behind her, cradled her head on his arm and brought the salts under her nose.

She took one breath, hardly visible. Two. Gave an audible gasp. He snatched the vial back. She coughed. Coughed again, half choked, cried something, with the force of shock or pain. Opened her eyes.

Two took both her thin, knotted, sea-battered hands and said, *"Mother, can you hear?"*

She did hear: she recognized me too, as a woman if nothing else. I saw open relief. She tried to grasp my hands, got out some-thing else, with her hoarse, gasping pronunciation. And neither Two nor I could understand a word.

"Wave Island?" I said.

She understood that, and made a nod, a minute head motion, flicker of eyelids. Two said, in what must have been Wave Island patois, *"Where before?"*

She struggled for words. Someone put a cup over the healer's shoulder, he laid down the vial and held it to her lips. I could smell warm, salted broth.

She managed one sip but her eyes never left mine. I closed my fingers a little, signalling in body talk: You are safe, all is well as it can be. But I have a question I must ask.

Two said, *"Greenhill?"* Her eyes stayed blank. *"Summertree?"* Nothing. *"Redrock?"*

The look changed to shards of scorn. She said something, repeated it, clear enough to work out the syllables.

"Carsia."

Two had caught it. I said it back. "Carsia? Is that it?"

The slightest motion of her lids spoke assent. Mild complacency. Again, the husks of scorn.

*"Beyond sea,"* Two said. *"Whale road. Swan's path."*

I knew the sense, but the words I never heard before. She had. The eyes widened, in recognition, faint delight. A thankful smile.

*"How,"* Two went back to the patois, *"here?"*

Delight, animation vanished. I held her hands tight and tried not to shake, not to urge her beyond the limits even of need. "Mother, tell me? Let us try—let us know where to help. At least, try to let us know."

She had caught the plea, if not the sense. Her look paused on me. Two said, more urgently, *"How? How here? Carsia. Wave Island. Dhasdein. Why?"*

She was going to refuse. To close her eyes and everything else with them, and die with whatever it was untold. I tried not to over-tighten my fingers, but I could not deny our own need.

"Mother, please?"

She shivered sharply: the inception, if not the execution of a cough. Her eyes rolled up, I almost groaned aloud, and she got words out, the rasp of a whisper, on the cough's impulse and little else.

"Maer," she gasped. "Sthassa—" Her eyes clung to my face as if it were a rope. "Sthassa . . . maer . . ."

The cough overtook her. Her body spasmed, choking, the healer supported her, I held her hands as long as she could feel it. As long as there was need.

# CHAPTER VI

"I killed her," I said.

The wind howled over the lantern platform and whipped ice down my cheeks before it could dry the tears.

"I didn't mean—I didn't want—I never saw—" Anyone actually die before. Before my living eyes, rather than in Two's double-distance memories.

"And it wasn't any *use*—we still c-couldn't understand."

Azo put her arm around me. It should have dried my eyes from simple shock.

"Heads' work," she said.

"Head's—? How can that be Head's work? To kill—!"

"To decide."

My mouth shut on, Killing's your work. Troublecrew's.

"To decide what?"

She still had her arm around me. Hard, impossibly unaccustomed shield against the cold, even as she stared out to the sullenly darkening sea.

"The hard choices," she said. "The ones no-one else *can* make. Not just for the blood. For the—capacity."

She hitched a shoulder to the stairwell behind us, where Verrith was standing guard. "Like him."

Like Therkon. In that moment when he had deliberately chosen, with pity and grief and anguish, to take the weight of a life on his own shoulders. The blood on his own hands.

I looked at my hands, clamped on the gritty stone. My mother's palm shape, my father Sarth's long, strong fingers. The blood, as on Therkon's, invisible.

"Know it," Azo said. "Rightly, be unwilling. Rightly, grieve. And then, do what must be done."

Know what I did, I slowly understood. And carry the weight of that memory, as much a Head's as the responsibility for House or empire, and as necessary, if you are to rule. And if your rule is to be good.

Azo said, "Like Tellurith."

Another fury of air screeled over us while I worked out all that meant. Not simply a recourse to precedent. Full understanding of what I felt. Comfort, of the hardest sort. That I had done the right thing, however it hurt. Had done what my mother would.

When she felt I had mastered myself, she took her arm away. Reading her body language in turn, Verrith glanced from the stairwell. With an impassivity that carried its own signal, she said, "Chaeris, can you see them now?"

\* \* \* \*

Thankfully, they took us back down to the first floor, where the fort-commander and his staff evidently convened. A somber room with no adornment but the maps and charts on the walls, the piles of signals and reports on the commander's table-desk. We all stood, whether by custom, or respect. Whether for me, or Therkon, or something else.

"My lady," Therkon murmured, before the silence could grow painful. Very quiet, very formal. Knowing better than to express either sympathy or gratitude. "My lady, is there anything you would wish to say?"

Like Azo and Verrith, the officers were waiting. Trying not to appear greedy for whatever grains of value might have been won, but waiting, and hoping. That there might be worth for Dhasdein, at whatever the price.

When I could not answer immediately I felt Therkon give me one swift up-under-the-lashes glance. And turn to the fort-commander before he said, "The last word. Words. Did anyone recognize them?"

I only realized I had let my breath out when a voice among the officers replied, "'Maer'. That means Shadow. On Greenhill, anyhow."

The stifle of tension eased. Someone else added, "Most of the Archipelago. At least, where we know."

"And the rest?"

A wave of mumbles to which I could add visual signals: *Not me, unsure, Can't tell, Never heard before.* Then, hesitantly, another voice.

"'Thassa.' I think—that's something like 'sea.' On the Mel'ethi coast."

"Thassa," Therkon repeated slowly. "Not 'Sthassa'? Does anyone know . . ."

"*Sthassa*," Two said. "*Like 'S'hurre'. Something of the Mother. Sacred. Different.*"

Sounding startled, Therkon said, "Holiness?"

"*Not . . . necessarily.*"

In the tumbling pause I had time to think, Just another riddle with no answer, no sort of useable information. Just more loose, stray, uninterpretable words.

"Sea. Shadow. Something, perhaps, more." No way to tell if Therkon shared my despondency. But after a moment, more tentatively, he added, "My lady. Can you tell us? The other words? Carsia? And, whatever you said?"

"Beyond sea. Whale road. Swan's path." I could translate them now. I was thankful Two let me have the say. "I must have remembered them. From where, I can't tell, but they're names. I think maybe poet's names. Names for her island. Carsia."

The fort-commander stirred and let out a sigh. "At least we *have* a name. Or another name. If it's only one more," grimly now, "nobody's heard before."

I looked up and he saw more than I wanted, for his face changed abruptly and he almost gestured to me. "My lady, whatever we can find's a gift. We've begun a map, we can add on these. Beyond sea, it has to be a long way from whatever they call Centre in the Archipelago. Swan's path, I swear I've heard that before."

"West," somebody said. "The sea-songs, on Grey and Greenhill, they'll sing that. About losing, um, your girl. Or somebody like Deor or Ciannan, heroes. Taking the swan's path. Going away, lost, dying. But properly it just means, going west."

Another gust reverberated in the floorstone and the hair crept sharply on my neck. The woman from Carsia had indeed taken the swan's path, far past her own island. Further than any of us could go.

Therkon must have been intensely aware of every breath I took, for he shot me one almost invisible sidelong glance and asked softly but firmly, "And the center? Where's center, for the Archipelago? I thought maybe Phaerea?"

Phaerea meant nothing to Two, but it brought a rumble of general agreement. "Phaerea," summed up the commander. "At least, t'was in our day."

"Ah." I just had time to silence Two's, Where is it? What is it? Not *now*, I berated her, *he's balancing this group, this meeting, this entire fragile consensus like a half-blown bubble of glass on his fingertips. Wait.*

"So then. We advance, if by hair-breadths. We have another island. Maybe, a direction. And . . . a name."

With an artist's timing, he did not leave them long enough to consider the ill-omens of that name. Decisively, however politely, he addressed the fort commander.

"Pheis, we must commend your alertness, and thank you for your warning. And," a faint, decorous smile, "leave you most unjustly with the aftermath. You'll see her safely—kindly? Bestowed? Like our own folk." *We can*, the note said, *give her that tiny recompense.* "We ourselves should not, cannot linger. It must be past third watch?" At Pheis' nod his mouth stiffened. "We must not miss the tide."

Not if we, at least, were to reach the city before evening. If we, at least, were to find our safe way home.

The commander bowed in assent, but he was frowning when he straightened up. "Your Highness," diffident but determined, "that wind's making. It's a long pull through the channels, even with the tide. You'd not consider waiting? Lying over the night?"

Therkon nodded, but the way he pulled the cloak around him was signal enough. "You're very kind, Pheis, but if *Aspis* can't get us home through this, some Army designers will be finding another job." There was a quick, over-eager laugh. "Besides, I promised the fastest tidings possible. To the Empress."

The rowers at least had been briefly rested, and fed. Therkon politely but as adamantly declined refreshments for the rest of us, though he did allow the fort cooks to press on us a basket of bread and ready-heated soup. We clattered downstairs, over the now almost horizontal gang-plank, and they pushed us off.

The portcullis had hardly dropped behind us before I could feel the weather's change. *Aspis* did not merely bounce now when she met the outside water, she bucked. A great sheet of spray flew abaft the bows as she swung toward the channel, and the captain, who had been unusually quiet as we worked out the gate, cast a glance ahead and silently sucked his teeth.

Beside me, Azo said in my ear, "Find a stay or a belaying pin. And hold on."

I locked my hand around a belaying pin just below the gunwale, set to hold a brailing sheet. No-one, I could see, would try to raise a sail in this.

The wind shrilled and squealed around us, the spray flew from our bow no less than from the short, vicious little waves. The whole world had faded to the monochrome grey of the forts: sea, horizon, sky, pieced with white frills and scraps of foam.

Except in the wind's eye. To the north-east.

Therkon was watching the livid, broadening bruise over the horizon there. The white wall of rain beneath was as ominous as the furious boil of cloud above. He looked almost as grim as Azo. In a moment he said to the captain, "A squall, do you think?"

The captain bit his lip. Then answered brusquely, "She'll weather it. And the sooner we're in the channel, the better."

Therkon nodded. Then he too took a step back in grasp of the rail, and fastened his hand round a rope.

Whatever it was closed on us almost unnaturally fast: the wind quickened more fiercely, the light dimmed, we could hear the hiss of rain flying forward under the cloud's feet. The captain shouted something to the steersman and grabbed the tiller bar himself. They pulled the Nikonian round to make the first turn in the channel. As she straightened out the air went dark, the rain whipped into us with a roar and the wind hit like a very warship's ram.

*Aspis* literally staggered under the blow. The bow flew sideways as the whole ship reeled and ocean bucketed over us from fountains of mast-high spray. Even the captain's bellows paled against the din. The deck pitched and suddenly flung me sidelong against the gunwale, Azo grabbed me with a hand like a steel hook and my sight vanished in a choking wave of red.

It ripped away. I had been hit by the breadth of Therkon's cloak. He was wrenching it back around him and I would have been shouting at the captain, at anyone in earshot, but he was perfectly quiet: flattened to the rail just beyond us, eyes on the struggles of his ship.

And she was struggling. The wind-spasms gusted fit to break oar-looms as they whipped and whirled and the Nikonian was being mauled like a weaker boxer under a hail of blows. The captain and steersman battled madly at the tiller. I caught fragments of the rowing officer's yells. The oars beat like a winded bird's wings, to keep time, to meet or at least match the oncoming blows.

I had the belaying pin in both hands as the ship flung me to and fro like a pendulum until Azo yanked us both down on the deck. It isn't natural, was all I could think. I had no need of Two's memories, I knew already: this was one of the huge storms, the abnormal storms, that caught the freighters in open ocean. And now it was taking us.

With shattering suddenness the wind dropped. The sea roared and beat at us, the rain scourged down on us, but the wind had collapsed like a fallen tent. Suddenly Therkon and the captain, shouting beside me, were loud as heralds over the rest.

"—can't hold her! . . . afford to spend them! Not in here!"

". . . then? . . . make the fort?"

"—never do it—sea-room! Channel . . . tight! Have to run—!"

The captain gestured wildly ahead, then to the left, where the fort had vanished into a wall of rain, then behind and left again. Two and I understood together and my heart climbed right out of my throat.

The rowers could not hold her in the wind's face. Nor could we reach the fort, and the channel was too narrow to manoeuvre. He wanted to run: to flee for a beleaguered ship's only other, chancy safety.

Out into the open sea.

A minor gust screamed at us and fresh rain battered after it. Like his ship Therkon staggered. Then he swung one glance back to the fresh dark bearing down on us and as the wind quickened he shouted, "Yes! Now!"

The captain needed nothing more. He bawled something forward and as the next gust rose at us he and the steersman heaved on the tiller bar.

I know now that only something as light and deft as *Aspis* could have survived that move. She had just begun to swing when the wind hit and again the sea fountained round us, the bows flew up aslant. But the fulcrum moment had passed. The wind itself whipped her on past the deadly side-on broaching point, fatally vulnerable to wind and water both.

She crashed back level over the next wave's crest and the wind struck again, but this time on her quarter. The blow only drove her forward, oars dipping now to balance rather than impel, and she flew like a gull on the gale's impetus, up channel toward the open sea.

\* \* \* \*

I never saw the forts pass. They too were shrouded in the grey pall of spray and cloud and driving rain, but even my landlubber senses felt the Nikonian's stride lengthen and the wave patterns steady under us. It did not need the way the captain eased his back to tell us the first peril was past. We had sea-room again.

They rigged a stormsail then, a ferociously dangerous if brief struggle that nearly put men overboard. The captain was determined to conserve rowers while he could. When it came to securing brails, Azo and I found ourselves urged perfunctorily if politely toward the tiny kennel abaft the steering oars that served as a captain's shelter. The only cover on board. For all Two's panic at losing information, I did not have the heart to resist. No matter that Therkon was still outside, and even Deoren had not protested it. If they lost us overboard, I could tell, it would be the final straw in the load of calamity.

Two has the full count of time. I seem to have been numb for much of it, after the first few hours, when the terror of anticipation slowly dulled, under the endless noise, the wind and water's battering, the all-encroaching wet, the never predictable lunge or buck that would fling you against wall or deck. Break a doze, upset a position, and almost always spill the tiny precious rations of water or soup.

We blessed the Mother for that basket in the early part, despite the battle over its allotment. Therkon would take nothing unless his men did. Deoren insisted Therkon at least had to be fed. The captain claimed he and his officers would take shame not to match the sailors and rowers, who swore they could last on water alone. All of them were adamant that Azo and Verrith and I had no choice in sacrifice. And eventually, for the same reason we had stayed in the kennel, we gave in.

Two says the basket lasted three days. And that the mast snapped the first night, when they tried to rig a sea-anchor to slow us down. I do recall an unholy din of shouting and cracking, banging, crashing that reverberated through a hull which suddenly seemed to be lunging hither and thither like a riderless horse. That would have been when the mast went, and she lost steerage way, until they cut the wreckage clear and got her back on the first shift of oars.

Leaving two sailors overboard.

The sea-anchor rope parted the second morning, Two computes. To me nothing distinguishes it from the night, except a paler light creeping in the hatch cracks, and a view of salt-rimed, red-eyed, raggedly-wrapped wet and struggling scarecrows outside.

But somewhere in that light's span a sudden and even more untowardly savage spasm of wind and wave caught *Aspis* like a striking snake and smashed oarlooms like twigs, losing us half the upper starboard oars.

And men along with them.

We were out of the kennel that day for good. I still cannot bear to remember the sounds of the injured as they struggled to free them from the shattered looms and benches, to get them astern through the ship's bucking and the treacherously slippery spume, to lay them, close as packed fish, in the tiny shelter. And then the heart-breaking battle, with nothing but a bucket of water and a layman's experience and a few bandages, against broken arms, legs, stove-in ribs . . .

The lower-bank oars were too short to use on deck, if they could have been freed. By evening I was down in what had been the bilges, shouting signals in the fragmentary lulls, as guards and off-shift oarsmen fought to shove lower oars out their ports. And then to block the ports themselves, with bare hands, a ship-wright's maul, pieces of scavenged sail and broken oar-loom, naked swords.

That did give us more hands for upper shifts. With the sea anchor gone and the mast broken off short, leaving a mere rag of storm sail, she was almost unmanoeuvrable otherwise. As for the steersmen . . . Almost everyone took a hand at that, wrestling beside one or other of the red-eyed, sleep-walking experts who had been the captain and actual tillerman.

And by the fourth day, as Two accounts it, all of us could help to bail.

"Never spring a plank in less!" I recall the captain bawling at Therkon. "Most weatherly ship in the fleet!" His outrage was only rivaled by his injured pride. But even *Aspis* could not withstand the strain the torn-off starboard oars had put on her flank.

"She's working," I heard one of the sailors say hoarsely, as Azo and I came past him to the handles of the baulky, back-breaking, hand-mangling pump. Even deeper than the lower deck, dripping, raging gloom about us, the whole long submarine cavern stumbling and staggering under unseen blows, while we heaved to the point of exhaustion. And atop it, the terror that any fresh bellow of sea or wind might be the last. That those moving, twisting planks he pointed at would actually part, the water not merely leak but gush in from above and below and find us trapped there, with no chance but to drown.

"Keep pumping," his mate muttered. "Gotta be land somewhere."

They both winced. "Don't matter," the first growled, turning for the midships hatch, "which comes first."

Taking the weight of the first pump stroke I gasped at Azo, "Don't we want land? Surely?" Surely, any port would be a sanctuary in this?

Azo snorted with the remnants of her breath. "No say—how we'd strike it. Best chance. Lee shore."

My own blood ran cold. I had heard the old water-tales of Amberlight. Even on the River, there was no peril greater than a leeshore. Caught with wind behind you blowing onto the land, in a ship that had no way of fighting clear.

\* \* \* \*

It was no better on deck, battered by the implacable wind, the relentless rain, a shivering misery as salt crept in to abrade through every fold of cloth or flesh. And the exhaustion. The hunger's palpable weakening. The ongoing terror that never let up.

"Five days," I heard the captain whisper as he collapsed into the shelter of a bulwark at the end of his latest shift. "Has to drop *some* time."

Verrith measured him a cup from the water breaker. Rain we had in plenty, but the sea adulterated every drop that came aboard. The other scarecrow in a sopping red-black cloak put a hand for a moment on his shoulder, and I tucked my own blistered palms into my armpits and carefully did not meet his eyes, even though I knew he would not ask. Like me, he already knew the nature of this storm.

The wind and sea shrieked and cascaded round us, unremitting, undeterred. Saying for themselves, *No cause for this ever to end.*

That evening the worst injured rowers began dying.

The corpses had to lie among the living, with no more than the gesture of burial: Therkon, as most senior officer, reciting in a husk of whisper prayers they use in the Delta for the safe passage of a soul.

When he crawled out of the shelter the last time the light was going too, smothered in the maelstrom of wind and spray and endless, ear-breaking noise. I could feel everyone of us, from me to the off-duty oarsmen, literally dropping on our feet.

Therkon must have been near dropping himself. But as he straightened up with the now automatic clutch for a handhold, I saw his eyes go round the haggard faces, the eyes coal-red and inflamed as his own. Before he pulled himself a little straighter, and managed almost full-voiced words.

"Thank you, Deoren," he said formally, to his Trouble-head, who had met him with a steadying arm at the shelter's door. And then, more clearly, to the extra man on the tiller, "I will take this watch."

And I felt the rags of will and resolution tighten and re-firm in everyone around me, for if he went on, how could we not?

\* \* \* \*

I have no real measure for the span of eternity before the light came back next, only a marker for its end. Staring out from my lair under the gunwale with a muzzy sense of change. And then sudden, shocking comprehension, as the ragged stump of mast, the splintered midship bulwarks, the rags of fighting screen, the listing, paint-stripped figurehead assembled, above the clusters of bodies huddled among it all.

And the water that raged up beside us, cascading over the bows, doubtless the water still crashing at the slightest chance on our stern behind me, had changed color. Under the white spray and inlay of thrashing foam, it was green.

Ice-cold, bitter deep southern green. But no longer the eternal grey of the storm.

The light strengthened. I craned up over the gunwale. And for the first time in six days, stared out not into a wall of spray and rain but over a wilderness of heaving ocean. The wind still flogged, the sea tossed us fiercely, but the air had cleared at last.

The others were rousing too. I heard murmurs, faint and hoarse, from cracked, bleeding lips. The slow lift of attention, and with it spirit, that ran like an intangible wave down the entire ship.

Beside me Azo dragged her elbows over the gunwale. On my other side, Verrith did the same. With the swift scrutiny of troublecrew they stared about. Then across my head their eyes met in a long, expressionless look.

"What is it?" Alarm signals went off through every terror-strung nerve. I got one of my own swollen, blistered hands on the gunwale and heaved myself up. "What's wrong?"

After all, they did not have to explain. The light was creeping slowly but surely out into what, above the sea's furore, would sometime be a blue if cloud-wracked sky. And beneath it, on the horizon where sea and air met, low, swaybacked, and already far longer than it was high, lay a tiny but unmistakable shape.

"Land?" I could hardly whisper. "Is it really land? At last?"

Azo looked at Verrith. Verrith lifted a shoulder in a shrug.

"What is it? What's wrong? If it's land, we're saved, aren't we? It's all right?"

When neither of them answered, Two did the extrapolating for us both.

"Oh, Mother. You mean . . . it's right ahead of us? The wind . . . it's a lee-shore?"

After a moment, not looking at me, Azo answered.

"Unless the wind drops—yes."

* * * *

Therkon knew what hope there was of that, as well or better than I. Not that the rest of them needed urging to struggle with the tiller and set to the oars with all their strength. Double-shifts, even three men sometimes to an oar-loom, as they fought with their swollen hands and their exhausted muscles to turn and hold us across the wind's weight. To force us, however imperceptibly, to the right of that distant shape.

"Get past, into the land's lee," Azo did not have to explain, "get ashore if we can, lie to if we must." Her glance down the working deck, past the great gap in the starboard oarblades, added the rest: if we can keep afloat long enough to postpone beaching till the seas go down. "Do that, and . . ."

The shrug finished for her. In that unlikely event, we might still have some hope.

It seemed to go on for another eternity, in the knife-edged wind, over the thrashing green water, under that tormentingly blue sky. Cruelest of all, to fight the last battle in sunlight, in what would otherwise have been a fair, cheering day.

We did fight, all of us. At times I struggled with an oar myself. And for all our efforts, against the wind, with *Aspis'* dead weight of intaken water, the lack of sail or full oarbanks, it was not enough.

"If t'forsaken Adversary'd let the wind drop," I heard the next oarsman pant as I fell out. "Just a knot or two . . . 'd be enough."

And the man beside me gasped back, "Gonna all but clear it anyway. Just that last . . . bloody . . . cape."

The ultimate cape on the island's eastern side, the butt of the highest hill, that we could see so clearly now, sweeping down to the sudden bite of cliff. Slanted rock stacks black in the wave-spray, taller than a lighthouse, reared up from the welter at their feet as the waves raged in and exploded, throwing spray higher than the very cliffs. We could even hear the seabirds wheeling round them, a cacophony of indifferent, high-octave shrieks.

"Not just wind," gasped the captain, struggling in his turn at the tiller bar, as I gravitated astern, where we all did, when we had a chance. "Got a—bloody—current—under us."

Therkon hung on the bar beside him. The imperial rings had cut deep around his salt-caked, swollen fingers, but he was still pulling. Still sharing the load.

"Can we—ride it," he panted too, "round?"

"Round?"

"Setting in—like that. Has to turn—doesn't it? Off cliffs?"

Wind and birds screeled in eldritch dissonance. But the captain actually dragged his head up, squinting through the sunlight, forward over his failing ship.

His head dropped. His shoulders dropped too. A fresh gust took half his words away but I caught, "too dangerous. Like this."

*Aspis'* failing resources, I understood, left too narrow a margin for such risk.

Azo had been peering landward too. Suddenly she left her post, never six inches from me since the storm began, and moved over to the pair at the tiller bar. Stretching as if to throw her gaze up through the air like an arrow, she pointed landward. The wind robbed more of her woman's voice, but her gesture and the fragments made sense enough.

"Eddy, back along." She was pointing left, along the base of the cliff. "Hill this side. Bet money, inlet—beyond it. Under cliff."

The captain said something, his head-shake demurring. Azo snapped at him, tone if not sense clear enough.

". . . see it. *I* know how to look!"

He shook his head again, actually letting go the bar as he straightened. Therkon's back stiffened under the load, though he did not lift his head. Azo yelled, pointing, all but growing agitated. The captain looked and looked again and shook his head furiously, doggedly, then bellowed back.

"Can't risk it!" He jerked an elbow at Therkon. His eye and hand picked me out as well. "Oughta know that—yourself!"

Not dare such extra risk, with such precious cargo. Not with me aboard, as well as his own crown prince.

The intonation had been final. Azo did not demur. Just came back to me and Verrith.

And pulled my cloak undone, beginning to fold it in neat, tightly compacted squares, snapping something to Verrith. Who fossicked along the rail to find lengths of flailing rope, sliced them loose and handed them to Azo. Then sheathed the knife, her precious second throwing knife, and began undoing its straps from round her wrist.

Before she grabbed my own left arm and started buckling it on.

"What are you doing?" I was too stunned to argue, let alone think. "Azo? Verrith?!"

"Could need 'em," Verrith was never less than expressionless, "more than me."

She had the second sheath free, the one that went above her elbow, was scrabbling with my sleeve. Azo yanked rope under my arms and across my back, knotting corners of the cloak package, tying me into a virtual harness, I tried to stop them both and only managed a stagger on the shifting deck. "What in the Mother's name are you *doing*? What is this? I'm going to freeze—!"

Neither of them replied. Azo just glanced round, then slid halfway to the mast-foot to scoop up a broken oar-loom that had washed up and lodged there, perhaps for all the previous night. She brought it over to stow under the bulwark beside us. Said flatly, "Taking precautions," and gave me a look that added like a slap, *Shut up*.

Then she went back to staring through crystal-sharp sunlight across the tumultuous sea.

I opened my mouth and shut it again. The wind strengthened: and suddenly my cheek, attuned through those six days' purgatory as keenly as any ancient mariner's, picked up an alteration. I felt Azo twitch and raise her head even as I lifted mine.

The wind was shifting. Swinging, now, at the bitter last, slightly from the endless north-east. Coming round to east-north-east.

Pushing harder on *Aspis*' injured quarter. Driving her prow in, that last fatal fraction, toward and not away from the land.

The captain had felt it. In his off-watch stupor the steersman, all but comatose under the bulwark, had begun struggling to sit up. And Azo and Verrith had caught it too.

*Aspis* took a fresh wave and stumbled, worse than before. A vision of those working planks flashed before my eyes. Therkon hauled his own head up and addressed something to the captain. The wind gusted, they both heaved instinctively on the tiller bar.

And the port steering oar snapped.

Both oars must have taken untold stresses in the length of the storm, I would have expected the tiller bar itself to go first. But it was the oar that broke, with a crack like firing qherrique and a shower of flying chips.

Then the tiller bar was slapping, even I could tell how much looser in the steersmen's hold, the great blade and half the loom bobbed forlornly astern, and the rest hung down, like an amputated bird's wing, at the Nikonian's side.

Nobody had to gloss the calamity. Nobody shouted, or screamed, or even swore. All along the deck there was only a final, exhausted hush.

Then uproar broke out as the captain and officers started shouting, flogging numbed brains for the last desperate chance to compensate. I caught fragments of "deck-oar!" "double-watch!" Something about the sail. Men began running, or at least staggering, sailors, guards, off-duty rowers, the trembling deck reverberated to their hurry as the voices beat at the whistling air.

Therkon had heaved himself up from the tiller bar. The steersman had almost respectfully pushed him aside, taking the captain's place. Somebody had found an upper-deck oar, they were running it astern through the ruck. Someone else was scavenging for unbroken rope, half a dozen others had begun heaving in the massive steering-oar loom. They meant to rig a jury oar, to hold her at least partly into the wind. They meant to fight to the bitter last.

The loom came up against the side and somebody swung himself astride it: hands proffered ropes, lashings were passed round the loom, then a dozen other hands shoved the rowing oar through the loops. Frantic with haste and weakness, several hands began to pull the lashings tight.

The knots were fast. The men around me touched breast or forehead or lips with knuckle-backs and I heard the mutter of invocations, to the River-lord, to sundry other gods. The big loom slid back through its port, and the blade hit with a splash.

Suddenly it was almost wholly quiet. Everyone had gone mute, waiting, watching, as the tillerman and his offsider took up pressure on the bar.

And *Aspis* moved. No more than a point or two, but her bow came round for all that, slowly, so slowly, pointing away toward the east.

The uproar this time was yells of glee, relief, furious delight. They scrambled about the deck as if they had never known six spent and starven days at sea. They even crowded over, at the captain's shouts, to make her starboard side weigh heavier, to counteract the thrust of wind and sea.

The cape was close enough to see the seabirds now, a whirling white and grey flaked cloud. To hear the strike of each separate wave, the thunderous, reverberating impact of ocean on naked rock. But its seaward butt showed now, almost on the nearer side of the bedraggled figurehead. We had, again, a chance of getting past.

Azo and Verrith exchanged another look and leant on the bulwark, some unspoken purpose ebbing from their stances, postponed, if not revoked.

"Can I get out of this now?" I demanded. The ropes under my arms had already begun to chafe. "If it's not bad luck?"

Azo answered brusquely, "Not yet." Verrith muttered, "Don't test the Mother too far."

*Aspis* wallowed on, even I could tell how unhandily, her wounded, over-loaded hull struggling against the sea-scend. I had a painful memory of her leaving Riversend, that gay, bright fighting cock, and closed my eyes.

And felt through my feet the moment it happened, even before a pair of sailors burst up the hatchway, wild-eyed and dripping from head to foot, screaming, "She's opened! Midships starboard! Planks gave way!"

I heard the uproar, and it beat on me insensibly as wind. Even for Two my brain had stopped. But Azo and Verrith's eyes met over my head, one quick wordless look.

Then Azo yanked the oar from under the gunwale and cast another loose loop of rope around the loom and Verrith put a shoulder under mine and heaved me bodily onto the bulwark too.

"What are you doing?" I was too stupid to do more than shriek. Azo said through her teeth, "Hold this," and slapped the oar-rope into my hand.

"I can't! I won't!" Understanding seared like lightning. "I won't go without you!"

Azo got an arm under my leg. I started struggling in earnest. "Let me back! Let me back! Azo! Verrith, I won't, I won't!" No time to shout that others would have no chance to escape, even if there were they would fight for the ship, no time to invoke Therkon's fate, the anguish awaiting the Empress. I fought like the proverbial maniac. And Azo and Verrith grabbed me either side and literally threw me in the sea.

The cold green water sank me, scraps of Azo's last shout ringing like a warcry in my ears.

". . . or what'll I say . . . Tellurith?"

\* \* \* \*

The sea drank me like a pebble. I have no idea how far down we plummeted before the oar and my own lungs' air-bladder drove us back toward the light. My head shot out into streaming, reeling vistas of green splashing water far too close to my nose under far too distant cloud-dappled blue sky. I thrashed aimlessly till by merest luck one arm hit the oar loom, that the rope had kept close by.

I got some sense back then. Enough to work my arm over it. To understand why Azo had tied my cloak on my back instead of leaving me to wear it. To realise why the oar had come with me. To comprehend that they had put me clear of the ship now, to avoid, if it foundered, any chance of being sucked down. To understand Azo's last, so chancy plan.

To hold my head a little higher, and stop fighting for air, and let the sea bear me, as it would bear me, if I let it. Two had the memory of water-wise generations. She translated the tingle and push around my calves. It was the current. Taking us in, where the ship could no longer go.

Into, I realized slowly, the eddy Azo had so madly, so desperately gambled on. Into what she had guessed or intuited or just prayed would be an inlet, under those cliffs and back behind the intervening hill.

Because I, at least, was so low in the water that now the wind could not come at me. The ocean alone would take me to what might be safety, our other, most inveterate enemy at last annulled, the ocean's indifferent malice turned against itself.

I shook water from my eyes and tried to see *Aspis*.

Green hills surrounded me, moving, sometimes colliding, ever-changing green hills with foam strung like sliding daisies on their flanks. The seabirds screeled, much closer, filling the register above the waves' thunder with their din. But no human voices wove amid their clamour. The shifting horizon showed no barest glimpse or fragment that might be the work of humankind.

The eddy did set along the cliffs' feet, though it was so close I shut my eyes and committed my soul to the Mother if Azo's guess proved wrong. But then I opened my eyes again, unable to help myself. And the great rock stack that had been straight before me was perceptibly further to my right.

It seemed another eternity before the water motion steadied. Until the making tide carried the oarloom in, over yeastily thrashing shallows where my feet touched, where I could at last, with the onward swing of the tide, get my feet firmly set. And wade, stumbling, staggering, breast, waist, calf-deep, towing the precious oar-loom after me. To reach, at last, the brief, coarse sand-margin. Where I fell down, weeping, cloven between relief and anguish, but understanding to my bones' marrow what it means to be cast up—disdained, thrown back, regurgitated—by the sea.

# CHAPTER VII

Two insists that we came ashore some time in second day watch, as sailors count the time. But when the rising plaints of skin and bone and muscle forced me to wipe my streaming nose, and shift position, even consider trying to sit up, it was early afternoon.

The wind was still blowing, however thwarted by the lesser cape. Still, my internal compass verified, from the malevolent north-east, and despite a watery sun little past its zenith, still colder than the sea. The sheets of blown sand and spume drifted from the breakers' thunder forced me, eventually, to begin struggling with the cloak harness. To remember, after uncounted ages, that I had a knife.

Verrith's wrist-blade slid smoothly from the sheath. It was salt-rimed but the steel was intact. Its razor-edge parted the rope. I saw, heard, felt, smelt Verrith, close as Azo, as watchful and taciturn: their Uphill but not House-born accents, the crinkled Amberlight hair, Azo's unruly left eyebrow, the gap in Verrith's teeth. Their troublecrew solidity. Permanent as history, my bulwark on this journey. The bulwark of my life. Of my mother's life. In Iskarda, before I existed. Even in Amberlight.

Eventually the tears ran dry. I got the ropes off. The cloak was wet as the rest, but its oiled goat's-wool worked as always. Drawn round me, it cut the wind solidly as a wall, almost with a fire's relief.

I felt Azo's hands knotting it tight. I felt the cold space at my right elbow, empty as the one at my left. I heard their voices, and saw again that last moment on *Aspis'* deck. I put my head back on my knees and wept.

That time my belly brought me round, with a pang that overrode even grief. Inside the cave of hood I scrubbed at my eyecorners, trying to tell myself I must get up. That whatever the desire to lie down here and die, I must not squander Azo and Verrith's gift. I must get on my feet, and go inland, and try to find . . .

People? Refuge?

Help?

They're gone, I thought. They're all gone. *What*, I cried to Two, *is the use of going anywhere? Of doing anything?*

Two had no reply. The wind had none either. But suddenly another sound overrode the sea and air's untiring rumour. Fast, broken, thudding crunches in the sand. The sound of running feet.

Then a body thumped down against me so hard it nearly bowled me over, arms smothered me like a wave and a hoarse voice cried into the cloak folds, *"Chaeris!"*

\* \* \* \*

We both cried then: I know that, because his tears were wet on my hair after I finally fought back out of the cloak. Then I buried my face again and tried to lose all but the sound and smell of him, sea-hoarsened voice, reek of salt water and human fear and indelibly persisting sweat. Anything to credit that someone else had survived. That at least, I was no longer alone.

That at least, I would not have to take that news to the Empress.

He was babbling, "Oh my lady. My lady. . . The River-lord be thanked, the Lord be blessed." I re-wiped my eyes, and managed to look up.

He was looking down at me with as fatuous, as unstrung an expression as I could feel on my own face. The once immaculate hair hung in elf-locks, its clip naturally lost. A week's stubble improved that gaunt, haggard cheek. Salt and tear-reddened eyes squinted, come-and-go smile breaking over it all like the first of that morning's light. He had not lost me, after all. His word, at least, remained intact.

"How?" I achieved at last. I could not seem to let go of him. A handful of sandy, sodden cloak, a corner of irretrievably filthy shirt. "How did you *get* here? How . . ."

The joy snuffed. He shut his eyes. The one remainder of the crown prince was those dark smooth crescents of lash.

"Deoren," he answered, just audibly. "Suris. They saw . . . your troublecrew."

He bowed his head and his hand clenched on my shoulder till it hurt and I saw the tears run as mine had done, and understood.

His troublecrew had done as Azo and Verrith did. Somehow, they had got him and the cloak, at least, overboard. Consigned him to the sea, and hoped.

I put both arms round his neck. Tanekhet's warning, my own hankerings, Two's reaction, did not matter. It would not have mattered if both of us had been men or both women or each a hundred years old. It was human solace, answering desperate human need.

"It's what," I whispered in one ear, through the lank tangled hair, "they meant to do. What they would have wanted. The same as . . ."

I lost words then too. We hung onto each other and discovered the second miracle. That after everything, there were still tears.

When that tide finally ebbed, we could at least begin to look around.

The dry beach was a mere crescent above high water, its coarse, pale reddish sand backed by a dull green scrubby fringe. Some sort of ling, I guessed. Left hand, his footprints receded into dark wet sand, where the sea creamed pallid azure and silver behind the ebbing tide. Further off, the land rose precipice-steep to the main cape, a towering vista of slanted, sandy red, fissured and fragmented stacks. Waves still shattered along their bases, seabirds still gyred round them, keening like the undaunted wind.

To our right scattered boulders marred a somber, not to say sullen green. More ling, or perhaps low-growing shrubs. And a crest, like the other slope, bearing not a track, a fence, a roof. Not even a distant twist of smoke.

In a while I said, "Do you—did anyone—" I could not bear to mention any name, "have any idea where we might—where we are?"

Mutely, he shook his head. I swallowed hard and shut my eyes. Far, far into the Archipelago, reason answered bleakly. Six days before a storm like that? No telling where this might be.

I clenched my teeth on the new wave of grief. We would have to help ourselves. We would have to walk, climb that unwelcoming hill, look for succor. For news, and directions, and a bath, pray the Mother, and fresh clothes, and food.

Therkon had let me go at last and turned a little, still sitting tight against me, but now with heels dug in the sand, arms bowed between his knees. He had gone quite still, almost as if he had forgotten me, along with the land, with himself. His eyes were staring out to sea.

Staring, in more than grief. Dilated, as at some horror just come into view.

I jerked my eyes down the beach. Flotsam was emerging behind the tide now. Kelp wreaths, ancient driftwood, sanded and salted white and smoothed like a craftsman's work from the natural form of trees.

But not painted, on the baulk's facing side.

Red, a rustily faded red, picked out with shreds of white. The heart-stoppingly familiar shape of a volute from a galley's stern fan, its inner side scoured whiter than the paint.

Sea did that, something announced, so far away from me. Wind, and salt, and sea.

I jerked my eyes away. I jerked my hand too, fiercely, brutally, in Therkon's shirt and cloak and almost spat it at him. "No! Don't look!"

He might not have heard. He was still staring down the beach.

Then he said abruptly, hoarsely, "I should have known."

"Known what?"

His right hand released the other and thumped, almost viciously, against his thigh.

"The River-lord forgive me, any backstreet brat would have known. Straight out of the sagas, told on any street-corner. A survivor. One survivor, and a message and a mysterious—clue." It came out nearer a curse. "And the messenger dies that moment. No follow-up. No questions. Dhe, how many tales, how many times—"

He punched his knee again and suddenly sank his head between both hands. "I should have listened." He almost whispered it, into the uncaring sand. "I should have stayed, at the fort. But I *ordered* it. Dhe pity them, *I* brought them here—"

He fought the tears this time, though now they were almost convulsive sobs. When I tried to touch him he half-turned away and too many of Two's memories warned, *No. When a man cries in earnest, an outland man, he wants no witnesses. Especially this man. He hasn't just lost friends or a ship, he was the one who commanded it. It's pride broken as well as grief. Give him the only kindness possible. Let him be.*

I got up as quietly as I could and wove away, stumbling in the sand and trying to find my land-legs, further up the beach.

\* \* \* \*

He came to me in a while, moving as shakily as I had, the sodden cloak battering in the wind. Trying to hold his head up. To re-assume, whatever the lapse, his responsibilities. To recall and reassure the one he thought still in his care. Looking at me with those freshly reddened eyes. Trying, however pitifully, to smile.

"My lady. Forgive me. I've neglected you . . ."

"No," I said and could not help it. I put both arms around him again and held him tight. "You *didn't* neglect me. You didn't neglect anyone. Nobody could have foreseen this. Nobody could have done more to stop it. You—we—had to go out to the forts, we—it was a message nobody could have chanced. Do you hear me?" I actually managed to shake him, just a little, on his feet. "*It wasn't your fault.*"

He was looking at me: uncertain, but listening. Willing, perhaps, to believe. To accept it. But Two had broken in before I knew.

"*This was not chance.*"

Therkon's face very nearly blanched. His eyes seemed to pierce me through.

"Not chance? Then—"

"*It was planned.*"

It was no longer the sea's hobbledehoy, but the imperial hatchet man. I wanted to step back. Especially when the voice dropped another note. "*Who?*"

"*We have insufficient data.*" A teetering pause. "*But it may have been, What.*"

Therkon almost gasped. Then his eyes slitted.

"The, the thing? Whatever it is? Sthassamaer? In the Archipelago?"

Two pulled me back a step. "*We have insufficient facts!*"

Therkon was breathing hard enough to hear. He just managed not to shout, *Don't tell me you can't guess!* He did get out, through his teeth, "What *proof?*"

"*Wind . . . the wind thinked.*" Two was losing words along with grammar, I clenched my hands and panted, trying not to shout at her, *Not here, not now, you have the inference, find words for it, or let me tell him—Think!*

"*Wind . . . Too long! Then change—at the worst. And the sea. When the oars broke . . . TELL him, Chaeris!*"

"Wind, sea, the wind thought?" Therkon was on the edge of violence too. "How does that mean, What?"

"*Two-legs!*" Two screamed at him. "*Two-legs can't change wind!*"

We stood shaking, glaring at each other like a pair of gargoyles. Then suddenly my legs melted. I was down on the sand and Therkon had both arms round me, hatchet man vanished, the crown prince babbling, "Chaeris, I am so sorry, I should not have done that, I beg your pardon—"

He stopped. Neither of us had to go on.

Two-legs means, Human.

Human beings cannot rule the wind.

Selfishly, despicably, I let my forehead rest against Therkon's shoulder a minute or two longer. Letting myself linger in that physical presence, the delusion of safety, warmth. Anything to avoid thinking. Drawing the conclusions. And then, from that worse place, repeating the inevitable question. Now, what do we do?

It was he who finally pulled himself straight. Released me. Carefully not looking seaward, he struggled to his feet, and offered me a hand. And somber beyond dourness, gave me the first words of any reply.

"Lady Chaeris, let us get off this beach."

\* \* \* \*

The ling was wind-dwarfed and thick with horizontal, twisted but wiry twigs, as difficult to cross as it was infuriating. We struggled up the first rise, tripping, stumbling, in our sodden, salt-rough boots, feeling six days' hunger in every step. And at the top, the Mother finally favoured us. The shallow transverse valley below held a footpath, a thread of white sand among the ling.

At its edge Therkon glanced left and right, and then at me. Saying silently, to me or Two or both of us: *Which way?*

Two had no suggestions. I turned my back on the wind and said, "Down there."

Skirting the next hill's swell, the track reached a deeper, seaward running valley, with shrubs and occasional trees in its seam. Thick, green, seeding grass grew among tall wet-spangled ferns, and from them came the sweetest sound I could have prayed for. Water, running over stones.

"Praise the River-lord," murmured Therkon, wiping his mouth at last. It was a mere rivulet, its water spate-ebb, cold and pure-tasting but brown as peat. Brown as Amberlight eyes.

I cut the thought off as the spear transfixed me all over again. No Azo to scout before us, no Verrith standing watch as we drank . . .

Therkon's head was bowed above the water too. Still kneeling, he scooped out another double palmful, and let it trickle away among the ferns. The whisper was almost inaudible, but I caught the River-lord's name, and guessed it was a prayer.

After that we did wash, the bliss of clearing salt from limbs and hands and feet and faces, if not a complete bath. But as we re-laced our revoltingly soggy boots, Therkon eyed me, considered his own shirt, rasped a hand over his chin, then produced a rueful laugh.

"My lady, if we even *had* a comb . . ."

It would take hours to untangle either of our heads. We had no razor either. Seeking charity from strangers, we would win no favor for prepossessing looks.

The path went across the rivulet's three stepping stones to the further valley side. Over the crest, down, up. I plodded after Therkon, feeling my eyes blur, my muscles soften with every climb. He had naturally put me behind him, and I was past protesting that I had the knives, and he was precious too. Soon it did not seem to matter. Every so often the dull green ling, the great, silent, lichen-patched boulders, the watery, clouding sky would swing slowly round me. I literally walked into Therkon when he stopped.

He said, "There's a house."

We had mastered a particularly stony crest. Before us stretched another dull green and grey-spatched valley, but this one ended in silver-blue reflections through a lattice of taller trees. A pool, if not a lake. Framed in grass rather than ling. And tucked neatly into the slope above it, a roofline and a haze of smoke.

House? I thought. Two amended, *Perhaps*. With a stone-walled—yard? Greenery in a further enclosure, and this side the lake, an oddly dancing series of varicoloured patches, brown and black and white.

Someone said in my ear, "Goats."

Smoke meant fire. A hearth? What possible connection could unite goats and hearth-smoke neither Two nor I could imagine, but one of us managed, affably, "Goats brew tea?"

Therkon drew in his breath. Then he gathered me by an arm and, just slightly the steadier, started down the hill.

The house kept swimming in and out of focus, but it grew stranger with every glimpse. Long, low, single-story. Roughly rounded ends. Stone walls, the color of the brindled roan cliff-stacks, but not squared either. Unshaped, miscellaneous slabs.

I stopped short, head reeling to memory of the wildest yarns spun in Iskardan winters. Fragments older than Amberlight, tales of the scree folk who dwelt on some lost mountain, in houses of stone and grass.

*Thatch,* Two insisted. From one end to the other of the sway-backed roofline, it was a deep shaggy covert of age-pallid thatch. End-poles stuck up like masts, and rope laced round above the wall-rim, held in place by a necklace of big dangling stones.

Therkon urged me on. The yard-wall was more unshaped stone. The sapling-frame wicket gate had a leather loop over a standing rock. Beyond it the doorway confronted us, a rag-edged rectangle, under a particularly long slab for lintel. A portal on silent dark.

Therkon cleared his throat. Hesitated, and almost managed a shout.

"Ahai!"

Wave Island dialect, Two informed me. Neutral signal at an unknown threshold.

A woman came out.

She was pale-skinned as some of the Riversrun folk, tall as I and gaunt as Therkon, and though, once past the lintel, she held herself upright, her face was deeply seamed, her coronet of braids iron grey.

With no hint of surprise, she said, "There ye are."

Two very nearly came apart. I was past reaction. But my companion had kept some wits.

Therkon said, "You saw the wreck?"

I felt his voice falter over the word. I did see the odd look cross her face, but in a moment she answered, again in Riverspeech, if with an almost unintelligible accent.

"The wreck. Aye."

"Did anyone—do you know if anyone—"

He could not go on. But the break seemed to make her refocus: next moment she had me by one arm and him by the other and was saying in that gruff deep voice, "Ye'll be better inside."

The doorstep was a wide stone flag. The wall was thicker than my forearm-length, breathing the cold of stone, that vanished under the inner fume. Smoke, I identified, gasping. Human fug, dried herbs, drying meat, a whole history of food. And smoke, a haze that overlaid the air like mist, white in the glare from some window, red-lit above the rock-burning fire.

The flames sat at the room's heart, under a tripod and hanging chain. They filled a stone-rimmed hearth, and the right-hand wall was broad slabs of stone, with a doorway blocked by what must be an unshaped hide. The cupboard against the back wall was all stone slabs, and the saddle quern to the left was not a mortar, but a huge, recumbent boulder like those outside.

We're underground, I could not scream. In the scree-folks' lair, and it may be five centuries before we get out.

The ensuing blur Two cannot reclaim. I myself can recall sitting down, a bliss of rested feet. A huge pot swinging against the hearth-glow, a hot bowl in my hand. Broth, barley and meat and vegetables, finely seasoned, and a miniature loaf of gloriously crusty, rough-milled bread.

Also a grey blob sliding past my feet, the brush of fur against my wrist. Lunatic commonsense observing, *The scree-folk keep cats.* Therkon biting into a mouthful and faltering abruptly. And the woman opposite us, her face uplit devilishly by the fire.

Consuming rock rather than wood, the blaze glowed rather than flamed. Of the five hundred questions seething in my head for eminence, Two reached that one first.

*"What is that fuel?"*

"Peat," she answered, with an expression, even on that face, that anyone could read. How could anyone not know?

There I must have greyed out again, because the next thing I recall is Therkon saying, "Woman of the house? What do they call this land?"

"Sickle," she said.

*Never ask banefolk where they live!* I try to scream it, and my vision clears in shock. Therkon's face swims close, looking blank as I felt. And suddenly, more than a little sick.

"You mean, the island—some—call Scythe?"

"Aye." She answers after a too long moment. "They do call it that. Beyond the Isles."

I clearly see Therkon's expression. Before she rises, speaking crisply enough to pierce the fog.

"Best not fill your bellies yet. Best . . ." Words blur, and motion is drawing me away into the outer dark. Someone fumbling with my boots. Then a horizontal surface, thick, soft, and warmer than the fire. Fur. A deep, deep fur with level stone under it, all drowned by the oncoming swells of sleep.

* * * *

I came awake with a pop. A sinking net-cork cut loose. I actually sat straight up and sound came out of me on a wordless yelp that would have become, "Azo—!"

Memory struck on the breath. Sound became a sob.

Something rustled in the gloom. Close to me in unfamiliar gloom, fur and stone instead of planks under me, no light of wave-crest or ocean, no motion at all. Only salt persisting in my matted hair, my vilely salt-caked clothes, and a grip on my wrist over Verrith's knife-sheath that I just kept Two from sparking loose.

"Y're awake."

The beach, the ling, the stone-house. The woman with iron-grey hair. I managed not to gasp, Where am I? I could make out the inner door now, its curtain pulled back, the glow of fire beyond. My heart slowed, then jumped in fresh panic. "Therkon! Where's Therkon, is Therkon all right?"

"Just outbye." The hand let go. "Come now, and break y'r fast."

Pale light was creeping through the outer door and the back window, visible now, its shutter drawn back. The brume endured, but the fire was burning high and hot, a pot over it and a grid below, and on the hearth rim an indubitable iron pan.

*"You cannot suffer iron."*

Two had harvested all those wretched stories and got loose at the most inapposite time. But the woman actually laughed aloud.

"Aye, a score o' mothers past! But there's use in it now."

Beyond the hearth Therkon rose from what must be a block of stone, softened with another hide. He looked twice as disreputable as I felt, a ragamuffin rather than a crown prince, let alone the gorgeously apparelled Dragonfly: but his expression was clear relief.

"My—Chaeris."

As superfluous to ask, Did you sleep? As, Are you all right? I seemed to circle the hearth without volition, as if homing into his arms.

I tried to tell myself it was to reach the one familiarity left. He did grasp me lightly by the shoulders, and after a pause just not long enough for a hesitation, bent and kissed me on both cheeks. A formal, or perhaps a kinsman's salute.

No time to weigh that. Two was already rabid to record the house from end to end, to drain its owner of every fact about herself, the island, the Isles. *Not* yet! I ruled fiercely. Just as the woman herself said behind us, "Ye can begin now."

Porridge she gave us first, thick and hot and salted from the pot, then eggs, tossed neatly in the iron pan. Therkon hid a shudder at the sizzling fat, but when she handed him his wooden platter, he braced himself to eat.

I gulped back any version of, Should you leave that? Clearly, the disaster of flouted hospitality out-weighed his stomach's possible vagaries.

Bread followed, with cheese to spread on it. Thick soft white cheese that set Two loose again, demanding, *"From the goats?"*

*Blight and blast you,* I yelled, *don't ask point-blank like that!* But the woman, looking amused, answered only, "Aye."

She measured our meal like a groom gauging water for an over-ridden horse. Then, returning the cheese and bread to that stone cupboard, she brought back a big wooden comb and a lidded basket so tiny it left me speechless. *Where,* Two wanted to yell, *do you find work like that?*

"Happen ye'd wish a bath? Then," with a drolly straight face, "best fettle y'r hair first."

The basket held fragrant salve. "Goose grease, wi' a touch of lavender," she annotated, at our dubious looks. "Later, we'll try it elsewhere." Her eyes dropped to our blistered, still swollen hands.

We had to "fettle" each other, for the back knots were beyond either of us. We rubbed in grease, and combed, and re-combed, ignoring the hideously gooey results. "Though I hope," Therkon muttered as I worked over the nape of his neck, "she does have soap."

She had soap: she had also heated the big cauldron, so we had hot water to dilute the double yoke of wooden buckets she had unobtrusively filled from the lake. Then we could strip down, out on the flags between the house and peat-stack, to scrub and rinse to our heart's content.

Therkon naturally insisted I go first. There were even fresh clothes, for me an ankle-length robe in the softest imaginable undyed buckskin. When Therkon disappeared in turn I was happy to loll barefoot on the wooden settle by the door, shake out my wet hair, and look around.

The yard was trodden earth, with stone-rimmed garden beds against the outer wall. Herbs, my nose read, including the lavender. A hazy sun enhanced their scents amid the warm breath of grass, a wet-hay smell from the thatch, the cold presence of that stone wall. And a definite drift of ammoniac byre stink, across the scent of new-turned earth.

Our host appeared, little basket in one hand, in the other, my discarded boots.

"I washed these fresh, last night. Work t'grease in well now. An they dry, they'll be fit to wear."

What is more precious to a traveler, a castaway, than your own fitting, well-worked, intact boots?

She brushed my thanks aside with a little upward shift of her chin, and produced a distaff and spindle and a dusty mass of— wool? The same dark brown as her smock and the peculiar skirt. But Two had no time to question. My left sleeve had slid back as I worked. She observed, "That could use grease, too."

She knew what she had seen. She was right, and it was both risky and stupid to dispute. I unbuckled both sheaths, and slid knives and all onto my knees.

Both blades were salt-rimed but intact. The hilts, carved bone dark with use, needed wiping at once, and the sheaths were as direly soggy as my boots.

"Work them with this." She gave me a handful of unspun wool. "Within and out." Adding with satisfaction, "T'will serve your hands as well."

If I had never owned knives, Verrith had taught me both their upkeep and use. I wiped and rubbed in silence that kept blurring out with tears. Then caught her glance, saying she recognised my training, and let Two loose almost with relief.

"*Who are you? What is this place?*"

One small wave accepted and dismissed my look of apology. We spoke very well, I realised, without any speech.

"This is the ban-house of Evvamoor. And I its keeper. These last ten years."

Two nearly exploded on the spot. She anticipated, with that small, suppressed smile.

"Evvamoor's t'village. Over there." Southward. "But the old ones, the bones, are here."

"The *bones*?" This was a graveyard? I could not help the wild glance round. She smiled a little grimly, and pointed a thumb earthward.

"There."

No tale of the scree-folk had been this bad. Could she possibly mean what it seemed? "The, the old ones are buried under the house?"

"Nay." With a deft twist she sent the spindle twirling and the distaff began to turn. "On Sickle, time out of mind, bones go to the ban-house. Flesh goes to the air."

Even Two could not find a question to expand that.

"The birds," she said. "The dead lie on the ban-rock. The clean bones come here. For the ban-keeper to grind, in the under-pit, and lay to sleep and ward."

I just managed to keep Two quiet. In a moment, with ebbing irony, she added, "The under-gate's t'other end of the house. Past the quern."

I could not possibly exclaim in relief. After a minute or two's sedulous rubbing and wiping, I could almost get the hush out of my voice.

"How, uh, do we call you?"

She gave her sudden almost-laugh. "M'name's Nouip: ere I was ten they were callin' me tall-as-a-peak."

"Oh." Could this woman ever have been ten? But the return courtesy was pressing. "I am called Chaeris."

She nodded. She had heard Therkon use it, I realized, and in any mannerly exchange my origins came next. But could I, should I open the door to the questions that would follow that?

With relief I saw Therkon reappear, rubbing at his hair and trying at the same time to carry his boots and pull tight the laces in a long buckskin shirt.

* * * *

We made room for him on the bench. He shook his hair out. Sighed, as I had, in near luxurious relief, then remembered his manners, and turned to Nouip.

"My lady, how can we thank you? Your courtesy, your gifts—"

She made the little hand-twist again. Castaways: who could do less? "T'is the custom of the land." She nodded at his boots. "We've the goose-grease here."

I nearly hiccupped at the thought of Dhasdein's crown prince oiling his own boots. A sharper shard of thought slashed the mirth: she had read my experience with the knives, she would pick up his inexperience here. What would that tell her? What should we tell her—belatedly I reclaimed Iatha's, Tez's caution. What should we tell anyone in the Archipelago about either of us?

Therkon's wits were warier than mine. He made a little motion all grace, but equal parts dismissal and request. "My lady, if you please. First, if you could tell us. What you saw." He did swallow. "The wreck?"

I lowered my eyes in shame. I had been thinking ahead, taking the past as given. Done with. Lost. He had not yet relinquished it.

The spindle rose and fell. She said, "I Saw it. Aye."

I heard the capital and my heart spun right over. She was not just scree-folk, or a ban-keeper. She was a Seer. She Saw it, as she Saw the two of us.

Two said, *"How long since?"*

Therkon frankly gaped, but the woman's eyes slitted. Grey eyes, by daylight grey as her hair.

Then she answered, evenly, "Twa, three days past." The gesture pointed up and seaward behind the house. "On t' Head. Rack Head. At the Giants' Dance. The Long Stone. Speirin' the Quarter star."

Two and I were flying at her sentence tails in literal giants' leaps. Giants' dance, long stone, stones even bigger than the quern stone inside, she had been seeking the mark of a year quarter. Spring? Far behind ours on the River, Two extrapolated frantically, we must be far, unthinkably far south. And she?

Two, or I, or both of us, drew in a long, almost ecstatic breath. She was a true Seer. One who knew how to do it. One who might pass that knowledge to us.

I made the gesture by which, in Amberlight, you would acknowledge a woman of the Mother's. Not merely Craft, but Calling. What Dhasdein terms priests.

She inclined her head. Therkon had reached, Two, *three* days past? Now he repeated, uncertainly, "You saw the wreck?"

Her brows made a little twitch.

"I Saw a ship. Sore touched by storm. In t'Rackstream, that aye sets into the cliffs." Another eloquent turn of a wrist. Knowledge enough to forecast the rest.

"But when it happened? Did you—"

He broke off short. He still had his wits, and he had been some time round me. He did not burst out, So you *saw* nothing? But went on, almost composedly. "There was . . . wreckage. On the beach."

The spindle ran up and down again. And up. "Naught else?"

"Not—before we left."

He was watching her with more than a heart in his eyes. After a moment she said quietly, "Evva beach. T'Rackstream flotsam comes there, aye." She shook her head a little. "Eh, man, t'is no surety they lived."

"But one more chance they might." He clenched his hands. "My lady. I am importunate. But to have lost them—lost them all, and not be sure—"

"Aye." Her face had softened, but the next question came smoothly as a stab. "Where were ye bound?"

"We—" Therkon balked. Then he suddenly shook his head with a tired little laugh. "I think you know this. We were blown out of the River mouth. Five days south-west, without a sight of land. We are," he took a visible breath, "from Dhasdein."

"Outlanders," she said, but not in surprise. And Two got loose with, "*Did you See that too?*"

Her eyes turned, considering. "Nay," she said.

We had hardly shorted her of common clues, after all, from our accents to our ignorance. Or our clothes. Or . . .

Therkon was sitting bowed as he had on the beach, hands clasped between his knees. Knees clad in the semblance of those elegant black trousers. Swollen, blistered hands that still bore the glint of rings.

The Empire's spousal ring. Worth a fortune, anywhere. The imperial signet. The last thing he should wear in any island of the Archipelago.

"I beg your pardon, uh, Nouip." I wanted to call her Lady, at the least. "We've been mannerless. I told you, my name is Chaeris. This is—"

"I am Chaeris' brother Therkon," he said.

I just controlled the gasp. The lightning flash of comprehension woke a stupid jet of relief: that's why he didn't hug me this morning, he's starting as we must go on, he means to protect me. And the irrelevant counter-flash, she already knew his name.

But the courtesy was what mattered. And the distraction. He had sat up, making an abbreviated Court bow, his ringed hands were out of sight.

Nouip turned the distaff deftly and the spindle ran up and down. She said, "Aye."

"My, our family are merchants. Chaeris sailed with us, just to the Delta mouth."

He stopped again, catching his breath as on him too the past fell like a wave. Azo. Verrith. Deoren. The captain, the steersman, the rowers and sailors. Ten men of the Imperial guard. Gone. Lost.

Dhasdein, the Empress, left not knowing if we were with them. The River beyond. Iskarda.

Nouip looked once at us and dropped her eyes to the distaff. After a moment she asked, "What think ye to do now?"

* * * *

"Now?" Therkon laughed raggedly and shoved a hand through his hair. "My lady. There's hardly been time—"

I saw the thought hit him, almost physically. He spun on the bench and almost grabbed for her. "My lady, can you See what we should do?"

Such a desperation of hope as would have broken my heart. Nouip's eyelids did flinch a hair's-width. Before she slowly, sadly, shook her head.

"The Sight comes to me," she answered, "at its will. Not mine."

Therkon did not have to reply in words.

I was saying, too loudly, "Then could you show me? Maybe I can look? Could you show me how?"

She put the distaff down altogether and turned to face me. Understanding was in that look. And with it, reluctance. Regret.

"I would show you, Chaeris, and welcome. But I think, it will not help."

It was disappointment, not shock, that left me mute.

"Sights . . . come all of a piece to me. Once and only. Most often, at the Dance. I've to, to put the pieces together, for myself."

She reached a hand out suddenly and set it lightly on my wrist. "With you, I think t'will be very different. To begin with, there's two of ye."

She nodded, wryly, not making me try to marshal words through the shock. "T'one's a fine well-raised maid, smart with If-you-please and Thanks. T'other's mad to know things, and no carin' how."

Therkon had got up. I felt him twitch, but she only smiled faintly, and let go my wrist.

"I've no way of tellin' how, or when. But one day, aye. You will See. And I think, t'will come from that. From the two o' ye. And knowing things." Her hands shaped piling up something. "But t'is naught to do with mine."

Somewhere a strange bird whauped. Up the hill came a drift of wind, the jingle of a bell, an irritated bleat and unmistakable smell of goat.

Then Therkon let his breath out in a long soft sigh, either disappointment or anticipation, and Nouip said, "Now, whither would ye go?"

Instinctively I looked at Therkon. And Therkon looked at me.

I had ado not to scream at him as I wanted to scream at Nouip: *I'm a girl, I know less than you do, you're used to asking councillors and experts! I'm somewhere I know nothing about, and I can't even ask Azo!*

But he had no other counsellor. If Two and I could not See the future, if we lacked data even for a solid extrapolation, surely we could lay out the logical choices? The necessities?

I took a very deep breath and tried to make my voice steady. "Shouldn't we, uh, let Dhasdein know?"

Therkon sat slowly down on the bench again. Familiar warmth and solidity beside me, and the anomalous smell of lavender and lye soap.

He said, "First, we would need news to send."

"But we know—Oh."

About ourselves. Not about the rest.

Therkon looked past me at Nouip and said, "My lady, the main harbour on Scythe—on Sickle island. What is its name?"

The mere fact that he had to ask told me just how far south we must be.

"Hranhaven?" Nouip had begun spinning again. "In t'Sickle-crook. West of here."

Therkon's face set. "The current. The Rackstream. It would not carry that far?"

The spindle sank down, and up again. "If ye're bent on speirin' after your folk, ye'd ask at Grithsperry." She pointed south and west. "When the Rackstream carries aught round t'Head, t'will drift down there." She added, after a moment, "T'is the southern harbor. The traders call there from Eynholm. And Phaerea."

I saw Therkon's eye flash and my own heart leapt. At last, a name I knew.

"That is," Nouip went on precisely, "if any lived."

Goat bells fell like punctuation into the quiet. What chance had there been for the others, if Azo and Verrith had taken such a desperate risk with me?

Therkon straightened his neck and said, "We must ask."

He had brought them here. He would not, till the bitter end, renege on his responsibilities.

Then he looked at me and said, "But my—Chaeris. If we went to, to Hranhaven, you could take passage. For Riversend. You could tell them, what we know."

Go back to Riversend. Tell them we lived. Abandon all this sea and strangeness, go right back to Iskarda. Go home. Be safe.

Tell Iskarda I had failed. Had lost Azo and Verrith. And what would I tell my mother?

*What would I say to Tellurith?*

The world flew away on a cross-waft of lavender and back on a jet of absolute wrath.

"You want *me* to go back? To run off, not knowing anything about the others, not knowing *anything*? Just to be *safe*?"

"If you were safe I could be—"

"And what will *you* do? What do I tell them about that?"

"We cannot risk us both! They must know, they need to know we are alive. And they will need *you* as well! If the worst comes, they will need you, not me!"

"Claptrap!" It was Iatha's word and I never savoured it more. "They need *you*, didn't you see that? On the River? At the forts! Dhasdein can do without me, they've done it before, but they can't—"

"And I swore to protect you! Lost in some squall, some spawn of the Adversary catches—if I ever did get back, what would I tell your mother, about you?"

"What'll I tell *your* mother now?"

"She will understand—"

"She won't understand! Blight and blast you, you won't be there. I'll be no use to her and *I'll* have to tell her! I'll have to say, Empress, I've lost your—!"

I choked, but it was too late. Therkon's eyes blazed hotter than the house fire. Then he gave a groan and sank his head in both his hands.

I had jumped off the bench. I wanted to yell, to cry, to bawl, *I'm sorry!* To bang my own head against the stones. But it was too late for Sorry now.

The silence vibrated like a mis-struck drum. Into it, Two spoke.

*"No-one can go back."*

All three of us jumped. Nouip actually let the distaff fall.

*"You have been brought here by another's plan. Nothing you have done could gainsay it. If you could not steer events this far, then it does not matter what you decide now. You will move only as the plan allows."*

Therkon whipped his head up. I could see Where? forming. Two already had the reply.

*"The only way you can go is as you have already come."*

Therkon's eyes were black as pits in a cream-pale face. Neither of us needed words to finish. We knew which way we had come.

South.

*"You have been brought here from the Seaforts. From Riversend. From the River. From Iskarda. There is not enough data*

*to say how far back the pebbles began to fall. But they fell to bring you together. The plan includes both."*

My knees were shaking. My heart was pounding like a water-mill, something had parched my throat. I took one step and Therkon grabbed me as I collapsed.

\* \* \* \*

Eventually my heart slowed, my breathing eased. But I was still propped like a rag doll in the coign of Therkon's shoulder when Nouip spoke.

"Whose plan?"

We both turned. At whatever our faces said, she lifted the distaff an inch and let it drop.

"Ye've let cats enough out already. And if yon—creature—will prophesy before me . . . might ye not as well finish it off?"

I did not feel myself flinch, but Therkon did. His arm went iron hard and he spoke over me as I had heard him address Deoren.

"Chaeris is not a 'creature.' She is—"

"I know who Chaeris is. T'was not she I meant."

Therkon balked. I turned about in his arm and spoke for myself. For us.

"The other is Two."

She had not recoiled. Revulsion, I realized now, had never been part of her response. Her eyes almost skewered me. Then she said softly, "And who is Two? Or what?"

"That is Chaeris' business." Therkon sounded more than redoubtable. "Of your courtesy, let it be."

Her long unblinking look retorted, I have a right, as your rescuer and host, to know what I have let into my land, taken to my hearth.

"My lady." He very nearly managed conciliation, if not outright plea. "Two may be, may be more than any of us understand. But what she *is*—"

Nouip turned the distaff over and back. Met his eyes again and said evenly, "Haps ye'll tell me, then. What's the Empire's Heir, and a maid that's maybe Sighted, and very like not his sister, doing here?"

I could feel Therkon thinking, faster and more redoubtably than Two. Calculating, running projections, deciding what, or who, could be sacrificed. Then his muscles tensed. I knew he had cut a thicket of losses, and chosen to be brutal too.

"Do you know the word, Sthassamaer?"

Nouip stared. Then her face went blank with shock.

"Water." It came out the barest whisper. "Black."

Ice blocked my throat. I was belowdecks on *Aspis*, trapped in the howling rocking gloom, the inky water sloshing, welling, rising, engulfing everything . . .

My hands were clenched in Therkon's shirt and I was trying to bury my head in his chest. His arm was tight and hard around me and he was saying fiercely, "Not like that!"

Nouip answered beyond him, distant in more than space. "Ye asked what I knew."

"Yes, but—!"

I almost literally felt him bite his tongue. He added dourly, "What else?"

I sat up in time to see Nouip produce a quarter-shrug.

"What everyone knows. There's trouble, south. Storms, out of size, out of season, folk ship-wrecked, castaway, fled. Whole towns, whole ports ruined. Isles lost." She met his eyes. "But that word, nay."

Two said, "*You fit pieces. With the Sight, do those pieces fit?*"

Nouip twitched a little, but she met my eyes, too. "Aye."

The clear rich air breathed over us, the goat bells rang down hill. But the silence round me had opened like a well, and past, present, future were cascading into it. Not merely confirmed disasters and direction, but a Sight. A Sight to amplify disaster's name.

When Therkon spoke, his voice was steel. "We think that is who—or what—made the plan."

Suddenly I was shivering again, uncontrollably. Two said we had no choice. We had been driven or drawn here, willy-nilly, we would only be allowed to go one way from here, and that way . . .

Blackness relinquished me, with a surface-breaking jerk. I clung to the bench, to Therkon, to the reeling, dancing daylight world. Anything to forget what Two had said.

But I could not let them forget what Two had said.

"Two—Two said—the plan—"

Therkon's arm clenched. But Nouip watched me in silence a moment. And then she said suddenly, "Have ye thought, that this may not all be so?"

"The storm?" Therkon sounded bewildered as I felt. "The wind, the sea? They changed, at the worst moments. Two said, no human could do it. Two said, it wasn't chance."

"Aye. T'was maybe *something's* plan, that ye were storm-driven, on Sickle, and the ship lost. But that ye came ashore, ye two, and ye alone? How did ye manage that?"

My heart rose suddenly, quivering in my throat. I could not tell if it was hope or fear. Beside me, Therkon was tense from head to toe. It was almost a whisper, when he spoke.

"Our troublecrew. Chaeris' people guessed there was a bay. Under the cliff. And the current. Before—the wreck—they put her overboard."

"His," I said for him, "did the same."

Nouip looked from one to the other of us. "A What," she said, "might rule wind and water. Could it foreguess living hearts?"

A heart that would put another's life before its own? So quickly, so unexpectedly, even that other might not guess?

The sun had slid out from behind a cloud. Or the air had cleared, miraculously, from its midday haze. The sun was blinking through my tears, bright, shadow, bright. Could even a What have predicted Azo and Verrith?

Therkon said, "Two, what do you think?"

The world whited out. Came back. Two said, *"Without more data, it is impossible to say if troublecrew's action was expected. Or not."*

They were staring at us, Nouip and Therkon both. It was Therkon who spoke.

"So—it—might have planned the wreck. It might even have expected troublecrew." He took a breath. "But even it might not have foreseen—that."

*"That is so."*

"Ye're missing the point," Nouip said crisply. "If t'was planned, for whichever end, it could only have intended one."

Therkon wheeled on her, his own wits sparking. "Either we were meant to go with the, the ship? Or not?"

"Aye."

"So perhaps, the plan failed?"

Two answered for us all. *"Perhaps."*

Therkon drew a great breath. "Then perhaps . . . Two was wrong?"

*"Perhaps."*

Nouip gave a sudden little splutter of a laugh. "A canny oracle, to take misreading so quiet!" But Therkon was tense as a sight-hound with prey in view. Or a philosopher, a conclusion within touch.

"Then if Two can be wrong. If the plan may have failed. We have a choice."

A genuine choice. A will of our own. However strait the door, there was some play within it. If we had overset the plan once, we might do it again.

Perhaps.

Nouip was watching Therkon like a cat with a mouse. "I'll ask ye again, then," she said, softer than a cat's tread. "What mean ye to do now?"

Therkon's eyes sprang back to her. For an instant I glimpsed again that dark, elegant deer, head poised, scenting the wood for traps.

Then he drove both hands into his hair and shook his head fiercely. "Of your grace, my lady," he said. "Give me a little time. A little space. I need to think."

\* \* \* \*

"As if *I* don't need to think at all!"

Nouip courteously handed me another turnip. As I started carving with her oversized kitchen knife, she added mildly, "Chance he thinks he already knows, what you think."

"Oh."

Therkon would have gone barefoot up the hill, had she not commanded him into a pair of larger but shorter homespun trousers, and weirdly all-of-a-piece boots—"hunting shoes"—bidden him check her fish trap, and added bread and cheese to eat.

Then she gave Two that craved tour of the house, and suffered the ensuing fusillade, yes, the outer garden grew vegetables, the bothy folded the goats who yielded meat and wool and milk, yes, her kin, "grandsons, the most," farmed barley in her two little fields beyond the lake, whence came water and fish. The cat brought rabbits off the "moor" as well as mice. Yes, she wove her own cloth—"the loom's back there." Beyond the quern, the one place we did not go. "And now we'll need to wash those clothes."

A giant's toil. We hung them on the wall till late afternoon, then went out on the lake path, where Nouip's storm-volume whistle raised the goats, meek as sheep between two broad, shaggy dogs. And behind them Therkon, face weary, somber but composed, carrying a pair of fish hung on a withy through the gills.

"I beg your pardon, my lady," he said, as the dogs sniffed his legs, but, I noted, neither hackled nor barked. "I would have cleaned them, but—"

But he had no weapon. I thought about that, while I fossicked the herb-beds for fennel and dill, then watched Nouip gut the unscaled fish, coat them in mud, and fit them into the coals. *Who,* I burned to ask, *taught you to cook without pot or pan?*

Peeled from their clay jackets, the fish accompanied the turnips, boiled complete with greens, and then a sweetener of last season's hazel nuts. We did not talk until the end. But at last Therkon set his platter aside, and rose to stand across from me and Nouip at the hearth. In the fireglow I saw his jaw go tense.

He said, "I have thought."

Nouip inclined her head like a priestess giving audience. I tried not to glower.

"There were so many, so many paths to map. But the first step on them all: we must seek news of the others. And—Chaeris—was right. We must send word to Dhasdein."

He pushed a hand through his unbound hair. Almost silky again now, it fell like smoke on the pale buckskin shirt.

"The lady Chaeris," a hint of tired, wry smile, "has made it clear she will not bear the news herself. Even if it were safe."

Two said, *"Against the plan would be unwise. For either or both."*

"Yes." I will not, his expression added, see more innocents drown for my sake.

"So we go south."

I had thought my voice steady but Therkon gave me one piercing glance and said swiftly, "We send word north. A letter would be best, but—"

Nouip said, "I can manage that."

"Goatskin," she said, as we both gaped. "Oak-gall boiled with soot. Beeswax." She meant, to take his ring as a seal. "A carrier to Hranhaven'll come soon enough."

"My lady." Therkon rallied. "That would be more than we could repay. But even if your folk could carry it to the port . . ."

Who would carry it on, or pay its carriage over the sea?

"T'will go," she said.

I could see Therkon meditate questions about means and costs, and courtesy silence them. "My lady. That would leave us free, yes. We can go to Grithsperry."

A last, forlorn but tormenting hope. My heart leapt at thought of Azo, dour and solid as the walls of Amberlight, stumping down some island quay.

Two said, *"For the main choice, that is irrelevant."*

Therkon gave me a look more indignant than shocked. And then, at my confusion, began setting out, colder than the hatchet man, what Two meant.

"Yes, to go back will be as dangerous for one as for two of us. To the travelers, to those they travel with. Iskarda will not wish to hazard the lady Chaeris. Dhasdein will wish to recall me."

He looked past me into the fire and it made his eyes glint like stone.

"But we are here. At our foe's behest, but far further south than we could otherwise have come. What advantages—it—also vantages us."

He looked straight at me. "And in what resources we do have, it may find a double edge."

Two. Me. He had always considered us as among his, Dhasdein's, our resources. But we might be what the enemy deemed a resource as well.

Far away, Nouip spoke. The words were lost in black water, welling up around me, deep, deep water, the bilge of *Aspis'* lower decks, the depths of ocean, of abysses beyond ocean, and it was not merely depth but an awareness, sentient, deliberate. Seeking, drawing, wanting.

Wanting me.

"Chaeris! Chaeris!"

Therkon had me in both arms this time, clamped against him, squeezed all but breathless as the black cracked open and I could breathe, gasp, pant and try not to sob aloud.

"Chaeris."

I got my head up, eyes swimming in the firelight. Almost finger by finger, he set me back a little. Let me go.

"My—You will not go back. I know that. But you could stay here. My lady Nouip would," I felt him lift his head and her nod in response, "would care for you. You could be—I could know you safe."

Safe, Two echoed, and ran before me the projections and calculations, the map of islands and ocean and irrefutable deductions, tightening like the meshes of a net. Safe ashore, safe from the sea.

Safe for how long? Safe for those around me, if what ravaged the Archipelago was looking firstly for me?

Safe here while others were where?

I sniffed hard and said, "Will *you* stay?"

The fire muttered in tiny sub-audible clucks. I could hear the silence beyond the stone walls, with their illusory safety. The black water, listening.

Therkon lifted his head and his jaw set so he suddenly looked ten years older. Twenty years sterner. Not a prince, not a philosopher. Perhaps not a warrior. The images that Two ran past me were halo-ed in story, legend, myth. Faces of hero-kings who, in threat and battle, did not hold back from fighting. From death. From sacrifice.

He said quite quietly, "I do not know what resources I will have. Or what the enemy plans. Or what I can do against it. I only know, that every other choice is impossible. For the sake of Dhasdein. And the River. And the Archipelago. Whatever anyone else does, I cannot rest here. Alone or companied. I must go on. And do what I can."

I said, "Then I'm going too."

The hush fractured as suddenly as if peat had fallen in the fire. Nouip must have moved. I know I did. Beyond the quern a dog roused and shook itself in its sleep. Then Nouip stood up and came round the hearth.

"Aye," she said. Therkon looked up, startled, and this time she bent her head as to a king.

"Dhasdein." It was a title, I belatedly realized. "An I read the weave right, ye say true. For us in the Isles, as for the Empire. Not twice in a twelvemonth do I See as I have with ye. If t'is ye the enemy seeks, has called: then t'is ye are our hopes as well."

She spoke quietly, yet my skin chilled and my hair rose as to the cry of trumpets. She means both of us, I realized. She spoke to him, but she had used the plural. Always, for the two of us, she used, "ye."

Nouip turned on her heel and went with a decisive sweep of skirt to the front wall and the great wooden kists atop which Therkon had slept.

* * * *

"Chaeris' gear is well enough, but best go no further in the Isles, Dhasdein, in that cloak." The Empire's own uniform, I understood, in color as in cut. She opened hasps, lifting the lid on a sweep of darkness, a throat-clutching scent of cedar and beast and perhaps, sea. A glitter, a clatter and clink.

"My lady," Therkon said in something like awe. "This is too much—"

"What's in keeper's hold and Seer's view is mine to give." She measured it against him: an ankle-length cloak of some short fur, fluid as silk, glistening like water itself. "T'is fitting, that ye garb against Sea-banes in a sark o' the sea."

The hood was trimmed in long pewter-colored fur, probably, Two thought, wolf. The front had leather ties, but the throat fastened with a great brooch of interlaced gold, at its center a hazian's sullen fire. When it showed among the fur Therkon began to protest in earnest. Nouip simply shook her head.

"Chance this will make ye a way where dry clothes cannot. Will ye cheapen the Isles, when River and Empire have already staked so high?"

Making grace of necessity, Therkon gave way. Looked past the cloak as she laid it down, and caught his breath.

"Aye." Nouip picked the sheath up, its dull silver tracery snagging at the fire. Interlaced stylized snakes and gripping beasts, wolves perhaps, even one of the seals that had gifted us its "sark."

"This comes to me by blood as well as place." The hilt glowed dully cream. Ivory, I realized, once sea beasts' weapons, walrus and sea lion, now dark with use and age. She drew the blade slowly from its sheath.

"The name is Hvestang." She sighted dispassionately down the suave, darkly gleaming length of steel, with a ribbon of serpents beaten from tang almost to tip. "Sharp-tongue. For that it puts an end to dispute."

"My lady, I can *not* take—!"

"Say me not, Nay, Dhasdein. The maid's steel comes from her own folk. But you," her eyes lifted and her voice changed. "You will have use for this."

The fire fluttered. I saw Therkon swallow. Then, mutely, he reached out and received the sword as he would any treasure, reverently, across both hands.

# CHAPTER VIII

Entering Grithsperry was like crossing into another world: stone houses, but square, worked stone blocks, straight rooflines of grey slate or dark red tile, never a sign of thatch. No fortifications, just whitewashed house-walls lining narrow paven streets threaded above a milky blue bowl of bay, with shipping busy at its quays. But for the sea beyond, it could have been some middle-sized town in Riversrun.

When we paused atop the last bare rolling hill brow, I said what had burnt in my mind ever since we left Nouip's house.

"Do you think we really were Under the Hill?"

Therkon shifted Hvestang's belt on his hip. He was still over-careful, though he had borne it there the last two days, over empty uplands, on footpaths, through way-stops, never letting it out of reach.

In a moment he said, "It was like a saga. The wise man, wise woman, who helps the benighted hero." His mouth-corner curved before I could retaliate. "Heroes. Shelters them. Feeds them. Gives them," his hand shifted a little, "cunning weapons. Advice."

We had slept the night in a rough stone hut, and taken care to bar its door. "There are wolves," Nouip had warned us, "all over the moors." It was why she folded her goats and kept her dogs in at night. And if I had babbled of scree-folk while we walked, at Two's demand he had told me Delta sagas in return.

"So do you really think . . ."

Therkon surveyed Grithsperry again. Then he remarked, judiciously, "She did have a latrine."

"She what? Oh!"

I was still laughing when we reached the town.

I might have been afraid, approaching the sea for the first time since Evva beach. The window-boxes, bright with royal gold and purple crocuses, might have stabbed me to the heart with recollection of Iskarda. Both were lost amid Two's frenzy to catch every passing detail, and then the appalling realization that here, now, with Deoren gone, out from under Nouip's shield, I was all that could serve for Therkon's troublecrew.

A low blow won the tussle when he wanted to deposit me at the first decent inn. "Deoren would know: *I* should be looking after *you!*" If our two days' solitary travel had dispelled all constraint, it had also won Deoren my true sympathy. At least my mother dared to train me as both guarded and guard: Therkon knew the principles, but all too often he strayed like a sheep, staring at the shaggy ponies trotting in one-horse carts, the homespun skirts and wide-legged trews and peculiar knitted brimless hats, the people pale as Nouip or darker than either of us. Not to mention the market's riot of new turnips, dry apples, pens of hairy little black cows, and sounders of invincibly ignorant pigs.

About then the fragile sunlight dulled with a now familiar speed. We donned our cloaks. In a regular deluge I shepherded Therkon through bollards and net-mounds and stalls of emphatically stinking fresh fish, onto the actual quay.

Two was unsurprised that, from the long façade of solid stone fronts and heavy window shutters, he should choose a door whose frieze showed a ship wreathed in grapevines between sheaves of grain. Shippers, as my mother had known, always get the freshest news. If the sign read true, this one might trade as far north as Wave Island. Or Dhasdein itself.

The open door revealed a smallish rain-dimmed room, a sort of desk, ceiling-height shelves, records no doubt, half the back wall lost to a wide arch that emitted the fragrance of wool and spice and, beyond doubt, wine and grain. The three men at the desk swung round, two donning a polite habitual smile.

Then the man in sea-jacket and heavy boots gulped audibly. The man before the desk smothered a gasp, the one in the other modest version of Therkon's dark coat and once pristine white shirt nearly jumped off his stool.

Therkon said, "Give you good faring, sirs."

Dhasdeini phrase, Dhasdeini accent. To my wonder, it evoked plain relief.

The man behind the desk came back hastily, "And a fair wind to you." The speech was ours, the accent not quite so thick as Nouip's. "Ah. Um?"

"Of your kindness, sir. My sister and I are merchant folk. From," it came quite steadily, "Outsea." Nouip had told us the word to use, but it did not seem to work as it should.

"We are seeking kin and, ah, house-friends. Caught in a great storm, driven south. Might you have news here, these last few days? Folk brought or blown ashore? From a, a wreck?"

He had pushed his hood back. The fur framed his face spectacularly, but the cloak still swung round him, its sleek dark fur beaded with rain. He was tall and slim enough for them to do each other justice. But hardly to warrant a response like this.

The two neat men exchanged frantic looks. Therkon's slight, enquiring frown became pure crown prince. The seaman breathed in as for a dive, and broke out, "Wreck? Where?"

"Off Rack Head. We were told, the Rackstream might bring . . . things here?"

Their faces spoke volumes, had I been able to read past the shock. Then the seaman blurted, "Where'd you come ashore?"

Therkon's little breath put memory's dagger in my own ribs. "On Evva beach."

The second neat man changed colour. Therkon said earnestly, "We had help and shelter from Evvamoor's ban-keeper. She—"

At that the man behind the desk did gasp. "You were in the house?"

No time to say, *I knew it was Under the Hill*. Therkon's brows rose a single warning notch.

"She was very kind to a pair of castaways." *And would you*, the tone added, *wish to asperse our benefactor at all?* "She suggested we ask in Grithsperry."

The desk-man winced. Therkon's frown creased: then he slipped the laces and doffed his cloak, gathering it over an arm. Doubtless a courtesy, to keep wet from their fine mosaic of grapevines and dolphin, as well as to show his empty hands. The hitch at his sword-belt was as automatic, but it made them notice Hvestang.

The seaman backed into the desk so papers or tallies went everywhere, the second man gasped out loud. All three made a finger sign, what Riverfolk would call the horns. I cleared Therkon's left arm and loosened Verrith's wrist-knife in the sheath.

Then the man behind the desk recovered nerve and voice at once and gulped, "My lo—Your Maj—ah, ah—if it please, ah . . . what might we—"

Therkon stared at him. Crown prince, emperor's heir. Almost, imperial hatchet man. Then he demanded, quite softly, "Who do you think I am?"

I think they would have run if he had not already nailed them to the ground. Their eyes went round like mill-wheels. The desk-man gripped his table for courage, but he got it out.

"Outsea. You said. But . . . the ban-house . . ."

Therkon handed off the cloak as if I were his valet. Unbuckled the sword-belt, handed it after. Still staring at them, he held a hand out, palm upmost, and said, "Will you cut me, to prove I bleed?"

The man behind the desk made a kind of squawk and began gabbling, "No, no, m'lord, but the beach, the sea-sark . . . They say He comes ashore there, seeking his own, after the big storms. And that cloak, the Winter Man wears it. In Evvamoor. For sun-turn. The, the old feast." And." He gestured to me. It went almost inaudible. "Sharp-tongue. When there was a king, a king on Sickle . . . that was his blade."

*This comes to me by blood as well as place.* She had gifted us her past along with Evvamoor's, and the island's with them. The hair lifted on my neck. I had ado not to salute.

Therkon's face had gone quite blank. Imperial composure. Imperial arrogance. Moreover, they had slighted his benefactress. Worse than taking him personally for some haunt or revenant.

"I," with a slight emphasis, "am a Dhasdeini merchant. Honored by strangers' bounty. Seeking news of my own folk. Can you tell me, then? Have any from Outsea—come ashore here?"

Their eyes still spoke more than awe, but the authority made all the heads shake at once.

"Not—not—"

Not bodies. He could not quite manage that. But the flaw did what armor could not.

"No, sir," the desk-man answered almost gently. "There's been nothing, flotsam or jetsam or—come in here."

"Thank you." Therkon managed courtesy, at least. "Is there anywhere, anyone, anyone else—we might ask?"

They volunteered names, a handful of shippers, the latest vessels from the north. Eagerly, by the end almost falling over themselves. Therkon did not demean them by offering money, also one of Nouip's gifts, but as we walked away I felt them watching us with awe, with fear. Perhaps with yearning as well.

* * * *

Therkon was so ruffled he went straight back to the inn and hired at least one room where he could cache Hvestang. I persuaded him to leave most of the money with it. After that, though my leggings drew some odd looks, we searched in relative peace. But if everyone remembered the storm, no-one had any other news.

In late afternoon we plodded back to the inn. The weather had closed in, bringing a sour little southerly. Everything was grey, without and within. We tramped past the tap-room door to the steep stairs for the sleeping quarters, and I was bracing for another fuss over the shared room, when we turned a twist of passage. And found the door ajar.

The walls were stone, the door wood, as seemed usual in the Isles. The wood was unbroken. There was a latch-string, and we had a key, in Therkon's pocket. And clearly, there was another key elsewhere.

After a truly pregnant moment he put out a foot and gave the door a solid shove. It swung open on its prediction: two beds, our scanty belongings, the tiny window, intact. Hvestang, its gear, and the little bag of money, were gone.

After another moment I sat down with a thump on the closest bed and put my head in my hands.

I felt Therkon sit down too. Presently, his arm came round me. Just audibly, he said, "You still have your knives."

And the other loss was my fault, but it was the thought of Nouip that I could not bear. To lose her family's, perhaps her father's blade, like this . . . Better to deplore the lesser loss.

"The money!" I almost wailed. "What are we going to do? We probably can't pay our reckoning, let alone passage—!"

Therkon sat still. He, I thought with a moment's compunction, must be tired and despairing too. He had lost people, as I had. He had lost Hvestang. We had both considered him in charge. Whatever went wrong, he would take as his responsibility.

Ignominiously, I considered putting my head on his shoulder and dissolving like a true Dhasdeini woman into tears. But he had already removed his arm, and was clambering off the bed, with a little, wry, but visible smile. "Two said, we were intended to go south. If so, this is also a setback to the enemy. Let *it* find us a way."

And what, Two wanted to know, if we were not meant to go south?

But Therkon was already crazing the inn-folk with demands for a screen between the beds, chamberpots, heated water, private hire of the inn's bathhouse, not least to use the razor he had just bought. Distraction, I realize now, that lasted till the evening meal. Since, he also decreed, the fastest way to be taxed with an unpayable reckoning was to behave as if we could not pay.

\* \* \* \*

Unlike River inns, the taproom, as they called it, served both food and drink. The thick bare beams and the fireplaces' copious soot umbrellas were familiar, at least to Two, though the carving on mantle and door jambs was strangely angular, and eating happened only in a series of booths along the wall. Beer and food did come from a single servery, but beside the outer door was an alcove where every incomer lit a candle, of the most pungent kind, before a pair of images also dark with soot. The Mother, I decided one might be. Of the other, Two had no idea.

There was also some odd seating etiquette. Azo's precepts in mind, I headed for the shrine corner, which was least busy, half-masked from incomers, with a good room-view and quick possible exit. But the beer-seller frowned and told Therkon, "Winter corner, sir." We had to take the next best, a booth halfway down the wall.

Wonderful to relate, the servery offered fish: fish baked, fried, rolled in breadcrumbs, shellfish for the eccentric, and with it all a grainy, dark and heady beer. "Barley brew," Therkon observed when I gasped. His slight frown came and went. "No hops down here."

No wine either, despite that shippers' frieze. But Therkon had intelligencer's reflexes, at least. He was trying to catch scraps from the next booth: "worse than last year!"—"Nothing left on . . ."—"The Yarl . . . forgiven taxes"—"But what about the *fleet?*" I was chasing the opportunity to hiss, "What's a Yarl?" when the outer door opened, and I found out.

The four men who came in wore knitted hats and dripping cloaks like everyone else, but when they pushed the cloaks back, unlike everyone else, they were carrying swords. The one in the lead glanced casually round the taproom, nodded to the beer-seller, and headed straight to us.

Therkon froze. I gripped a table-leg to curb my knife-hand. Two was in emergency mode. The leader loomed over us. Sketched a perfunctory courtesy and said, politely enough, "The Yarl wants a word. If ye'd come with us?"

Our eyes flew about in unison. Nobody else looked guilty. Or alarmed. Or in fear. This was not unusual? But who was the Yarl, was this incursion danger or routine, what was I to do?

*Suppress Two.* Azo's voice was crisp as in my living ear. *Keep surprise's vantage and manners' defense. And pick better odds for a fight.*

Therkon's eye caught mine. Without a blink to reveal collusion, he stood up.

We tramped through the rain, which was blowing now, all muffled in our cloaks: uphill first, then left-hand along the slope, Therkon and I stumbling behind the leader's lantern over unfamiliar stones. The street had a roaring central gutter, echo to Two of Amberlight. We swung past a door whose reek of beer and bawling voices warned, low-level inn, mere drinking-house, perhaps dangerous. Another doorway. A dark shoal rose athwart the gutter, somebody coughed, and the leader stopped.

He said something to the cougher, invisible in the rainy dark. Then he held the lantern low and asked, "Would you know that, at all?"

Silver glinted to the lamp-glow, a shining tracery. Below a hands-breadth of sheeny, wet grey steel.

Therkon gave a grunt half shock and half relief and retrieved his wits with it. "What is Hvestang doing here?"

In a tone that made further claims of right and ownership superfluous.

"We thought," the lantern-carrier answered, still non-committal, "you might tell us that."

Therkon said, "Will you hold up the light?"

The gutter-shoal was a man, wrapped in a cloak, arms wide. His face lay in the water that foamed round his sodden hair, and a red tinge spread downstream from around his throat.

Therkon drew a little, comprehending breath. "Was there money?"

The lantern wavered. The cougher in the dark spoke, hoarse but unsurprised. "Just t'bag."

Therkon looked back at the corpse, and down at the sword. And said, in a still, cold voice that would have graced Nouip, "It puts an end to dispute."

The men all moved, as if they had somehow been released. The lantern came down. The cougher emerged from the dark, took up Hvestang by the middle of the sheath. Silently, held it out.

Therkon wiped the hilt and scabbard gently on his cloak. He did not don the sword-belt, just tucked it all, like a child or an heirloom, into his arms. Then he said evenly, "It was a gift."

All the men seemed to sigh. The lantern-carrier said, sounding suddenly far more matter-of-fact, "Aye, sir. But there's a man dead of it, and another gone wolfs-head. A matter for the Yarl."

Authority, Two extrapolated. The town's ruler, the island's ruler? Are these men his? Warriors, or civil authority, on patrol in the streets? No time to ask. Therkon was answering as calmly, "It seems so. Shall we come now?"

We trekked back to the right through the narrow, winding, now slippery paven ways, and then upward. When lamplit windows began to pick out a taller shape above the roofs, Two knew what it was.

We had seen it from the quay, almost atop the southern headland, a stolid drum-shape of rough-hewn stone: old, I had guessed, if nowhere near the age of Nouip's house. The alleyway twisted, skirted a handkerchief-size enclosure, and the lantern-carrier pushed open a tall iron gate.

The entry itself was low and lowering, with an iron-braced door that opened to a screep of wood and stone on a reddish glow of fire. A voice bellowed, "Vanni, that you? You turn up this bugaboo, or what?"

The lantern-carrier returned something brief. A sort of passage-tunnel emitted us on a circle of stone floor amid bulky heaps of shadow, with a fire at their midst. This one blazed in a semi-circular fireplace with a mantel, a hood, and presumably a chimney to draw off the smoke, limning a man in a chair big enough to call a throne. With a cluster of retainers at his back.

* * * *

"Come on, man, where are they?" He was already rumbling in a near-bass voice as we appeared. There were candles, gratefully, on the mantelpiece, revealing a redoubtable black beard and a nose to match, carving on the chair arms, the colour, as he leant to the fire, of an almost purple coat. "Couldn't've picked a finer night for it . . . ah."

We had reached the glow. He was looking Therkon up and down.

"So." The voice had changed a fraction. "That *is* the cloak. And who in heyill's name are *you*?"

Therkon's back was already stiff. I tried not to groan aloud.

"I am a Dhasdeini merchant. We were wrecked here. We are seeking news of our folk."

With one push the man was on his feet.

"You're no merchant." It came so flatly the men behind him tensed and my own hand flew to my wrist. "Dhasdeini, true. A lord, or an officer." He grinned suddenly, wolfishly, teeth a fire-red flash in his beard. "I've heard enough of 'em. I was in your benighted navy, m'lord *Yabbie*." It is what they call the Delta shrimp. "Ten blighted years!"

An Archipelago sailor, or marine. In the Imperial navy, groaned my sinking heart, far too conversant with Dhasdein, the River, recent history, he might even have left at the cataclysmic end of the war, when half the navy deserted, from under Therkon's own command.

He might know the crown prince by sight.

My lungs froze. My sight blurred. Two was in a whirl of projections that might pre-empt everyone. I fairly screamed, *Shut up! Wait!*

Therkon was only just answering, as coldly as before.

"I was a lord. Yes."

There was an almost abashed hush. Then the Yarl exploded, "So what're you at, sending my town crazy with that cursed sword? Folk jumping at shadows and crying Bogle and a man already dead!"

"Will you at least tell me who I am supposed to be?"

He had known better than to move, but it came out a whiplash all the same, tension and exasperation breaking loose.

"*Tell* you?" The Yarl's eyes actually bulged. "Wander in with the old King's sword and the Winter Man's cloak 'n say you've toured the ban-house coming from Evva beach . . . A pox on your Outsea brains, Yabbie. They think you're the Ash Lord, of course. The Dead-Thane. The King of the Sea!"

His retainers seemed to cringe away from the words. The very fire seemed to dull, as if a wind blew past us, a thinly creeping nor-easter, in the hot shadowy room.

Two said before I realised, "*Sthassamaer.*"

That time everyone jumped. Then the Yarl whipped round and roared, "Don't dare name him with that *thing*!"

"But," I stammered, "but—"

"Fetch and bogle he may be but t'Sea King's *ours*. Come of Isle folk, fed on Isle folk—nothing to do with *that*—!"

Then he heard himself, and broke off short. "And who," now he was truly glaring, "may *you* be?"

Therkon took a swift sideways step that made all the sword-hands jump. "This is my sister—"

"Stand away from her, Yabbie. 'N keep quiet!"

The shift of men behind him added warning enough.

Silently, Therkon stepped back. Gulping, cursing Two, I confronted the Yarl alone.

"Who are you, woman? Girl? What's your name?"

"I am called Chaeris—sir." Any title was better than blank discourtesy. "I am m-my brother's sister. At least, I mean—"

With any other leader, the hirelings would have laughed. The Yarl twisted half round and the single snigger choked.

"Y' brother's sister, eh? 'N what's *his* name?"

This was moving too fast even for Two. I looked desperately at Therkon. The Yarl snapped his fingers and said with steely affability, "Talk to *me*, girl. What's his name?"

"My sister is not used to this. Dhasdeini women seldom go in public. Allow me—"

The Yarl's eye swiveled. "She's not y' sister, any more'n you're a merchant. She don't talk Dhasdeini at all."

"My *half*-sister—"

"Don't palter with me, heyill take you! What *is* she? Your thrall? Your mistress? Both at once?"

With one economic twist Therkon dropped Hvestang's gear into his left hand and drew the blade.

The hiss cut like a snake's. As the blade flared retainers snarled and surged, swords flashed, feet thumped, I jumped myself with a handful of wrist-knife just as the Yarl bellowed, "Stop!"

His men just managed to obey. The first sword-blade shook upright, six inches from Hvestang's edge, and Therkon was already in the soldier's crouch. Not expecting room for a duel: prepared to take his enemies massed, as he stood.

The air quivered to fire-flicker, the tremble of men's breath. The Yarl glared at his retainers' backs.

"Might you," with awful courtesy, "wait on *me*, Vaskyr?" His eyes switched. "'N you, Yabbie. D'you mean what Sharp-tongue says? If you do," his eyes narrowed, "how'll your sister fare?"

Therkon's face was rigid as ice. Mortal rage. Mortal threat. Then he drew a sudden shuddering breath and eased Hvestang back into its sheath.

The Yarl half-relaxed. "Vaskyr?"

His men backed clear. Swords went home in a straggling scrape. I buried my own knife. The Yarl sank into his seat, tilted an elbow to a chair arm and his chin to a fist, and confronted Therkon, I saw in amazement, with the suggestion of a smile.

"Fight for her, whoever she is?" Therkon's jaw worked. "Stand easy. I'll not bait you again. But if she's not y' whore *or* y' sister—who is she, then?"

Therkon gave me one swift glance and tilted his chin in imperial hauteur. "The lady Chaeris is my companion," he said.

*Don't*, I prayed the Mother, *let this creature sport with that.*

"Companion," the Yarl repeated. Dear enough to fight for, the tone added. To die for? He glanced over to me. "Companion in what?"

Therkon drew breath and bit the words off in his teeth. The Yarl nodded at him, acknowledging a lesson learnt, and looked back to me.

"*Sir*," Two said, "*will you first tell us? The ban-keeper. Evvamoor. What are they? What do they matter? Why is the town overset?*"

The Yarl almost recoiled. He did blink: then, while I stood in terror lest his wits be acute as Nouip's and Two have started an even more dangerous hare, he gave a smothered snort.

"Questions to keep off answers, eh?"

He paused. Then went on with a jerk. "Evvamoor's the last Old Place. They live there as we all did once, in the Isles. Dark-houses. The Stones. The old—workings. Summer-height. Sun-turn. The keeping of—the dead."

I felt the shiver that went through the rest of them. I shivered too.

"But the keeper." He gave me a sudden piercing stare. "They say she comes down in direct line from Langlieve. The last of the kings. The one," he jerked his chin at Therkon, "who carried that."

There was another pause like a boulder-fall. Into it Therkon said a fraction too loudly, "Why should the town be—why would a man kill, for this?"

"Dumb as a block, like all the rest." He sat forward suddenly. "Look'ee, Yabbie. D'ye know what 'King' means, here? Langlieve's kin held all Sickle, true. But Langlieve's sire was Lord o' the Thirteen Isles. Overlord, from Sickle to Foldbay and clear down to Phaerea."

He flapped a hand. "'N Grithsperry, Grithsperry's not just quiet, the day. There's lordless men 'n run Navy-men here, there's ousted folk from south'ard. There's merchanters with their trade wracked 'n fishermen starved from the gales. There's talk—there's always talk! But d'you know what they're saying now? 'The King's come! The King's come back! Down with the Yarl and his like. Beer in the streets'!" He flapped the hand again. "D'you wonder some gangrel lifts it when you turn y' back, and gets his throat cut by some other fool that's sure he's but to lay hands on Sharptongue, and he'll down me and Phaerea both, sit a golden throne and be King-come-again!"

In a moment Therkon said, sounding small as a boy, "Oh."

"Yes, *oh*. So, d'you see why I might just wonder? If y' knew what you were at?"

Slowly, but awkwardly, Therkon disengaged his grip from Hvestang's hilt, and took it by mid-sheath. "If this belongs on Sickle . . . If it will bring quiet . . ."

The Yarl jerked his chin. More than acknowledgement. "Just tell me. Where *did* y' get the things?"

Therkon answered tiredly, "I have said already. They came from the Evvamoor ban-keeper. As gifts."

There was another plummet of a hush. Then the Yarl grunted, "Easy to say, 'the keeper.' D'you have a name?"

"She told us to call her Nouip."

That time I actually heard someone gasp. The Yarl's brows certainly rose on end.

"If y' have it, so. It belongs to you." He hesitated. "But they say, she has the Sight . . ."

"She told me," Therkon said, "I would have use for this."

I could almost feel the retainers' hair rise along with mine. The Yarl looked from Therkon to me and said the inevitable. "Use it for what?"

"We do not know."

Therkon spoke before I could. Flat, if without offence. A stall-off, if not quite a bluff.

The fire flickered and phutted. The Yarl stared at him, brows coming slowly down.

"Look'ee, Yabbie. Ahhhh." Half apology, half exasperation. "What *is* y' name?"

Therkon stared back. I could see, as in a counterpoise, his chin go up.

"Therkon," he said.

The Yarl frowned outright. "Therkon? That's not Dhasdeini, either. Therkon? That's province or upRiver. Quetzistani. What's a Quetzistani lord at, playing merchant—Come here. Into the light."

Two was going crazy. I gripped both wrists behind my back and tried not to shut my eyes, told myself Nouip would name him anyway if they asked, tried not to yell, Did you *have* to tender your imperial pride now?

Therkon took three steps forward, full into the candles' range. The chin was higher than ever. Mother, I cursed, why afflict me with a prince who's never had his edges smoothed?

"Huh. Quetzistani, sure enough. Know those eyes anywhere. *And* a lord, ah, plum-in-the-mouth as the Riversrun Suzerain. High Quetzistani. What was y' clan?"

*He knows too much*, Two was screaming, *in a minute or two he'll add the last facts and realize just what he has in hand, stop him, stop him!* Therkon answered, words slicing the white roil.

"I was of Jhuir clan."

"Jhuir! The same as—"

He stopped dead. "Y're close kin to the Empress."

Therkon said with bitterness, "If I had been acknowledged. Yes."

The Yarl's jaw dropped. "Y're a by-blow? Some lord's bastard? Got in the rebellion, when the clans changed—? Never! There's no lord in Riversend'd acknowledge, let alone raise one. And y' were raised in Riversend, don't try to tell me not. Therkon, Therkon . . . What is it I'm thinking?"

"*Sir*," Two burst out in pure desperation, "*what is the Sthassamaer?*"

"What?" But he did swing round. "Girl, what in heyill's name makes y' think y' can spout questions hither and yon?"

"*Sir, we need to know what you know.*"

*Stop it!* I screamed. Too late.

The Yarl's brow literally darkened. "*You* need to know. 'My lady' Chaeris. If y' were raised in a decent household—"

"The lady Chaeris may be a Seer."

"What?"

Therkon had made the supreme counter-diversion. But did he have, I bawled to myself, to draw the hounds off by exposing me?

"A Seer. You mean like—like—"

"My lady Nouip," Therkon was as precise as ever, if he had muted some of the disdain, "said she would See. One day. But— differently. The lady Chaeris needs information. Everywhere. As much as she can get."

I tried to keep my face calm and hoped the pulse was not hammering visibly in my throat.

"*One* day." The Yarl had fastened on the crucial point. "She's not a Seer yet."

"She still needs facts. In particular, about—Sthathamaer."

"Sir, if you could tell us, we know hardly anything but the name."

"The name. Uh." Give him that, he was resilient. We had bounced him from one shoal-edge to another and he was still on the scent. And he was a ruler. He gave me a stare half affront, half recognition. If I were a Seer, even in the future, information now might help his own folk.

"Comes from south'ard. The outed folk, some'll say it. Most—not."

"But do they say what it is?"

"No."

Two clenched my hands. I tried not to swear aloud. In a minute the Yarl would start a fresh chase, and there were too many vulnerable spots. *Do they, does anyone say, it has something to do with the storms?*

"Everything's to do with the storms. Heyill's luck. Somebody saw a merewife. Somebody shorted the Mother a candle. The gods weary, and the world ends." It was exasperation, but under it was something I knew all too well. The first struggling sprouts of hope. "Is that anything y' can . . ."

*"Perhaps for Nouip."* Two was being too honest again. *"Not for us."*

*And will you*, I bawled, *stop saying Us! How long do you think before he wakes up?*

He did not say, Oh. Or lament outright. His face merely dismissed another marsh-hope, before he turned away.

"You. M'lord—Therkon. What, exactly, did y' plan?"

Therkon parried the new thrust with hardly a twitch. "We came asking after our folk. From the wreck."

"That was before. This is Now. What'll y' do next?"

"We will try to find our folk . . ."

"If they're not in Grithsperry," the Yarl said brutally, "they'll not be anywhere. What then?"

Therkon opened his mouth. And then, slowly, shut it again. And said nothing at all.

The pause stretched and stretched, filling gradually with men's movements, the flutterings of the fire. The creak of my own joints. The coil of fear in my belly, as the Yarl realized Therkon was not going to reply.

*He can't say any more*, I told Two flatly. He can't say, We'll go home, because we can't. He can't say, We'll go south, without raising worse questions. Not least that we don't have passage money. And how can he say, the way will be opened by Sthassamaer? This man is too sharp and already knows too much. Disaster is a breath away. If he just remembers why he knows Therkon's name . . .

Almost casually, the Yarl said, "Don't want to say?"

Therkon actually seemed to relax a little. He dipped his head. Acknowledgement as well as agreement. Quietly, almost ruefully, he answered, "I cannot."

Calamity, one half of us groaned, while the other remembered my fathers playing castles, and bawled, The only safety is to end this. At whatever sacrifice!

The Yarl sat up with a short if tumultuous sigh.

"A maybe-Seer. A Dhasdeini—lord-merchant—with a not-sister. From nowhere. Going, who knows where? Carrying a brand to fire the Isles. M'lord—Therkon. If the ban-keeper gave y' that blade, only a fool'd try to part you. But for the moment, y're best under ward. For all our sakes." He jerked a thumb downward. "Vaskyr, see 'em downstairs. Blankets. A necessary."

His eye came back to Therkon and I knew it would be granite hard. "And I think y' know the rest."

Almost soundlessly, Therkon sighed. Then he offered Hvestang hilt first to Vaskyr and answered resignedly, "Yes."

* * * *

"This would probably have happened, whatever we did."

"At least it got us out of there. If he'd asked more about me. If he'd remembered why he knows your name. If they'd searched us!"

No need to tell walls that, even in the dark. A search would have found Verrith's knives.

"Downstairs" proved to be the tower's undercroft, barricaded behind another iron-strapped door, beneath stone steps whose crooked edges and single unshaped slabs hair-crispingly recalled Nouip's house. Older than the tower itself. At their foot Vaskyr's lantern revealed a big semi-circular space as full of miscellaneous shadows as the room above, another man dropping blankets on the stone slab by the door, while a third set down a bucket, then pulled back a stone lid to reveal their equivalent of a latrine. Then they took the lantern and locked the door, and left us to the dark.

"They must not search us," Therkon said.

Not merely for Verrith's knives, but for the rings. One of those our sole source of funds, the other a betrayal worse than his name.

"Oh, if only Azo—"

I bit that off in earnest. Along with the stab of memory, the panic and lamentations and all the other unwomanly cries, curses, tears. You are *in* the blighted fix, I rated myself. Put your mind to getting out.

Therkon said, "I am sorry, my lady."

For more, I could tell, than my loss, or even our situation. For what he considered his own lapses, his own failure. As he had been on the beach.

Two said, *"There were too many dangers. You did what was best."*

The pause was startled, even in the dark. Then he said, sounding strained but somewhat rueful, "I never did things like this, face to face."

Never confronted an enemy or opponent without the insulation of his troublecrew, his officers. The court, his rank. I dropped the search for some mealy-mouthed version of, It *was* rather flashy, to challenge for me like some touchy court-gallant. Two had exonerated him. A better pardon than mine.

And Two should not get off scot-free either. I said, "Two didn't help."

"At least once, she did."

He still sounded odd. Fatigue? Stress? But I heard him move then, a boot scraping stone. A hand touched my arm. Human touch, seeking and giving reassurance. *At least, I know where you are.*

I bit down even harder on the impulse to swing round and plaster myself abjectly on his chest. No doubt that he would receive me, as he had on the beach, in Nouip's house. Probably it would ease him, to play the protector. But I was a woman, if a newly-made one. A scion of Amberlight.

But, Two lamented, he would be so *warm* . . .

I just managed not to let my voice shake. "Should we try to look, ah, feel, around?"

His hand clutched and released. It was a good long moment before he spoke.

"Yes." It came with effort, with untoward resolve, but it came. "You are right. We cannot risk more questions. We have no safe answers. We have nothing for bribes." Nothing we could afford. "We cannot even risk him remembering, before morning." Who a high-bred Quetzistani called Therkon and raised in Riversend had to be. "We have to get out. Tonight."

He had jumped farther ahead even than Two. I had only meant to scout our surroundings, not work for immediate escape.

"But the door. The lock. And I think they barred it. All those men—"

Two shut me up, that time. *How do you know what will fail, till you see what you can try?*

"Well, I could hunt around."

"I will do that." I could feel him physically pull himself together. After everything, he was a Dhasdeini man. "If you would speak when I ask? To show me the way back?"

I stood with one calf against the blankets and listened to fumbles, the occasional clatter, once a muffled, "Adversary take it." He seemed untowardly slow. But at last his hand touched my elbow: he put a foot out, then sank down on the slab with an audible outgoing breath.

"Barrels." He sounded muffled, and still strained. "Not beer. Heavy, though. Timbers, of some sort. Planks. Stacks of peat."

The silence thickened like the encroaching cold. Waiting for one of us to say it. *There is no way out.*

"Blight and blast," I heard myself say, thin and quakily, "If only Azo—or if I had her tinderbox." Or the one from a ship's chandler, cached in our room. "If we could just make them open the door."

Therkon did not enquire, And if they did, how do you propose to overcome the Yarl and six or eight grown men, with one unarmed helper and a pair of throwing knives? Therkon did not say anything at all.

"We can't stay here." I could feel panic rising like the cold. "If it's supposed to get us south, this is hardly the way to do it! If—anything—goes wrong here, who knows where this could end?" The Isles' hope dashed along with the River's? The enemy left to advance unhindered, while, at best, we sat in the Yarl's under-croft, waiting the fulfillment of a ransom demand?

"Maybe we could bang with timber? Or roll barrels? Or . . ."

"My lady." Therkon sounded very odd indeed. "I think I, may have the diversion, at least."

"You do?" I thumped down beside him and grabbed a hand by pure chance. "What?"

The hand was clammy. It clenched suddenly under mine, his breath caught in a gasp and his body went into a rigid hunch.

"Therkon! What is it? What—!"

"My stomach." I could not tell if it was shame or chagrin or simple pain. "I hoped not, but . . . It is about to—misbehave."

"Oh, Mother!" I leapt back up. "Not now, it can't, I don't have any—" any help, any supplies if I could use them, any idea what to do. "Is it—how is it—what—happens . . .?"

This time it was definitely a gasp. I felt him twist as if, however bowed together, he could not hold himself still.

"Sometimes. If I just lie down. Others: cramps. Much . . ." He let that go. I already knew. Much pain. "The—" It was coming word by word now. Not just pain but reserve. Having to bare this to someone else. Someone new. "With the worst. I throw up."

I did not have to finish, This is going to be one of the worst.

"Something new. Perhaps the fish."

Resignation now, at a cycle all too well known. Then, with a tiny glint of black humor, "But good cause to bang the door. You could even," dryly, "scream."

\* \* \* \*

I screamed. I banged the door too, with the heaviest plank I could carry stumbling and teetering up the steps. I shrieked till my throat hurt, with my heart behind the simplest distress call: "Help! Help! *Help!*"

And just before my voice gave out, the door emitted a rattle. A scrape. A crack opened on light and a querulous voice demanded, "What in heyill's wrong?"

"My brother!" I had no need to act. "My brother needs a healer, quick!"

Silence. A mutter. Another rattle. Panic spurred my wits. "He's ill, he's been poisoned! For the Mother's love, get *someone!* He might, he might—"

Genuine tears choked the rest. I had heard Therkon throw up once already. It sounded fit to tear his stomach out.

More muttering, but "poison" had done it. The light broadened suddenly. The voice ordered, "Stand away from the stair."

I stood away. At least, I danced from foot to anguished foot while the lock worked again, while the lantern descended, all but step by step. When it reached bottom I could not help darting for-ward. "Here, he's here!"

I would not have cared if it had been massed retainers led by the Yarl himself. But it was a lone man who held the lantern high enough to get a clear look at Therkon, and let out an involuntary gasp.

He stepped by me. In a single slide I was behind him with my sheath-arm round his neck and the drawn knife at his throat. "Don't move," I said, and heard Azo's casual, pitiless menace in the words.

He gave one grunt and froze. He had not known I was armed. He never dreamt a woman might attack. He knew Therkon was unarmed, and one glimpse of Therkon, a mucky beige color, knotted on the blankets with a pool of vomit at his feet, had done the rest.

Therkon got to an elbow, then, teeth bared against a new pang, struggled to his feet. I said in my prisoner's ear, "Hold the lantern out to the side."

And only realized then that I expected Therkon, like Azo or Verrith, to know what to do next.

But Deoren had hammered some things into him. He moved hunched and shakily, but he circled to reach the lantern and pluck it loose. Set it on the slab. Got out huskily, "I'll get," a breath, "his belt."

Whatever his body did, his wits worked. We would need to secure this captive first of anything, and we had no other bindings. I could have cried with relief.

\* \* \* \*

Only after that did I wonder where the rest of them were. How long before this one would be missed. How we would get further, except with the simplest and most unlikely bluff: take him with us and threaten his life to get us out the door.

And then, where would we go?

Away. Anywhere. To a healer who would know what to do when Therkon doubled up in another spasm and collapsed back on the stone.

He struggled up again, hands shaking, body clenched, but still thinking, despite it all. "How many," he got out, and gestured overhead.

I shifted the knifeblade. The prisoner said in a hurry, "They've all gone home."

Despite everything, Therkon's brows climbed into his tangled hair. Pure crown prince.

"It's the store-tower! Nobody'd stay." I could hear his own resentment at being left with the task. "Cold as the ice and draughty as Shivell Straits. They thought, till morning—"

With a lock, and a door, and no weapons, we would be safe enough.

Therkon looked at me. I looked at Therkon, and gave the point another fraction shift. "Likely," I said, mimicking Azo when dangerously bored.

"It's the truth! I swear, sir, m'lord!" He had spoken throughout to Therkon. Not only was I a woman, his resentment at my capture was coming out. "Nobody's up there. Nobody thought—"

Therkon got off the slab, with a hand clamped to his middle, and gathered up our sodden cloaks.

He took the lantern and went first. Having demonstrated I could throw the knives, I made the prisoner climb behind him, with me a good six steps below. And those six steps, given his resentment, must have seemed opportunity enough.

I heard the crash and tinkle and a thoroughly recognizable grunt the instant he went out of sight. I cleared the stairs in two leaps and hurdled Therkon's fallen back in time to see lantern oil fan in a burning cascade across the main room floor and pile like a wave around the first bulky shadow heap.

Sacking kindled at once. Flame went up the heap like a treed cat to burst in a rosette of fire and the vilest imaginable stench, and the prisoner let out an anguished, "No!"

Therkon threw the lantern remnants at him. As the man reeled back I caught him by the belt fastened round his elbows in the usual Imperial restraint. I had the knife at his throat in earnest when Therkon grabbed my knife-wrist, jerking it up and round into a soggy crunching thud.

The man folded through my hands. I stood paralysed, unable to think past the woman in the Seaforts. A second time that someone had died by my hand.

"Just hilt. Behind ear." Therkon had both hands on his knees and was gasping in the throes of another cramp. "Get cloaks!"

I snatched them off the floor and beat at lingering sparks. The prisoner was out cold. The heap, it must have been wool bales, was enthusiastically alight. Raw wool, Two informed me, full of natural oil. We would burn out the tower . . . Therkon staggered past me to the prisoner and gasped, "Help!"

The outer key was on the man's belt, easy to see as the keyhole, by the escalating flames. Therkon threw one desperate glance around and I knew what he was thinking. Secured prisoners or not, they would never leave Hvestang here.

His face twisted in a different pain. Then he started struggling with the man's legs.

I nearly ruptured my back helping to get him outside: nothing had prepared me for an unconscious human's weight. Therkon heaved the door to behind us with a bang, and tried to straighten into the still enthusiastically pouring rain. "Come!" he gasped.

"Come where?" He was moving already, half reeling, half crouched as the next pains hit. "Not there, the town's the first place they'll look!"

He checked, no more than an intimation of movement in the inky, streaming street. The voice was contorted by his stomach's work, but the brain behind it was still razor-sharp.

"No use go up. Catch us . . . fast. Not expect—down here. Fire not showing. When it does . . . Run up. Not down."

"But down? The, the port? The sea?"

"Got to get off—*island*. No use stay here!"

No, we had no means of travel or flight on land except our feet. And whether or not it was planned, we had to keep going south. Over the sea.

"A ship? But the money?" He could not mean to expend the ring on this?

"Stow away."

# CHAPTER IX

If that next hour was nightmare to me, for Therkon it must have been the Mother's hell on earth: stumbling, slipping, floundering through those pitchy street caverns, cannoning off walls, blundering into dead-end after dead-end as we tried first to double back leftward, then blind-stab to reach the quays. With the rain still streaming, and hardly a house showing light.

The rain and dark at least were a double-edged curse, blinding us, but emptying the streets. The hue and cry was unequivocal. A rumor, then definite shouts. Then a great spurt of fire as some unwary soul forced the tower door open, and a sudden wounded-bull roar.

No mistaking the Yarl. We ran until I thought my heart was burst. How Therkon bore it, half-doubled up even between cramps, I cannot guess, but at the end of eternity, we staggered out onto the wharf.

The strengthened wind told us, and the glow night-water always brings, however slight. With riding lights added, we could actually guess at shapes. We took the first ship moored rather than anchored, and without a light. Even in terror's befuddlement I thought her alarmingly small, but she had at least one mast, and a gangplank. That should have warned us, had our last strength not gone in getting aboard.

The deck heaved slightly, disorientingly, gloriously, under my feet. I groped for bulwarks, for ambushed ropes. Therkon crossed before me against a distant lamp, a doubled-over silhouette that wheezed, "Down here."

Black as *Aspis'* lower-deck. I would have jibbed. A hand grabbed my wrist. She was a merchantman, not a galley: it was the sail-locker, up past the hold on the foredeck, with a hinged, raiseable lid. We thudded down together in a heap and stink of moldy canvas, on a relatively soft floor of bundled sails. At least, it was softer than naked stone.

In a minute or two I regained breath to get disentangled. As I squirmed clear of Therkon's legs, an importunate arm, a double ell of wet furry cloak, my hand caught on suddenly yielding cloth. Wet cloth, soggy in a single spot.

He had gagged himself with a shirt-sleeve. I could hear, now, the wheeze of his breath. And feel too clearly how he lay, limp as a shot deer, too exhausted even to try to get up. Until the next spasm doubled him over, muscles rigored, grabbing the shirt and stuffing his mouth again to muffle the groan.

When it finally began to ebb I said, "I'm getting a healer. Now."

"No!" He still had a man's strength. His hand grabbed me like a trap. "Wait! Will pass!"

"And will it—"

*Will it kill you first?*

I bit that off. In cold reason, he was right. He knew his body. He had suffered this how often before? We had already dared to the limit of the Mother's luck. Escaped the tower. Reached sanctuary, and nearly killed him doing it. How could I ask him to suffer more?

Two might know the number of my second thoughts, after we sorted out the cloaks and huddled down, trying to find some bundle of canvas halfway comfortable. The myriad irks of weariness, hunger and a full bladder joined forces with the cold. Worst of all, I had to listen to the muted sounds of spasm after spasm, and wonder how either of us could possibly last till dawn.

Therkon had just relapsed back into fresh exhaustion when the canvas conveyed a faint, sudden tremor. Then, even in the sail locker, we heard the clump of boots.

Therkon grabbed another mouthful of shirt. I had just time for terror to sear right through me, Not just coming aboard, they're coming here! Then the sail-locker lid rose like a vertical dawn, light burst in our eyes, and a deep voice commanded, "Come out."

No hope of fight, let alone flight. Four shadowy heads looked down on us. The locker was lit from end to end. Nowhere to hide.

I tried to get my feet under me. Wobbled up against a wall. Looked up the further two feet to the hatch rim, and managed a very small, "I c-can't."

Not unkindly, they laughed. Someone made a pointed remark about getting in there well enough. Someone else tossed down a rope. Another said, "There's two of 'em."

"My brother. He's been—he's ill." Two shot a bolt of memory's warning and I gabbled, "Not plague or fever, something just upset his stomach, it's very sensitive—"

"Ah?" The first voice again. Not unkind, but not overly friendly either. Then, "Skappi, you'd best go down."

It took two of them and another rope and a very considerable slice of imperial pride, before they finished fastening him in a series of half hitches and then steadying him while those overhead hauled. One of them legged me over the coaming, as if onto a horse, and I scurried after the two carrying Therkon, down abaft the mast, into a companionway.

"Present for ye, Mither," one was saying, as they lowered Therkon onto some kind of wall bunk or seat. A hanging lamp lit a shadowy, crowded but warm room that smelt of wet wool and man-sweat and sea-salt, peculiarly dashed by whiffs of mint-tea and geraniums.

A female voice retorted, "Ah?" But a bigger, solider presence ducked under the lintel behind me, and the now familiar deep voice announced, "Here's our stowaways."

"*How,*" Two got quite away from me, "*did you know?*"

All five of them laughed. The big man even slapped my back, all but knocking me down. "Next time you take the rat's path, boy, before you run up the cable, wipe your boots!"

Mud. We had been so spent, so bent to the limit on other endurance, we had completely forgotten that. I could feel my face burn hotter than the lamp.

Therkon was struggling to sit up. Lamplight showed his face an alarming beige, all sunken eye-pits and baulks of cheek. "My," he managed, just as the big man realized for himself.

"You're a girl!"

I was past anything but a mumbled, "Yes."

His eyes narrowed. He was tall enough for that to show, so close to the feeble lamp. Darkened slits in a beefy but not bearded face, under a knitted cap releasing strands of some dark-colored hair. He swung suddenly and caught up a handful of Therkon's cloak.

"Ye're Skatir's bogles," he said.

Therkon got one hand on the table and tried to push himself up. The table swung sideways—it was on gimbals—and the big man pushed him firmly back.

"Less the blade, o' course." An appraising glance. Then something that might have been a chuckle, sunk in his chest. "Finest I've heard a man swear. That fool Stoth out like a candle, the birds flown, and his whole poxy wool-tithe alight!"

It became a full-chested laugh. He actually slapped a thigh. "And here's the pair o' ye, fetched up on the *Tolla,* snug as rats!"

Under the cloak my hands moved without volition, sliding loose Verrith's knife. Driven less by the words than the look on Therkon's face.

"Whisht, man." The big man had read it too. "Only fall on your nose. The whole town heard Skatir bellowing." Another chuckle shook him. "Same as they heard the rest."

"But you." Pain and throwing up had reduced Therkon to a whisper, but the panic and defiance were clear as a shout. "How did you know—where were—who *are* you?"

"Me?" It had brought another general laugh. The big man out-bellowed them all. "Oh, I'm his misbegotten, meddling, tight-fisted Phaerean marriage-kin!"

Therkon's face said it all. Two had us on my toes, tension shooting bolts down every nerve, fingers tightening on the hilt . . . But then the woman moved round the table-end.

"Colne," she said, "let him be now. Light the galley fire, and heat me some ballast stones."

\* \* \* \*

"Skatir is the Yarl. My brother, yes." She spoke almost resign-edly. Quietly as she had issued every order from the first, which sent the big man off with hardly a word, before she dispersed the three younger ones to fetch blankets and drying cloths and "my herbs." While she herself moved in and began, as calmly, as irresistibly, to unfasten Therkon's cloak.

"We were at his house. 'Supping.' Him and Colne, telling jokes. A new way to squabble over harbor dues. Take this, Skappi." She handed the cloak behind her, and did something that swung the table aside to stay. "Now, you. Therkon, is it? Can you lie down flat?"

Therkon was past questions, let alone demur. She touched him lightly but carefully, temples, throat, chest, then bent her head and pressed an ear to his solar plexus. Straightening, she did not bother with so little verbal confirmation as a grunt.

"You, girl, come here."

I got my hand from the knife-hilt and hurried to her side.

"Take that off, t'is streaming wet. Skappi." Without raising her voice, but he was there instantly. "Hang this with t'other. And keep your hands off those furs." Then, re-directing her voice to me, "A belly upset, aye. Ye thought right." She must have observed him all through the men's talk: made her diagnosis, and decided, without a word, what she, and they, would do.

As calmly, she drew open Therkon's coat, pushed up folds of shirt and found the trouser buttons. "Be still." With a flattened palm as Therkon came to life and tried weakly but wildly to protest. "Girl, rub your hands warm."

I obeyed in a hurry. She already had enough buttons undone to loosen the shirt, and was easing the trouser flaps apart. "Give me your hand. Here, where I've put it." Therkon let out a yelp. "Rub with the heel of your palm. Slowly. Very gently. This way." Down in a circle from right to left and up. "Not any other. Keep doing that."

She turned smoothly but swiftly to the thump of things on the table. I was left kneeling beside Therkon, the heel of my right hand pressed to his naked belly, to a final brusque, "Rub."

Therkon gasped and tried to wriggle, then, wordlessly, to protest. The muscles under my palm were ridged with denial. With ongoing pain. The skin . . .

The skin was warm. Smooth, soft as velvet. Far softer than the shaven stubble of his cheek. Far more delicate than my own palms. The velvet touch of protected body skin, the body of a man whose people almost never strip.

I clung to my orders for dear life: rub here and thus, only the heel of the hand, this much pressure and no more. The crest of a pelvic bone nudged my wrist, and my fingers wanted dizzily to slide upward, over ribs and breastbone to trace the swell of a pectoral, smooth, firm, warm, all but assembling under my touch, but Two was insisting as dizzily that I move *down*, that just a hand-span lower would find skin more delicate, even more deliriously velvet than this . . .

The Mother preserved me. A step sounded, a voice, then the ship-wife slipped down to sit by Therkon, saying, "Can you lift your head?" And to me, "Don't stop."

*Don't stop!* Two howled, only barely not aloud. *Don't stop!*

*Shut up!* I bawled back and tried to concentrate as Therkon struggled up on his elbows, and the ship-wife held a cup to his mouth.

"Slowly, now." I could smell whatever it was, sharp, pungent, but pleasantly warming, even as a scent. Meekly, Therkon sipped.

She lifted the cup away. Told me, "Enough." Gave me the cup, and herself tidied Therkon's clothes. Said quietly, "Close your eyes, now, and keep still." She took a blanket from the pile on the table, shook it out over him, folded another to go under his head. Slightly louder, she said, "Colne, do you have the stones?"

They were big round stones, not hot, but warmed to last. Therkon tried to protest when she pulled off his boots. As she settled the stones under his feet, he did manage to whisper, "What was that?"

"Good for sea-qualm. And belly-spasms. In the Isles they call it," the irony said she knew as much about us as the rest of Grith-sperry, "imperial spice."

The men were at the stern end of the room, beyond the lamp. Handling, I realised, as the ship-wife led me over, Therkon's cloak. One was saying, "kill to work skins like that." The big man rumbled, "Done the old way. From Evvamoor, sure enough." They turned guiltily, Colne asking, "Well, m'dear?" The other one, Skappi, I thought, hurriedly hung up the cloak.

"Upset belly," she said, "aye. He should settle now."

Two broke in before I could insist on prudence, on keeping options clear. *"What will you do with us?"*

The big man spluttered. "You've a rare tongue, for a stow-away—!" The ship-wife turned toward me, still little more than a smearily colored shadow under the tallow lamp.

"Ye will do as ye please," she said, in that quiet, even voice. "But we're away to Phaerea, the morn. Ye might be wise to come with us."

\* \* \* \*

Phaerea at first sight was green: green as spring grass, as early summer leaves, green-gold under the dawn light when I clambered on deck, fragile and lovely as the gold and tangerine splendors of cloud from behind which burst the coming glory of the sun. Low and softly green, rolling with crops and pastures, as gentle a land, at first glance, as Sickle had been harsh.

They had cast off in Grithsperry at first pallid light. As they towed us out with the ship's dinghy, Therkon was still asleep. So I stood alone beside the ship-wife at the helm, looking back to the whitewashed walls, the rain-pure hill-crest, the black wisp of smoke still sulking from the tower, hoping fervently that Colne was right. "Skatir wake? Hah! You're safe till noon!"

And remembering the great diminishing prospect of Rivers-end. Thinking, like a knife in the side, of Verrith and Azo. With protest, and grief, and bitter reluctance, finally saying goodbye.

When Grithsperry had quite disappeared I slipped below to find Therkon waking, however drowsily, at last.

"It stopped," he murmured, as I sat down where the ship-wife had, by his head. "Just . . . stopped."

The pain. The spasm. Ceasing, that voice told me, as it never had before, for any remedy. More than a cure. A miracle.

I touched the loose hair straggling half across his face and whispered, "I'm glad."

The touch brought him round like a cold-water dash. A hand came out of the blanket to restrain mine. He actually tried to sit up. "Chaeris—my lady—I am not fit—" Filthy, unkempt, still vomit-stained. Only a crown prince would worry. I had ado not to laugh aloud.

"It doesn't matter." But to him it did. "I'll ask Frotha for hot water." But the new razor he had bought with the tinderbox was back in our inn room, along with the precious clean underclothes and shirts. "Oh, fry it! Well, one of the 'boys' will have—"

"Chaeris." Still husky to the edge of breath. But forceful enough to stop me in mid-step. "Don't—ask much."

Two, he meant. Don't turn her loose as she already ached to go, bombarding them all with questions about the *Tolla*, the family, the Yarl, Grithsperry, Phaerea.

"But, but, we should, we need to know—"

"If you ask, then they can. Don't."

He slid back against the blankets. He still looked drained as a corpse, but those wits were most definitely awake. The rest came in a dour whisper.

"Don't tell them anything."

\* \* \* \*

"Tolla" actually means Sticky, but with a ship, it stands for Holds-well: keeps the wind. I learnt that from the ship-wife, whose name was Frotha, which means something like, Well-informed. I did manage to suppress Two there. And I could avoid questions in return, trotting to and fro after Therkon instead.

He was hardly fit to move for two whole days: not merely the attack's aftermath, but the arrears of the storm, when he had labored and starved far worse than I. After one determined effort that left him wilted on the cabin floor, he bowed to Frotha's decree and kept to a temporary bunk in the forward quarters, where "the boys" slept. Like me, he had to bear dowering with our latest necessities from them, or Colne or Frotha. I even had to ask her help when my courses came. I could tell the charity galled him still worse.

And far too often, handing clothes or a towel or helping him waver to the head made Two replay those moments in the main cabin: silk and velvet skin over warm solid muscle under my palm . . . But the forward quarters' other benefit was space, at least in daytime, to work out. And at night, if I was firmly steered to the spare bunk in Colne and Frotha's cabin, I hardly had to feign exhaustion before I dropped asleep.

Even for the *Tolla*, on a fair wind Phaerea was barely four days run. With landfall made, the wind comfortably behind us and the wide bay of Jurrick opening celestially blue under our lee, Therkon finally made an extended foray on deck. Wrapped in Nouip's cloak over somebody's shirt and trousers, he clambered aft to Frotha, who had the steering oar.

As a matter of course I went too. When he settled against the rail Frotha decided, with a glance, that he was fit to stand. After Colne materialized, and Skappi and the other "boy" on watch dawdled aft, I realized it was, by intent, if not consensus, a gathering.

The ship heeled and hissed louder to a flaw in the breeze, and after four days my body had unlearnt storm reflexes far enough not to tense from head to toe. Giving lightly to the oar's push, Frotha echoed Nouip, that short age past.

"What think ye," she said, "to do now?"

Therkon glanced forward and starboard, where Jurrick town was beginning to coalesce in the bay's curve, a cluster of white and steel-blue and perhaps distant red, the squared shapes of wall and house.

"We must ask after our folk."

Frotha did not repeat her brother's cruel refutation. She merely asked, after a moment, "And then?"

"And then," the chin tilted a little. "We must acquire funds. What we owe here . . ."

Write that off, Frotha's gesture answered, casual but firm. She tipped her plain, sea-burned face into the breeze. She was a deft and experienced helmswoman, but at times I almost expected to see her tuck the bar, like a farm-wife with an errant fowl, under one arm.

"And then?"

"And then, my lady, it depends on what we find."

Like the expression, the nuance was pure crown prince. Remote, coolly courteous. Cutting insistence, like curiosity, off at the root.

Then, to Two's utter outrage, he began asking all the questions he had so straitly forbidden us.

At the stop-royal Frotha's mouth had not quite opened, and shut. Now there was a distinct twinkle in her eye, but she answered gravely enough.

"Town's called Jurrick, aye. Chief port o' the north. In Jurrick bay. Though t'is more like some call it, the Sway in Phaerea's back. Aye, by here t'is all green and pleasant enough. Wheat fields as well as barley, and pasture. Cattle, sheep. Horses, too. Rare, among the Isles, surely. Jurrick counts as rich, with all o' that. And the trade, aye. Everything from the South Isles, going North."

"No, at the moment, t'is more often coming south. Not just grain. Cloth, and timber. Even rope, sometimes. Aye. But whichever road, Jurrick takes its cut."

"Not a king, nay. After Langlieve, Phaerea swore t'would never bide a master's word again. But Jurrick leads the north 'o the isle, and the lords' council leads Jurrick. Rich folk, some o' them, aye. They buy in their crafts, like their wine and music. There's few fine workers here."

"The south? They go their own way. Thring's Deep, and Mirkadin, Ve Pool and the rest. Folk enough, but not the pretty lands up here. Sheep ashore, mostly, and barley where it'll grow. More often, they work the sea."

"Pirates?" With a slight look of amusement. "I'd ware where I said that, in the south."

"Nay, Jurrick'll not o'ermaster them. Phaerea, it's sweet enough along the Sway, but inland there's hills like the crests of a porcupine, clear from east to west. The lords o' Jurrick can run a claim into the foothills. The hills, nobody owns."

I stared away over the smiling roll of pastures, of grain fields not yet in ear, up the slight ridges to a smiling blue sky. No rough heights announced their presence yet.

"Aye, if ye've goods to chaffer, fine goods, Jurrick's the place." Distinct speculation in her eye now. I was on tenterhooks lest Therkon ask after some particular craft—Two judged that to barter even Nouip's brooch would need a king's goldsmith—but Deoren had taught him that much. He thanked her courteously, and moved, slowly but decisively, to leave the rail.

"So," Colne said from his place opposite, "ye're welcome to go ashore when we berth. No toll," his lip twitched, "for ship-guests who never paid passage." Therkon began, slightly but visibly, turning red. Colne caught Frotha's look and waved a hasty hand. "Just japing, man, that's all! At the least, you'll not need to chop divots from *my* deck-beams again."

The workouts. Shut doors had muffled the sound of Verrith's knives thunking home, but they had left their mark in the big hammock-beams. For a moment Therkon looked honestly flabbergasted. Then his mouth opened and shut and mortal embarrassment changed its target. He ducked his head and dug at a board with a toe, muttering about, "apologies."

"No matter." Colne grinned, magnanimous now his barb was home. "I'd've offered a whetstone, had ye said."

"Colne," Frotha said, in a tone I knew now too, "the lad's been long enough on deck."

Colne buckled immediately, even, contritely, offering an arm for the companion ladder. I forestalled that, at least, though my heart still hurried with relief. They thought Therkon owned the knives, his bluff had worked, Frotha had stopped Colne's teasing, she would not ask anything more.

Then Skappi broke out, "But ma? Pa? We still dunno: what about his sister, not-sister? Where's *she* from? And where're they going? An' Sthassamaer . . . ?"

Frotha turned on him fast as I ever saw her move. "A word with the passengers. Ship courtesy. They've spoken as they choose. That's all!"

Skappi shut himself off in mid-breath. At mention of that word I had tried to turn, Two growing quite unmanageable, and Therkon's hand shut on my own shoulder, both message and propulsion, pulling me, Two or no Two, down the companionway.

* * * *

In Archipelago terms, Jurrick was indeed well off. The tiled or shingled roofs, the white-washed walls and narrow, climbing, paven streets replicated Grithsperry, but the sea-frontages carried far more decoration, and if they did not gild the mooring posts like the imperial wharf in Riversend, money and manpower spoke from new-painted dock-frames and all but polished bollards, the smartly fettled ships and tidy piles of nets.

*Tolla* came in without pilot, using the dinghy at the last to carry a warp ashore. The berth was hers, reserved. Or so Frotha told me the letters carved along the quay-edge said. What more it said I read in Therkon's expression, and hoped we would get quietly ashore.

But we had only to endure a few more barbs from Colne, arrange with Frotha to hold Nouip's cloak, as much for a pledge in answer to Colne's jibes, I guessed, as precaution against another stir like Grithsperry, and then rediscover our land-legs on the quay.

It was a bright, breezy but not inclement day. The long waterfront bustled with stevedores and sailors and merchants and passing loads of produce that almost distracted Two from our chief task, but Therkon at least glanced to and fro for himself. Rubbed both hands up his sleeves, as if unconsciously cold, and eyed the narrow mouths of half a dozen unfamiliar streets.

"Deoren," he said, on a sharp little sigh. Then he drew a palm between his brows and headed inshore.

I tracked a pace behind his shoulder on the street side, which left my throwing hand clear. I knew the stiletto memory had used on him: Deoren would have scouted already, found the fine wares quarter, picked out a shop fit for a crown prince to chaffer in. Deoren, like Verrith or Azo, would be a bulwark now at our backs. But Deoren was gone. A gall this time, as well as a grief.

Since we used eyes rather than mouths it took a frustrating time to reach the craft shops, tucked along a single street parallel to the quay, opposite a worrying number of tall chimneys and blind outer walls with heavily built gates. A couple even had a guard-house in the entry-bay. Therkon eyed that vista a long, frowning moment, then shrugged visibly before he turned away.

We chose a jeweler, eventually: a small shop whose stout bars spoke louder than the glitter catching candlelight inside. In his borrowed clothes Therkon looked the merest sailor, but the shop-watcher was at his elbow halfway across the floor.

"If we might assist m'lord?"

Therkon considered him: white shirt-sleeves, an indoor vest of fine-spun wool, a solid gold but quietly elegant seal ring. Attentive, not cringing. A merchant of substance, Two concluded. Perhaps a Crafter, sib to his wares. Surely a judge of customers as well.

Therkon inclined his head an imperial degree. "Sir. You are the owner? Then I think you might assist us, yes. I am an Outsea merchant, ship-wrecked in the Isles. Hence in need of funds, as you may imagine, and in Jurrick our house has no credit. But there may be funds, perhaps."

The crown prince, not condescending but drawing the other to his own status, confiding, though with dignity. Not suing charity, but certainly not expecting to be refused.

The jeweler kept dignity too, but there was no hesitation as he indicated an open side-door. "If m'lord will come this way?"

"In other circumstances . . . I would pledge this against an advance, if circumstances required such a, a measure. But I may not return to Jurrick." Something bleak had slid under the words. I saw the jeweler's head lift with a quickly mastered twitch. "Therefore, I must seek a complete sale."

He drew his hand from Skappi's coat and slipped the Empire's spousal ring onto the velvet pad over the jeweler's table top.

The thillians caught the lamp with a flare of diamond blue and white. The jeweler caught his breath.

"Summer's Lady!" He looked for permission before, carefully as it had been laid down, he gathered the ring up. "But these are . . ."

"Thillians. A matched trio. From the—Empire. An heirloom of, of our house."

Almost superfluous, all of it. Especially the last. The jeweler's eyes came back to his, concern and understanding and more in his square, dark but smooth Archipelagan face.

"M'lord, an heirloom?"

*Are you certain?* the inflection finished. This was more than a treasure, this was a heritage. Selling this was as near blasphemy as the son of a great house might approach.

And heart-break, it went without saying, as well.

Therkon moved a hand slightly. His voice was almost steady. "The sagas say, Outsea. He is in chains, who cannot cast a treasure away at need."

The jeweler escorted us out, even breaching discretion to mention "your lady" amid his wishes for a safe voyage. At first Therkon had proposed to sell the ring entire. Then, at the jeweler's protests of lacking even capital to match its true value, to extract a single stone, which made the jeweler squeeze his eyes shut as at literal blasphemy. Finally they agreed on as much cash as the jeweler could raise, with the rest in smaller gems: blood-red hazians, a half-dozen finghends greener than the southern seas. "Far easier to trade, m'lord, and still good worth." I did not need the avowals to know he was in truth trying to return full value for his gain.

Therkon was very quiet when we reached the street. I crept behind him, my sympathy mixed with shame and guilt. He would provide for us both, at such a price, and what had I contributed? Under that, another voice was ignominiously exulting: *He's not married to the Empire now. Forget whatever pattern of a Riversrun daughter might get him someday. He's not married to the Empire any more.*

When I tried to silence that by telling, however stumblingly, my other shame, he stopped dead and stared.

"Chaer—my lady. You are not . . ." He stopped. Pulled a very rueful face. "Very well, it is doubtless different in Iskarda." He shook his head a little. Another stress, I interpreted, yet another difference to keep in mind: Iskardan women rebuff charity. "But. You *have* contributed." A sudden, heart-stoppingly real smile. "You are the one with the, ah, arms. And the one," it became an open grin, "who sheep-dogs me."

Whether to ease my embarrassment at that, or because his momentary lightened spirits had woken the philosopher, a few minutes later he nodded me up beside him. "Tell me," he began. "When you 'work out.' Or—at Grithsperry. Does Two join in? Or how does Two . . ."

"Two keeps out." There had been some alarming early episodes, especially when Azo, I remembered with yet another pang, began to teach me hand-work. "There's no time for her." Not for talk, or advice, or any memory, except the body's own. "And it's safer. For us both."

I actually meant me and the opponent. I had never been in mortal combat, but the last thing needed outside that is an ally who can over-damage from simple fright. Two had learnt that, once and for all, with my father Alkhes, when in human time I was three years old.

"I see." The philosopher, charmed by pure interest. "So Two *can*, uh, be still, at need?"

"At need, yes." Suddenly I was the one alarmed. Too close, too reminiscent of those moments by the qherrique, when we kissed and Two showed, told, wanted me to go on as men and women do, far too searingly reminiscent of the *Tolla*, that silken skin under my palm.

The Mother sent me another boon: a two-horse wagonette was lurching down on us, haphazardly piled with hides, far too wide for the tortuous street. "Careful, let me near that horse."

* * * *

Once discovered, the ships' chandlers and haberdashers did well from us. My sober Iskardan shirt and leggings were durable as my cloak, but Therkon's white shirt and noble's coat had passed reclaim, and we both needed fresh extras from the skin out, not to mention travel necessities. And bags to carry them. Before the *Tolla* hove back in view it was past noon. I was hoping to re-view the succulently scented market cook-stalls, on the way to what had looked a decent inn, when I noticed the crowd on board.

The whole family was clustered at the gangplank head. Colne blocked the way, Skappi and the next-largest son flanking him, Frotha craning past his elbow. Their body language alone would have alerted me, without the package Colne held.

In both arms, as if it were a baby, or a scepter, or something too fragile yet too dangerous to release: a long narrow package, carefully wrapped in oil-cloth and trussed with twine. The central knot was clinched by a big red wax seal.

Two and I understood together, on a dizzy blast of shock, wonder, disbelief. We might lose Nouip's gifts. However impossibly, they would not lose us.

Therkon had read the situation at least. His head came up in that wary-deer pose. Then, his first sign of troublecrew sense, he veered a little, bringing me up by him at the gangplank foot.

Colne said, "This came for you."

Therkon's face went imperially blank. In a moment he said, "From Grithsperry?"

"From Grithsperry, aye." In stress Colne would turn red himself. "Signed by the Yarl, sent by war galley. Two days and nights at sea. Right past us! Delivered with a poxy escort! All to get this—this—into someone *else's* hair!"

"I apologise," Therkon said very softly, "if this has made trouble for you."

Colne's cheeks swelled to explode, Two caught the whole subtext and nearly made me laugh aloud. Skatir had turned the joke on his brother-in-law, avenged himself on the one who took us beyond Skatir's reach, skipped the seed of trouble out of Grithsperry and back onto the troublemaker with an emphasis Colne's own lords would not miss. And now his salvage, with that regal condescension, had also repaid those jibes about charity.

Colne bit off a splutter of consonants. Turned almost purple, then gave the package a ferocious shake. "Come up and get this—thing."

"I will have my cloak as well," Therkon said.

The inflection implied not merely dishonesty but contempt: *I will not leave you a second cause for fear.* Colne did turn purple, but Frotha tapped the nearest son's shoulder. Pushed past, revealing the cloak in her arms, and came down the gangplank, snapping, "Colne," as she moved.

"We've not the weight to ply among council-lords." The tone added, *And these things will make you lords' business.* She handed Therkon the cloak. "Colne." She still did not look round, but he put the sword into her outstretched hand. She waited till Therkon had the cloak arranged before she held it out.

"Ye know your plans, whatever ye intend. We cannot help ye further." She stopped, then spoke with sudden intensity. "But if ye're meaning to do with the Seabane, we—*I*—wish ye well."

\* \* \* \*

The White Grebe was palatial, in Grithsperry terms. It had stables for lordly guests' mounts, and hence a back-door as well as a separate guest entrance, with a courteous watch-keeper. Its bath-room water ran hot from a cistern-tap, and we found a room with alcoves for troublecrew, as well as a lord's bed. The one thing it refused was to serve food or drink upstairs. The custom wrought too much havoc, the watch-keeper told us apologetically, with nautical guests.

"I could run back," I offered, as Therkon at last relaxed the imperial affront that had borne him clear through the crowded streets and over the Grebe's defenses, as if lordly strangers in sailors' gear stalked round Jurrick with an armful of seal fur every day. "It's not far to the market-stalls."

"Oh. Yes." He had let the cloak slide onto the wide main bed, and subsided almost limply after it. His hands moved, perhaps meaning to seek the jeweler's pouch inside his new, sober if fitting coat. He made an odd noise and went still.

Then he said, "The brooch is gone."

"It can't be—" I bit down on my tongue, hard enough to draw blood. I had wanted to trade the brooch from the start. He had steadfastly refused. More charity, I had guessed. It would be worse than his own cost, to lose Nouip's second gift. And perhaps this, at least, he might, one day, have returned.

"Colne?" I said.

He made another noise that became a startled little laugh. "My lady. I always forget."

That I was Iskardan, trained as troublecrew. To draw inference from calamity, and act, rather than question and lament and blame.

"I think . . . Skappi, perhaps." His hands clenched in the fur, and released. "He wanted this. Wanted answers he never got. And he saw the family—his father—"

Have a joke back-fire. End in trouble. Be shown afraid.

"Do you think Frotha . . .?" I could understand why she cast us loose, but she had returned us the gifts. Had wished us well: even nodded to me, there on the quay, and I had sketched her a troublecrew salute in return.

"No." He had been feeling that abandonment too. But his voice was quiet, with conviction rather than grief. "She would not have known. Put her people first, yes. Steal, no."

It made me feel a little better, though losing Frotha had been a small version of losing Verrith and Azo. Dogging Therkon down the wharf, I had felt outright panicky. The heart of the Archipelago, a town of lords unknown if not outright hostile, and here was I, left alone to ward Dhasdein's heir as well as myself.

"Well." I carefully removed my hand from Verrith's wrist-knife. "I can go to the market, anyhow. With," I gave him a meaningful eye, "the money I already have."

And alone, I meant. They would stare, but knowledge that you carry weapons can change a woman's bearing more effectively than any escort.

"Frotha said, you have to eat."

But when I came back he was asleep where he had sat on the bed, the cloak under one arm, the other hand shut, firm as a clamp, over Hvestang's sheath.

* * * *

I ate at least one of the pies. Scouted the inn. Dispatched our borrowed clothes back to the *Tolla* with a pot-boy for messenger. The supper smells from downstairs had me ready to rouse Therkon when he finally stirred of himself.

This time we took all our valuables, including Hvestang: my tentative question about raising trouble made Therkon buckle the sword-belt with a positive snap. Trouble, the sound retorted, might get more return than it sought.

It was raining outside, lightly but persistently. As we ducked into the taproom I wished for a candle to light at the Mother's feet, but when Therkon headed for the shrine corner, I hung back.

"That's the winter corner." Frotha had answered some questions, at least. "For people who don't want to be sociable. In grief, or trouble or—"

Or expecting worse, like a blood feud's return strike. Therkon gave me an eye-corner as if I were Deoren. *Are we not in trouble,* that look demanded? *If not trouble made flesh?*

When we walked over, with Hvestang's sheath catching the lamp-light at every stride, the half-full, convivial room went suddenly hushed. But I judged us lucky. In a minute or two the patrons turned to their own business, and the server was hurrying over, a waft of fresh-cooked chowder at his back.

Next morning we both woke early, in my case after a restless night. Another strange bed, no ship motion, sufficient rest, for once, and too many concerns to drop off again. When Therkon's voice asked from behind the far alcove's discreet screen, "Shall we look for breakfast?" I was glad to slip into my clothes in what felt like the first full morning light.

So we came down the Grebe's guest stairs in time to catch the street-crier in full voice.

"Hear ye, hear ye, all Jurrick folk! The council cries wolfshead! Be ware, be ware! Yield no help or house, aid or ask, for any or both of these: a man hight Therkon, claiming to be Outsea trader. Six feet and two fingerwidths tall, black hair. Bearing the blade hight Hvestang, garbed in a seal-fur cloak. A woman hight Chaeris, claiming herself his sister, six-feet less three fingerwidths tall, Outsea accent, black eyes and hair . . ."

I missed the rest. Shock and alarm-fire coursed through me, over-ridden clear as life by Azo's voice.

I grabbed Therkon's sleeve and hissed in his ear. "Walk out. Don't stop!"

He gave one jerk and moved. In emergencies at least, Deoren had trained him well.

We had Hvestang and the money but not our cloaks. The tap-room was almost empty. Long odds that anyone here last night would be back so soon, or would know us at a glance. We were past the door. I hissed, "Stables!" and tweaked Therkon right.

"Back stair. Get our things and go." I shot Azo's latest order at him as I leapt the first two steps. The stair was narrow and odorous but it went right to the guest floor, doubtless for servants' use, and thank the Mother for Azo's lessons, I had scouted it yesterday.

We shoveled gear into bags and hurled on our cloaks. Risk upon risk to walk out garbed precisely as described, but good chances multiplied, if we could only reach the street.

Therkon was shuffling money. Jurrick coinage was mongrel, Dhasdeini silver or gold, coppers of all ages from a dozen mints. He dropped a jingle of coins on the big bed and swept me out.

The Mother had emptied the short upper hall. We shot down the stair: the street, I was thinking desperately, then a bolt-hole, or better, the quay, a ship, any ship . . . Therkon grabbed my arm and Two half sparked as he swung me about and muttered, "Wait."

The stable-yard was narrow as a well amid high building backs, age-grimy cobbles scattered with straw. Six stalls at the rear. And in three of them, a horse.

"Can you ride, Chaeris?"

"I, uh—I've been on a mule. You want—you mean—!"

"They've cried us outlaw. We'll never get out of town in these clothes. Not on foot."

"Oh, Mother!" One thing to stow away, or leave an unpaid inn reckoning. Another to steal, to actually lift a horse.

"We can't reach the quay. Or a ship." He slung his new canvas back-bag on a handy hook and the cloak after it. He was down the stall line, pulling at the adjacent door. "Only one way—one place—to go."

South. Two fired it at me in a lightning bolt. We were supposed to go south, by whosever's choice, and south here need not mean the sea. It could be inland, overland. The hills, up there we might escape. Wolfs-head, that might just mean outlaw but the lords might try to trap us, pursue us. Our best chance of escape, again, was the unexpected direction, the most unlikely means.

"Chaeris!" I just caught the flying pouch. "Count six imperials." Dhasdein's major gold coin. "Guess a match if there aren't. Put them in the manger here."

He vanished. Reappeared with a bridle, a saddle over one shoulder. The look added plainly: Come on.

For a moment the world went blank, and then it opened on a blaze of enlightenment and a jet of sheer relief as Two clarified at last: we were troublecrew. Therkon was the strategist. Just so, in Grithsperry, he had seen the bigger patterns, far faster than we. His role was to shape the plans. We had only to make them work.

I started shuffling furiously through the clutch of alien coins.

# CHAPTER X

We walked our horses out of the stable yard, then trotted through the streets. Both of us had bundled our hair up under yesterday's last belated purchase, a pair of the usual knitted caps. Therkon was wearing my cloak, half-concealing Hvestang's sheath, I was wearing a sulky expression and my shirt. The seal-fur was crammed with our other impedimenta in Therkon's saddlebags. He had, by chance or skill, picked the livelier horse. Mine, which he claimed had acted like its friend in the stable-yard, was the slug content to trail along.

It was so early that the crier might have just begun his rounds, and in any case few people were abroad. Errand boys, housewives sweeping steps, lambs or pigs coming to market, the occasional wood or vegetable cart. Therkon wove expeditiously among them, I bumped along behind. The glances we caught were at best briefly curious. Lords' men, they said, on some errand. Better left alone.

Unlike Grithsperry, Jurrick has an inland wall, and of stone, if low. With a gate. It was open, but I saw with a bump of the heart that it also had guards.

Women did not seem to bear arms in the Isles. Two men, in leather vests and some sort of steel and leather warcap, with at least a sword apiece, were lounging in the little roofed shelter just beyond the gate's iron-shod right leaf.

I sought desperately for a diversion, a shield of some sort, any sort, even another sounder of pigs. Therkon gathered his horse up with a kick and made straight for the guards.

"Clettri farm," he called, at the limit of hearing range. His shoulders had sunk a little and his chin jutted. He sounded dour, sullen, thoroughly Outland, and exasperated to the point of wrath. "Which way?"

They both came out of the guard-house, half-surprised but not alarmed. Two understood in another lightning flash that they knew the horses. As Therkon had gambled that they would.

"Attric got you exercising his 'charger'?" The first sounded mild, but he had a suspiciously straight face. I did not know enough about horses to gauge if he was jesting, but whatever Therkon did with his own face, both men laughed.

"New, are you?" The second one asked.

"Hired yesterday." Therkon had dropped his voice three or four notes and turned his accent to something Two claimed was broad Delta. "The lord said, Clettri farm. A message. Take the horse."

In one brief twist his shoulders conveyed resignation, irritation, a professional verging on insult at the quality of his mount. "Where in Dhe's name do I go?"

*Dhe?* My heart hit the roof of my mouth, but to my complete shock both men nodded. "Outland, eh?" the second said. "This far south?"

"The Empire." Therkon said through his teeth. "No wars. Less troops. No pay."

The outrage reached even to me. The men nodded again, somehow eager, in a way Two at least recognised. Provincials identifying a sophisticate. Amateurs encountering something that might be a professional. And a simmeringly irate professional. Not a safe man to tease, let alone balk.

"Your lad there?" the first one did ask, the tone making it mere formality. "He along for the ride?"

Therkon glanced once over his shoulder. The look said, from a more than professional scorn: *If he lasts so long.*

They both laughed again. I deepened my sulk. The first man stepped to Therkon's stirrup and began pointing beyond the gate.

\* \* \* \*

The first part followed the rutted track that passed as Jurrick's main inland road, and by the Mother's grace, it topped a ridge within the first half mile. Halfway down the dip beyond, Therkon glanced back. Then he let his horse drop to a walk, and let out a great, shaky sigh.

"How," I breathed, kicking my own horse in speaking-range, "did you know to do *that?*"

"I didn't." He actually wiped his forehead. "I've never had to." He tried to laugh, or something like it. "Sheer terror? It just—came."

Sheer terror? Pure invention, at the very least. Of course he had never had to go under-cover, even in training. Deoren would never dream he might have to do it without help. "Clettri farm? Where did that come from?"

"People talking. Last night."

So he had listened in the taproom, again. "But. The lord's name." In retrospect, my hair had begun standing up. "If they hadn't said it, what on earth would we have done?"

"Found something else." He scraped up a half smile, though his hand trembled on the reins.

Small wonder, there was still a trip in my own pulse. Daring, inventive, but beyond reckless, to try such a ploy without warning, untrained. Nevertheless. "To claim yourself Outland, a soldier. And the accent. *That* was smart. Where on earth did you get that?"

"Harvis. The army commander, when I was a boy. He was Delta bred. For the rest." A jerky little laugh. "I just reversed Skatir."

A discharged veteran, but Dhasdeini rather than Archipelago. I nearly laughed too. I came near patting his back, more in wonder than congratulation. Strategist, Two called him. I had never expected a tactical stroke like this.

"Well, it worked." I did not add, despite being past dangerous. I glanced up the road. Grey gravel and pot-holes, rushes in the ditch, a low skyline ahead. "How far is this farm, do you think?"

"Ten miles? Maybe more? And westward." He pulled a face.

"We'd best try for supplies, then." As he gathered his reins I kicked my slug again. "Pretty soon."

* * * *

We both knew we must have food for the hills, and find it while the Clettri-farm story would hold. We slugged the horses past one, then another farm-house, tree-bedded in their clusters of folds and pens and out-buildings amid green pastures and the threadbare green of rising grain. Three times Therkon proposed, "This one." And three times Azo's training, Two's instinct, something, answered, "Not yet."

The track branched and branched again, hemming us among ploughland between drystone walls. The fourth choice was smaller than some, with trees on the hill below it, masking the road. By this time the farm folk would be mostly about their business, even fewer witnesses. "This one," I said.

By the time we regained the road I almost had Two, at least, under control. As Therkon turned his mount westward, I could keep myself to a mere, "That was—*That* was—!"

"My lady." He gave me an apologetic glance. "Deoren would say, Hide under the lamp. I only thought . . . it worked at the gate?"

"At least she didn't set the dogs on us." I could feel that a laugh would get out of control. "It worked at the gate, to claim we were Attric's hire, yes. But out chasing *us*—!"

"She will know soon enough."

"Oh, yes." When he began to repeat the crier's notice I had nearly fallen off my horse. But, Two insisted, we would dodge off this track no later, whenever the real hunt brought the truth. And to claim patrol-duty let us ask for food that would last: bread, cheese, but also cured bacon, flour, oil. And about passes and tracks. However perilous that instant when the white-skinned but weathered farm-wife had checked. Stared. Then said, "Aye, ye're outlanders, I was forgettin'. Aweel, ye can ward the foothills, but there's no passes," she nodded sharply, "up there."

I squinted sidelong to the jaggedly looming horizon, rising now with every stride of my horse. "Did she mean, no passes at all?"

He gave me a swift glance. "There must be passage. For deer, for rock-scramblers, if nothing else. We will find a way."

He did not have to finish, *we must*. He glanced behind, and added, "At least, there will be no trouble with tracks."

The clear morning had begun to cloud before we passed Jurrick gate. Now the eastward farmland was disappearing under a steadily darker curtain of rain. We could take the second track, not the one we had told the farm-wife we would try. Turn the horses loose up beyond the settled land. After that, trust our cloaks for shelter and the weather to obliterate our traces, and walk, with the saddlebags over our own shoulders. Into the hills. In the rain.

* * * *

It did not get truly bad till dusk. We loosed the horses after the rain reached us, sometime not far from noon. By then the track had climbed onto open hillsides of bracken and that sullen green ling Sickle had grown, pressing deeper and deeper between crags that beetled over us as the valley closed. High crags, stacked and fractured sometimes as Rack Head had been, sometimes worn down through three or four kinds of rock, grey or black or cinnabar red, weathered to chimneys and flying buttresses, and more and more often, a precipice only flies could scale.

By the time dusk came we had found the boulders as well.

Amid the ling, smaller stones had threatened toes and ankles, especially in the rain, but up the valley the ling ended and earth rose like a cresting wave. Now we faced crevices, crannies, foot-catching narrow spots between slippery, bulging boulder-faces. Naked, massive stone.

We might have made a quarter mile, through the battle to find and conquer scaleable places amid our dangling bags and entangling cloaks, before the light began to fade. As we panted atop the latest monster, I caught Therkon's cloak and gasped, "Need to stop!"

If we went on in the dark we would break our necks: he did not have to be told. His hooded head swung to and fro, scattering drops as the seal-furs shed rain like glass. It was not denial. He was seeking any possibility of shelter. Of protection against the cold.

My own scratched and battered hands were already almost numb. I tilted my head to peer through the hood-drips. Dark, glistening rock faces, jagged and crenellated all the way to the cloud. Grey cloud, wisping close over us and twining through their battlements, steadily shedding rain. But now there was a draft behind us, a whistle and rustle in the boulder-field. The wind was rising too.

The best we managed before full dark was a kind of slot between two leaning boulders, close against a cliff. It did face cross-valley, cutting down the wind, and its top was narrow enough to stop most rain, leaving the base just wide enough for two people to edge, single file, inside. And then huddle in our cloaks with the thankfully retained saddlebags under us, to extract, finally, the bread and cheese and my wrist-knife, and amid the drip and splatter of water and the rising wind-howl, swallow the first real food of the day.

We also had a short but fierce skirmish over who went furthest in. Therkon won, mostly because I dared not shout, *You're likelier to catch pneumonia!* Nor, *I'm troublecrew, I'm supposed to protect you!* So it was he who had his back in the outer opening, while to get him in as far as possible I was banging my elbows on the rock at every move.

When we had managed, the final straw, to catch the only drinkable water by putting our cups out for raindrops, he said ruefully, "My lady, this may not have been the best way, after all."

"*It was the only way,*" Two said.

"Two thinks so?" I felt his side relax. "I thought—no. I did not really think. It just seemed what we should do." A sudden little pause. "I did wonder, why you, um, agreed so easily."

I had fussed and fretted over his fecklessness too often, too visibly. I was glad of the dark. But Two had given me the answer to that as well.

"Two says, you're the strategist. You see the big plan. We're troublecrew. We just have to make it work."

"Oh!" He might have been flattered. He was certainly surprised.

"But I wondered." It had nagged me in the fleeting pauses from necessity, all day. "Do you think it *was* your plan? Or can—it—turn people too?"

More silence. Silence so long the wind went through an entire cycle of rising scream, squeal, skirl and fall. While the rain pattered unrelentingly, and my longbones measured the encroaching nether cold.

Then he said, almost under his breath, "I have wondered that."

"Two," I swallowed hard, "Two can't say. *Insufficient data.* But surely: if there was a plan, and it did go wrong at Rack Head. Everything since then couldn't have been, uh, set up?"

More silence. At last he said, "The chain would be so long. Nouip's gifts. Hvestang's past. My—attack. The *Tolla*, perhaps, yes. A good guess that we might escape, a possibility we would try that ship. But that Frotha would take us? That horses would be at the inn?"

"Maybe it can only push where there's a, a weak spot? Like Hvestang?"

"That would seem sensible. But," he moved sharply, "who is to say what is sense in this? Or what *it* considers sense?"

No-one, if Two could not. Cold comfort, even shared. But talking was better than consciously waiting for the cold to penetrate, for muscles cramped in position to complain, for mind to trace out the still-unexpended span of night.

And better, far better, than the treacherously rising awareness of his side and flank and hip crammed so tantalisingly close. The memory of that velvet skin, the present, tangible human warmth.

"At any rate," he said, and for a moment I heard the crown prince who had also led an army, who would have been expected, however minimally, to support and reassure his troops, "we made our own choice. And whether that was helped or not, we are going south."

\* \* \* \*

Talk lapsed after that. Eventually weariness must have won out, and I dropped asleep. Because I know I had been dreaming when I came round with a strangled shriek and limbs flying upright from the black about me, not lightless air and darkened earth but water, black water, welling, rising, still and soundless as death, black water reaching to engulf me, knowing what it sought . . .

Something had my arm, noise was in my ears, a voice. All that stopped Two sparking was that known, familiar voice. "Chaeris. Chaeris! It's all right. I am here. You are safe."

My lungs still wheezed for air. I clutched frenziedly around me, my knuckles struck rock, my other hand met cloth, hair, flesh.

"Oof." I think I had hit him in the mouth. But the sound rallied me. We were on Phaerea, not the *Aspis*, in the rocks, far inland, at night. And I had just punched my charge, my troublecrew trust.

"I'm sorry, sorry—"

"Not your fault." His hand found mine, closing on it lightly enough to keep Two quiet. He did not have to say, That was a dream? I did not have to ask, You were already awake? But some things are too much to bear alone.

"It was like, at Nouip's house." I could not control the shudder. "She said, Water. Black water. Only rising round me. Like—like *Aspis*. Belowdecks."

"That is over. A memory." His hand shut hard on mine.

"Yes. Yes." I tried not to shut my eyes on the night's unbroken but earthly black, the wind's keen, the pattering drops of rain.

In a moment he said, very softly, "But?"

"But," it broke out like water spurting through those started planks. "It wasn't just water. It knew. It thought. And it was l-looking. Looking for me."

His hand clamped this time like a vice. He did not speak. He did not have to. But once begun, I had to go on to the end.

"At Nouip's house, it was like something Two sees. A, a projection. I was awake. But th-this time—it was a dream."

A time when my mind would have no defense.

The rest simply would not come out. Does this mean it's getting closer? Does it mean the thing is more aware? Getting close in more ways than one?

Therkon stirred, then began to rub my hand between both of his. "It's night. And cold. And cursed uncomfortable. If not as bad as *Aspis*." His own voice skipped away from that. "With wind. And water. The noise, the wet. Small wonder you dreamed."

"You think I was just remembering *Aspis*?" I could not keep the disbelief, the verge of disillusion, from my voice.

There was another stretching quiet. But in the end, for all the temptations, he did not fail me. He sounded flat, and very tense, but he said it out.

"No."

Cravenly I thought, I wish I'd never asked. I wish I'd let him try to fool us both. Oh, Mother, I wish I could crawl over there and hide in his shoulder like a baby, like I did at Nouip's house.

And in that brief memory of muscle's weight and warmth under my cheek, I felt the almost imperceptible vibration in his fingers. Not a tremor, something less controllable.

He was shivering.

"Fry it." To flee into concern for another was more than a relief. "You're cold, I knew you'd be cold there, you're too far out in the wind—Are you wet? Let me change places. If you get pneumonia, what will I tell the Empress?"

"My—Chaeris." Surprised, almost enough to be amused. "I am not wet. The furs are better than a tent. I am not wholly feeble—"

"But you are in the wind there—"

"If *you* get pneumonia, what will *I* do?"

A Dhasdeini man, who could never let a woman shield him, rather than shielding her. More fragile than I, after the storm and his stomach's damage. But this time, I had a face-saver to use.

"I live in the mountains. I'm used to it." I took a handful of fur and gave a little pull. "Either you come further in, or I go out." I let the silence add, *Which will it be?*

He sighed, audibly. But he had read that silence too.

I shoved my own bag to the cleft end, we tangled and untangled feet, trying to dovetail the baulky masses of cloak-wrapped shoulders and legs. Two pressed infuriatingly with memories of how much closer two people could get if they both straightened their legs and lay side by side, sharing cloaks. Shut *up!* I told her, maddened by the recall of his shoulder, his body against me, at Nouip's house, on Evva beach. I'm not getting any closer. I won't! I can't!

Then it struck me that he too was holding back. And with greater shock, that it might not all be misguided Dhasdeini courtesy.

"Two." My voice had gone so small that in a new wind-flurry I could barely hear myself. "Two won't spark. She'd never—"

Hurt anyone in this situation. Least of all you.

I felt him move again, an almost ungoverned jerk. Then, rougher than he had ever spoken to me, he said, "I am inside. This is close enough."

I could find nothing to answer that. It hurt too much.

\* \* \* \*

I woke cold through, despite the cloak, hams bitten despite the saddlebag by unrelenting pebbled stone. But I woke because, with a skill taught me on *Aspis*, I had felt the weather change. Before my eyes opened I knew the rain had stopped.

The wind had dropped too, in volume, in pitch. And Therkon had slid over, or fallen over, in sleep. He was half lying next to me, his breathing sleep-steady, his head's full weight against my cheek.

If I don't move, I thought. His shoulder was under mine, slack-muscled but solid, his hair in silky strands against my face. He was snoring a little, and bristle roughed my collarbone where his jaw had displaced my cloak. It was miserably cold, just creeping into light. But if I don't move, I told myself, I can make a dream from things Two knows. That we're in a Tower room of Amberlight, garnished with rich cloths and furs, warmed through by qherrique. That I'm a Head and he my husband, we're in the big men's-quarters marriage bed, and we can stay like this, if I choose it, every morning of my life.

Was it a minute, or five, or a yearning century? Before Therkon gave a snort and a grunt and either from a weather signal like mine or just bent muscles' complaint, came awake.

With another snort as he jerked his head away, coming almost upright on a gasp and a smothered "Dhe—!"

"I told you," I could not help it, "Two wouldn't spark."

The pause fell between us like a cataclysm. I could have bitten out my tongue. He—I could not tell what he felt. But the words were more than stiff.

"My lady. I beg your pardon." He started to struggle with the gear. "It will not happen again."

* * * *

We each sortied into the rocks. Tried to tidy ourselves up. Carved up the last bread, both probably silently cursing the lack of fire for hot food or even water. As we donned our packs I could bear the other chill no longer. It came out whisperingly small, but it came.

"I'm sorry. I only thought—it would be better—warmer—"

He turned round with a jerk. His hair was in elf-locks as on *Aspis*, his face stubbled, his new clothes the predictable wrinkled mess. But of a sudden the rigid expression melted away.

"My lady." Two steps and he had my hands. "I do beg your pardon. It was nothing to do with you. It was . . . No matter what it was. Forgive me. I did speak truth in one thing. It will not happen again."

He found a smile for me. A true smile, as he would have given me on *Aspis*. He still looked a perfect ruffian, but the sudden, redoubtable barriers in those eyes had gone.

So at least we confronted the boulders in something like the accord of yesterday.

The moraine finally topped somewhere in mid-morning. Puffing, sweating despite the wind and cold and prevailing damp, we looked out the through the low V of sinking cliffs. Into another unrelieved landscape of boulders, rising to a perfect boar's chine of jagged, unbroken rock.

"Blight and blast it!" I gasped.

Therkon heaved at his pack. In a moment his eye turned westward, and I knew his thought.

"We'll have to find another gap, or whatever this was. Work sideways, through that mess." The pack dragged at my own shoulders. "Oh, Mother. Do you suppose, at least, there's water? Anywhere?"

And again, the Mother answered. The wind gusted along the hillside, bringing a faint tinkle and gurgle. Somewhere to the west.

It was a little spring, a freshet, perhaps, falling out of a boulder interstice like a city tap. Cold, pure, fresh. Best of all, dropping into a tiny rock oasis: ling, some bracken, a spindly white-barked tree.

We had gathered twigs and dead wood and sacrificed some precious tinder, Therkon had unearthed the new little cooking pan, I had dug out ingredients for pan cakes, before the next calamity struck.

"Flour. Oil. Water. Salt, if you have it. I've watched mess-cooks make them." Therkon actually scratched amid his mare's nest of hair. "But the proportions—!"

And to invade Shia's kitchen would have been more than my life was worth.

We cooked bacon, in the end.

* * * *

What I would have given, by sunset, to see that little bay again! We had kept westward, taking the spring as the Mother's sign. By sunset we might have made two miles, or maybe two and a half. Every inch was a giant's labor of prospecting a possible route, then climbing it. Then, blocked again, having to cast, and search, and scramble, for a further advance. Not counting the back-casts, the simple dead-ends, from which I had begun to think we would never escape.

Sheer exigency, if not gravity, had pushed us steadily downhill, deeper into the boulder maelstrom, lower under what, on our side, had become cliffs again. There was no shelter. There was no water. The sky greyed, the wind probed and prised at us, and the jagged skyline beside us had never showed a sign of breaking in the length of the day. The sole blessing was that it did not rain.

We were in the bottom of the dip when the light finally began to fail. My feet were bruised to the bone, my thigh muscles felt to be falling off their bones. The pack had cut my shoulders to infuriation point. My eyes ached, my head ached. Every fiber of me ached to simply fall down, give it all best, and expire where I lay.

Therkon was staring up at the next impasse. His hood was back, his shoulders bowed. He looked as tired, as disheartened, as near the end of his resources as I felt. The only comfort that remained, perhaps, was to share our misery.

I took a step closer. I did not have to ask, Do you see anything? It was his turn to lead: he knew I would wait for a suggestion. That when he found it, he would speak.

I stood still, close behind him. Then, without thought, almost without volition, I leant my head against him, somewhere between his shoulderblades. And like the most water-hearted child, half-whispered, "Will we ever get out of this?"

I felt his breath catch. His muscles clamped. I was past caring if he took offense. But in a moment, the tension changed. He drew in a long breath and spoke.

"We will get out." His head lifted, ever so slightly. "We will find a way. However long it takes." Softly, so softly, with that steel-cored resolution I had heard on *Aspis'* deck. "We will come through, my lady. We will not *let* ourselves be stopped."

For the sake of Azo, and Verrith, and Deoren. And the Empress. And Dhasdein. And Iskarda.

And perhaps, for Nouip, and Frotha, and the Isles, as well.

I leant my head a little harder and shut my eyes. He set himself to sustain my weight. It seemed natural to slide both arms around him, as round a tree, a column, a support. But trees do not have their own hands, that closed, warm and firm however grazed and bruised, over mine.

Two can only guess how long it was before we both shifted, drawing breath again. And he let go, and I stood back, and he turned about and said quietly, "For today, this is far enough."

We mixed flour with water from our bottles, added salt to the paste and ate it raw. We drank half the remaining water. Then we curled up at the boulder foot, on the only half-flat place in sight, and he put his arms around me, and I fitted myself into his side as if he were one of my fathers, an uncle, a friend like Tanekhet. I was far too tired even to have listened, had Two brought up thoughts of anything else.

\* \* \* \*

It took a good hour to unkink next morning. But as I sipped the last breakfast water, Therkon, trying to tie his hair back, turned sharply and said, "The sun."

It had topped a skyline behind us, and the overcast had not yet come right down. Light streamed over the boulder-field, sharpening the salients with rose and gold-leaf, deepening the shadows to cobalt and velvet grey. Highlighting the western horizon, between the right-hand cliffs and jagged spines of range crest, opening a ragged but golden-edged door of celestially pale sky.

And suddenly Therkon grabbed my arm.

"Under the wall there! By the hedgehog." We had christened the massif in exasperation the day before. "Do you see there, Chaeris?" He almost shook me. "It's a gap!"

A slot, a mere crevice, at that distance. But if nothing more, it offered a goal. A possibility. A hope.

We were half the day getting there, struggling over the same old obstacles in the same maddening way. Tired out, now, bellies starting to rumble. Bruised, as well as weary. But struggling on, between awareness that we had little resources left, and the lure of that chance.

We reached the foot of our landmark buttress with hope stopping our throats. Both of us stared upward. Neither of us dared to say, *It is a low spot.* We just scrabbled and scrambled yet again, up between two more enormous boulders to the flattened third between. Panting, rising, to stand on top.

Then I yelled. Therkon whooped. We held on to each other and laughed like maniacs.

Because ahead of us, long slopes of ling, shields of pocked, naked rock stretched down and out and round to our left about the prow of the massif. And beyond that, rugged, sometimes wooded hills fell green and russet and occasionally golden toward a half-world of shimmering blue sea.

\* \* \* \*

"Oh," Therkon said.

"The Mother blight and blast it!" I cried. "From top to foot!"

We had near broken our necks scrambling cavalierly over the last downhill boulders, we had found water on the first open rocks. There was fuel in the adjoining ling. We mixed flour and water in slapdash proportions till one lot would hold as cakes, and then we ate, sprawled out in what passed for midday sun.

Lumbering afoot again, we found what the rock-shields had hidden. Our first unskirtable cliff.

A hundred feet, Two estimated, from top to foot. Not sheer, or even stacked rock like Rack Head, rather a fall of earth-faults and rock outcrops with a brief glacis of scree beneath. Obviously descendable, with care and stubbornness, but one final obstacle we had not thought to meet.

In a while Therkon said, "I think I can get down that."

"We can both get down it." Every troublecrew instinct fired to life. "But not in cloaks and packs."

He opened his mouth. Shut it again. "You mean, drop them over the edge?"

"I mean, lower them on the rope." We had fifty feet of light line, a final security buy in Jurrick. "I climb halfway down, you put them over. I tie the rope there and lower them the rest."

"*You?*"

He broke off. Gave a little grunt. *You would think so*, it said. And, *You have named yourself troublecrew. You will not, you cannot let yourself sit up here and watch me take the risks.*

"Have you climbed," he enquired sternly, rearguard action, "round Iskarda?"

"I have." Yes, on beginner's work, with Azo or Verrith or someone else, and a firm hand on the safety rope. But it had to be more than Deoren had ever allowed him.

He gave me a long stare that became resigned halfway through. Then he crouched on his heels and began prospecting the cliff face. "You will at least allow me to work out the way."

"I'm expecting it," I said, and unfastened my cloak.

The edge was shaky, old crumbling sandstone under earth and grass, but Two exhumed a score of memories for dealing with bad sandstone in Amberlight. What matter those were from a mine? I persevered, slowly as I could manage, heeding Therkon's directions. Despite this final hold-up, it was almost bliss to move without a pack.

Astonishingly soon I heard him call, "Far enough, Chaeris."

"You are near halfway down," he added, when I looked up. "Find a tie-stay and I will lower."

We made one drop of it: the two packs, laced together, cloaks bundled between, Hvestang buckled atop. He had carried it on his back the last three days, but he had more sense than to try to wear it now. I settled myself behind a sort of stone-hedge outcrop. When the bundle arrived, I had found a handy belaying rock. After it all bumped safely among the scree I called, "Now you come down."

While he was where he could keep at least token guard. We did not have to speak that either. I heard him make a little dry noise before he began to climb.

And when he had settled into my temporary fort, I stood up and stretched sore and bruised limbs in anticipation and added the final caution. "Wait till I'm down."

It was partly the sandstone. Old, crumbling, and toward the bottom, damp. And partly the weathering that had undercut the cliff so even Therkon did not notice, and partly the chimney, as Two says real climbers call it, that she knew how climbers would descend, and that looked faster than spidering sideways to find the next properly inclined place. It was perhaps twenty-five feet to the bottom. If I told Therkon, he would argue and dispute and demand I tie the rope on, wasting even more time. I braced my boots against one side and my rump against the other and started down.

Fifty heartbeats later the chimney-side gave way.

\* \* \* \*

Two recalls everything going very fast though what memory I have is slow. My boot's sudden sickening slip. The fall's foresight coursing pure terror in vein and nerve. A sudden gyre of revolving rock and sky and the searing knowledge I would land face down and then a lightning dazzle of white.

The world resumes as if coming awake. Fingers sting. Nails broken, where I must have clawed the stone. Black and white flashes, eyes reclaiming light. Shadow, pattern, place and objects coalescing round me to a frantic, familiar voice.

I managed words, eventually. The world was dizzily remote, and the indrawn breath hurt, but I got out, "All right."

The voice stopped. Resumed in an undertone. Profanity and prayer mixed. Something touched the upper of my two shoulders. The other seemed bedded into the ground.

"Did I break—"

"Keep still. Dhe fry you, you've no business being alive." His voice shook. Gratitude's wrath. "I don't dare move—where do you hurt?"

"Fingers." I shut my eyes to get the signals clearer. Two had memories of disabling blows, injuries far worse than this, but these damages had been imprinted on my own, original flesh. It had never encountered such a shock.

But now Azo's training revived. Eyes shut, I tested hands. Arms. Toes in boots. Cautiously, whole feet. Legs. Bruises screamed on a thigh, a hip, the lower shoulder, I wanted to rub six places at once. But bones came first.

Hands would move. Arms. Head—

"Don't move that!"

"Have to—find out."

I opened my eyes again. Rock confronted them, inches away. Mossed, lichen-stained, fallen rock. And rock that might this moment have been cracked apart.

"Everything where you fell . . . Two blew it up."

"Wha—"

"Two blew it up." His voice was shaking now too, the hand back on my shoulder as if to confirm I was breathing flesh and blood. "Pieces went up like—chips. You're mostly on bare dirt."

"Oh."

It would make sense later. My head rang, blood was seeping from somewhere into my mouth, but Two insisted that was no more than consequences of a mild impact. I was awake. Therefore I was not concussed. I could sit up if I chose. I took in a whole breath.

The world went round in a black kaleidoscope. I had to keep very still till it came back.

"Think . . . cracked a rib."

I could just whisper. I heard him spout a new gush of maledictions: I knew he was thinking, what if it's worse, internal damage, liver, spleen, heart?

"Two says. Inside. All right."

I heard him move. He had sat back on his heels, shaking too now, down to the indrawn breath.

"Chaeris. You reckless, Dhe-forsaken idiot—"

With a more than human effort, he cut it off. When he spoke again it was, if not the hatchet man, at least an approach to the crown prince.

"You landed on your side. Two says things inside are all right. Does your head hurt? Your neck?"

"Feels . . . all right." I had to speak in very small sips. "Neck . . . try."

His breath hissed but he kept quiet. I moved my head a fraction, then carefully, further, to and fro. Tried flexing whole limbs. He first protested and then helped me, eventually, to straighten out. Then, even more carefully, with a pack under my head, to turn on my back.

The cliff was a half-dozen yards behind me, the circle of shattered stone well out in the scree. I had either fallen wide or bounced, and I did not care to find out which. The bruises yowled in flesh's complaint, there was a gash up the outside of my right arm, that had torn my precious shirt. And with every breath my body informed me more and more clearly: I had cracked or broken at least one rib.

"I don't dare touch." Therkon was still kneeling beside me, more frantic now I had him in full view. "Gods, that I never bought physic, even bandages. Poppy syrup . . ."

I think he almost wrung his hands. Then his head went up. His eyes swept wildly once to and fro, and he started to yank at the gear scattered about.

"Let me tie that up." He meant the gash on my arm. He wrenched clothes from his own pack and I almost flinched at the rip of cloth. Not, I wanted to wail, another new shirt! But he was doing a masterly job of bandaging, spitting orders as he worked. And seeing them carried out.

"Put my cloak over you. Yours under. Put your head on your pack. Drink this. You still have the knives?" He checked that for himself. His other hand shot somewhere behind me, he yanked Hvestang to him as if it were a rotten stick. "Chaeris, you must keep still. Do you hear? You are *not* to get up, you are *not* to try to walk." As if I were truly his troublecrew. He had ordered Deoren about just so. "I will bring help. You are to wait. That is all you are to do." An anguished check. I could see, *What if there are wolves?* flash behind his eyes. He said harshly, "If anything comes—you have the knives. But I will be back. On Dhe's name I swear it. I will be back here by dark."

He sprang up to buckle Hvestang on. Then of a sudden he plumped back beside me and whipped something from his inner coat pocket, pushing it into my pack. "If you *are* troublecrew," he was trying valiantly for lightness, "you should ward this."

The jewel pouch. I had just time to recognise the shape and shade of it before he dropped a sudden fleeting kiss on my forehead and leapt up like a literal deer. I heard his feet receding, thud and crunch and reckless slither, down the lower slope.

\* \* \* \*

Two can reclaim very little of the next few hours. I think, despite the plaints of minor damage, including what I found was a bitten left cheek, that shock and the previous days' effort overwhelmed me, and I actually fell asleep. Or at least dozed, roused ever and again by the ribs' scream when I tried to move naturally, or draw in a full breath.

When I woke fully the passage of time spoke from my stiffened wounds. Even in the warmth of the furs, I could hardly bear to move. Until I craned to read the colour of that distant patch of sea, and realised, with a hop of the pulse, that it was nearing dark.

And Therkon had not come back.

He will come, I promised myself. He said, by dark, and he keeps his word. Even if he doesn't find help, if he can't find anything at all, he'll measure by the sun, and turn back when he knows he must. He'll be here by dark.

Except if he lost his way. If he tripped, fell, injured himself in the hills, if he did meet a wolf, some other hazard, outlaws, bandits, just an unwary step on an unknown path and he's lying out there now, truly incapacitated, with a broken leg?

Or unconscious. Unable, if scavengers found him, even to resist.

Impetuous unschooled lunatic, he had left his pack, his cloak, the saddlebags, food, water. If he fell or disabled himself, how would *he* survive the night?

I did some pungent cursing, envenomed by fright and helplessness. Crazy chivalrous Dhasdeini, to rush off with nothing but an Outland accent, a princely manner, Hvestang and a few coins in his coat. We knew nothing of the south, but Frotha had said "pirates." What if he walked straight into such hands? And with no ward at all?

It was the worst moment, till then, of my young life. Not simply the physical pains, the friend's, the more than friend's loss, the knowledge of failure and mistake. Worst was that so much was my own fault.

If I had not let him go. If I had not tried that chimney. If I had not been so cocksure as to do it without the rope. If I had thought to make him take at least his pack. Amid Two's more and more frightful scenarios the indictments seared like blazing brands.

But one attempt to push the furs off enforced the bitterest truth of all: I could hardly move. I had two packs and Nouip's cloak, all our possessions and food as well as the gemstones, and I could not carry them. I could not even totter off down hill to search for him. On the mere chance that he was close, and that I could find him, I could not hazard all that in the dark.

After a while I did get up. Hauled, cursed, battled my impedimenta round me, up against the cliff. Drank more water, warned by Two of the drain that follows wounds and shock. Sacrificed one of my own shirts, to girdle my ribs, so I could at least trust an unwary breath.

After that, I crawled out to hunt deadwood in the outliers of what would have been our first Phaerean wood. Then with bitter, bitter guilt I used our flint and tinder to light the first sticks. Settled Verrith's knives beside me, and braced myself to pray out the night.

\* \* \* \*

That is the only time in over seven hundred years of memory for which Two refuses to retrieve anything at all. My fragmentary human recollection tells me that it seemed an eternity, as you might expect. That I wept a great deal of it, as you might also expect. That, even more predictably, every bone and muscle in my body pained, but not so badly as my conscience or my heart.

By the time the sky paled, less predictably, I had a plan. I stirred up the last coals left beyond the packs. Heated my last water to drink. Pushed, with travail and trial, both packs in against the cliff, tied the last flour and the water bottles up in Nouip's cloak, made a sling, and got it on my back.

Walking was possible, however the ribs panged. Azo had long since taught me to track, and Therkon's trail was blatant, skids, heel-prints, crushed tuffets, overturned stones. Downhill straight as water. I cut a withy for staff among the first saplings, and shuffled into the wood.

The trees were writhen and scrawny, from aridity, I thought, as well as wind. The tracks led me among them, except for some reckless bound or spring I could not match. And where he had leapt across the little pool of seep that started a brooklet, I stopped to drink and fill my bottles amid the croziers of new spring fern.

Straightening up, I heard the shout.

Below me. No great distance, perhaps just beyond the wood. A man's voice, a clear and carrying Halloo.

For one wild instant my heart leaped. And dropped again. Therkon's voice I would have known anywhere.

But if it was human, it was help, however dubious. I braced both hands on my shirt girdle and produced a breathy wail.

They came bounding up into the wood like the proverbial hounds on a scent. Two young men, muscular and fit as trouble-crew, with farmers' sunburnt, weathered faces under the ubiquitous knitted caps. And they were trackers. The leader had run his eyes right to me along Therkon's traces before he jerked up his head and stopped.

In a moment he said, "You're the girl."

My heart almost jammed my throat. But caution or joy alike, there could only be one answer. I managed to whisper, "Yes."

He scanned me, a hillman's quick expert check. The face was frank enough, broad cheekbones, open, curious expression, pale skin bearing a healthy flush. He was barely breathing hard, though his sleeveless jerkin and rolled shirt-sleeves bore leaf and twig wrack as well as sweat.

"Aye, y'r brother found us." No doubt my face had been an open book. "Tumbled out o' Kjelfield spinney flat on his face." The accent was thick as Nouip's, with a slight but different drawl. "An' near as short o' words. But he tell't enough to follow." He made a brief gesture behind him. "Skeag 'n me back-tracked."

No huge task, from what I had done myself. But the corollaries were pressing away my breath. "M-my brother. Is he—where is he?"

He should have been back with if not before them, if he had not been able to do it last night. Had Two's worst projections become reality, had he fallen, slipped, injured himself?

"Nay, lass." The first one was beside me. "He found us in ane piece, did ye not hear? No thanks to the track he took." Another glance back. "We had him to the house, but he was aye beside himself about ye. An' we've no healer ourselves, m'cousin's off down-coast. So we fed him, and lent him a field-coat. And he was off, down to Ve Pool, before yestreen eve."

Ve Pool. A southern town. A port? Frotha had mentioned it. He had gone after a healer. He could not have come back in the time. "He, he asked you to come up?"

The pause, their faces, made my tongue dry in my mouth. "It's far to Ve, Ve Pool? He could not come back?"

The silence was worse than their looks. I took a step forward, nearly losing all control and bawling, What is it, what's happened, what do you know?"

"Ve Pool," the first said in a hurry. "It's a way, aye, but we tell't him the healer's house." He took an audible breath. "If he made haste, an' he did haste, we thought, he'd be back before dark. So. We waited." He gave me a hangdog look. "'Till t'was too late to start."

"So," Skeag picked up, in a matching accent but a note or two deeper, "we were away up here the morn, soon as we could track."

*Forgive us,* both faces said, *for the delay, for leaving a stranger injured and alone in wilderness we at least know well.* Then Skeag worked his shoulder, and for the first time I noticed the packs both of them bore.

"We brought what we thought handy. An' right glad, to see ye up o' y'rself, an' this far to the fore."

Oh, Mother, some distant voice was crying. O, Mother, O Dhe, O Lord of the River and all the other world-gods, let it not be true. Let it be a story, a misunderstanding, a mistake.

My lips were cold. I seemed to fumble the words. "But he—my brother."

The first one took me lightly but firmly by the arm. Only when Two did not spark did I realise I was swaying on my feet.

"He went," he said quietly, "to Ve Pool. He knew his way. An' he'd find it, if he found us."

"Then what—how—why hasn't he—"

There was pity in that look, and something more.

"T'would be the will o' the gate-watch—an' mebbe t'lord Stokka—that he's not come back."

# CHAPTER XI

Could I have run headlong out of their farmyard down the seaward cart-track to Ve Pool, I would have outstripped light itself. But when they undid the chair of linked hands that had borne me the last two miles downhill, my own traitorous legs gave way.

They were very patient. They carried me into the dour grey farmhouse, sunk amid its ancient herb-garden, and deposited me on a settle by the central hearth. "No' Ve Pool today, lass. We'd take ye, an' welcome, but we've not time now. We're fair athwart the lambing. Can ye not hear?" And indeed, the house rang with the bedlam of orphan lambs squalling from the nearest byre. If lambing had taken them up the fields to encounter Therkon, and they had already spared precious time to retrieve me, I could not ask more of them now.

"Were Veenn home to fettle 'em—but Eemis said, Cross-birth. She'll maybe be back the night. We'll get y'r gear then. Dath," Skeag finished, "start the milk heatin'. I'll see to this."

He found me some bruise salve, washed my arm and re-bound it, with a bandage this time. I managed to keep my own shirt at least half on, until he brought me a voluminous replacement, under which I could slip the knife-sheaths quite off and bundle them in Nouip's cloak. With its rounded ends and unshapen stone wall-slabs, the house was eerily like Nouip's, but its slate roof had a fire-vent, the furniture was all wood, there were rugs and woven cloths. And the ache in my heart was infinitely worse. As Skeag set down the salve I caught his sleeve.

"Who's Stokka?" I said.

His face changed. He answered flatly, "Master o' Ve Pool. An' half the bay lands round."

"Why would he—my brother—" But I could imagine far too many causes why Therkon, with Hvestang at his side, imperial hauteur in all too close reserve, and in a perfect panic about me, might fall afoul a town lord. Especially one who invoked a look like Skeag's. "I have to go!"

"Small help," a new voice snapped, "to run y'rself arse over head into Stokka's brangles. If ye didna break y'r own neck first."

Skeag said, "Mam, can ye see to this?" on a note of clear relief. As he scuttled round to Dath by the warming pots, the cracked old voice retorted dourly, "See to it. Aye."

She was creased and bent and shrunken as a mis-cured lamb hide, but her eye was alert as her speech. "An' a bonny lass for breakin' bones over: as ye'd likely guess." She passed the salve with one hand while the other propped her stick on the settle. "Small wonder that—brither—o' yours was in a fuss."

My head ached, my heart ached worse, panic was a fire in my gut. But none of it would help me here.

"Stokka, ma'am." It was not quite what Skeag had said, but 'ma'am' might do. "He, what's he like?"

She cocked an ear to my voice. Then she took my hand, turning it up and down, running her fingers to the wrist. "Such fine skin, both o' ye. Smooth as petals. An' regular blackamoors." She actually sounded admiring. Her eyes came up, rheumy and sunken and sharp as tacks. "Outsea, would it be?"

"Outsea, yes, ma'am." Would I have to fence here as we had with Skatir? "Stokka?"

"Stokka's greedy as a herrin' gull an' cold as three-day fish. An' a fine Outland lad wi' such a blade droppin' in Stokka's back gate'll not smooth out for a pretty look." Another piercing glance. "Put the salve on. Then ye'd best have somethin' to eat."

They ran sheep, with just a couple of milking cows, their sole cultivation a tiny field of gold and bronze brindleflowers. A precious crop, petals for the Isles' most exotic perfume, pollen for their own four hives. She directed me to honey and sheep-cheese for the day-old bread, with a herb-tea to follow—"helps the aches"—and chattered throughout: the neighbours who shared the "high vales," the seven mile cart-track which brought up the community's flour. "For we work naught but hides and wool." The virtues of her grand-daughter, who had drawn two fine lads to the farm. "And she'll have it after me, as she should."

I fidgeted through it all, maddened alternately by the pang of my ribs and the fire in my brain. At this very moment Therkon could be embroiling himself beyond salvage, captured, imprisoned . . . would Stokka recognise Hvestang? What would he do if he did? What if Therkon's imperial dignity ran riot again? If his stomach misbehaved, with neither healer nor healing to hand?

Her own hand caught my shoulder as I tried to scramble up. "Look'ee, lass. Ye're hirplin' sidelong an' breathin' like a lung-sick ewe. If ye *could* get down there today, ye'd bring him more trouble than help."

She was right. Bitterly, cruelly right. But I could not help the stifled protest.

"I let him go. I got myself hurt to start with. It's my *fault*."

"Aye. Times we think so." The hand tightened. "Veenn's likely left the willow-bark. Now, ye can help me make a posset—I don't get about much better than ye are—an' then, middle-day or no, ye'll be best tryin' to sleep."

\* \* \* \*

Veenn came in late afternoon, a brisk, silent, compact woman with an elusive likeness to the men and her grandmother both. Between greetings and starting supper she felt over my side. Nodded to my, "I think I cracked something," said, "Ribs, aye," and held up two fingers. "But ye've not started the bone-joiners, an' they're worse than crackin' a bone. I'll strap ye up, for surety. Take more willow tea. Here's a needle to fix y'r shirt-sleeve. Ye can try to walk, the morn."

And with the lamb-stew bubbling steadily over the renewed fire, she sat down by me on the hearthside, and speared one steady grey-blue look into my face.

"How came ye," she said, "to be on t'Fell Cliff?"

I stammered. Her gaze sharpened. "Ye ne'er came up this way."

"No. No . . ." That look told me I was facing the true House-head. And she would have answers, whether I chose or not.

"We, we're Outsea." Whatever the risk, safety might lie in truth. "We lost our folk in a wreck. We came to Jurrick, to see if there was word of them. And, um, we had to come south. Overland."

Her eyebrows climbed to her short brown hair. "Ye came from Jurrick *overland*? Right through the Brettabreck?"

"The hills up there? Yes."

She breathed a while. Then, "An' where were ye bound?"

This at least was easier. "We hoped to find a port. Take ship. Go on south."

"South?" This time her grandmother, in the settle behind her, stirred too. "What did ye want down there?"

Desperation winged my wits. "Do you know an island called Carsia?"

"Ye mean, Kaastria?" Her brows went up and stayed. "What d' ye want with Kaastria? Especially now?"

"Now?"

"Kaastria's waste. The ports're gone. Hondeland town's gone. The folk're gone. The wave—They've talked of it all year. What d'ye want *there*?"

"*What wave?*" I could not have stopped Two if I had wanted. The first actual details of a destruction, at last. "*Where did it come from? What did it do?*"

She stared as if I had run crazed. "What did it do? It o'er-ran Hondeland, that's what it did. Took half the town folk, and most o' the farms. An' foundered the fishin' boats. They had to turn off, those that lived, an' take ship for elsewhere."

"And where did it . . ."

Her face shut. "Where d'ye think it came from? Waves come out o' the sea."

The stew bubbled. The fire cracked. Black water rose silently behind my lungs. I tried desperately not to let Two voice the final too betraying word.

"I meant: was there a storm? A—and which direction? North, west, south?"

She made a hand-push. "Storm, not that I hear. Hondeland looked east. Behind Bakki cape, to ward t' sou'easterlies." She shrugged. "T' wave came west, I suppose." Her brows came down again. "But what did *ye* want there?"

I scratched frantically for truth, at least as a base. "There was a boat. A wreck, on our shores. Someone gave us a message. We were to find Kaastria . . ."

"Why'd ye not take ship in Jurrick, then?"

"It, ah, I—" The headache had fuddled me, the willowbark had slowed my wits. "We, ah—"

"Had this sword I'm hearin' of aught to do with it?"

The answer must have been plain enough. She frowned openly. "What happened in Jurrick?"

I held my temples with both hands. The herb tea had eased some aches, but the urgency was unslaked. And perhaps the only safe way of fencing here was truth. But not all the truth.

"We wrecked near Sickle island. We got the sword there, and it made trouble in Grithsperry—"

"Girl, ye're worse than a cow for holdin' up milk. *How* did ye get the sword?"

I looked in that steely grey-blue eye and knew she would not let be until she knew.

"It was a gift. From a, a Seer. She said, he would have use for it."

The eyes went suddenly wide. "The Seer of Evvamoor?" She almost drew back. I could only nod. When she spoke, her voice had hushed.

"Aye, that'd put an orca 'mong t'herrin' for Grithsperry. An' Jurrick too?"

She knew something of what Hvestang was, if her family had not recognised the blade itself.

"The lords—they called us wolfs-head, yes."

"So ye took to the hills. An' carried it right across." It was something close to accolade. Then her shoulders rose. "An' now y'r feckless lad runs it right in Stokka's mouth!"

"He didn't know, he—! What will Stokka do?"

"Sit, girl. Nothin' you *can* do, right now. As for Stokka, no sayin' what he'll do. He's a creature o' humours. Most of 'em bad." The frown was back. "Tiran's luck him seein' it at all. But if the lad's not here—"

"The gate guard?"

"Nay, they'd take Stokka aught such that caught their eye." The frown blackened. "Tiran's luck indeed!"

Two broke in irresistibly. *"Who is Tiran?"*

"What, ye've never—?" She swung round on the hearth coping and pointed to the coign of the door, central in the long wall, as so often in the Isles. "D'ye see that?"

It was the household shrine: a small wall cupboard held the familiar crowd of candles, the familiar unfamiliar shapes. The Mother, if only by the figurine's largely symbolic skirts. And the other, the unknown.

"The Mither, you know her? The Lady o' Summer? Aye? Well, t'other has to have his honor too. That's the one chases her, and fights her, and beats her and is beaten, year by year. That's Tiran. The Winter Man."

The Winter Man. The Winter Man's cloak, Skatir had called Nouip's other gift. No doubt my own eyes popped, for she gave me a shrewd stare and I stammered, "We know the Mother, she's our own Lady, but I never heard of that."

"Belongs to the Isles, maybe. *Of* the Isles, surely." Her lip curled. "Stokka's own lord, they say down there." Her eye returned to me, holding a frown. "When the boys come we'll eat, and then ye're for bed, girl. Little enough ye'll likely do with Stokka. But ye'll have more chance, in a day or so."

The woman of the house, indeed, I thought. In more than one sense, I found, when they settled me on a pallet and pile of bolsters by the hearthside, the grand-dam creaked off behind the curtain at the room end, and Veenn and Skeag and Dath all climbed into the big main bed across the hearth.

Skeag must have seen my face. He looked surly for the first time, and growled, "Not like the Empire, hey?" And sudden tears stung my eyes.

"Not like the Empire, no. But I live beyond it. And in my place, my own mother—she has two husbands herself."

Iskarda. It stabbed me harder than the cursed ribs. Snow and mud along the streetline, my own hills rising above. My own folk, my own family, my mother, my fathers, returned safe from their own quest, out to meet me at the gate.

I lay holding tears back in the big bed's confounded silence, feeling suddenly more at home, and at the same time more bitterly alien than ever before.

\* \* \* \*

Veenn was out with the men before daylight, leaving the matriarch to shepherd me. Yes, there was porridge in the breakfast pot, and no, I could not go out till Veenn saw me again. "Ye've eyes on ye like a wood-owl and if ye slept two winks t'wasn't one by next. If ye're buzzin' to do something, wash y'r face in the bucket there."

And comb my hair. Laborious enough, if with my own new comb. The men had retrieved our packs while I slept. Bolsters and blankets had to be folded, the fire stoked, orphans' milk pots prepared. Scraps thrown from the door for fowls. Mild exercise, thankful distraction, for perhaps half an hour. From thought of where Therkon might be, and with whom, and what he was doing now.

I looked desperately round me. Then Two's reflex dovetailed with Azo's schooling: this time, there were crucial questions to ask.

Like the men, the matriarch had a civilian's recall. Ve Pool lay at the end of a bay behind a long hilly peninsula, welcome shelter from the southerlies. Of its relative size she had no idea. "Bigger than Jurrick? I've ne'er been north." One land gate opened from the outer wards, beyond the market-space, at the end of the inland road. Guarded, yes. "Stokka'd not leave a mouse-hole without ward." But his close retainers lived with him, round "t'brech."

The "brech," presumably a fort, sat on a hillock, with a prospect over the peninsula's quarter-mile neck. The healer's house was on the street to the brech's single door. She had some idea of the size, but further questions made her stare. "Iron or wood? Bars? Eh, lass, how'd I know? How many paces from the gate to the healer's house? To the brech door? How many guards at the gate? With what gear? When do the watches change? Lass, why d'ye ask? How d'ye *know* to ask all this?"

I tried not to grind my teeth. The cheek would hurt. And then the anxiety became too much to contain.

"Ma'am, my brother. He's not my brother. He's . . . an ally. A great ally. Of my folk. He's, highborn. He's never been alone without, uh, watchers. Troublecrew. My folk at least trained me. I'm the only ward he has left!"

Her eyes had got almost round, but she was shrewd, however ignorant. "Never thought ye were kin," she said, with some satisfaction. "Ye talk different. An'," she eyed me, and let that go. "Guards, is it? 'Troublecrew?' So ye're thinkin' to skirl down on Ve like a winter southerly, an' spring Stokka's trap?"

"I don't know what I'll have to do. I only know I've got everything except his sword, and he—" I nearly did tear my hair—"he needs me *back*!"

Doubtless she passed it all to Veenn, when the other three swept in halfway through the morning. Because Veenn paused long enough to examine my arm, listen to my pulse. Have me raise my arms, walk a few paces, try to lift a pack. At that result she sucked in her lips. Then she took a second look at my face.

"Thursis," she said to the matriarch. "He'll be up with the flour, aye?"

The grand-dam's eyes snapped. "Aye!" She tapped her palm. "Lass, have ye a penny or so? Yon Thursis lives two hills across. He'll take ye and y'r gear to Ve Pool the morn, he's goin' down for flour. But he's mean as a half-starved billygoat. He'll do naught open-handed, even for us."

"I have money." I could have cried with relief. I scrabbled through my shirt's inner pocket for the last of my Jurrick allowance. "Silver, if he takes me to an inn." I would never walk far with both the packs. My fingers found coppers, something smaller. Brushed the gem pouch, and stopped.

What these people had given us was beyond pennies: not merely help, and kindness, and a minimum of questions, but some of the farm's most precious time.

I worked a stone out. It was a hazian, red as fire on the horizon, even in the dim-lit house. "I have money for Thursis. I—we—would like you to have this."

"It came from Jurrick," I said, in the hush. "We, uh, sold an heirloom. It's," I felt my face flame, "honestly come."

Veenn moved abruptly, cupping her palm. When I set the stone in it she glanced quickly, in something that might almost have been awe, into my face.

"Ye," she said softly, "ye're highborn too. Are ye not?"

"If I am, it's no matter. Not for something like this."

"What's y'r name?"

"Girl," she said, when I hesitated, "t'would be mannerly, for our givin' thanks. In somethin' like this."

So what could I say but, "I am called Chaeris"?

"And whence do ye come?"

"My, my home place. It's called Iskarda."

Naturally enough, she did not know it, though even in Phaerea they might have heard of Amberlight. Her brows knit in another frown.

"How old *are* ye, Chaeris?"

"I'm"—twelve years old, and seven hundred. "I've trained since I was little. I'm old enough!"

I gave her a stare, she gave me one back. After a moment, her look cracked in a rueful quarter-smile. "Aye," she said, and tucked the hazian in her grandmother's little hearthside kist. "For what ye're ettlin' to do, ye're old enough."

\* \* \* \*

What I was supposed to be "ettling" I did not ask. Thursis was as dour as he was mean, and his twin donkey-yoke slower than the sun itself. I did not grudge the apparently outrageous five pennies hire, but even Two could not get information out of him. Between impatience and the bumps that jarred my ribs to mutiny, I was almost screaming before Ve Pool came in sight.

Amid grey boulders and scrubby treetops the last descent offered glimpses of a white, unnaturally perfect semi-circle of beach. The inland hillock blurred against the peninsula beyond, but a boulder-hump on its foreland had to be the brech. The town beneath fell from a huddle of market-crowd into a haze of smoke, blurring a further, untoward amount of white. A rudimentary quay shielded galleys, perhaps, moored inside. Fishing boats, like other small craft, were relegated to the beach.

The farm-women had not cut me completely loose. "Put y'r hair up," Veenn ordered, "an' wear that cap. Ye're a cousin." She made me learn a genealogy obscure as it was intricate. "I've sent ye to Vithre for some belly gripe I've not the herbs to fix." That would explain my hunch and slow movements, even the frequent curse. And get me, not merely past the gate-watch, but directly to the first place for questions. The healer's house.

When we reached the market in mid-afternoon, most people had already left. The donkeys plodded through scattered booths up to the ditched rampart and palisade, with the outer gate's single leaf of heavy tree-trunks set in the midst. A lackadaisical watch, all leather jerkins and quarter-staves, waved Thursis through unchecked. And Vithre was at home.

He came at Thursis' hail, a slender man almost as brisk as Veenn, dark of hair and skin, with the eyelid fold I had last seen in a Sea fort, silver flecks in his hair and a chased silver bracelet on one wrist. "Veenn's kin, is it? A gripe-pain?" He nodded me down from the cart. "I'll see what I can do."

The amount of baggage did raise his eyebrows, but he heaved it up unquestioningly. Thursis grunted and poked the donkeys. Ill-mannered to the end. I followed Vithre and the packs inside.

The "street to the brech" had been barely wide enough for the cart. The houses were stone, I thought, as usual. But these had been whitewashed to a dazzle, and the side-ways opened on a warren of passages and alleys under a dome-bubbled stretch of common roof.

Domes, I realised, blinking at Vithre's heels, because the actual houses were round, rooms and roofing both. And white-washed inside as well, almost blinding white. Vithre led me past a central hearth in a space crowded with household gear, into one in a cloverleaf of subsidiary rooms, each with its own dome, each lacking more than a curtain for door. He dropped my packs beside the cunningly curved wall cupboard, its pots and clay bottles reeking of assorted herbs, pushed a pestle and mortar along a slab of stone work-counter, and said, "Where does it hurt?"

Then he took a second look and said, "You're no kin of Veenn's." A third. "You're a girl."

"Yes, sir, not kin, sir, no. Veenn thought this best. I only want to ask about my brother, sir—"

"But you are hurt."

"Just cracked ribs but he thought it was bad, Skeag and Dath sent him here—"

He pulled the mortar back up the counter and reached for a pot on the nearby hanging shelf. "Your ribs," he said, "first."

"But my brother, sir—!"

He turned from the mortar, the refracted light limning his face, with its healer's reserve, and something more.

"I've seen no stranger," he said, "but you."

* * * *

It was willowbark again: I knew by the smell. When he nodded to the three-legged stool by what was clearly his bed, I sat numbly till he fetched a steaming pot from the hearth. He had set the mash to steep before I managed, "But—where can he be?"

If Therkon had not reached Vithre, he must have run afoul the gate-watch. Who must have taken him to Stokka, and neither Two nor I could bear to extrapolate what might come next. *Oh, Mother,* I was screaming silently, *why did you take Azo and Verrith and even Deoren away from him, why did you leave him no recourse but me?*

Vithre had heard the panic behind the words, the tears almost out of control. But he was a healer, who thought methodically as Azo herself.

"When did your brother set out?"

"Three days," he repeated when I had told him. "You're Outsea." It was not a question. "I've heard naught of outland travellers in Ve. Not these last three days."

"But, sir?" I could not find the diplomacy to point out he was a healer, not Stokka's right hand. How would he know?

His eyes flickered with a brief, almost boyish smile. "I think I might hear." He was inwardly, deeply amused by a private jest.

"Yes, sir." I had no time for superfluous enigmas. The next steps loomed ahead, a vista that crushed me into the stool. Veenn and the grand-dam could get me in the gate and through to Vithre, but to confront Stokka? Trace a possible prisoner? Take on the assembled force of Ve Pool to get him out?

I had known better than to ask. Two had the memory of troublecrew and Trouble-heads, back through centuries of Amberlight. But they had been fit, healthy, groups of fighters. What could I do, a single, still almost immobilised girl?

Azo's voice said, *Start at the beginning, like anyone else.*

And the beginning, here, was the gate.

If Therkon had ever reached the gate. If he had not fallen, injured, immobilised himself tearing helter-skelter down those hills that first night, if he had not lain invisible by the cart-track this very day, starving, mute, savaged by passing wolves, already dead?

I don't believe it, I told myself. I won't believe it. He's alive. He has to be alive.

In that case, I knew where to start.

"Sir, is there a, a tavern? An inn? Where the gate-watch might go?" Impossible to walk up to the gate and ask outright. As crazy as to enquire at the brech's own door.

"Not the brech?" Vithre asked.

The cock of his eyebrows, my answering look, was all he needed. He handed me the posset. "Bide a spell. Later, someone might bring news."

I sat till the posset took effect, managing to keep my shirt on, if lifted, while he checked the rib straps. There was an anxious moment when he caught the bulk of dressing in my right sleeve and wanted the shirt right off, but I pleaded modesty and only slid the arm free, thanking the Mother I was right-handed: the knife-sheaths were on my other arm.

Sight of the gash made him add a poultice of comfrey and mutter under his breath. That done, he asked after Veenn and the farm, and pointedly, not about me. I suppressed Two's fountain of questions about him and the house and Ve Pool and Stokka, and did my mannerly best to reply, but once the ribs settled I could bear no more.

"Sir, if I could ask a favor. May I leave my, our, packs here? And look about the town?"

He gave me a piercing healer's look. He did not say it was no place for a solitary girl. He did say, "You'll not be asking much."

Meaning, my accent would betray me, beyond a question or two. "No, sir, but I might see something. Maybe overhear . . ." And I could scout, if nothing else.

He flicked his brows up, but he was as sharp as Veenn. He saved his breath and let me go.

\* \* \* \*

Supplies and livestock, I guessed, were traded in the marketplace. In what seemed more a fortified village than a town like Jurrick, I had little hope of craft shops. The irregular, tunnel-like house-connections would have lost me anywhere bigger, but I processed haphazardly up the short central street, sallying briefly to right or left. My gear and cap made me almost invisible, though the traffic was all pedestrian, and light. Mostly men, with Vithre's dark skin and eyelid fold, a good number armed. They had the indefinable air of a place lacking law, where streetgoers allowed for trouble, and expected to handle it themselves.

Down one alley an entrance-smell announced, *Liquor*, but the room was empty beyond. One doorway brought a clacking rattle Two identified as a loom. Another door, shut, the usual solid unpainted timber anomalous among the whitewash, had carven over its lintel a crossed pair of oars. Ahead the hill rose, and over me loomed the oddly amorphous hummock of the brech itself.

It was not whitewashed: the outside was worked grey local stone. It went up, Two and Azo's estimates told me, perhaps three storeys. A cat-walk circled the top, round a roof that might be slate, from the great patches of lichen splashed across. The granddam's words echoed in Two's recall.

"Round, aye, what brech's not? An' they have double walls. For strength, aye? Inside? There's the hearth, an' livin' rooms round the wall, an' the lord's quarters upstairs. How many floors? I'd not know that!"

The door's great stone lintel would have trebled Nouip's. Metal glinted below it in the afternoon sun. Helmets, perhaps, or sword-hilts. It was closer than bow-shot, in a moment I would either have to go right up, or retreat. And I was not going to walk straight in on Stokka, however anxiety ate at me.

The opposite street-side did have an opening. Near its corner, a smaller door gave out clinking, clanking noises, and more than a single voice.

The doorway had no insignia, but the sounds told me before I reached the jamb and peeked around. Metal on metal, whetstone, hammer. Ve Pool had a swordsmith's shop.

The actual workers must have been in a side room. Instead of a hearth, the main room had a cleared space between a pair of thick but battered wooden posts, and a rampart of long, solid, narrow chests, backing the counter where the smith showed his wares.

He stood behind it, a burly fellow with his trade's cropped hair if not the apron, a blade in his hands. Its sheath glinted atop the counter, through the chancy indoor light. The customer, half-facing the door, had a hip against the counter in an indolent sprawl. A tall, thin to gangling, fairly young man with short hair and a neat cock of black beard, in a fur-trimmed half-coat and calf-high, gold-buckled boots. The clothes spoke louder than the smith's stance. I had run on Stokka himself.

As my belly melted and I shrank by pure reflex a second voice cut the smith's rumble of, "good work, aye, old, indeed, but well-balanced." Sharp yet soft, the other voice demanded, "Who's there?"

My shadow must have intruded just far enough, motion had caught his eye, I could not flee or even retreat and I could not answer or he would hear what I was. As vision whited at the edges I screamed at Two, *Fry it, don't burn things, be some USE!*

"Who's there?"

He had straightened. Tautened, hand dropping by instinct to his dagger-hilt. In a moment he would be on me and everything would fail.

Two said in a gruff octave-higher version of Deag's voice, *"Only m-me, m'lord."*

I am quite sure my heart stopped. I know my breath did, for the endless instant before Stokka's elbow relaxed. The smith's head turned, both stances saying: A boy. Nothing to worry about.

And Stokka said, "Come here."

Oh, Mother, I had time to pray, as I slunk round the door jamb. Help me. Help us both.

I kept my head down. I could not look up. Nor did I think. I waited on Two.

"Who are you?" said that light, too light voice.

*"M kin o' Veenn's, m'lord. Up to Fell Farm."* The acme of half-grown yokels, Two mumbled it at the floor. Stone-paven, dark-edged flags. I could trace the shape of each one now.

"What are you doing here?"

*"I, ah, we come in for flour, m'lord. Finished loadin'. An' I heard . . . I heard . . ."*

The sword-sounds in the workshop, still heedlessly going on. She had the embarrassment, the inarticulate, adolescent male longing perfectly. I did not think I would ever breathe again.

"Ah."

A world of grown male, lordly male comprehension, condescension and pitying amusement at once. "So, boy. Look here."

A gesture. The smith, astounded, disapproving, masking it all behind that suppressed apprehension, set the blade down beside its sheath.

"D'ye know what that is?"

Silver on the black-dark scabbard, in an interlace of gripping beasts. A darkened-ivory hilt, above an armslength of dark grey, serpent-patterned steel.

Lungs, heart, my every muscle locked. *I know what it is, yes,* something screamed silently. *I know far better than you!*

"Well, boy?"

The first hint of impatience, wind-breath before a lethal, habitual squall. Two cringed my shoulders as the smith's had and gulped into the floor, "Ah, ah, m'lord—a sword . . .?"

"A sword, aye." The smile was back, fragile and deadly as a predator's calm. "Never seen such before?"

Two let my eyes slide over it, linger over it, longingly, despairingly, while the grief and fear choked us both. The blade was here, however lost. It had found me, Nouip's deadly returning gift. But where was its owner now?

"N-no, m'lord."

Artful deceiver. She got in far more than rustic awkwardness. Recognition, transmitted knowledge, transmuted longing. Desire. The yearning of a farm-boy for a blade whose status he might guess from song and story, but could never hope to possess.

Stokka laughed suddenly and swept Hvestang from the bench. With a scissoring Shhh! it went home in the sheath. He held the scabbard out by the middle and said, "Here."

Neither of us had to dissemble. We gaped by reflex, my eyes, I should think, almost falling down my cheeks.

"M-m'lord?"

He was smiling: a light, casual, blood-chilling smile, fey and perverse as the act. "A fine blade, Starrin says. Fit for a young champion. Take it, boy. It's a gift."

He did not say that he himself had it unjustly, perhaps by force, certainly not by law, that its mere possession ought to be a curse. Even if he did not know its reputation or its name. But to outward appearance it was precious, an heirloom. Anything less fit, more deadly for a farm-boy, could not be dreamt.

And he would pass it on, like poison, whether or not it threatened his town as it had Grithsperry, and smile over the gift.

"D'ye not want it, boy?"

The smith's jaw clicked up almost as fast as mine. Odd humours the lord of Ve Pool might have, to say the least. But we could hear the wind rise, both of us.

Two was wordless in sincere earnest, but she got my hands out. Reverently as in genuine awe and gratitude, closing round the sheath.

"M'lord—"

"Eh, boy. One day, I'll claim the toll."

Still light, still smiling, that threat fit to rob a court lord of words. He left the counter. Gave a nod, as if they had merely exchanged day greetings, to the smith. Two managed to move us, as he passed, into something approximating a clumsy bow.

"M'lord . . ."

We could not have done more than breathe it, anyway. Stokka half-smiled. Inclined a head, flicked a finger on my cap, crossed the threshold with a soft, easy predator's tread. His shadow vanished.

From deeper in the alley came a steely clink, and the shuffle of men's boots.

* * * *

When lord and guards' steps had faded, the smith let his breath out in one explosive, "Whoof!"

"*What—why—how—where—*"

Two was barely articulate, but I could have done no better. The smith gave us a dispassionate, perhaps jaded, certainly comprehending stare.

"Stokka. D'ye not know y'r lord?"

'A creature o' humours. And most of 'em bad.' Temper, caprice, I had expected. Nothing like this.

"W-where did he—What is—"

Two turned the sheath, with as much disbelief as a farm-boy, with grief that could masquerade as bewilderment, in our hands. The smith pulled his shoulders to his ears.

"Come down with it from t'brech just now. Judge me the blade, he says, an' set a price."

"But how did he—"

The smith dropped his head between his shoulders and his voice lower yet.

"Come here with an outlander. Queer fella, maybe crazed. Got crossways wi' Forthir at the gate an' they hove him up the brech."

My belly was solid ice. I strangled projections neither Two nor I would be able to bear. But after all, it hardly needed more explanation. Any of it. Therkon had run afoul the gate guard, and their master after them. Whatever Stokka did with its owner, he had taken Hvestang: but not to keep. Because, Two's comprehension flew in lightning leaps of precedent from among, powerful, vicious men, Therkon had stung his pride or his fey humours so badly he would take the crueller revenge. He had been going to sell the sword. As if he deemed it unworthy to retain.

Until a more delicate, more absolute stroke of contempt offered. So he had given it away. A prize among swords. To an ignorant, yokel youth.

The dark-bordered flags were all swimming in a pool of tears. The weight of Hvestang was a millstone. I think Two hardly considered, either, what we said.

"What do I—what am I to—"

"Keep it," the smith answered curtly, not looking up. "More'n *your* life's worth, to do aught else."

"*But the—what happened to the, to—him?*" Two would have gone on, *Did you hear, does anyone know?* The smith had already jerked his chin out and added an elbow thrust. *Don't ask, because I can't answer. Don't make trouble for me either. Get out.*

I stumbled often on the way back to Vithre's house. Tears, grief, blurring our sight. Over my shoulder, Hvestang's unaccustomed length and weight. Desperation in my wits where What-nexts whirled like leaves in a drain, and under all, recollection's shock and the wake of terror's relief.

Two *had* been of use: Two had done what I could not, what I would never have dreamt to do. Impossible as Therkon's ruse at the Jurrick gate. And she had deceived Stokka, she had used Stokka, she had retrieved Hvestang in the world's unlikeliest way.

Or had there been the unlikeliest help?

The grey-walled, shadow-patched street went round like a top. I got a hand to a wall and tried to stay upright amid the maelstrom in my head.

Full of odd humours, Stokka. True enough, perverse, unpredictable, capricious as a whirlwind and more vicious in intent. How could anyone—any thing—have foreseen his act?

How could anyone or anything have set it up?

The world whited out and Two's logic stepped in lightning jags through my brain.

The black water. Water that wanted me. A sure way to bring me where it wanted. Take Therkon from me. Ensure I would follow. Remove any cause for delay, by returning the sword.

And where would I be meant to go?

My fingers relaxed on grey hewn granite. The street coalesced. Calm was around me, the calm of concluded logic, or the eye amid a storm.

Either Stokka has Therkon somewhere, or he has discarded him like his sword. If he is here, we can find him.

If he is not, then only in one direction will all intents coincide. We reasoned it on Sickle. However perverse, however backhanded its achievement, the logic holds. If Therkon is no longer in Ve Pool, we know which way he went.

I swallowed a snivel and drew a careful longer breath. Then I re-settled Hvestang over my shoulder and made for Vithre's house.

\* \* \* \*

A flock of children swirled about the hearth-space now, while amid their herring-gull shrieks three women peeled vegetables beside the built-up fire. Their eyes grew round at sight of me, and wider at the sword. I managed a wave toward Vithre's door and a mumbled, "See the healer, have to," and one opened her mouth, one half-rose in apparent consternation, but I was already past.

Vithre's curtain was drawn, a darker shadow in the waning light. The house was intrinsically dim, despite whitewash as well as the fire. I found the curtain edge and without pause drew it softly back.

Vithre was home, yes. Pressed up against the wall beyond his bedside with a male knee shoved deep between his thighs and being enthusiastically kissed by someone whose antique but recognizable mail-coat shouted, No common guard.

I eased the curtain down as if it were poisoned, throat choked on my held breath. If Vithre saw, reacted. If his companion, like Stokka, noticed the change of light . . .

I tiptoed back a half-dozen paces, and stood trying not to shake. I could not leave, Vithre had my packs. I could not join the women, Two might not be able to change my voice again, or manage extended conversation, and they might already know I was a girl. But nor could I stand here, in earshot of what might happen. I had seen my fathers kiss, and learnt what its various signals meant. The stranger had more in mind than a warm, Give you good day.

And if that mail-shirt signalled aright, Vithre might indeed get news that mattered. From Stokka's true right hand.

I smothered the embarrassment. Eased Hvestang off my back. Hunkered down, as well as I could, against a further door-jamb, and prayed the Mother that if I had to eavesdrop, the stranger would justify soldiers' name for haste.

Through the child shrieks and women's chatter came a deeper mutter, a smothered laugh. An endearment, by the tone. Something that might have been a question, then a louder, rougher laugh.

"Up the hill just now, smirkin' like he's drunk t'creampot. He'll not be needin' me the night."

Vithre murmured something, sounding smooth as a scribe after a stable lout. From the other came a thoroughly boorish hoot.

"Him! He'll not trouble Ve again. Down the wharf this mornin', an' ye mind Thralli docked yestreen? Ha ha!" A regular donkey bray. "Trust m'lord to make the shoe pinch. Put him on the auction block!"

Vithre said something startled and the other gave a snort.

"Outland, ain't he? Outsea, at that. None to trouble for him, naught to trouble us. An' ye flout our Tiran-son, ye'll pay a merry price!"

The firelit whitewash went round and round again. Sheer horror blurred my sight. Therkon, the Empress' son. Dhasdein's crown prince. Sold as a slave. Put on the auction block.

Two had knowledge of slavery, Two's appalled projections shot across my sight. I would have sunk into the abyss myself. But for Therkon to be stripped, prodded, examined like a beast, sold to the highest bidder . . .

And who had bought him? From where?

Vithre or the Mother heard me. Vithre said something more, and his lover answered in that brash, careless voice.

"Nay, Thralli's away the night. Sailed on the midday tide. He'd near a cargo, and don't reckon to get its price in here."

Stokka had not just sold his victim through a slaver, he had sold him *to* the slaver. And the slaver was gone. While Thurkis' accursed donkeys were snailing downhill, Therkon had already been aboard ship, and by midday, the ship had sailed.

The firelit room was red-shot and quivering like light through water. I tried to breathe, and wondered, from the pain in my temples, if my heart had stopped as well. Tears filmed the light right over. Pit, fundament, nadir of calamity. Therkon was indeed gone from Ve Pool, gone where I could not follow him: even if I could find ship or boat to take me, I had no idea where to go.

* * * *

The ribs brought me round when nothing else could. I had been crouched and hunched too tightly, too long. Unheeded, the pain came, then deepened like a drill until I might have gasped, but I had to straighten up.

I leant my head back on the door jamb and a child pack thundered past me in a cascade of shrieks. Supper had begun cooking at the hearth. Fried onions, perhaps, a crisp smell of fish. Sound and smell infiltrated, while the tears dried on my shut lids. And behind them, Two made herself heard at last.

Almost she used actual words: the amazement was clear enough. Had we not worked through the logic? No matter what we knew, or what the slaver planned. There could still be only one direction to go.

South.

It would help, I was thinking sourly, if "south" included some sketch of islands, of possible ports, of distances and direction. Then my eyes shot open as the light changed, and someone was standing over me. A blurry trousered shadow, with a permeating odor of fish.

"Lad? Lass? What's to do?"

My hand shut automatically on Hvestang, making it a stick to help me up. He was about my height, gaunt, it seemed, in a thick, perhaps knitted jersey instead of a coat. Short hair gave him a halo, though his features were against the light.

"Are ye here for Vithre?" He had dropped his voice as if he knew what was behind the curtain too. "Ye can come to the hearth." The glance, the nuance added, Vithre may be some time.

Speak as boy or girl? I had no time to waver. Two simply fell out of sight.

"Th-thank you, sir. Veenn. Veenn knows me. She sent . . ."

"Does she so?" It was more than interest. Understanding, and to my over-strained ear, yet more. Because he did not exclaim, *You're a girl.* He did not even ask about Hvestang. Merely pointed his head along the wall-circle, beyond heaps of household impedimenta, and led the way.

So when he turned at another dark but uncurtained doorway, Two burst out instantly, "*Sir, where has Thralli gone?*"

I bit my lip and wanted to kick Two as well as myself. But I had still under-guessed his knowledge, or else his wits. It was a bare five heartbeats before he spoke.

"Ye'd be the sister. Aye?"

He had seen Therkon, spoken to Therkon, or simply shared the wave of sensation and scandal that must have washed Ve Pool from edge to edge. He knew enough to argue backward from my question. Relief left me all but breathless. So much less to explain.

"Yes, sir. But Thralli. Does anyone know . . ."

The slight tilt of his head said he might have caught our voice switch, but he answered readily. A heavy accent, but assured authority in that deep, composed voice.

"He'd maybe go down-coast, to Thring's Deep. Or up, to Mirkadin. Ye'd say, west or east."

Still on Phaerea, then. My lungs seemed to empty with hope. "Not—not somewhere else?"

A heart-sinking pause. Then he said, "For that, ye'd need to know whence he came."

Hope collapsed again. I could just limit myself to a single, "Oh."

He looked over my shoulder. I guessed at what from the angle of his head. "There's one might tell ye," more than neutral this time, "in a while."

Vithre? His lover? I could never ask direct. And what risks to be here, visible, when the lover came out?

Two took the opportunity before I could speak. *Sir, do you know the next island south?*

"South?" Startlement, perhaps. I braced for a reprise of Veenn's response.

"Eh. There's Terrace, an' the Fleshes, though they're more sou'west. An' Rostack, but that's sou'east?"

Three islands, and how to choose, and which way would our enemy's intent skew Thralli's own choice? "You don't know? You can't guess? Which way Thralli might . . ."

He understood then. His head lifted, his shoulders went tense. "Ye're never meaning to—"

"I must." I could stifle the shout, but the tears welled again. "My brother, I have his gear, I have his sword, I have—there's money, I can buy a way. I can find, I can guess that, but I have to go. I must!"

"Girl." It came out almost on a hiss. He rubbed hard at his chin. Stubble, probably. "If ye *could* go. Could travel. Find him. What could ye do?"

For an instant all the obstacles and terrors I had foreshaped loomed up again. Then I cast one thought at the alternatives and fairly fired at him, "What could I do here?"

I literally heard him grunt. Another scud of children screeled past. I stared at his shape with the tears of fear and resolution teetering on my lashes, and through their film saw him rub his chin again, and suddenly lift his head and shift his feet.

"Aye." It came heavily, but sure. "Ve Pool's no place for a—" an isolated outland girl whose nearest known kin had already mortally offended Stokka. He glanced over my shoulder again. "Wait ye here. There'll maybe be word, later. If not, I'll speir about myself. There's folk I know. Ye say, ye've money?"

"I have, I can get money, yes. I can go now?" And if Therkon had kept the jewel pouch, might he have bought off trouble for himself?

"Ye're goin' nowhere, the night. Tide's awry." He gestured into the dark, uncurtained room. "Bring ye that—brand o' yourn, in here, an' bide till I call."

It was his own room, or at least, his family's room. I fumbled my way in the shadows through scents of fish and children and soap and some kind of aromatic oil, past a cradle and truckle bed to the big box bed, as they call it, a kind of walled enclosure on the floor. But it held at least three down quilts, and a couple of soft pillows, "down o' the southern geese," and when he had settled me, with a pillow for bolster and a hand free to find Hvestang, he drew the door curtain. Leaving me in comfort, and, I realised, concealment. With at least a glimmer of hope.

# CHAPTER XII

I woke with a heart-stopping jerk. Dark enveloped me, swallowed me, pitch-black darkness deep as water was sucking me down.

Not water. Softness underlay me like Nouip's fur, but solidity sustained it. Hard, unyielding, rock or earth. Horizontal, more uneven than her bed shelf. And the dark was paler overhead. Rimmed by a solid edge of shadow, higher than I was, peculiarly curved.

*Hearthside*, Two said, matching memories of Nouip's, Veenn's, Vithre's houses. Curved hearthside. Above us, because we're horizontal. On a quilt, on the paven floor.

They must have moved me from the box-bed while I slept. Reaction almost over-rode the too-familiar complaint of jostled ribs. Jostled, and Vithre's willowbark wearing off. Had I slept so deeply they could have moved me without a murmur, had they stripped me too, searched me, found—

My hands flew in pure fright, but the sheaths were on my left arm, intact. The jewel pouch bulked under my palm, the cloth on my breast was my own wool-and-linen Iskardan shirt.

The house was utterly quiet. All in bed, room curtains drawn, no light left but the last faint afterglow from the probably banked hearth. Even Vithre's lover must have gone, or surely, they would never have moved me out here?

In the darkness, something creaked.

My heart all but came out my ears. Stone floor and walls would not creak. Wooden furniture creaked, but only under an impulse, a weight.

Leather might creak. In someone's belt.

Azo's skills and schooling fired like nerves themselves. Night-training, ambush, we had done it over and over. Especially, being ambushed in a bed.

The wrist-knife flew into my palm. I sighed softly and rolled as a sleeper would, getting my back to the hearthstone. Low, but still a ward. By the Mother's mercy, with my right arm uppermost. Knife folded against my breast behind a quilt edge. Perfectly palmed to throw.

A long, long pause, while my blood thumped in my ears and I worked to keep my breathing loud, even, sleep-like. At last, a whisper in the darkness. The brush of touching cloth.

A needle stabbed overhead so brightly my eyes squinted. Moved down, but my eyes were shut.

Another eternity when I used ears alone. At its end, again, a rustle. And this time, on the flagstones, the whisper of a tread.

My eyes shot open and motion hinted in the all but extinguished hearth-glow, air shaped the body approaching, big, solid, bending toward my shoulders, the arms' swing down to my pillow, my face.

I slammed the knife home where all those drills had taught me, whipping upward with the blow to put my body-weight behind it, right where motion and mass triangulated a human throat.

Darkness screamed and mass whirled up and back. I was out of the quilts with the ribs' shriek unregarded as my hand flew up my sleeve for the elbow knife, darkness spun about and pottery clattered, metal banged, furniture crashed in a perfect avalanche. But from somewhere near my quilt-foot new ferocious motion launched itself, visible if inaudible, and I palmed the knife and threw.

I dived for the hearthside to the soggy carrying thump. As at the targets, both ear and muscle affirmed it had gone home. I did not wait for the choking, bubbling sounds to confirm it, I was swarming round the hearth with a hand out to ward spit or cauldron, praying the Mother for a replacement weapon, a pot, a piece of wood, or, acme of desire, a kitchen knife.

Something bumped down, heavy as a falling tree, on the stones. Something else bubbled, coughing, rustling, scratching like weight dragged over rock. From my right hand, where I knew now the inner rooms lay, rose sudden human noises. Sounds, babble, outright shouts. And presently, the wavering glow of light.

* * * *

Someone was weeping. Someone was praying, by the tone. Someone was babbling, all women's voices, but none of them mine. With light at hand the emergency alarms had shut down, and now my abused ribs were exacting their full toll. I all but doubled up on the hearth edge, clutching my side, feeling tears run, trying not to scream aloud.

Male voices deepened the noise. Light came suddenly toward me. As suddenly the hubbub stopped dead and I saw what they had seen.

At first it was just a bulk on the light's rim, another motley heap of household goods. Then details opened out of it: the dark base, spreading, glistening. Then, more sudden than dawn, identifiable pieces. A hand. An outsprawled boot.

And another hump in the half-light beyond. Dead men. We—I—had killed them both.

I doubled up in earnest as shock's aftermath and horror struck together. Trained, yes, I had trained for trouble, for attack and ambush, but in all that stringing of nerve and reflex no-one ever bled. No-one had ever died. Not by my own, active hand.

The light came closer. A male voice, vaguely familiar, said, very deep and low, "Thrif."

Silence replied.

The light moved. The voice spoke again.

"And Tjofor."

Some shock in it. Some regret. No grief. And no surprise.

The light stooped lower. So low that he, and I, and those beyond him, saw Verrith's knife-hilt, upright in the upturned throat.

My stomach rolled. Dimly through the struggle to control it I heard exclamations, more than shock and surprise. "—killed each *other*?"—"Tjofor?"—"but his knife's there!"

The light swung round. Swooped abruptly. Its bearer set the candle on the hearth rim and held something else up, a lantern, to show my face.

"Lass," he said, quite quietly, "did ye do this?"

"I—I—w-woke up—there was s-someone here. I heard—they tried to, to grab me, I think, one came—there wasn't *time*—!"

Time to ask, time for second thoughts, margin for mistake. Troublecrew training is made to eliminate that. For troublecrew, at the crisis point, there is never time to doubt.

Hubbub broke out again, astonishment, consternation, disbelief. A nuance that made the dead neither strangers, nor well liked. Known, for things that made this outcome horrifying, but not a surprise. Then one voice burst atop the others, a woman's shriek. ". . . let them in, the wicked besom, t'is all her fault!"

Another yelled back and I lost the sense. Through it the man beside me said curtly, "See the door." I almost tried to get up before motion in the dim air told me he had addressed someone else.

He half reached out, and stopped himself. "Bide ye, lass," he said under his breath, and then, louder, "Heima? That's enough."

The woman's clamor eased. In the relative quiet Vithre said behind me, from across the hearth, "The bar is snibbed." And, slightly louder, "As I left it when I let Rekkir out."

The women burst out again, louder with fury at being baulked. The man beside me ignored them, but he tilted the light-source in his hand away from me, up toward the roof.

As the light circled slowly I heard steps round the hearth. Beside me Vithre said, "You've jarred your ribs."

A healer's tone. A healer's conclusion. A healer's single-minded concern. I felt a laugh near hysteria catch in my throat.

"Let me see." He eased down beside me, waiting a moment before he touched my shirt. I could just straighten enough to let him lift it. His fingertips brushed the strapping and I winced, and he drew back. "Willowbark." Another brush of fingers over my left wrist. "So." He sounded almost amused now. "No wonder ye'd not strip yestreen. Arm-knives, eh?"

I managed a gulp that might mean, *Yes*, and he stood up. Went to the nearest body, and with a healer's coolness, slid the knife out of the throat. Turned it once in his hand, moved on to the other. A longer examination there, then he brought both back to the hearth.

"Home to the hilt. Into the gold. In the dark." He sounded more wry than amazed, let alone shocked. "Girl, where did ye learn that?"

It was almost a relief, for once, to tell the truth. "In my—home place. The, the guards. They taught m-me. From when I was young."

Verrith's knives, Azo's council, Zuri's unrelenting drills. The sinews and spine of Iskarda.

"Young?" Vithre was saying softly, and now the amusement was plain. "And ye're so old now?" He broke off. "Fiskri, what's there?"

The circling light came down. "Smoke-hole," said Fiskri, in that deep voice I had identified at last. "A line fast up there."

"So the lass never let 'em in."

Fiskri did not dignify this with any sort of comment. The light simply swung back to the bodies. The other onlookers had come closer, a shifting wall of shadow-feet and hands and sometimes white garments blurring the light, so only Vithre's presence kept my hand from springing for the knives he still held in his lap.

"This," Fiskri said soberly, "may be my fault."

The onlookers got no further than gasps.

"I speired round Drek's taproom the night. About Thralli. I'd to let out . . ." he paused, and went on. "Had to let out, there was maybe another outlander, seekin' passage. Ready to pay."

And these two had been there, or had heard from someone who was.

"Lass, I'd ask ye to forgive me." Fiskri's voice had gone deeper yet. "I never saw this pair around the booze. I never thought such—illdri—would break house-faith. Guest-faith." His shape straightened a little. "For my house—for Ve Pool—I am shamed."

I tried to find a disclaimer, courteous or not. But his kindness had been the final straw. All I could do was whisper, "not want—bring trouble here."

"Trouble, aye!" The woman burst out again as if a cork had popped. "Ye outland hussy, we're the ones with trouble, left wi' these blothgra on our hands! What'll the lord say, what'll we do the morn—!"

"Heima!" Fiskri still did not shout, but his voice was a slap in the face. She gave a gasp and stopped.

"T'is Ve Pool's wrong," Fiskri said grimly, "come of Ve Pool's work. My work."

"If she'd never—!"

"Heima, I'll not tell ye again."

He waited to confirm the silence, before he went on.

"Outland or kin, a guest is a guest. And a healer's charge is his bond." He was, I realised, defending my first appearance at the house. "Would ye have y'r brother deny his craft?"

Heima knew better, at last, than to reply.

Fiskri turned a little, the lantern beam swinging, and not, I thought in a moment, entirely by chance, across my face.

"The lass is grieved as any would, at such a thing. To come on her by stealth, in a guesting house, by night." The anger burned up in that somber voice. "If she defended herself, t'is no more than a guest's right. Man *or* woman." Cutting Heima off at the butt of an objection about women bearing weapons, let alone being able to kill with them. I could guess that all too well.

He paused, letting the lantern trace other faces in the dark. Two more men, one darkly stubble-faced, the other with tousled brown curls. Three women in toe-length night rails, their hair in braids, a scad of awe-silenced older children, all teeth and eyes. Fiskri was, I understood, delivering judgement: as head of the house. Thinking out the terms that justified it, as he went.

"For these two," his toe touched, so lightly, the edge of a boot, "t'is this house they broke, and through my fault." His eyes moved through the lanternlight. "Kerlin, will ye see the children settled? And y'rselves as well?" The other women, I realised. His eyes moved again. "Sheinn, Halri, come ye here?"

The quick, low-voiced men's talk must have gone some time. I missed most of it, for almost immediately Vithre went off for willowbark, and then coaxed me to sit on the quilts, my back against the hearth. Despite the aftermath jittering through me, the proximity of the dead, even the illogical fear that this place was no longer safe, I must have dozed, then. For I came to with another start, pulse if not limbs leaping, as someone hunkered down by me and Fiskri's deep voice said, "Lass?"

"Vithre says, ye're fit to walk." The slight upward ending added, *Is this true?*

I nodded, gazing into the pools of shadow that held his eyes, sunk deep amid gaunt, broad cheekbones, high, corrugated forehead, all caricatured by the upward-thrown light. "If ye put that cap on, an' y'r hair up, soon as it's light, Sheinn'll take ye down the beach."

The beach. Outside the gate, so we must wait for the gate-watch to open for the day. I had to gulp.

"Yes, sir, I'm so sorry to have brought this trouble on you, I never meant to do it, but—the beach." Did they mean to cast me adrift as Frotha had? My left hand had suddenly, unintentionally, shut on Hvestang's sheath. "If you please, sir? My packs?"

"Sheinn'll take the packs for ye. Ye've a cloak? Aye. Put—that, then—underneath."

"Yes, sir." Another who thought ahead. I took a careful, thankful breath. "But—the beach?"

"*Aerful*'s buoyed, but t'is low-tide. She'll be half aground. Sheinn'll see ye aboard. *Aerful*'s my boat. Herrin' boat," he expanded belatedly. "Ye'll find stores there. Vithre'll give ye herbs."

Herbs, stores, a boat. My head swam with fatigue and stress and hope. "Yes, sir. What am I—"

"Bide ye till we come. Belowdecks, aye?" A somewhat self-conscious pause. "Ye'll maybe mislike the reek, but . . . T'is these." He gestured briefly, the direction clear from the distaste in his voice. "First we'd a mind to leave 'em in the street, an' let the clack fall as it would. But there's too many questions loose an' too much known already. About ye, an' y'r brother, an'—what I've blabbed. So we'll let the loobies come, an' gowk an' squawk an' carry the word. Thrif's father, he'll be grieved, but I doubt he'll cry blood-debt. Not with 'em lyin' here, dark lantern an' line an' dirks an' all. An' the door full snibbed."

My head reeled as Two caught us up: they meant to get me out of the way, of gossip, of retribution, of Stokka's undoubted interest. They meant to run the gauntlet of talk over a pair of locals dead. But in Ve Pool, where slavers landed as a matter of course, men slain in blatant burglary would not warrant an open feud.

And they would decide all this themselves.

"Will the lord not say, not judge, what's happened? Who's to blame? To pay?"

Fiskri snorted softly. "For this pair o' line-snippers, off his own grounds, an' maybe trouble kept from him after? Nay."

"Oh."

"So ye're away out, and no word left o' ye, Stokka'll let it go."

"But—but!" The reality spun back on me. "How were they killed, what will you say happened? And—and—"

And would everyone in the house tell the same tale?

"Ne'er you mind for Heima. She's a tongue on her, and flings blame about. But she'll not tattle over this."

"Yes, sir." Could the children be so suppressed? "But about what happened? What will you say?"

His shadow shrugged. "Happen they'd a disagreement, an' fell out. T'would no' be the first."

"No. No. Wait." Even if no-one made a true, ruler's enquiry, how would they explain the wounds, the men's own, clean blades? More vitally, what they had been doing here?

Then light burst on me, with the blaze of a full dawn.

"Sir, sir. Say they came to rob me and I killed them. Wait." The next connection struck and I clutched Hvestang off the floor. "With this."

His mouth fell open. I yanked Hvestang to me and almost laughed aloud.

"If they doubt, if even Stokka doubts, say the sword led me. Like in the stories, the outland stories." I could hear Therkon in the Sickle uplands, reciting the Delta saga of the sword that fought by itself. "I just had to hold it, it made the kill. And now it's gone, we've both gone away!"

And Stokka, Two was almost making me laugh aloud, Stokka gave me the sword, it's Stokka's loss, for the deaths it's Stokka who'll be to blame.

Fiskri's mouth was still open, but he was catching up fast. "Aye. Aye." His face spoke the conclusions back to me, Stokka muzzled by his own deed, motive, means, both evident: everyone could blame the absent outlander. "Aye, lass. So long as ye're out o' the way, that'd be best of all."

Out of the way. Abruptly the malice and pleasure quenched. "Yes, sir. If I could stay on your boat. Just a day. Perhaps, then,

I could walk to Mirkadin. Or Thring's Deep? And, and try to find a ship." With the packs, and Hvestang, how far would I get? But I could not stay to endanger them. And to follow Therkon, I could not delay.

"Walk?" Fiskri all but toppled off his heels, he straightened up so fast. "Did ye not understand, girl? Ye'll walk to the *Aerful*, aye. I had no time to tell ye. They were talkin', round at Drek's. Thralli, he sailed for Rostack. Thinkin' a sale, maybe, in Eithay town. Once fettle this, we'll be down the boat wi' ye, the three of us, an' so the Mither smiles, we'll catch the noonday tide."

* * * *

Sheinn solved the pack question by calmly hitching them together, wrapping a swathe of net around, and hanging it all over his shoulder like a pair of saddlebags. At the gate he jerked his thumb to me and observed, "Some o' Veenn's kin. Wantin' a passage to Mirkadin." He rolled his eyes and the gate-watch swallowed his yawn in a laugh and a glance at the damp, louring grey sky.

"He'll maybe regret it, aye! But ye're never goin' to Mirkadin just for him?"

At which Sheinn cast his own eyes heavenward and answered resignedly, "T'is Fiskri taken a bee in the ear this time. Swearin' sure, somewhere by Rostack, we'll find fish."

"Fish?" The watch's answering eye-roll died in an expression I had not expected. Then he touched knuckles to his breast and said, all but under his breath, "Mither grant him sight."

* * * *

*Aerful* means Sea-fowl, but she was no flyer, only a three-man fishing boat, even smaller and slower than the *Tolla*. She took five days to make Rostack, and for the first three I was more than happy to obey Vithre's commands. "Get aboard, get below, take this when it's needed." He had made me a whole flask of willow-bark, already compounded and stoppered with an actual cork. "And let yourself heal." With a pause, and a wry glance. "The ribs as well."

The flask survived upending in my packs, and in those three days I commended him to the Mother over and over again. Not merely for the surety of sleep in the cramped, fish-acrid quarters among three strange, if reticently respectful men, or for the drowse that cocooned *Aerful*'s constant saw and pitch in what Fiskri called "a sour milk wind," but above all, for a way to ease the shock. To break the memories' cycle. The terror of death. The sounds of dying. Worst of all, the thud and sink of a blade in naked human flesh.

By the fourth morning the fug belowdecks outweighed that slow subsidence. I crept up the two-step companionway and turned Two loose on deck.

*Aerful* sat low in the water, with a pronounced rake from a higher stem, her paint a faded blue with now dingy white trim, and black seeing eyes. She had a single tall mast and gaffed mainsail, and her living quarters were far rougher than the *Tolla*'s, though most of belowdecks was also devoted to holds. She was one of what, a bare five years since, had been a twenty strong fishing fleet.

"Gale took 'em," Fiskri told me. "Southerly, out o' season, out o' strength. Put the fifteen of 'em straight on Skeia Rocks." He stared somberly forward, past the tall leach of the dark-red sail. The sky there was grey, as it had been since I came out of his house, grey as the miserly, restless sea. "Never picked up more than a couple o' boys."

Fiskri had told me all I asked about Terrace, about Mirkadin, about Thralli. Above all, about Rostack and Eithay, and Two and Azo's tenets made me near insatiable. But I knew better than to demand, What brought the gale? Let alone to mention Sthassamaer. When it came to the Why rather than the How of the steady calendar of calamities, Fiskri would clam up faster than Veenn.

Rain spattered in constant drizzles, and the wind, tetchy as the ocean, chopped yet again from south to south-east. Fiskri shifted the helm and muttered tiredly under his breath. Halri stuck his head up from mending an over-mended net, and Fiskri shook his head. No tacking yet. I knew now why not. Why he himself looked so gaunt. Five years and more of calamities had brought Ve Pool near starvation. He would conserve all their strength.

Five years, Therkon had said, since the unseasonal storms began to wreck Dhasdein's ships. What had happened to drive the weather, the seasons, life itself awry, five years ago?

Too close to the brink that mystery had brought, Fiskri would not help me speculate. I looked into the eye of the wind instead, and said, "Do you think it'll storm?"

He gave me a slightly odd glance. I wondered if the memories of Sickle had somehow infiltrated my voice. Then he shrugged his canvas-swathed shoulders and said, "Pray the Mither not."

Cold comfort, after all their help. I tried to repay by working with them over the scanty meals, the nets, but I had found no real recompense before a smudge climbed from the persistently surly sea, and Fiskri said, for the first time letting me hear tension eased, "Yon's Rostack."

\* \* \* \*

At closer quarters Rostack was lofty and forbidding as Sickle. "Aye, well, t'is named Red Cliffs." *Aerful* had to beat long and hard down-coast from the prow of Nebin Head, with its swirling sea-birds and the crash of surf too vividly reminiscent of Evva beach, before the grey sea surrendered a beading of human work behind a lower point. Halri, at the tiller, nodded to me and said, "Eithay."

Grey, white, more somber blues, under yet another rolling hinterland, the dull green and muted browns of winter ploughing, only slightly touched with green. Spring was later still, on Rostack. I stared at it through the nagging wind and felt the heart beat in my throat.

Thralli would not travel fast, Fiskri had said. He might well have called at Mirkadin. We would not catch him there, with a day's handicap, but, "That tub o' his don't tack better'n a netter's float." We would catch up here.

And Therkon had been lost for three, five, eight days now. What sort of voyage had he made? How had they fed him? Had his stomach broken out again? Had he been chained, beaten, battered, atop almost certain hunger and cold?

Had he managed to keep the crown prince suppressed?

I shut my eyes on the image of that imperial hauteur confronting a slaver's mind. A slaver's powers. My hand clenched on the wrist-knife and I bit my tongue on, Can't we go faster than this?

Eithay did have a short mole and quays, but in a stranger's port *Aerful* naturally had no berth. We dropped anchor by a covey of similar boats whose rigging Fiskri read for me like a book. "Somethin' from Hamair. Two out o' Cuwen. A Hivell trawler. An' the last two'll be Kaldr boats."

"Kaldr?" The timbre of sadness caught my ear.

"Been movin' north this last year."

More about the reason, I knew he would not say. "They're all from further south?"

"Aye."

Strangers, as we were. But unlike us, dispossessed.

Fiskri was still scanning the inshore shipping. Now he gave a grunt. "See ye the schooner, in the mole-coign? Gaff-rig, black upperworks. That's *Hraffn*. Thralli's keel. He's still here."

I had not regained breath from the shock of realising that Thralli might not have stayed, after all, when Fiskri called, "Sheinn? Get the dinghy set."

He flatly me forbade me to go ashore with them. "Ye'll do no good speirin' after him yourself. Thralli's past carin' for kin."

Thralli had been a slaver for a decade or more. I had not been able to help exclaiming at the mere thought of slavery accepted as just another trade, and Fiskri had given me a wry look. "Happen ye'd sell a child, sooner than watch it starve. Especially when ye've neither net nor furrow to feed it y'rself."

Silenced, I remembered the children in his own house. Looked again at his gaunt cheekbones, and wondered if that choice already haunted his nights.

But when I asked, "But Thralli? What will you say?" He looked sourly amused.

"Tell him I've kin aboard, seekin' a brother sold in Ve Pool. He'll understand that well enough. And," wryly, "t'will be better I do the chafferin'."

Because he knew Thralli. And the market, vile word. Because he would not let sentiment get the better of him, and show Thralli how much this kin meant.

Hard, bitter sense, yet again: Two conceded it. I swallowed hard and muttered, "Yes."

On deck the dour wind chilled to the bone, but I was too fraught to go below. Halri was splicing another ancient rope. He let me help, and had wit or tact enough not to talk. It still seemed an eternity after they reached the *Hraffn*'s stern, parleyed, then made fast and climbed above, until *Aerful*'s shabby dinghy pushed out and headed back.

When Fiskri swung himself over the rail the look on his face sent the heart into my throat. "Is he not there? Is he . . ."

"Belay, lass." He still looked somber, but he knew what I could not say. "He's alive, aye. But." He set his chin. "He's been sold."

If I had burst out already like the merest boy, I did manage to contain it then. The words hardly wobbled.

"Sold where?"

He jerked a thumb inshore. "Herself."

"Her? You mean, the Woman? The Woman of Eithay?"

"The Lady." He said it sharply, with a warning look. "Call her the Lady, here."

He had said, "Woman" when he told me Eithay's lord had inherited her father's lands and chosen to rule them alone. Despite various attempts to oust, unseat or marry her, willing or otherwise, she was still there, scandal and gossip of the Southern Isles, as much for Eithay's increased prosperity as the address and ferocity that defended them both. I ducked my own head hurriedly, as if the wind had ears. "The Lady, then."

Inwardly, I wanted to wail aloud. Another redoubtable ruler, another fortress unknown as Ve Pool's brech. Another desperate sortie to organize, for another impossible rescue, and once again, alone. *Oh, Mother,* I cried silently, *could you not have delayed them one more day?*

But Two was going on, beginning where Azo would.

*"She bought him? How do you know?"*

Fiskri gave a snort. "Thralli tell't me."

"Thralli—! He just *told* you?"

Fiskri gave the dinghy's mooring rope an automatic jerk, and his own head another. "Come below."

By the time we settled round the tiny table, and Halri had silently set a kettle over the brazier that counted as galley stove, my wits were halfway to working again. "Thralli told you? You just walked up and he—Why?"

In the half-light, Fiskri's dour look became a hint of almost vindictive grin.

"Because I tell't him the kin wi' me was Outland, too. A lass strong as Sheinn an' tall as me, wi' a pair o' knives up her arm that did for Thrif an' Tjofor at my own hearth-stone. Tough as Rekkir an' fey as Stokka. An' beggin' to carve the gizzard out o' *him*."

"Oh!" The image was inconceivable. But Sheinn and Halri's faces spoke a grim amusement that was not laughter at the indulgence or exaggeration offered to a child. I almost exclaimed, Do I look like *that* to you?

Then the real concern revived. I could have groaned aloud. "But he'd already sold . . ."

Fiskri snorted again. "Aye, he did. 'An' curse the day I let y'r lord cozen me into buyin' him!'" Now he was caricaturing someone with a higher voice and almost wailing accent. "'Not clear o' Ve port an' he starts heavin' his belly up! Two days runnin' for a healer an' payin' for pap an' milk at Mirkadin! Lyin' to o' nights to save his precious guts! An' him carryin' on the while like Langlieve come home! Fresh air an' washin' water, straw to lie on, tantrums if he'd to wait a blink! An' makin' trouble'," it climbed in outrage, "'in the hold! Tellin' the others, get the manacles an' trip us in the dark—get free an' take the ship!'

"'An'," Fiskri was almost as breathless as Thralli must have been, "'when I locked the witch's besom in the bilges to shut him up, him sneerin' and fleerin' and lookin' down his long Outland nose at me—*Lay a hand on me,* he says, *an' I'll bruise like young mackerel. An' where's your profit then?* By the Mither's eyes, if I'd not let your cursed lord chouse me out o' such a swingein' price, I'd ha' run him out an' tipped him overboard!'"

"Oh—oh!" I was trying not to laugh and cry at once. Sheinn and Halri really were laughing, with deep, savage glee, but for me terror was only a breath beneath. Therkon had made his weaknesses both offense and defense, he had scourged Thralli with imperial arrogance and made him rue his buy every inch of the way. And come within a breath of losing his life for it. If Thralli had not paid such a swingeing price . . .

"'So'," Fiskri was weirdly repeating Thralli's mingled outrage and vindication. "'I cleaned him up an' took him ashore, aye. An' he'd not reached the block when Herself clapped eyes on him. So if I've not the profit I deserve'," now with a hint of detestable smugness, "'I've no' the pestilence either. Send y'r Outland catamount after *her!*'"

Sheinn and Halri had stopped laughing. Their eyes on me held pity, concern, sympathy. But also expectation, a kind of wary apprehension. And with it, hope.

I took a deep if shaky breath and had to keep my hand from touching the jewel pouch under my shirt. I had stopped Thrif and Tjofor, I told myself. I had met Stokka, and Two got us out of that. I could deal with the Woman of Eithay. If Therkon was sold, he had been sold here. He was going no further. And I had the money. I could buy him back.

I said, "Are there craft shops, in Eithay?"

\* \* \* \*

Instead of craft shops, Eithay had an actual changer's mart: a solid block-house of the reddish-grey local stone was sited conveniently on the waterfront, just beside the long, low buildings raised to hold Eithay's new and richest merchandise. The slaves.

Fiskri would not let me ashore alone, either. "Y'r knives might stop two men, lass, but show money in Eithay an' ye'll have five on y'r neck." He and Sheinn marched each at my shoulder, with a belaying pin thrust through his belt.

We had to land beyond the fish-market, in the only place open to small boats. But as we threaded the carts, tables, stands of fish, jostling buyers, stink and earsplitting clamour of fishmongers, I heard Sheinn almost explode, "See that!"

I jerked half about. He and Fiskri had both baulked, staring up a regular pyramid of barrels. To me the stink said only, Fish, but their faces cried aloud.

"Herrin'," Sheinn gulped. And Fiskri, with a longing, an envy near desperation, "Someone struck a shoal."

The din around me went away. A dozen memories dovetailed, Fiskri's gaunt face, the gate-watch's prayer, Fiskri's talk of slaves, the tally of Ve Pool's calamities. Herring. Salted herring. That they would not need a fleet to catch.

"What is it, lass?" They had almost cannoned into me, alarmed in their turn.

"Fiskri," I said, "could *Aerful* carry all those?"

"*Aerful?*" He broke off short. The stare became outright shock. "Lass, what d'ye mean?"

"Those fish are for sale." It was all clear now, lifting my heart against the weight of Therkon's plight like the opposing side of a balance beam: recompense, more than recompense, better and more immediate than I had given Veenn. "You know what I owe you. All of you. Will *Aerful* carry those? And should you put a lien on them now? Or will we get the money first?"

For a minute they could have been stricken to stone. Then Sheinn suddenly started trying to wring my hands and babbling incoherencies. Fiskri just stood there, staring, while two tears tracked down his fleshless cheeks.

The mart had a cramped front compartment with a barred window and tiny counter, but the sleek well-shaven face at the grille nodded unhesitatingly when I asked, "Will you change gems for coin?"

Nor was the rate niggardly. But Fiskri handled the fish-sale with a vigor and parsimony that at first astounded me. Why pinch pennies, I wondered, when we had the money? Until I remembered he was buying Ve Pool lives.

"There, lass," he said, reappearing all but breathless. "They've a berth down quay, we can bring *Aerful* in to load. Have 'em aboard before dark. An' aye." Suddenly, shyly, he grinned at me. "The lot'll fit."

The three of us stood there, obstructing a whole aisle's traffic, smiling, grinning at each other, faces shining like sunrise breaking through a storm. Finding no need for words.

Until Fiskri drew in a great breath and straightened his shoulders and said, "Now, lass. Your turn."

The Lady was nowhere so accessible as her money-changers. We had dropped anchor not long after noon, and there were still perhaps three hours till night, but Sheinn, sent into the town as herald and harbinger, came back dourly shaking his head. The Lady of Eithay received uninvited visitors only from second to third morning watch.

\* \* \* \*

We took *Aerful* to load instead: the ribs had settled far enough for me to help despite the protests, trudging to and fro with heavy little barrels or passing them down into the hold, amid gusts of steadily increasing rain. The wind had risen too, making *Aerful* push and twist unexpectedly, doubling the effort. I was quite sure I would sleep without stirring till dawn.

But once in my makeshift bunk I woke far too often to riving anxieties. Was Therkon safe now? Better cared for? Would the Lady see us? Could I make her listen? Would the money I had changed be enough?

Nor could I rush ashore the moment Fiskri called us up. "Ye'll not go to the Lady," Fiskri told me firmly, "without a tail." Wild visions of a dragging rope-end doubtless marked my face, for he amended, "Without a following."

All three of them were coming. "Ye should rightly have a banner," Fiskri pronounced, "but I'll be y'r bailiff." Meaning my herald and negotiator. "A lord'll never speak first for himself." My actual "tail" would be Sheinn and Halri, good clothes under their canvas weather-gear, and boathooks in hand. "An'," Fiskri gestured forward, "ye'll carry that."

"Hvestang?" I was startled enough to use the name outright. Propped beside my packs, up beyond the bunk, it had been determinedly ignored by them all. "Fiskri? It's not mine?"

"Aye." Fiskri said, and held my eyes. "But it's his."

"She'll know it?" His expression made me catch my breath. "So: it makes him someone? In the Isles? But then, won't that raise the price?"

"Better a higher price than have her count ye a nithing." A flicker of grin passed almost too fast to catch. "Bein' mere Outland's too little. An' carvin' up a couple o' house-blades with y'r knives'd be too much."

So I wore Hvestang, hitched weightily and uncomfortably over one shoulder under my cloak, as in still gusting wind and persisting rain we ploughed through narrow, curling streets, among shabby whitewashed cottages and past tall gables rising beyond new-cut walls of reddish stone, to the Lady's gate.

The gatehouse was temporary. The court beyond was littered with building apparatus and long banks of rain-darkened red stone: the Lady was expanding, or perhaps improving her hall. But nobody was aloft on the steeply slanted tile roof, or round the peculiar sharp feather-shapes rising from the gable ends, or scrambling over the scaffolding today.

The two sentries at the main door's decorated lancet arch read us as strangers, but Fiskri's introduction and a couple of coins took us past. Though dark and smoke-laden the hall beyond was, Two considered, comparable to that of an Amberlight House. Trying to disentangle Hvestang gracefully from a wet cloak, I squinted through the murk.

Beyond the long central hearth the Lady sat, like Skatir, in a carven chair. If the hall was busy, the fire was high enough to light even the recesses beyond the double line of roof supports. Her face showed roselit though sharp featured, with a glitter from some kind of diadem over short, straight, dun-coloured hair.

My heart hurried. My mouth was dry. Fiskri, cool as at the tiller, began working his way among the knots of warriors in mail and sword-belts, sleek persons in double broad-cloth, and harassed scribes or serving-folk, toward the Lady's chair.

She received four petitioners ahead of us, apparently with both incisiveness and calm. But as we edged along the hearth I could tell she watched us every step of the way.

"M'lord." Fiskri stood at the hearth-end, inclining his head one scant inch. The traditional title, whatever the gender. And the salutation of a man elsewhere vowed. "I bring here the lady hight Chaeris, from the land of Iskarda." We had settled it in the din-ghy, rowing ashore. "She has traveled far and long, and she comes now seeking aid and grace in a matter of her kin."

Her eyes had been on me all the while: narrow eyes, probably a light color if not simple blue, and her skin was pale as Veenn's. One of the older people, Fiskri said. The pale ones, who filled the Isles in other days. Her voice, I knew already, was carrying and clipped despite the Isle accent, and her decisions spoke a fast-moving brain.

When Fiskri finished she said at once, "Some back-water o' the Empire, ye mean."

"Nay, lord. Iskarda is beyond the Empire," Fiskri said.

One brow went up. "An' what's the sword?"

I had not expected her to waste time but my heart jumped all the same. Fiskri answered calmly, "It hight Hvestang."

This time both brows rose. Then she looked direct at me.

"An' whence had *ye* a blade o' the Isles?"

This time, I had to answer for myself. I took a steadying breath and let my voice reach the hall.

"It was a gift. To my brother. From the Seer of Evvamoor."

She might not have known the place but the title she under-stood. Beside us I heard breaths go in.

"Ye don't speak like him."

Fiskri had warned me she was sharp. Veenn's grand-dam had prepared me. I still had to master my hands' twitch.

"We were raised apart."

The riposte I myself had worked out, in those latest days' voy-age.

"Aye?" The lifted brow spoke skepticism, irony. "An' what d'ye seek here?"

She had already told me, like some reckless gameplayer, that she knew who I was. Who Therkon was. So why make me spell out what I wanted? For amusement? For pride? To bait me?

Or because she meant to refuse?

I took a deeper breath and Two got there first.

*"You know."*

**Not** *like that!* I cursed in silent consternation. *If you must butt in, be polite!*

"Ye're not loose wi' words."

She had sat up a little, but the curious half-twist of expression was almost a smile.

*Shut,* I threatened Two, *up*.

I must have looked conciliatory enough. In a moment she said, "An' what'll ye offer, for this—brither—o' yours?"

*"What do you ask?"* said Two.

Even Fiskri drew breath that time. I struggled not to squeeze my eyes shut as I screamed, *Shut up,* **shut up,** *you just played right into her hands!*

"How if I say, the sword?"

She really was toying with me. I cursed Two again and with too much distraction. She had answered before I could.

*"The sword is not ours to give."*

This time the Lady's lip curled in a definite if unpleasant smile. "Oh, aye?"

"It came to my brother," I got control before Two could make worse trouble, "from the Seer. Who is of Langlieve's line."

She had sat back an inch, perhaps despite herself. Her brows climbed again, but I could tell that name carried weight.

"And did she say t'would stay with him?"

"The Seer said, he would have use for it." The rest leapt at me as from the sagas that Two remembered so vividly well. "The sword speaks for itself."

*It puts an end to dispute.* That corpse in the Grithsperry gutter. Colne on his own gangplank, face purple with impotent rage.

"Does it so?" She could not have known what I remembered, but she read the intonation more than well enough. The eyebrow had climbed again. "An' so ye'd give him back its use?"

My heart did a dolphin leap somewhere under my chin. "If m'lord so please." Even "m'lord" did not choke me as it might.

"Ye'd have me name a price? Any other price?" She leant back again into the high-backed chair. The hand wave appended, Anything other than the sword?

Don't offer an actual price, Fiskri had beaten into me. For the money price, let her come to you.

Silently, I bent my head.

"Ye've coin for a ship-load o' herrin'. I doubt a brither's worth less." My eyes jerked up. She was smiling, a little, smug, ambushed-cat smile. "Pity I've no way o' testin' that."

I did manage to keep my hands still. I hope, to hold my face still. To swallow the breath that seemed to choke in my throat. To look, and nothing more.

"Y'r brither was here, aye. For an Outlander, a fine piece o' man. Vinegar tongue an' uppity ways an' all. I'd like fine to have had the breakin' o' him." Her smile flickered like an adder's tongue. "But happen I found him other uses. To pay, ye might say, a debt for m'self."

The hall was wavering about me as if clear water rose over my head. I dug the nails into my hands and concentrated on that to keep my head up, since I could not bite my lip. It was Fiskri whose deep voice intervened.

"M'lord?" He at least sounded steady. "What d'ye mean?"

She glanced once at him and back at me. The enjoyment was delicate, but gloating all the same.

"Y'r brother's gone to the Lord o' Skall," she answered sweetly. "He sailed this mornin'. I'd need for a fine partin' gift."

* * * *

"South, aye," Fiskri said wearily. "Skall's south an' west o' Sandouin. T'is said they trawl the Hamair traffic, them tryin' to dodge the Fleshes comin' north."

"Trawl traffic? What?" My brain was refusing to work at all. "What traffic . . . Oh." My heart sank. "Oh, no."

You'd best not call them pirates, Frotha had said, in the south.

"Angrir," Sheinn growled, and spat over the side. "What in Tiran's ice brought *that* limb o' misdeed up this far? Now?"

"Hraffni," Halri retorted, and spat over the opposite side.

"Ravens," Fiskri told my bewildered stare. The curl of his lip added the rest. Carrion birds, both lords. Feeding on slavery, on piracy, on the slow unraveling of the Isles. What likelier than that, nowadays, they should make common cause?

"Aye," Sheinn grunted. "But hap she'd no' bid him here, either. There was need," a hard stroke emphasised it, "of a fine partin' gift."

"You mean," neither Two nor I were thinking well, "she didn't want alliance? He just came? And she had to get rid of him?"

None of them looked at me. But presently Sheinn growled in his throat. *Yes.*

So Therkon had been traded as a bribe, a sweetener. To a pirate. From a woman who would have taken pleasure in breaking him.

What manner of creature had him now?

I bent over on the thwart and laid my face in my hands. Let me go home, I besought the Mother, as the tears began to well. Or let this all be some longdrawn nightmare, and wake me, now. To the fire with the Isles and Dhasdein and the River and Sthassamaer. I have made nothing but mistakes from beginning to end and now it's beyond me. I've lost Therkon, again, maybe beyond recall. I've used and jeopardized all these other people and now it's just too much. I can't go on. Let me go. Take me home.

A hand settled across my shoulders. Nobody spoke, but the silence in the dinghy was solid as its touch: not condemnation, but silent comfort. Determination. Trust.

Then Fiskri said above me, "Sheinn, we'll be needin' stores."

"*No.*" Two spoke before I could. Two had my head out of my hands regardless of the tears, Two was saying what I should have, had I had either resolution or words. "*You have cargo. It must go to Ve Pool. You must not go further south. You are needed northward. You must be home before the storm.*"

They were all gaping: Fiskri by me in the stern-sheets, Halri in the bow, Sheinn at the oars. This time, I thought as my belly went to water, they'll know it's Two beyond all doubt. And what will they do then?

It was Fiskri who spoke first. Steadily, as Fiskri could. Evenly, too evenly.

"Lass? Is that ye?"

I bit my lip on craven evasions. If anyone did, they deserved the truth.

"She's—part of me. Me and not-me. She—comes from Iskarda. From long before Iskarda. She—we—were born together. I—we—sometimes she speaks for me. Instead of me. She has—memories. Sometimes, she knows what I—we should do."

They had stopped breathing. Sheinn had stopped rowing. Their eyes were round as bilge-stops. Now, I thought wretchedly, it's over. Now they'll name me for a witch and toss me overboard.

Fiskri got breath, audibly, first. "Ye mean—there's two o' ye?"

When I nodded, beyond words, he breathed in again. And then almost burst out, "An' t'other. *She.* She knows what to do?"

All too open portents of disaster, every past warning about silence and discretion fulfilled. I could only say desperately, "She can, can, put facts together. *Sometimes* she knows. Yes."

Fiskri caught his breath again. Halri flung his glance from one end of Eithay harbour to the other and almost shouted, "Storm?"

"You can see that yourself!" I nearly shouted in turn. "I'm sorry, I only meant, you know the sea, you can tell—" their stares were thoroughly discomposing—"I mean, if I can, you must, too!"

And after another aching pause, Fiskri said somewhat shakily, "Aye. Aye. The lass is right. There's somethin' comin', ye can feel that. Don't need some—some—We can see that, aye."

"Then you know what we have to do." It did not need Two now. "I have to go on. To Skall or wherever it is. You have to go back. Your family. Ve Pool needs you. I can't," I felt the tears return despite myself, "I can't take you with me. Not any more."

Fiskri patted my back, absently but gently, while Halri made comforting noises. Sheinn rowed. But as we came under *Aerful*'s quarter he shipped oars and said, "The lass's right."

The other two made protesting, disapproving sounds. Sheinn looked at Fiskri and gave a snort.

"What speed'll *we* make, wi' a hold full o' fish? But we can find," his eye glinted, "somethin' better. An' be sure t'is better for her."

# CHAPTER XIII

I argued my way on board, belowdeck, abovedeck again. Clambering back into the dinghy, Fiskri just looked over his shoulder and asked, "Are ye comin', lass? Or not?"

Left to myself, I would probably have leapt to the nearest deck and paid whatever they asked for passage anywhere south. By the time my companions sieved half the port, I had learnt better. Not a fishing boat, too slow, not the fast fore-and-aft rigged schooner, she would be sailing north for Inganess on Terrace, and not the schooner from Cuwen, because "her skipper's a rascal." Nor the solid-looking brig. "She's another slaver, lass."

When they did make a choice, a well-kept sloop whose captain's name they knew, we met a flat head-shake and a, "No' headed that way." With a look south-east, into the eye of the wind, that added, Who in his right mind would?

"T'is no' the gale," Fiskri said grimly, after the fourth refusal. "The Woman's been busy."

Spelling from oar-work in the bows, Sheinn glowered. "So t'other sells him on now, what's it to her? She gave the man away." But Fiskri shook his head.

"T'would have been a pledge. She'd no' want him thinkin' she's changed her mind."

By the time we rowed, tired, damp and crestfallen, back to *Aerful*, I was frantic. Every hour was taking Therkon further away. With the wind making, every hour lost here would increase the gap, and if a storm was coming in truth I desperately wanted *Aerful* out, off, homeward bound before it struck. But, "We're goin' nowhere," Fiskri said flatly, "till we've sorted passage for *ye*."

We were belowdecks, waiting in glum silence for the kettle to boil, when something bumped alongside, and a shout sounded overhead.

As we stuck our heads up he came scrambling lightly aboard and straightened up: an old man, I realized, startled by the lithe, assured movement in contrast to the long beard, the equally grey hair, an old man seeming well into the spindling, muscle-wasting phases of age. But his dark eyes were neither faded nor filmed, and he stood straight as he said, "I hear ye're wantin' a passage south?"

"Aye." Fiskri's answer was slow. He would be scanning the usual heavy trousers and boots, well-kept if not new, the jacket under an equally well-kept weather-canvas. The dinghy and rower alongside. "Where're ye bound?"

"*Anfluga*, out o' Munen. We're a sixer, but new-scraped. An' the wind's workin' east."

I had no idea what any of it meant, but I could read Fiskri now. Favorable, so far.

"We're wantin'," he said slowly, "a passage to Skall. To Yinstey, aye?"

The old man combed his beard. "So we go soon, aye. We'll run as quick for Yinstey as Munen. So it's worth our while, beatin' back."

"The passenger," Fiskri said after another thoughtful moment, "'ll make it worth your while. So ye get her there, soon as wind'll carry ye. An' in one piece."

"What do ye take me for?" The old man straightened with a jerk. "We're no' coggers or slavers. Or rude men, either, d'ye see?"

Fiskri produced one short wicked grin. "I've no call to worry for *her*. I'm thinkin' o' the craft."

The old man paused, then shrugged. "I've run to an' from Sandouin all m' life. To Eithay, often enough, wi' the whalebone from Hivell an' Kaastria. An' wi' *Anfluga* six summers now. Ye can ask ashore. What ye're doin' here, I can't say. But *we'll* be comin' back."

Fiskri nodded, even more slowly. Then he said, "*Anfluga*, aye. An' who'd you be?"

His name was Rathi, which means something like, Advice, but he was normally taciturn, to my relief. *Anfluga* was beached beyond the port: a six-oared boat, though bigger than *Aerful*, high-raked and pointed at both stem and stern. Uncomfortably, Two's ancient Amberlight memories informed me, like a River raiding craft. She was broad-beamed, with hardly a keel to speak of, and a single square-rigged sail like *Aspis*. Most daunting of all to me, she was undecked.

Fiskri and Sheinn seemed undeterred. They examined her clean, "new-scraped" outer planks, her rigging, then her crew. They actually did check with a shipper: then Fiskri negotiated a fair price to Yinstey, and I produced half the coin.

When we returned to *Aerful* for my packs, they loaded me with spare willowbark, a flat tin of tallow—"Keep the sea out o' them boots"—and a cascade of advice. We rowed back to the beach. And then, with half her crew and my packs already aboard *Anfluga*, it was time to say goodbye.

None of us could find many words. Sheinn and Halri did produce weak grins and sallies about not carving up the oarsmen before Skall. I did try again to voice my thanks. Then I consigned Two to the fire and hugged them all, careless of whether their bonecrushing responses made her spark or not. Wished them good wind. And torn between loss and relief, that it was little past noon, that they would have half a day's light to run before that blustery wind working steadily easterly, I watched them row away.

* * * *

At first *Anfluga* was more than daunting: an open hull lacking even *Aspis'* hencoop, no foredeck, no sterndeck, neither hold nor cabin. No belowdecks at all. Most was filled by benches and oars, a sail that now seemed rudimentary, the minimal freight lashed to the sides and wrapped in weather-canvas, as I half feared they would do to me. Worse still, waves heaved up higher than the ship and near enough to touch, and worst of all, the entire frame worked like muscles to every shift of the water beneath.

But however she worked, *Anfluga* did not leak. With relief, I found the crew remote, but neither crude nor importunate. Like the rowers, I learned that snugging close under the gunwale kept off everything but rain, and of that we had little enough. Like the sail and ropemen, I would snug down amid my packs to the squalls. The ribs seemed mending at last. Beyond cold dry-rations, the stale tasting water-butt, and trying to relieve myself over the bow while chastely wrapped in a cloak without being pitched overboard, the most frustrating part was the impossibility of workouts, lacking either partners or space.

And the best part was the speed. With the wind set ideally on her aft quarter, *Anfluga* ran the sea like a wooden form of her namesake: Loneflyer, the great southern albatross. When I asked, rather timidly, if we would be far behind Angrir, Rathi almost achieved a snort.

"A wind like this, *Anfluga*'ll do Eithay to Munen in four days or less. An' another to Yinstey." He patted the vibrating tiller bar. "In that barrel he calls a skaw, he'll no' land under a week."

Munen was the main northern port on the big isle of Sandouin. Skall lay westward, a small island, one of Rathi's rare speeches informed me. Yet again I added the days, and prayed to the Mother on my own account. Surely, Therkon could not come to much harm, even in a week, on an ocean-going boat?

We made landfall off the cliff-girt point of Oddi, Sanduoin's broad westernmost promontory, on a dour, chilling day that had already tightened my nerves. *Anfluga* altered course then, pushing on west across a last narrow strait into the murk that waited beyond.

Skall came out of grey sea and sky behind the grey smoke of a receding shower, like a towering, jaggedly-crowned grey ghost. 'Cliffs an' seabirds,' Rathi had said in a more loquacious moment, 'an' not much else.' In those long minutes as the outline coalesced, all I could see was cliffs: broken, deeply indented, uninhabited ciffs, rising sheer to the edge of sight.

But the ropemen were standing by, calm and collected, the rowers still lounging off-bench. At the tiller, as if he did this every day, Rathi was laying a course by eye to angle slightly further south. Pointing the bow into what had become a cloud and rain-veiled gap in the shoreline, that with the wind almost due easterly would make its southern cliffs *Anfluga*'s leeward shore.

I swallowed Two's alarm and got down amid my packs.

Another shower overtook us, hissed into the white-flecked waves and passed, veiling Skall in turn. The wind had grown steadily more bitter. The oarsmen had donned their weather-canvas, I was grateful in earnest for my knitted cap. Now, whirling past on a truly vicious gust, I saw white flakes that were not foam.

Snow. My first snow outside Iskarda.

Behind the shower the cliffs re-solidified. Much higher, they seemed, even higher than Rack Head, and far more rugged, though oddly immaterial through rain and cloud-light and the continuous sheets of spray. I had a sudden fear that if I took my eyes off them they would dislimn like a hallucination, and vanish quite away.

And the port, Yinstey, would be down in the toe of this recess, which had made Rathi more voluble than anything else. "Proper bear-trap, the Gnufe. Good shelter from t'southerlies, aye, but let the wind go half north and ye're better headin' home. There's too many craft come to grief when the wind backed, on that cursed southern arm."

I stared at it as *Anfluga* ran in, one long unbroken parapet of menacing black rock and heaving spray. Yinstey was still lost in the brume, but now I could catch a hint of the short northern cape. We were properly in the Gnufe, the maw of the Gulf.

My stomach turned over. I looked back into the bitter white eye of the easterly and wondered yet again, What made the wind turn that way? So helpfully, so advantageously for a south-west bound sixer? So helpfully for me?

Or had it been to help something else?

* * * *

Yinstey emerged reluctantly even from the earth. The Gnufe ended in a narrow cup of bay between slanted rock palisades, spatched with what looked like moss, flanking a scant grey beach. Above the sealine, a shelf green with the unhealthy tint of too much rain bore a couple of long tucked-down roofs. "Boat-sheds," Rathi conceded when I asked. "They'll no' risk much here afloat." One vessel was literally on the beach, rollers showing under her keel. "Angrir's skaw. They'll be heavin' her up soon, too."

Not that far ahead of us, then. I swallowed hard and looked for Yinstey itself.

Beyond the shelf a slope rose into the gullet of the cliffs, branded zigzag by the pale line of a track. The crest showed only a clutter of grey and green roofs, and evanescent sheets of smoke.

Rathi ran *Anfluga* in under oar, hovering a hundred yards offshore for the precise wave that would carry her furthest up the beach. The bow rowers leapt over and ran calf-deep in foam to lasso boulders, the rest heaved her clear. Then small cables replaced the carry-lines.

And Rathi turned from the tiller to meet my eyes for the first time that morning, and said, "Now, lass. What do ye mean to do?"

He sounded more than dour. My own belly squirmed, as it had since Skall hove in sight. But I made my voice as calm as I could.

"I'm going to Yinstey. To find my brother. And get him free."

Rathi very near bit a lip. "Are ye so? Just like that?"

"I'll pay you the rest of the passage first." I had assumed he would know that. I bit off, *Did you expect me to renege now?* "You, the ship, whenever you're ready, you can leave."

Rathi tugged hard at his beard. "An' ye'll be off, into that nest o'—gull-gropers—strand-lopin' gangrels, an' fetch y'r brither off. All by y'rself?"

He spoke too near the core of my own fears. I blurted, "You've done as you agreed."

He scowled overside. "Agreed, aye." He scuffed the deck with a boot. "Lass, ye've a knife or two, an' a fine hand with 'em, Fiskri told me. But there's likely twenty, thirty men up there. Sea-scum. Wreck-pickers. As fell a pack as the Isles hold. An' ye're only one."

Two found the words a fraction before me. *"More than one will only make it worse."*

Rathi threw up his chin and stared. "Aye," he said in a moment, sounding startled. "Happen, ye're right. Bring a tail, raise a brawl. But." He maltreated his beard again. Then literally flung both hands in the air.

"Ah, pest on it! Go then, lass. But we'll stay for ye. Be sure ye tell 'em that. Ye've a sail waitin', an' eighteen hands aboard it. An' Yinstey's whistlin' trouble if they try aught amiss wi' ye."

For a moment my throat shut. There was only the wind's fluctuating ice, the screams of seabirds that gyred above us like feathered mist. Then I gulped and managed, "But if the wind turns?"

"Pest take the wind too." He lowered at me. "An' the payment. Get y'r gear, lass." He thrust his chin out suddenly. "Get y'r gear and move."

I had the knives already: the packs I had to leave in trust, but when the moment came, I found I had pulled Nouip's cloak from the pile. He'll need clothes, Two or I were thinking, or at least, warmth.

Then my hand met the hilt of the sword.

Over my head Rathi said, "Take that too."

Startled, I looked up at him. He glowered, but repeated firmly, "Take that too."

A new gust howled round us amid flecks of snow. Half *Anfluga*'s crew were already at shelter under the ship-side. I looked from Rathi to the uncommunicative remaining faces. Then my hands began to move, without, it seemed, even direction from Two.

Lifting, donning the seal-fur over my own cloak. Swinging Hvestang's baldric over it, so the hilt rode above my shoulder. Drawing the hood up, over my head.

Rathi took a sudden pace back. From an eye-corner I saw the port stroke oar push his fingers into the horns.

I stood up, trying not to see their faces. Rathi said huskily, "Aye," and I heard in his voice what they saw. What the three men in that Grithsperry shipper's office had seen, what Skatir had seen and named for us. What Yinstey would see.

Rathi did not make the horns, but he did not invoke the Mother's aid for me either. He merely repeated, barely audible, "Go."

\* \* \* \*

"They've to ship in their wood along with their flour," Rathi had said about Yinstey, "an' they eat gull when there's nothin' else." Toiling up under the soaring cliff-planes, I could see why. On every cliff-face, every ledge, every niche, seabirds plumed or squabbled or brooded, and they all screamed and excreted continuously, including those expelled or abroad, circling like bees round a hive. The easterly only partly curbed the stench, and did nothing for the noise.

When the slope topped Two halted us, no more than my head above the crest. We looked into a shallow upland valley, treeless as usual. A circle of rough wall divided ploughed fields from probable pastures, with a central string of low grey roofs imitating a street, and the biggest building at its end.

It seemed half a small fort, half a natural green mound: a turf roof, I realized, turf growing down over some of the walls, its dome-like shape a cross between the Ve Pool brech and Vithre's house. Before it a half-circle of stone walls met at a solid timber gate. Open, at the moment, with people moving in and out.

Angrir's hall, or brech, or whatever he called it. If I had caught up at last, that was where Therkon would be.

I took a deep breath and relaxed every muscle as before combat. Then I pulled the hood up high, lifting my shoulders with it. And started to walk.

If I was five finger-widths shorter than Therkon, I was still tall for a woman, let alone a girl. The cloak-hem did not drag. The hood would hide my features, my entire face. All that Yinstey would see was the cloak, the tall, anonymous, advancing figure. The hilt of the sword.

I had time to wonder what they had done with their lookouts, why no-one even noticed we were ashore. I did not know that Yinstey watched the outer strait from the southern cliffs for passing shipping, when they watched at all. For the beach, the neglect had other cause.

The first to notice me were four ragamuffinly boys with sticks and loops on long poles. Approaching the street end, they first stared at me. Then pointed. Then stopped, then stared again, and then ran like literal hares. I could hear their cries diminish, blurring into the skreel of gulls.

If adults confirmed their reports, nobody showed themselves to do so. By the time I reached the first houses, the street was deserted. Up its length came the last faint clap of slamming doors.

The courtyard had been abandoned too. The gates were open, but along with the traffic, any possible sentries had fled. I paused in the gateway, trying not to tremble, both Two and Azo already flicking my eyes frenetically around.

An ordinary court would hold bothies and guest-cells, storesheds, the smithy, perhaps a byre. And people, all the hold-folk about their work. This one held motley heaps of planks, beams, oars, or anonymous sea-junk. Rusted metal, bits of net. A couple of pens, a sheep-stink, but no animals. And no people. Except one old man, squatted under the unshaped lintel, on the single step.

I walked across. The cloak swirled round me in a twirling gust. The old man cringed. From the hood's dark I said the words that came to me, and Two deepened them near a masculine bass.

"Where is Angrir?"

The ancient howled thinly and tried to hide his face. Doubtless he would have run, had he the legs for it. I pulled the sword-sheath slightly forward and he gabbled, "Not here, not here. Away, he's away up the ceat—!"

"Where?"

He crawled to show me. Literally crawled, on hands and knees to the gate side, where he got one wavering hand up to point along the wall. "On the head there. At t'prospect . . .Lord, d'ye no' . . ."

Do not touch me, see me, notice me. He was already curled like a frightened porcupine, arms folded over his head. He did not have to say it out. Ignore me, as your greatest favor. Pass over my cowardice, my complete lack of loyalty. Take my lord Angrir instead.

I swung the cloak and walked away.

I had no idea what a ceat was, let alone where to find it. I simply skirted the yard and followed the building side, heavy going among untilled earth and ancient grass. Before I reached the rear wall the bay of male voices told me I had found Angrir. And the gate guards, perhaps, and the beach watch as well.

It was the whole "fell pack o' the Isles." Fifteen or twenty of them, massed on the right-hand slope that would rise, beyond the wall and the brief pastures, into the great shoulder of the first inland hill. Some tall frame towered above the crowd, cutting the line of dull brown and green and grey-patched slope that glistened with rain and wind-spume, towering bleak as the livid sky.

The wind snatched around me, swirling the cloak in sharp little gusts like a winded man's gasps. The crowd of backs, dun and grey and brown, homespun cloaks or weather-dark canvas, heaved like wreckage on a wave and more noise came out of them. The bay of hounds, of beasts scenting more than blood.

I opened my mouth and Two spoke for me. A truly masculine bawl.

Backs whipped about but not as alert fighters do. These were men caught in some private pleasure, unawares.

They were uniformly squat and broad and almost a carica-ture of saga villains: unkempt, unshaven, straggling dark hair, low foreheads, ugly mouths, porcine eyes. And porcine temper, surly and perilous as boars. Among them Angrir stood as a living refutation of the archetype, tall and straight, pale-skinned as sun-light, fine-featured, with deep blue eyes and beautiful red hair.

"Lord," he said. And while the others stood petrified, he made a perfect courtier's reverence. "Ye're a little before y'r time."

The pack gasped. I nearly gasped myself at the effrontery. The perfection of the retrieval. The speed.

In my own shock, I made the perfect retort.

When I stayed silent, the curve deepened in that smile.

"But ne'ertheless, welcome," Angrir said. His voice was light as Stokka's but far cooler. The ice in it nearly froze my blood. "We're just halin' the badger from his lair."

He gestured. The pack were stunned, but not so stunned as to disobey him. They parted right and left and I saw the ceat.

A low, open-stonework shed, its turf roof straggling long blades and seedheads into the wind. Hardly high enough for a sheep, let alone a human. Swinging open before it, a rough-made but solid wooden door.

And running from the dark within, a rope.

An ordinary ship's rope. With the curls of its last use still in it, and some of the cabling marked with dark, fitful patches. Too red for tar.

Angrir did not give me time to react then either. He waved to the men either side, and shouted to them as he must have on numberless ship-decks. "Haul!"

They had been stunned with shock, with fear, with his profane audacity. But this they understood. Had done before. With shouts and yells they tallied on the rope.

Angrir called the pull. The men heaved, the rope jerked, once, twice, thrice. On the third, "Ho!" they almost fell backwards as a heap of debris flew out of the ceat.

It thumped down among their feet, a tangle of black and brown and Isabella dun that might once have been white cloth, a sprawl of suddenly identifiable limbs and trunk. A living, moving entity, a man with his hands bound before him at the rope end, shoeless, naked but for something like a breech-clout, filthy as a midden, with black animal eyes glaring from a cave of half-grown beard and elf-locked hair.

And bare skin dark with bruises, with half-scabbed wounds. Fresh scrapes on shoulder and thigh, and the slashes of older whip-work visible over his ribs.

The men bawled. The captive spat at them. Angrir took one long stride and kicked him solidly under the rib cage and shouted, "Heave him up!"

The timber frame stood right beside the ceat. A gallows, Two blazed a lightning trail of images past me, L-shaped wooden frames laden with men hung by the neck, or with butchered heel-hung sheep—At that vision of naked red flesh sense nearly left me. But the Skall men already had a toss of rope over the hook on the frame and were hauling on its end.

Therkon came willy-nilly onto tiptoe and hung there, stretched ribs heaving, glaring like a cave-wight through the mat of hair. And Angrir glanced round to me and laughed.

I took two paces neither Two nor I remembered and flung the hood back and shouted, "Let him go!"

The pack nearly went on their backsides. For a moment even Angrir's mouth fell wide. In the hush I could hear birds screaming, far down over the cliffs.

Then Angrir seemed to rise on his own toes. His head came forward and he almost hissed, "Who're *ye?*"

"Never mind who I am." I could barely control my rage. "I will make you an offer. One offer. Name your price, and let him go."

Angrir's brows shot up. Thin brows, well-shaped brows. So handsome, surely they should have signaled a goodness as extreme as the evil looks of the men he led. "Ye're offering a *price?*"

"One price." Both Two and I had got a better look at Therkon: his head had fallen forward. He hung limp as a butchered sheep, and the edges of my vision were swimming in a red fog of rage. "One!"

"Ye . . ." Angrir lost words in the contentions of understanding, outrage, temptation. His eyes slitted. Then his jaw dropped again. "Ye're no' a man at all!"

I was past caring for anything but Therkon. I snorted at him fiercely as Iatha might. "Name a price and be done!"

"Ye—ye—" Angrir started forward and the pack started with him and my hands went without my volition up, back and over, so Hvestang whistled as it left the sheath. I opened my mouth for a war-scream to match any Isle man's, and Angrir brought up with a jerk.

Not fear. Not even caution. The eyes suddenly glowed like back-lit sapphire. Then the face changed, and abruptly, dazzlingly, he smiled.

And waved both hands, signaling the pack away. Outward, opening space, flanking us, an audience, to either side. Before he drawled, almost silkily.

"Is that what ye're wantin'? A price?"

I jerked up my chin. It was the only retort I could manage without losing control.

Angrir retired a step, and then another. Softly, suavely, never taking his eyes off me, but never losing his bearings either. In another moment he was almost at Therkon's side.

"An' what's this one," he half-murmured, "to ye?"

"*Enough to pay for.*" Two fenced for me. How, I was trying not to cry aloud, has he not heard? Did Stokka not pass it on to Thralli, the tale of the missing sister? Or Thralli to the Lady of Eithay? How can he not know?

Because for a slave, Two answered from the wells of remembered atrocity, neither Thralli nor the Lady cared.

"But ye came here for him." Angrir was almost whispering. The pack's eyes were glued to him: wits to match their looks, a pack's eagerness. They could not fore-guess his ploys, but they did not have to. They need only expect them, and wait to be fed.

"Ye came here, from—Sandouin, was it? Or Eithay?" Angrir was smiling now in almost pure joy. "Or even earlier? Aye." A long-drawn-out sigh. Of pleasure. Of anticipation. He put a hand out and casually as a lout with a worthless cow, slapped Therkon in the ribs. "Oh, no, ye stravagin' hussy, you. *Ye* tell me what ye'll pay."

Therkon's grunt ended on a half-choked cry and Hvestang was ready before I knew it, gripped two-handed and drawn back for the sweep-stroke that would lift the red-rimmed target clean off its supporting shoulders. Angrir's head.

But Angrir had skipped faster than a snake clean behind Therkon, yanking his captive's head back by a handful of hair and yelling, "See ye!" with a dagger pressed to Therkon's ribs.

It was not Two that stopped me, but Azo. One flash of trouble-crew judgment that clamped my muscles at fire-point, bawling, *Wait!*

All three of us panted. Therkon with shock, perhaps. Angrir, in pure excitement. For me it was head-swimming rage.

Angrir had the wit not to goad me then. To wait till the extreme last moment before someone else acted, and then to drawl, "Ye said, a price."

The red fog ebbed. He was grinning at me round Therkon's shoulder, the blue eyes brilliant, the white teeth a sparkling grin. His hand still clamped Therkon's hair, the dagger-tip was still in Therkon's ribs.

Slower than thawing ice, I slid Hvestang's point to ground. My throat was full of ash, but I sounded no more than husky.

"Let him go."

Angrir assessed that, and took its worth. The grin widened, but he let Therkon's head fall forward, and took one graceful step, not entirely aside. With the dagger still inches from Therkon's side, he cocked his head and asked brightly, "Aye?"

*Bargain now*, Azo said in my ear's memory. *Never mind saving face. No hope of a strike yet. Bargain, work for better odds, and wait.*

While Two shot zigzags of memory, white-hot flashes of Amberlight Heads haggling with kings and lordlings, past us both.

I said, "One hundred Phaerean silver." The equivalent of Dhasdeini darrins, though I did not know the proper name. But if a hundred had bought a ship-load of salted herring, it was an opening bid for a man.

The pack rustled. A wave of intaken breath: too high, I thought as my belly plummeted, too high and reminding them too well that what I offered, I must possess. And I am a woman, here alone.

Angrir's grin brightened. "Aye?"

I stared at him, blank-faced as a basilisk, and let my eyes say the rest.

For a fraction of a second the grin drooped. Then he laughed, soft as a sleepy cat.

"That's the best ye'll do?"

I went on staring, for reply.

"F'r a man ye've hunted clear from—Phaerea, is it?" The eyes widened, almost the clear cobalt of a sunlit sea. Wind waved a toss of red hair over his forehead, bright cornelian against the wet stone, the oncoming rain. "Or," the brows contracted, "is it further than that?"

I let him see my jaw clench, and hoped my eyes looked poison. And made the silence add, *Your price?*

"A hundred, ye say?"

I jerked up my chin. A Dhasdeini gesture, but intelligible enough.

"Nothin' more?"

"I said," it came out almost as low as his own voice, "name your price."

"So ye did." His lashes fluttered. "How if I say, I'll not sell?"

I could not restrain Two, let alone Azo. My hands clenched on the sword hilt and Hvestang came to guard with a hiss I could almost hear.

"Aye, aye, belay there, ye catamount." Angrir flapped his hands in a mockery of terror. "Ye'll be cleavin' us all in twain. A hundred, then? That's y'r best?"

"Give me yours," I said between my teeth.

"I'm the seller." He flashed his dog's teeth at me, white and glistening. "T'is for ye to offer. An' me to choose."

And he would go on choosing, Two told me with vicious clarity, as long as he found amusement in the game. Or until he thought he had plumbed my resources and my need to their foundations. And then reject whatever I offered, and let the pack's greed, that I would myself have kindled, settle the rest.

"I said, one price." It sounded overloud, even among the scream of gulls and whuffling wind and now, against the seal-fur, the first patters of rain. "One."

"Ye'll not give me a choice?" Angrir flashed his smile again. "One hundred or naught?"

Azo almost did it for me. But I shifted my hands on the sword hilt, and then I smiled too. And said, quite softly, "This puts an end to dispute."

He knew the tag. For an instant mockery, taunting, cruelty, all collapsed. But then he was laughing again, more harshly now, with a snap under the play.

"A cruel choice, that! Have ye not thought, then?" He flipped the dagger about and jammed its hilt quite casually into Therkon's ribs. "What y'r price'll buy for him?"

Therkon gasped and I had taken another pace before I knew. "Let him alone!"

"So I will, then; but he's hangin' here, every minute ye delay." The white eye-teeth, the slitted blue eyes glinted at me. "Kind, d'ye think?"

*He's baiting you,* Azo's voice said, crystal cold to my inner ear. *That's all.*

*But this is impasse,* I had no time to cry back. *How can I make it break?*

For Angrir the pause had been incentive enough. The fine brows rose. The smile dazzled.

"Or d'ye not know what ye're buyin'?"

He took one sidelong pace, gave a tug at the breech-clout and swept up his dagger blade. The severed rags tumbled at Therkon's feet.

Distantly I heard that magpie voice taunting, "Ye think, we'd best take a look?" It was lost in fog where white-shot images burnt in flame: the velvet touch of belly-skin under my fingers, Therkon's averted face in a film of vomit and sweat. His scrupulous courtesy on Phaerea, separate rooms, screened beds. Not merely courtesy, but ingrained modesty. The crown prince of Dhasdein, of high Quetzistani blood. Worlds that shunned, tabooed, abhorred nakedness. For women and men alike.

Angrir was still laughing, he had not yet drawn breath. Therkon might not have moved. Perhaps the rags were still tumbling to earth. My hands had already driven Hvestang point downward and whipped the wrist-knife from its sheath.

It took Angrir full in his right, laughing, bright blue eye. And it went home with the whole weight of skill and muscle and fury behind it, to the hilt.

He never had time to speak. He hardly had time to choke. His hands rose. His mouth gaped. The other eye shot wide, surprise, the death spasm. His hands beat the air once and his dagger went tumbling. Angrir made a wordless noise and fell full-length at my feet.

\* \* \* \*

As on the cliff-face, time went both fast and glacier-slow. There was space for reflex, to shake the other knife loose, back a pace, make room for the next assault. Time to hear Angrir's last choking breath and half-see the way his body slumped, and the determinedly not-seen shape of Therkon beyond him, instinctively trying to curl up and cover his nakedness. The tall cross of Hvestang upright between us. And the faces of the pack.

They had been stunned beyond thought. Motion. Speech. That time stretched out and out through the sough of wind and rain-patter and gull-scream, a living bas-relief of loutish features, dropped jaws, bulging eyes . . .

Then real time snapped back: the mouths closed, the eyes focused, the faces moved to sentience, understanding, purpose. They knew what I had done. What I had cost them. We all knew what they would do next.

Two and Azo were screaming calculations so fast the whole scene blurred. Fifteen or sixteen of them advancing, the hands grasping for or already gripping weapons, cudgels, belt-knives, a short ancient sword. The heads down, grim as a military phalanx, the purpose black as murder in each look, I had one knife in hand

and I had to throw that, I must not get to close quarters, and after the knife remained only a too-big, clumsy sword.

Two was over-screaming that with ancient images of night and a fiery necklace of distant lights, shouts and beaten weapons before us, the tumult of a roused palace behind. Something gripped, long as my forearm, a pyramid of triangles in my hands. The statuette of a woman in a long wide-hemmed skirt, arms raised, and in her hands, a crossed pair of thunderbolts.

And the bolts streamed fire white as lightning, stretching before us in a single deadly beam.

I had no time to reason. To wonder, to deny. The knife was in my grip. I sprang back and again back and as the image of Therkon's nakedness seared across vision and memory the knife lit like a veritable light-gun in my hand.

Light blazed outward, that searing, impossible white. The Skall men bawled with fear that became sudden outrage, and instead of shrinking back, they charged.

I swept the beam before me as I could not have swept Hvestang. Pure, intangible, lethal as no solid weapon could be, as it had been in a multitude of weapons, ever since Amberlight learned to work with qherrique.

The beam's traverse took the left-hand side of their charge out, waist-high. Slicing, physically cutting human bodies in half with a hideous unchecked facility, severed torsos tumbling before ever I caught the stench. Before a one of them could scream.

I screamed though, louder than I ever made a sound before, all but tearing my throat.

*"Stop!"*

They froze. At the sound, at what they already knew. The noises, the stench, the half visible motion beside them, their pack-mates crumpled, some of the severed bodies still writhing, too little blood but too many vital organs tumbled round them, on the sere wet grass.

My heart was clamouring in my ears. My hand was a claw on the knife. The tip still pointed upward before me, bearing that terrible white fire. The live men were frozen. It is too feeble a word for the faces, the color of milk, of clay, caricatured terror in the silently screaming mouths, the white-ringed, lunatic eyes.

Then with a wordless wail the man nearest the dead melted down in a prostrate heap, trying desperately to pull up his hood, and failing that, to wrap both arms over his head.

The rest fell after him. Some cried out. Some threw gear clean over themselves, as if, not seeing me, they could become invisible.

I was alone with my killing blade of light, the only human creature upright and free on a hillside of groveling men and fallen dead.

Two moved me. Two did not care about the bodies: Two had seen worse, at the final sack of Amberlight. And these bodies would have harmed Therkon.

Two took us to him in a handful of strides, swooping vengefully as an eagle that turns to cherish fledglings, having rent their foes. Two swept the light-beam once above his head and the rope parted. Therkon crumpled more silently than the dead.

Two pushed the knife back in the wrist-sheath and unfastened Nouip's cloak.

Therkon was curled almost as tightly as the living Skall men. When the sweep of fur and silk floated down over him, he too flinched.

I fell down on my knees beside him and laid my hands on him less for his than for my own sake, and it came out a whisper, a prayer, a thanksgiving, a plea.

"Therkon?"

* * * *

It was five minutes, Two estimates, before I gave up. I had called him by name again, by title. After the flinch at my first attempt, I had not dared to touch. I merely knelt there, while Two and Azo and my own memory beat on me more and more fiercely, crying, There are dead men here, hideously destroyed by your own hand. And live men with them, and you cannot expect superstition to paralyze them much longer. You must get out of here, now. But if your prize cannot hear you, cannot bear the touch of a hand, how can you force him to go?

I swept one desperately shrinking glance over the corpses, the crouched figures, the sopping, bloodied grass. Angrir lay beside me, face up-turned, the expression of pure incredulity blurring under fallen snow. The wind speared straight through my Iskardan cloak. In minutes I would be unable to move at all.

Then grass rustled suddenly behind me, a voice made some appalled exclamation, and another voice demanded deep and fiercely, "Lass?"

I whipped round on my heels, Hvestang suddenly under my palm. Rathi stared down at me, instinctively holding hands out and up, signaling, I am weaponless. I mean no harm.

Though behind him his massive tiller-second Segil gripped a pair of belaying pins, and a short sword was buckled at his own belt.

"Rathi!" I nearly wept with the shock, and then the relief. "He's here but he's hurt and he—I can't move him, and they—!"

He took one look across the shambles and went white-eyed. His growl shook like a flicked-tight rope. "Aye. 'They'." He switched his eyes to the fur-covered heap beside me, and his own captain's reflexes cut in.

"His head's sound? No bones broke? We'll carry him. An' quick about it. Nay, lass." With one white-edged glance about that said the rest. "We're no' lingerin' here."

Not trusting the seal-furs' strength, they bundled him into Rathi's own weather-canvas. My heart bled for the flinch when they touched him, the smothered cry. But I managed to sheath Hvestang, and lay it beside him, and they were strong, active men.

They carried him swiftly if awkwardly between them, straight back down the hill.

I had to retrieve Verrith's knife. Almost the worst moment of all. Then I hurried, less like a guard-dog than a mourner, at their heels.

The old man was gone from the fort step. The street was empty. Not a door opened at the thump of feet, the men's hard breathing, the occasional swallowed curse. Like ghosts we skidded over the stones, toiled up the little slope to the crest. Essayed the seaward path.

Recollecting myself, from the crest I glanced back, once. The street was still deserted. Behind the tower, the slaughter-field was out of sight.

Until we crossed the beach rim Therkon had been mere dead weight. I still thought him unconscious as they eased him onto the pebbles and Segil helped me work him off Rathi's weather-canvas, while Rathi himself snapped orders and the rest sprang to the ship. Cables were cast off, retrieved, stowed, hands to the gunwales ready for the heave: they meant to take her off sternfirst, the way pirates might after a raid, Rathi was coming swiftly back to me, with quick, anxious glances over a shoulder: not to the ship, to the sky beyond. The wind, burnt-in experience told me in an instant's attention, was already colder, stronger.

And shifting to the north.

"Get aboard, lass, an' him with ye, we've no' a minute to waste. Segil'll give ye a lift."

Segil stooped to get an arm under Therkon's shoulder. Therkon shrank, but when I put my own arm round him he seemed to understand. At least, he tried to help himself stand up. He even levered up his head.

Then he must have seen the ship.

He froze in our hands. Then he dug both bare feet in the pebbles and threw his whole weight backward as if he were still on that rope.

Rathi checked, stared. Cursed. Caught past me at a shoulder. "Lad, come on—!" And Therkon snarled at him. Wordless, mindless, high and ferocious as an over-frightened dog.

"Tiran keep—" Rathi bit it off. "Lad. Y'r sister's here. D'ye not know her? Come on, then. The wind's turnin'. We've got to go!"

Therkon bared teeth through the elf-locks. A madman's glare, a madman's face.

"Lass?" Rathi swung from him to me and back in more than exasperation. "Move him, can ye? Or we'll have to wrestle him. Whatever damage that . . . Talk to him. Be quick!"

My heart was choking me, beating like a bird in my throat. But he had raised his head, looked round, reacted, if with seeming madness. Recognized a ship. He might remember me.

"Therkon? Therkon, it's Chaeris. I found you. I've, we've, freed you. These are friends, we're getting off Skall. Just come aboard and we can launch. We can get away."

His head half-cocked. I dared to reach out, to touch his bruised, filthy hand.

"It's me. Chaeris." I dared not ask, Do you know me? "Can you hear?"

The ship was ready. The crew had stilled, waiting. Rathi was all but gnawing his beard. The wind and the birds screamed round us, and Therkon blinked.

For one moment sanity looked through those eyes. Recognition. Then he saw the ship past my shoulder and threw himself facedown on the pebbles with a thin frantic wail.

I flung myself beside him, an arm over him before I could stop myself. "It's all right," I was gabbling, "my dear, my heart, it's all right, it's all right."

But he was babbling too, whimpering it into his hands in complete abjection. "Not again, not again, please, no, not again. Please, no, no more . . ."

The ship. The sea. Thralli, talking about running into port for a healer. Having to heave to at night. Had he thrown up all the way to Rostack? Had he landed in Eithay, empty as a purged dog, and been left so? What had Angrir fed him, in the ceat, or at sea, for those interminable seven days?

I could feel the tears stream, but I did get my own head up. "Do you," I gulped at Rathi, "do you have any, any imperial spice?"

"Imperial *what*? Lass, are ye—Oh." His wits were redoubtable, especially in the moment's pressure and haste. He almost groaned. "Nay. Nay, lass. We don't carry such. We—" He came closer, bent closer. "Is that what he—sea-qualm? Ah, Tiran's curse."

We might never get him aboard. It might kill him if we did. I could understand Rathi's feelings all too well. But I could not let *Anfluga* go, either. We had no escape but to leave Skall. Now. On this ship.

Two flung the other memory like a javelin. Frotha's second remedy. Even without the spice, that might be sufficient palliative. Enough to get us off this beach.

*If he dies on the way*, someone neither Two nor Azo knew was insisting coldly, *it'll still be better than what awaits him here.*

I snapped at Rathi, "Turn your backs." Then I scrambled in as close as I could to Therkon and groped for the edge of Nouip's cloak.

I heard Rathi grunt. Start to protest. But the tone worked: I had no time to absorb the bizarre, the all but comic sight of eighteen hardened seamen fretting and fuming and fixedly looking the other way on a spume-wet beach. My hands were inside the furs.

"Hush, my dear, listen. Listen to me, clythx, caissyl." Heart, sweetness, the words my mother spoke to my fathers. I used the endearments without thinking, concentrating on the tone, the only message that might transmit. "Hush now, hush, it's all right, caissyl, it's only me."

My hand found ribs, far too prominent, the curve of waist and belly slope. Recalling bruises and abrasions I slid my palms lightly as I dared, without losing track of where I was. Muscles quivered and contracted, that dimple was a navel, this ridge the crest of the iliac bone. Warm under my touch, despite everything, still, despite everything, a shadow of that velvet-smooth skin. Therkon gasped but he did not jerk away or cry out or try to hit me. I shut my eyes to protect us both, and began Frotha's slow, circling motion with my palm.

Therkon went completely still. The sea rumored, with a rising emphasis every fourth or fifth wave, the wind was freezing my ears. The men must have been chilled to the bone.

But the muscle under my palm had begun, fraction by fraction, to relax.

I opened my eyes. He was looking at me, through the hair's black tangles on sleek grey-black fur. Eyes like caverns with deep-dwellers in them, blades of cheekbone sprung from the too-sharp nose, the rest blurred with beard and haggard as a famine-survivor. But it was Therkon, behind the face.

The tears dripped down on my fingers but I did not let my hand stop. I did whisper, not looking at him, "It's going to be all right."

In a minute more his own hand moved. Shakily, tentatively, as if testing that it was in his control. Fingers rough with dirt, and more than dirt, closed like claws over my wrist. He drew breath. I expected, hoped, prayed he might complete his return by speaking. Instead he sighed, almost soundlessly, and shut his eyes.

In perhaps another five minutes Segil and the brawny starboard stroke tiptoed over. We edged Therkon, cloak, sword and all, onto my own weather-canvas, they worked him aboard as if moving egg-shells, I scrambled to meet them by my packs. The wind was screaming over us, louder in the almost entire absence of human sound. But I felt the heave and grunt with which, at the impetus of men's shoulders, *Anfluga* began to move.

\* \* \* \*

They were rowing when I surfaced again: all twelve oarsmen and two of the ropemen, the starboard one's shoulders almost in my face. No need for a timekeeper to get their backs into it. Rathi's profile above us, etched years older by tension, said it all.

The wind was still making, still swinging northward. If we could not clear the Gnufe fast enough, we would be leed against those deadly southern cliffs.

Spray and spume dashed over us, mixed with snow. Rathi had not bothered with a sail. It would lose time to tack. He had simply pointed *Anfluga* as far off the cliffs as he dared and trusted to his rowers.

And he was pointing her closer and closer into the wind's eye, almost at right angles to the shore.

I had no time to panic. Her stern came right into the wind, she wallowed, and Rathi bellowed, "'Bout *face!*"

Only an immaculately skilled and experienced crew could have managed it. But all fourteen of them shipped oars together and whipped round on their benches to grab the looms again, dropping the blades back, heaving in exact unison to Rathi's shout of, "Give way!"

*Anfluga* plunged forward. Bow first this time, coming about in a short sharp curve to her previous course, but this time, with the steering oar where it belonged, astern. Balanced, poised, to meet whatever came.

I had just seen a manoeuvre, I realized, that all Dhasdein's navy could not emulate.

Then I looked into the oarsmen's faces, and shut my eyes and prayed the Mother: Let me not have brought them to their end with us. As I, as we did, with Deoren. With Verrith. And Azo.

Therkon was immobile. Eyes shut, the black smoke of lashes the only thing intact in that ravaged face. He needed food, my wits clamored, proper warm reviving food, and dry warmth, safe rest, somewhere off a ship where his stomach would settle, where I could get him clean, tend his wounds.

At the thought memory replayed: the image of that hillside charnel house, the bodies living and dead. The corpses that blade of light had left.

I just managed to make the leeward gunwale before I started throwing up.

When I finally slid back from the side and dragged myself together, the faces looked different. Rathi was still tense, the oarsmen still straining to the utmost. But something had altered, in the way they looked at me.

I put a hand on the nearest strake, that moved and worked like the muscles of a running horse, and heaved myself up. The wind hit me like a blow across the face. Spume and snow shrieked past, louder than the seabirds, and the cliffs of Skall loomed toward me, once again charcoal-grey as ghosts.

But almost abeam now, the Gnufe's southern arm ran down into a white rim of breakers, and beyond showed a flat horizon of white-flecked, raveled, menacing but open grey sea.

I looked at Rathi. He gave one brusque nod.

We were almost out. We would not be leed, we would escape the Gnufe. And Skall. I had Therkon back at last. For a little, we would be safe.

I inched myself upright at Rathi's elbow and croaked, "Munen? How long?"

He spared me one fractional glance. "Not Munen," he answered gruffly. "We'd ne'er round Oddi. I'll not kill rowers tryin'."

"Not—?" I tried to keep calm. "Where then? I have to get him warm! Clean, dry, ashore—! How long—!"

"Aye, lass." He was still gruff, but not hostile. "But wi' a north wind makin', we've no choice. Clear the Gnufe, 'n we can at least run down-strait. Wind like this, Gildair'll be less than a day."

Saving his rowers, and I could not dispute that. *Anfluga* ran stably, I had felt that for myself. "Gildair, where is that? What is it?"

He visibly remembered that I did not know the Isles. "South Sandouin. Gildair's t'far end o' Skall strait. No' Eithay, but no' Yinstey, either." He spared me another fractional glance. "They'll help ye fettle him, there."

I looked once into the shifting wind's eye. Southward, it was pushing us. Southward, and I dared not think by what means, with what intent. I could not face the questions yet. I looked to Rathi instead and gave my silent, all but irrelevant consent.

* * * *

When we were clear enough to wear ship, Rathi put *Anfluga* before the wind, they shipped oars, the sail went up, and we tore past the Gnufe's point like a hound unleashed. Segil took the tiller. Someone broke out rations, and as the water mugs passed, Rathi dropped down by me at Therkon's head.

"Let him sleep," he said, when I asked about trying to give him food as well. "Happen he needs that more." He laid his own head back against the side as if exhausted. But every muscle in his body was still wringing tense.

Someone brought him the usual helping of dry biscuit—hard-tack, the Dhasdeinis would have called it—and a moment later, with just visible constraint, offered a second to me. Rathi snapped a piece to bite-size, and began, less for need than recreation, as was the usual jibe, to chew.

Then he swallowed, and said, "Lass?"

When I twitched he made a gesture: No harm meant, be still. "Lass . . . There was eight, nine dead men up there." A wry kind of snort. "Ye've broke the back o' Yinstey, an' every straits passager'll thank ye. For that if nothin' else."

"Broke?" Then I understood. Nineeen, twenty men on that hillside, and Two—I and Two had killed the half of them. Half a village's manpower, half a skaw's rowers. Half a raider's crew. Yinstey, Skall, the fell pack of the Isles, might never raid again.

"I'd no' wonder," Rathi added after the next mouthful, "if they had to emigrate."

Appalling visions flew past me, Veenn talking about Kaastria desolated, Fiskri about hunger and slavery, the dispossessed boats at Eithay. But this loss, this emptying of a homeland, however wretched, had been my work alone.

"I never meant—I never thought—!"

"Nay, lass." Rathi sounded so sure I believed it myself. "We all saw ye. Back here aboard. Ye ne'er meant it so. An', I'd lay odds, ye ne'er did such before."

I could only shake my head and bite my lips desperately at the memories: Be still, go back, don't rise now. Not that windrow of mangled flesh on the hillside, not the cut-short cries, the bodies falling, the sick jerk of a light-cutter meeting flesh.

"But, lass. Segil stowed the sword for ye." I had not thought to ask how Hvestang came there, shielded against the bulwark, in its usual place. "An' he said. He said: there's no' a mark on it. No' a spot. But I know. I *know* ye'd but the two knives, an' one—I saw where that was. So." He looked out across the farther gunwale and the constraint in his voice told me how much this mattered. "Can ye just tell me. What did ye *do*?"

Not curiosity. Not to ease his own fear, if any such remained. He needed an explanation to keep the trust, and maybe, even the onward co-operation of his crew.

He was not of Iskarda. He was not Therkon, or even Fiskri, who in those few days I had come to trust more than anyone else. At thought of repeating the explanations, of their possible outcome this time, my very soul cringed. But I owed Rathi, owed his crew, who had gone with me further than Fiskri ever had to, not merely brought me to Skall but waited for me, come ashore to help me, and were now, unhesitatingly, carrying me on to refuge. Not for money, but simply because the weather dictated it. In answer to my and Therkon's need.

"I . . . have a companion," I said.

Rathi's face changed and Two shot me an exasperated collage of meanings, *companion here equals familiar, witch, witchcraft, solitary old women with cats twisted round their legs*—Two cut in before I could stop her. *"We are of Amberlight."*

Rathi lacked Fiskri's ear for the change of voice, and the name meant nothing. The pronoun was another matter.

"There's two o' ye? But where's t'other? Who are ye? *What* are ye?" His hand went down on the plank beside him, unconscious prelude to springing up. "How can ye be—"

*"We are together."* I felt the spark kindle, ominously familiar, tried to snatch control and failed. *"For what we are."* The familiar quotation. *"Your words do not work, do not work, do not work."*

Rathi was growing white-eyed, but the threat was unmistakable. He kept quiet.

*"We are of Amberlight. In Amberlight, they learned to call the fire."*

"*Fire?*" Rathi sat up straight. "That up there was no' fire. What d'ye—"

*"Not your fire. Mine."*

*Let me do this!* I bawled. *Do you want them to lynch us?* And for the first time in my life Two bawled back at me: *Be still!*

Then she lifted my hand, and I felt the spark gather as it had far too often, and tried to pull away before it jumped.

But this time, the thunder rose and the building spark hung, coruscating at my fingertips, white as the lightning, pure as the light in that retrieved memory.

*"In Amberlight, they used it."* A far too-familiar image in memory, the great blades of light-guns sweeping a glacis free of attackers, leaving a swathe of dead and dying that paled mine to insignificance. *"To defend the city. If there is a vessel, we can use it now."*

She slid Verrith's wrist-knife clear and held it point up, and the light rose above us in its perilous white scythe.

*"The fire can—jump. If we are—surprised. But when need came, it woke."*

Very, very delicately, delicately as a cutter or shaper with a qherrique blade, she inclined my hand. The very tip of the blade traced across the top-board of the gunwale, and a thread of smoke furled from the black mark in its wake.

Rathi had recoiled against the bulkhead. Every other man was a statue. Some had forgotten to chew.

The light vanished, swift and completely as I had seen a cutter or light-gun die when its Crafter signaled release. Two ceded me control. I shoved the knife into its wrist-sheath and tried to sound neither beseeching nor desperate. Only, at best, halfway composed.

"That doesn't happen with, with—friends."

For a second the very planks beneath us seemed to have solidified. An ice ship, a stone ship, manned by a stone crew, caught upon a distantly heaving sea.

Then Segil gave the tiller a slight twist. Spat, accurately but remotely, to leeward. And remarked, with all the straight-faced irony of which Isle men are masters, *"That's* ta'en a load off m'mind."

I gaped. Someone else gasped. Then we all collapsed in a squall of laughter that nearly strained our ribs.

Stress, fear, a release less humorous than far too near hysterical. But as the men moved again their eyes told me just what Segil had done for me: caution, those looks showed, and rightful wariness, but every time it shifted toward fear I could hear those words recur, and the fear would slither helplessly into mirth.

Except on Rathi's face. Where in the ebb of laughter, it was not fear or fear's recollection that had resurfaced behind the common amazement. In his eyes the shock had become wonder. And with it for an instant, inexplicable but unmistakable, something else.

Greed.

# CHAPTER XIV

Therkon came around just at the verge of dusk, about an hour, Rathi estimated, out of Gildair. It was colder than ever, and the wind had worked round nor-nor-easterly, buffeting *Anfluga*'s flank like fists. Sitting at Therkon's head, I saw his lashes flicker, almost imperceptible in the dingy light. But then his face shifted. A moment later, he opened his eyes.

Straight upon the gripping beast atop *Anfluga*'s stern post, the leach of the straining sail, and Rathi, upright and tense at the steering oar.

Therkon gave a gasp that strangled at birth, squeezed his eyes shut and tried to curl up with both arms over his head. I had just time to catch at a shoulder and almost exclaim, "Therkon?"

His eyes shot wide. The curling motion froze.

"We're at sea but they're friends, it's all right—"

He turned suddenly onto his back. A hand groped inside the cloak and he murmured, sounding half-dazed, half-dreaming, "Chaeris . . ."

I shut my hand over his. His eyes flew wide again. He almost yelped, "Chaeris?" Then he jack-knifed up and grabbed for me. *"Chaeris!"*

He smelt like the bottom of a dungeon, his beard scratched, his arms hurt, his hands were rougher than the stones they used for sanding planks. I seized him like a Heartland python, hard enough to start both our ribs. And then we both wept as if we were still on Evva beach.

Eventually I had to let him loose: I wiped my streaming eyes down the seal furs, my nose on the back of a wrist, and fastened the other hand back in the cloak collar. He was still clutching me, murmuring prayers, gratitudes, vows of devotion to every known god. But when I moved, the burthen changed.

"Oh, Dhe," he whispered into my unwashed, half-undone hair, "It was my fault. All my own benighted fault."

Before I could burst out in excuses and denials Two said, *"No."*

"What?"

*"Not the choice,"* Two said precisely. *"Not at the cliff. Not with those facts."*

Therkon made a fraught, dissenting noise. "But after—!"

*"After, yes."*

It stopped him on something like a grunt. I almost felt the fall of imperial frost. He had been half out of himself as I had seen him on Evva beach, and as on Evva beach, more than ready to blame himself for everything. He had not expected blame.

"Two didn't mean—" I stopped before Two could cut me off. Because at the point, I could not lie to him. Two had forecast, I had feared, Thralli's report affirmed it: what happened from Ve Pool onward had been, must have been, partly his own fault.

He was too honest to deny it. He had already dropped his head against my shoulder with a single wordless groan.

"It doesn't matter." I overrode Two and grabbed him, cloak and all. "It's over and there's no use blaming anyone. Oh, my—oh, Therkon," *my dear, my heart's ease, my darling*, Two recited the endearments while I prayed he had not been conscious to hear them on Skall beach. "It doesn't matter. We've got you back."

I tightened my arms. He drew me in against him. For an uncounted span of time we had nothing but a seal-fur cloak and some odorous clothes and dusk falling in the ice-wind on an open heaving boat. And I would not have changed them for anything on the Mother's whole wide earth.

* * * *

Tacking to make Gildair's harbour restored us to life. We both squeezed against the side as the ropemen heaved and swung and stamped to and fro, while the rowers stood by and Rathi, half-invisible in the twilight, called commands. Gildair was only a cluster of twinkles in the grey mass of western sea and sky, sliding above the gunwale, here and gone. I had my head shamelessly on Therkon's shoulder. He was making his best effort, from inside the cloak, to grip me round the waist. And presently, in the eddy from others' attention, the confessional of the half-dark, he began to talk.

"Ve Pool . . . Lord, I was such an idiot." Two wanted to agree but I silenced her with ferocity. She had already stated the fact. Facts were not needed here.

"With the gate-guard. It was late afternoon, I could see no way to find someone, and still get back to you. Not by dark. I was half-crazy *then*. I would have drawn on them, except one clubbed me. From behind." He massaged a shoulder, under the cloak. "But in the hall. That *popinjay*. That prancing, posturing, Archipelago fishmonger. And you somewhere on the hill, no-one to reach you, no-one to—I lost—I wholly lost my head."

All too clearly I could picture it, the imperial Heir in a paroxysm of wrath and panic and outrage, gainsaid, flouted, trifled with, by what he would consider less than a backwoods autocrat.

Against my cheek he let out a sudden, silent air-shock of a laugh. "I hardly believed it when they threw me in the 'dungeon.' But when they took the lamp. And I remembered it was already evening. And I could not get out . . ."

I hugged him desperately and let that cry, *Oh, my dear.*

"I think," he added ruefully, trying to rub his temple, "I actually beat my head against the door. But in the morning. Oh, Dhe."

"If you'd only known, if only I could have told you," I whispered back. "They came looking for me that morning. Skeag and Dath." I told him about the night under the cliff, the whole saga of the ribs, the farm, the downhill trip, missing him by so few hours in Ve Pool itself. "I almost went crazy, when I couldn't go on. And we almost *knew* what had happened to you."

We made my-blame-was-greater noises for a while. But to have him in my grasp, to know him intact in wits if not wholly undamaged in body, was sweet enough to counter horrors twice as bad. I did deliberately skip over his sale. I did say triumphantly, "Two tricked Stokka. I got Hvestang back."

"You tricked Stokka? You got *Hvestang*?"

So then I had to tell that story, at full length, and add Vithre, and Fiskri. And the thieves in Fiskri's house.

"You were set upon? You had to *kill* two?" His voice spoke more than naked shock. A Dhasdeini man, to whom women were almost irretrievably the slighter, weaker vessels, the beloved to be cherished, defended. From violence, whether others' or their own.

I just kept from retorting, *It was what I trained for, it worked, I'm alive, Azo would have been so pleased.* Honesty compelled me to amend: at least, she might have said, *Not bad.* But I could recall, all too shudderingly, how the bodies had surfaced in the lantern-light, the vile sensation of a knife cleaving flesh.

The other memory fell like a boulder. The scissoring draw of a light-gun, slicing not one but eight or nine men apart.

"Chaeris? Chaeris, what is it? My—what is it, my dear?"

"Skall," I said, and buried my face in the seal furs. "Two. We had to do it. It was them or us. And you."

The sea threshed, the wind squealed over us, almost as high a keen as Skall's gyring birds. His arm had tightened round me, but it was a good minute before he spoke.

"Chaeris? What did you . . ."

I tried to sidle round it. I went back to Ve Pool, and *Aerful*, and forward to Eithay. The Lady, the emptied cage. *Anfluga*, a fresh hope of pursuit. "I'm sorry, I had to sell two finghends, for the passage, for the fish." He made a wordless, impatient noise. What did gems matter? What else were they for? "We were five days Eithay to Yinstey, I could hardly bear even that."

Knowing Angrir still had a full seven days' space for whatever he did to you.

"The slaver," he said into a gout of spume, almost under his breath. "I was—still new, then. I could not believe someone—anyone could—do what they did." My heart bumped against my mouth-roof. Don't tell me, I wanted to cry, even to exorcise yourself. But I felt the quick, curt shake of his head. "Chains, and that—*clout*—they put on me. They took my boots." The first note of true indignation. Of memory being sloughed. "I could have borne the clothes, even Hvestang. But my boots!"

Made in Dhasdein. Almost the last remnant of the crown prince. The one absolute necessity, had he actually managed to escape.

He laughed again, another smothered concussion of breath. "Do you know, my—Chaeris? I was glad to have been sold, before the end. I was even glad for my, my stomach's work. I made that squirming heap of lard pay for it, the chains, that hold." He shuddered once, more eloquent than any words. "Even the whip. I reminded him, every time he was driven to distraction, that if he beat me, it would bring down his price."

I bit my tongue on, And it was only the price's counter-balance that saved your life.

"But to be sold . . . *again.*"

To a woman. Stripped again, no doubt, this time before a woman's eyes. He did not have to put the loathing, the humiliation, into words.

"I thought. I did think—the only thing I could think was, *If she keeps me, I could get away here.* Find a boat, get back. I *had* to get back. I tried not to think, what might have happened to you, how far away you were. Oh, Dhe."

I hugged him rib-squeezingly and said fiercely into his ear, "I was behind you. I didn't ever stop following you. Whatever I had to do, I was going to get you back."

Whatever I had to do. The shudder took me, uncontrollably: I had done whatever I had to do, and it was beyond any horror I ever conceived.

He leant his cheek to mine, and for all the husk of mistreatment, his voice came with a rouse of the crown prince's authority. "Chaeris, tell me. What did you have to do?"

I stared out into the grey and white spume that was merging into darkened sky. Gildair was a brighter constellation, but human shelter, its comfort and sanctuary, still seemed very far away. Once he heard this confession, might he ever count me human again?

"Skall," I said. And shut my eyes, and said it out in a piece, before I lost courage irredeemably.

"Rathi put me ashore, he said they'd wait, I wore Nouip's cloak, I took Hvestang on my shoulder, I remembered Grithsperry. So I went up to find—Angrir."

His shoulder twitched. He had had cause to learn that name.

"They were," I took breath. "At the ceat."

His breath came in hard, and his every muscle turned to stone.

"I tried to bargain. I would have bought you, I would have traded him every gem I, we, had left. But he played with me. And in the end. In the end—"

His silence, his muscles' clench gave me the answer: *I remember what he did, in the end. Yes. I do remember that.*

"So I threw Verrith's knife."

I heard his grunt, loud as a foot-trip. He had seen us, at exercise on the River. He knew an Iskardan knife-thrower's scope.

"The others came after me." I had to get it over with. "I had one knife left, and Hvestang, it wasn't enough. But Two, Two remembered how they woke the statue, at Cataract. She pulled the other knife and—the—the—she woke."

Therkon had his own memories. Dhasdein's history. I heard the breath hiss, as if I had hurt him, in his throat.

"Gods above, Chaeris."

"I couldn't—we had no other way. I d-didn't . . ."

I didn't want to do it, to remember is almost more than I can bear, if *you* think I am not human, how do you think *I* feel? I could not get out any of it. I clutched like a man drowning at the folds of sealskin cloak.

I heard his next breath suck in. Then he moved with the jerkiness of shock, and his other arm tried to come round me, to pull me right into his body's refuge. His face bowed, but not with revulsion, into my hair. "Oh, Chaeris," I heard him whisper, almost in the way I had whispered, *Oh, Therkon.* "Oh, my . . . Oh, Chaeris."

Wind and sea-sound washed over us. *Anfluga* tacked again: Rathi must have been sailing purely by the wind's feel on his cheek, for it was almost completely dark. Gildair's lights had grown, strengthened, larger than planets now. We were round on the next tack before Therkon spoke.

Straightening only a little, not releasing me, but I could feel him staring out over the rail, onto the lightless sea.

"*He.*"

I did not have to ask which "he." The one he would not scorn as a slaver, nor dismiss as a popinjay. The one who had taken more from him than pride.

"I kicked him," he said softly, "the third day. At sea. He told me then. What they would do to me. When they had me ashore. When they were on—Skall." He said it as if the very word burnt his throat. "He would not just whip me. Like a dog. Or chain me. Like a dog. *We've a kennel for you*, he said, *on my island. Fit for an Outland cur. You'll taste the pleasures of that a day or two. And then.*"

I did not say, *Go on.* I could envisage, far too clearly, what that portal might unseal.

"When they pulled me out of the—kennel," Therkon said very softly, "I knew I would die."

He shifted his arm over me a little, as if to confirm I was still there.

"No more safeguards. No chances. Even if I chose—and I would have—to plead. *He*—Nothing would save me. I knew I would never find you. Rescue you. Know what happened to you. To you. Or to Dhasdein."

I had no words at all.

"So I spat at them." He was barely whispering. "And I prayed. To the River-lord. To Dhe. If it's all in ruin, I besought them, my charge lost, both my charges, my life's work, my mother's life work, the whole Riverworld lost. If it's all ruin, only let me die. As fast as I can."

I could only tighten my handful of cloak until my very fingerbones cracked. And I had thought myself sorely overtried.

"I meant to jump. To bang my head on the gallows. They told me about the gallows. To strangle myself, to—but when they pulled me out, I was too cold, they were too quick."

Now I could feel him trembling, a fine vibration that seemed to start in his very bones. His breath came in abrupt, fitful pants against my cheek.

"Then," he said, "you came."

He left me the dark to understand the fullness of that. Not merely his own survival, not merely the greatest of individual debts. Not merely rescue from torture and a prolonged, hideous death. But also the chance to redeem his honor. Recover the charge for whom he had pledged his life. And with it, a renewed hope for his greater charge.

For Dhasdein. For the Riverworld.

In silence Two rehearsed the rest. The price for us was great, almost as great as for those nine who lost their lives. But did this not go some way to redeem the debt?

Tears trembled on my lashes, blurring Gildair to a row of golden stars, more fitful and far blurrier than the torches that had burned for us along the imperial wall in Riversend. Tears of horror and sorrow and loss. Tears of a wormwood gratitude, such as Azo brought me on the tower of the Seaward fort. Yes, what you did was bitter, an eternal stain upon you, she too had said. But you did what you must.

*Anfluga* turned again, far more slowly this time, almost majestically. The lights were close upon us, I could make out the blocky silhouette of walls, perhaps a wharf. The shape of windows. The smell of smoke and tar and fish-guts, the sound of shipping, creaky planks, slap of ropes. Humankind waited for us. Warmth, perhaps some welcome. Even I need not despair of entering there.

In that slow rise of hope, the detail recurred with something near a slap. "The ring! What did you do with the ring? The imperial seal! You still had it, didn't you, at Ve Pool? Mother save us, if Stokka or Thralli found *that*—!"

"I ate it," said Dhasdein's crown prince.

* * * *

By daylight, Gildair was blue. A steely, dark grey-blue in both tile and stone, thick-walled, stolid houses snugged in startlingly regular streets above the harbour in its short arms of bay. From my upstairs window, its solidity spoke an aplomb, a tempered endurance, equal to every storm the south could unleash.

It was also a town sophisticated as Jurrick, the conduit between Sandouin and the bigger islands of the further, the true South Isles, a town with merchants and craft shops, and inns, from overnight dormitories to hostelries doubtless fit for lords. But even a dockside tavern might have refused our custom, a handful of bedraggled seamen, me in my hard-used clothes, and Therkon fumbling like an animated scarecrow in Nouip's cloak and Rathi's spare boots: had not Gildair, like Ve Pool, been feeling hardship's pinch.

"An' now, lass. What think ye to do *now*?"

Rathi had out-paced sun and breakfast both. It was scudding bleakly outside. Last night, I had been unable to think past getting Therkon clean, dry, fed, his hurts salved, and into a bed, preferably all at once. I had hardly noticed a landlord happy to fill even a few bunks and a couple of dingy rooms, and a healer willing to stir abroad in wind and darkness at a stranger's call.

A brisk, middle-aged, dark Archipelagan, he had seemed careful, if clinically detached. I had ached to hover, to tally the damage revealed and its repairs begun. But recalling that moment of rage and revelation on Skall's hillside, once he set to work, I had heroically shut the door on them both.

"Y'r brither'll hardly leave that bed today."

Rathi was right in that.

"The healer's coming back."

The healer finished, there had still been a bath to organize, cooks fit to cater for a near invalid, *Anfluga*'s crew to wrestle into conceding that, no, they would not sail on in the dark, yes, I *was* going to pay for passage from Skall, and yes, that price would include their bed and board.

They had just dispersed, leaving me to stay abruptly watery knees against the hall stairpost, when the healer reappeared.

"The skipper tells me, ye're in charge?" It had hovered between doubt and courtesy, a "lass," or perhaps, "ma'am." His face showed lines, even for middle-age, under the hanging lamp. "Y'r man's clean, an' I've seen to the rest. Ye'll need salves, for a week or so. I'll send some round?" I nodded and nodded, trying hard to summon suddenly elusive words. "He's abed now. If they've thin soup, give him some, an' a little bread. Not too much, at first! An' he says," suddenly he was eyeing me narrowly, "ye were hurt y'rself, a piece back. Ribs, was it? Cracked?"

"Ribs, yes. But they're all right now." His face was swinging slowly toward and away from me. "The soup's heating. May I, can I go up?"

"He's askin' for ye." He frowned. "But he was very firm. Made me promise I'd look at ye, as well."

I had shut myself out, but he had not forgotten me. He had looked for me. Thought for me, with that infuriating, ire-melting Dhasdeini concern, even in his own distress.

I had bitten my lip hard, and shut my hand harder on the stairpost. And managed, "I had two good healers, on Phaerea. But thank you. I can go up?"

Now I bit my lip again, still staring outside, as Rathi's boots shifted on the bare wooden floor. Too early, I wanted to exclaim, it's too early for this, before the healer, before breakfast, before Therkon and I even have a chance to talk. Do you think I, alone, can decree what we'll do now?

For some things, yes. I still had the gem pouch, and Therkon would not cavil at my sole decision there.

"I can pay the passages, both of them, but I may need a money-changer." The healer's reckoning waited, too. "Could Segil or someone escort—?"

"The whole crew'll convoy ye, if ye choose, lass. But—"

"In a moment. That's the door."

Therkon had been sitting up, against what looked like half the inn's pillows, when I tapped, bare minutes earlier. The nightshirt was probably from his own pack, its clean if now rumpled white a stark contrast to the dark veils of hair, combed but still loose over his shoulders, and the regular thicket of beard. It did match the hollow-eyed pallor of his face all too well.

I had known better than to try watching the night with him, just as I had known to bespeak my own room. I had officiated while he swallowed, almost reverently, his first mouthfuls of bread. Helped him spoon up soup. But when his eyelids began to sink, I had coaxed the sleeping-potion down him, and then, with what felt like tearing sinews, whispered a goodnight, and tiptoed out. If ghosts and nightmares plagued his rest, he would not want that further humiliation shared.

And if fatigue and relief had sunk me as swiftly, the memories had not stayed buried. Neither Therkon nor I had asked, *Did you sleep well?*

Now the door swung open. Helpfully, Rathi admitted the kitchen-maid. Unlike the White Grebe, the Lobster Pot readily served food upstairs. I did settle the tray myself over Therkon's lap, and inspect the barley broth, exactly as the healer had ordered. Toasted bread came with it. When my own stomach rumbled, Therkon said sharply, "Sit down, Chaeris."

The healer had said the same thing the night before. After a sharp stare, and a hand suddenly clamped under my elbow, while he sent a shout ringing down the rear passage. "Husvorth! Up here!"

Husvorth was the innkeeper, who brought bustle and exclamation and a hot, exquisitely poached cod fillet in his wake. Against both his and the healer's protests—"Y'r forespent, lass! Take a moment for y'rself!"—I had gulped it in time to follow Therkon's tray up the stairs.

Therkon's own expression now warned against further dispute. I sat on the bedside stool and purloined half the bread. A moment before he had been muttering about razors and rubbing at his jaw. Now I pointed magisterially at the spoon, and with a tiny smile that retorted, For the moment, you have the tiller, he began to eat.

Rathi watched in silence. But however villainous his looks, Therkon was rapidly reclaiming the crown prince: he took three mouthfuls, set the spoon down, looked straight in Rathi's face, and said, "Sir, I have much to thank you for."

Rathi grunted and shifted his feet again. In a moment he said gruffly, "T' passage was paid."

"But not the rest."

"Aye, well. None'd leave the lass to that."

Therkon's mouth crimped. I could see him thinking, *You saved us, and I could do nothing. I, who imperiled us both.* Whatever gratitude he assuredly felt had Dhasdeini self-esteem to balance it. Not to mention imperial pride.

Beyond the pretext for curtains, the sky had darkened. Now a sudden squall tapped against the casement's tiny panes. In Gild-air they burned bright whale oil in the lamps, however sparingly, and even a dockside inn filled its windows with glass.

Rathi was staring intently in that grey light: so an Isle skipper might evaluate a fellow man, and one he felt no obligation to respect, but something suddenly recalled that fleeting expression of the night before. Yet why should Rathi conceivably covet a rescued slave, an Outland enigma? Any more than a girl, at best an Outland curiosity, at worst a witch, with a 'companion' whose menace he had seen for himself?

Soup forgotten, Therkon was staring back. *What are you?* that look riposted: the prince, the imperial leader assessing a tool, an ally, a resource. *Who are you?* demanded the man behind the masks. *Who are you, to have helped, comforted, been trusted by my Chaeris?*

Because it was possessiveness, if not open warning, in that stare. Even, I realized, something near to jealousy.

"Ye're no'," Rathi said slowly, "much alike."

Therkon turned a wrist. The prince's gesture: a point I decline to explain. "And what are your plans, now?"

For all the snub, he had known better than to add, After you are paid. Rathi's look noted both points. What he said was, "An' ye don't *sound* alike."

"We were raised apart." Therkon looked down his nose as if he had never left Riversend.

"Aye?" Rathi raised his own brows. "But ye know about the lass's 'companion'?"

Therkon put the spoon right down. The stare chilled from prince to hatchet man.

"No affair o' mine?" Rathi looked half amused. "Ye take a fine toplofty tone when ye've a mind to it. No wonder ye stirred yon hoodie crow on Skall. Si'thee, *prince*." It was pure Isles irony, but Therkon winced. "T'was the lass followed ye, an' found ye, an' broke ye out o' that. An' t'was *Anfluga* brought ye off. I'm no' sure I'd do it again. But the lass. Ye've taken fine care for her so far. Is there any space, in y'r plans now, for *her*?"

Therkon sat up with such a jerk the soup spilt, but the manifold injustices gagged him the split second that let me get in first.

"He does take care for me, he *has* taken care for me! I'm the troublecrew, I should take care for *him*!" I swung on Therkon, spurting words that had waited weeks to be said. "I was stupid on the cliff, Two said it was quicker, the chimney, I thought, it'll just waste time to stop for the rope—What you did might have been wrong, but it began with my fault!"

He was almost as confounded as Rathi. He literally blinked. Then his eyes went black and hard as dagger-points and he said, "Are you sure?"

The question I had asked myself in the street at Ve Pool. Had I fallen by chance, or the consequence of my own choice? Or at the choice of someone—something—else?

I could feel the blood drain out of my face. Rain tapped and whispered at the window and black water was rising round me, touching, groping, reaching for my lungs, my breath, my throat . . .

"Chaeris!"

Therkon had lunged for my wrist. The yank threw me almost across the bed, the soup spilt definitively. "Chaeris!"

I managed to sit up. To nod, to gasp, to gulp wordlessly. *I'm here.*

He let go. His face looked hard as mine felt, stiffened onto the bone. I could feel Rathi staring. The air around us fairly vibrated. Doubt, suspicion, multiple tensions. More than a little fear.

Then Rathi said harshly, "Was that y'r 'companion,' too?"

Therkon shuddered once and took his eyes from mine. Looked vaguely at the soiled sheets, the empty bowl. Then lifted his stare to Rathi and answered bleakly, "No. That was what brought us here."

Rathi's mouth opened, and I felt my own jaw drop. Two had named, we had both thought we accepted Therkon as strategist, but his decisions could still catch us both unawares.

Therkon pushed bowl and tray away and began at the beginning. With the Dhasdeini wrecks, and the survivor in that Seafort bed.

When he stopped, Rathi had subsided on the forsaken stool, with both hands plunged wrist-deep in his beard, yanking it so hard his head swung to and fro.

"Somethin' brought ye to the Isles. Wrecked y'r ship. Saved ye, maybe. Sent ye on south. Maybe. So ye cannot say, flatly, Aye, or Nay. Ye only *think* this bogle's arranged things. Tiran's eyes, d'ye mean it arranged *me?*"

Therkon answered flintily, "There is no use trying to divide what was planned from what went awry."

Because if I had been manipulated on the cliff, with intent to part me from Therkon, why would I have been allowed to rejoin him? And if we were both meant to die, why would a rescue have been allowed on Skall?

"But ye can make no sense of this either way?" Rathi was almost ready to tear his hair. "Do ye at least know what's doin' it? Do ye have the faintest idea where ye're *goin'*?"

Therkon looked up with eyes black as midnight water, and said, "Kaastria." Just as Two said, "*Sthassamaer.*"

For an instant Rathi froze. Then he almost shouted, "What d'ye know—what have ye heard—how d'ye know about *that?*"

He had gone a clay-ish grey, and his hand had flown by instinct into the horns. Therkon stared at him, and then at me. But I was already staring at him.

He looked back to Rathi. Tiredly, he said, "The survivor said it. The Seer knew it. She said, Black water. My—Chaeris—sees—feels—black water. Rising. Around *her*."

Rathi gulped, twice. I said, flat and loud, "Kaastria?"

They both jerked round, but my own eyes were already fixed. "Kaastria. When did you think of—why did you decide on that?"

Therkon scrabbled a little higher among the tangled, soiled sheets. He still looked half invalid and half vagabond, but the hatchet man, the crown prince, the strategist, were all in that steely stare.

"That was the name she had." He spoke to me, as if we were alone. "The name we were given. The sagas' message. The clue. Whatever muddles, whatever tangles have befallen since, we have always moved toward Kaastria. Whatever we did."

"But t'is only one island, and half the Isles around ye! Why d'ye say *that*?"

"Because Kaastria is the only name *we* had."

He stopped, and stared past me into the grey mosaic of rain.

"And Kaastria," he added flatly, "is in ruin."

Where had he heard it? At Ve Pool, on Eithay, from Thralli's crew, even on the way to Skall? But in whatever extremity, the strategist had not mislaid the gift.

Rathi seemed to have been struck mute. Then he swallowed and croaked, "Ruins? Why ruins—?"

Therkon's back sagged, and he began to slide down against the pillows. The quick, unforeseeable ebb of over-tried strength. But he flapped a hand at me and managed, "Chaeris? Two?"

And Two was already answering for us both.

"*You are the strategist,*" she said.

Rathi clutched his hair and almost bellowed, "Will the pair o' ye just make *sense*?"

Two answered, but not to him, "*Because the name was given,*" she said. "*Because on Kaastria, there will be no-one else.*"

The casement rattled in a sudden little gust and a draft slid across the room. I felt the goosebumps rise on my neck.

No-one else to intervene, Two meant, for good or evil, as Azo and Verrith and Deoren had in the wreck, and Nouip and Frotha on Sickle, and Veenn's folk, and Vithre, and even Stokka, at Ve Pool. Or Rathi, at Eithay and Skall. No-one else to mar plans. No-one else to rescue us.

"Because," I said to Rathi, "Two or I can read information. But at the point, we are troublecrew. We just have to make things happen. My—brother—knows what the things should be."

Rathi hurled both hands in the air.

"So *he* decides ye're goin' to Kaastria? Now? Wi' him limp as a jug o' whey, an' ye no' much better, an no' a ship or hand between ye. An' ye want to go to Kaastria? To ferret in a heap o' flood-wrack and mud-fall an', an'—what are ye goin' to *do*?"

Between him and my own terrors, I was very close to tears. "I don't know! I don't know how we'll go or what we'll find or what'll happen and I don't care! I only know, we have to go!"

Therkon stirred, and tried to lift a hand, then his head. I put my own hand hard on his and stared at Rathi, who was staring, as speechless and over-harried, at me.

Then he pushed the stool aside and said flatly, "Nay."

We both stared. Rathi shoved fingers yet again into, through and out of his beard.

"If ye can find nothin' better, between ye, this part I'll tell. Ye may take ship for Kaastria." A sudden little shudder ran through him. "But ye'll do it on *Anfluga*, the pair o' ye. Ye'll sail wi' me."

Therkon heaved himself half up, and put in huskily but dourly, "*I* will go with you."

He let me shout, conserving his strength. When I finished he had slid almost flat again, and let his eyes close. But at the pause he opened them and added, on a note that had become familiar, "Chaeris, it wants *you*."

One of us had to go: we had no choice, he had already come to terms with that. Plan how we liked, the margin was no longer wide enough to think of reversing the tide. We had chosen to come south, on Phaerea. If we refused here, simply baulked, even took a ship and tried to sail back toward Dhasdein, how far would we get? In the teeth of that steadily northering wind?

So he would go. If it wanted me, then I was the more valuable, to the Isles, to Dhasdein and Iskarda. I must be left behind, protected, never hazarded. So if he did meet the enemy on Kaastria, I might still survive. Might still help the Isles, or if that was unnecessary, might go back, to bring the news, to become the next kingpost of Dhasdein.

Without him.

I might have screamed protests. I might have drowned in tears. Neither of them touched Two.

"*If it wants us,*" she said, "*will it take you instead?*"

Therkon's eyes flew open. Shock, disbelief. Disillusion. Something near despair.

"You can't—"

On my own account I snorted at him. "Do I have a choice?"

Because Two was right. If I did not go, would it even bother with Therkon? Might it not simply bypass him for some new ploy focused on its real target, now conveniently, perhaps utterly, even fatally alone?

I worked down Two's logic paths and wondered that I had not already seen it for myself. If staying had been an immoral choice on Sickle, it was outright impossible now.

Therkon put both hands over his eyes. Rathi stood abruptly back from the bedside and growled, "I'll find the healer. Whatever chances next, ye'll not be leavin' the day."

\* \* \* \*

We did not leave Gildair for a whole six days more. When I look back, it seems a time that swung like a pendulum between the Mother's heaven and the Adversary's hell. Because by day there was Therkon, safe, mine to cosset and tend and lovingly tyrannize over, recovering fast but still unfit or unwilling to rebel. But by night there was memory and dream to fling me back into Skall's freezing murk, to the sights, the sounds, the sensation of a light-gun shearing human flesh.

The third evening, after the healer had brought his salves and diminishing bandages, I found Therkon sitting, as he had most of the day, on the side of the bed. As I came in he said quietly, "Chaeris? Would you wish to sleep in here tonight?"

I could feel my jaw sag. Injunctions and recollections raced past me, divided rooms or separate cabins, that searing insight on the hill in Skall. Sharp panic as Two fired other memories atop them, the weight and warmth of him asleep on my shoulder, the muscled support of his back against my forehead, the velvet touch of belly skin under my hand . . .

"It's not correct, no." He spoke in some apparent embarrassment, eyes on the floor. "But," sounding rueful now, "after Phaerea, and the hills, ah, we may be past correctness, do you think?"

I could not suppress Two and speak as well. He looked up, and it was open anxiety now.

"We could make a partition. Hang a sheet, perhaps. They could bring another bed."

I found words, however foolish. "It—why?"

His lashes went down again. He had adamantly demanded to shave, the very first day, but his hair was still loose as I had hardly seen it before Gildair. Through its shadows even whale-oil light did not fully reveal his face.

"I would feel happier. If I knew. If I was at least in earshot—of you."

The strategist. He was thinking ahead of me, even of Two, considering some incursion here, as in Fiskri's house. And I was thinking, as fast as Two, that it was a more than cogent point. Never mind modesty, forget nightmares. What if the enemy decided to move, this time against him?

I said, "I'll ask Husvorth what they can do."

So when the next nightmare brought me gasping up in a pool of sweat it was not half-dark and solitude that met me, but the glow of a night-light. And Therkon, silent in bare feet and night-shirt, drawing aside the makeshift curtain to murmur, "Chaeris?"

He had known better than to walk in and touch me. Not troublecrew, fresh sprung from nightmare and still half-awake. Or perhaps, his own custom forbade breaking in on any female, however close she had become to him, in her bed.

In a moment I managed, "I'm all right."

"Of course." His head slanted, against the back-light. "But I, at least, could use a sleep-settler. Heillor showed me how to heat up milk."

In the peat coals of the brazier that served as fireplace, in a little brass pot, from the jugful on the window-ledge. A jug that must have come each night after I so tactfully left him to put himself to bed.

By the time the milk reached a bearable drinking heat, it seemed natural to sit on his bedside as we sipped.

"Ugh," I said, the only safe thing that came to mind. "I hate hot milk."

He laughed, a breath in the night-lamp's twilight. "Drink up. *It's good for you.*"

"My fathers used to say that." The pang of memory almost blocked my throat. Evenings in infancy, one or the other of them taxed with the job of "getting Chaeris to bed." Whether by cajolery, bribe or threat.

"My nurse," he said, after a pause that nearly over-charged the moment, "said it too."

His father was an emperor. Who would never do something as menial as bed down a son himself.

And I knew he had bad dreams too, and it would only embarrass him to say, Did I wake you? He would surely know better than to ask what had woken me. The past was forbidden territory. As for the future . . .

Rathi talked about thatt daily, mapping routes to Kaastria. "No' down t'west o' Hamair, though that's quickest, aye." Hamair was the one big island ahead. "But the chance o' weather's worse. An' ye'll no' want another turn o' the sea-qualm for *him.*"

So instead we would slant down Hamair's long, deeply indented eastern side, past capes and towns Rathi named with old familiarity. "Easy enough, wi' this wind settin' northerly. An' *Anfluga*'ll run better, on that reach." Faster, as well as easier on Therkon's stomach, I understood.

"If this pestilent weather ever turns." Rathi again, grumbling at the window with its vista of dull-blue tile and stone, dark grey sky, pelting squalls of rain. "Tiran damp it. Ye'd think, by this time, we'd be half into spring. Seems the whole year's turned hindabout, an' headed back to winter again."

And the wind still sat persistently from northward, a wholly untoward phenomenon in the Isles, whose weather came up from the west and south. Rathi had grumbled about that, too, if less than about the rain. "At least, if the cursed wind's still workin' westerly, it'll no' be in our teeth."

Now I looked abruptly along the bedside at Therkon, who was looking at me. When our eyes met he put out a hand and laid it over mine.

*Don't think about it. Don't wonder how and why the wind sits so long and so unusually as it is.* He had known where my mind went, as I could have guessed for him. To the future, the real future, the unknown that waited for us on Kaastria, at the voyage's end.

And he had not paused to consider Two's reaction, or mine, or his own scruples. Not this time.

I turned my hand under his and his fingers shut, gently but decisively. We sat uncounted moments, taking comfort in the simplest, most banal human contact, in the empty night.

* * * *

In truth, neither Rathi nor I expected to be out of Gildair in less than a week. But for all his damages and privation, the third morning Therkon was up, walking, however unsteadily, about his room. Coming downstairs at intervals the fourth day, and ready, the fifth morning, for a sortie outside.

Heillor firmly vetoed that. But at noon Rathi came into the taproom with a pleased expression, announcing, "Picked up a cargo. Naught but letters an' such, an' it'll take us clear in to Rangar. But we can take shore-rest there. An' the better for it."

He slanted a look at Therkon, mulishly established on a back-wall stool, meaning, too clearly, *The better for you.* Therkon returned crisply, "Can you sail tomorrow?"

"Tomorrow?" Rathi stared. "*We* could, aye."

"If the wind suits," Therkon said flatly, "so can I."

Rathi scrubbed his beard and looked anxiously at me. Therkon shot me one glance and got off the stool. "Tomorrow," he said, in the crown prince's voice, and whatever incompletely healed whip-marks and unfaded bruises he might be concealing, I knew better than to dispute.

Because I knew that he, like me, could not bear any more delay. Whatever was on Kaastria, whatever the outcome, he wanted it met. Done. Over with.

He did have to leave me most of the mundane arrangements, down to trading two more gems to pay the inn, the healer, Rathi and his crew for the two past passages, and, at my insistence, half the fair value of a further voyage to an unspecified port in Kaastria. I thought, with satisfaction, that I had learnt chaffering from Fiskri's example, as well as caution in taking Segil and both stroke oars as escort to the money-changer. Until I overheard Husvorth and Rathi by the kitchen, Husvorth saying, on a note of wonder, "Paid the whole score, for y'r men as well. An' never quibbled once!"

While Rathi responded, with something closer to respect than satisfaction, "Aye. Bountiful as the Mither, she is."

Therkon did have the better of me over his new boots. It was manifestly ridiculous to summon a custom-making cobbler to the Lobster Pot. Nor could he do without. So his first genuine excursion was "up-town," as Rathi described it, with someone's weather-canvas instead of Nouip's cloak—"we'll not want a riot, d'ye see?"—Segil and Rathi both in attendance, and me right at his elbow, all but biting my tongue in between trying to see five ways at once.

When we came back, the tap-room light showed him rather white about the mouth, but he made his own way upstairs. And when the boots arrived, altered from the best pair the cobbler had, he greeted them upright, if seated. "Now," he said, pulling his hair back into its usual tail, suddenly turning into an approximate copy of the man I remembered in Riversend, "we can go."

I watched the dawn break next morning, grey and wretched as ever, feeling stretched and jaded after a mostly sleepless night. But departure already had its own momentum. The inn-score was paid. Our packs were filled. Breakfast had been ordered. Heillor arrived for a final examination and consignment of salves. And with them, to my amazement, a little vial of brown powder that, when he lifted the cork, emitted the pungent, unmistakable scent of imperial spice.

"He's a fussy stomach, aye," Heillor observed complacently. "Ye'll likely need a store of this."

A greater boon than decent boots. I shut my hand over it as on a butterfly, and managed, "I can't thank you. How much—?" And he gave me an airy wave.

"Lass, ye've paid me o'er and above asking." A quick half-grin and a glance at Therkon, embroiled with Rathi over something. "Y'r man did most o' the work himself. You take that now." For an instant his look changed, into something that recalled the tone in Rathi's words to Husvorth. "An' remember us."

I would remember, I thought, with the last hot toast and delectably salted porridge warm in my belly, the rain beating futilely over my weather-canvas and knitted cap, and underneath, the heavy trousers and sweater Rathi had insisted I buy. "Those furs'll ward him in Tiran's own ice-house, but that bitty cloak an'—an' y'r other things—" in Gildair too, women all wore skirts— "'ll never hold an honest southerly." I would remember, yes, with as poignant a longing as I had preserved even the shape of *Tolla*'s cabin steps. Another sanctuary, so briefly found, so soon drawn away.

Rain sheened the cobblestones and pocked the puddles, wind beat our gear as we tramped dourly onto the wharf. *Anfluga* was moored rather than beached, with a spare sail for tarpaulin abaft the rowing thwarts. To keep, Rathi carefully did not explain, a place dry for my delicate brother, at least until we cast off. It gave me some amusement to watch how swiftly they had learnt to manage imperial pride.

We scrambled down and stowed ourselves, packs against the side, Hvestang atop. Only this time there were two of us to crouch beside them, as the rowers settled and the rope-men went into action, the warps dropped splashing, and Rathi nodded to Segil: *Cast off.*

In the unrelenting wind and rain, no-one had stirred out to watch. Segil put a boot to the wharf and pushed. *Anfluga* pitched a little, then the farther oars bit. She pivoted. The grey harbour waters revolved, as the River had beyond Marbleport, the somber blue tiles and stone walls receded. As silently as it had coalesced from wind and darkness, Gildair slid away into grey morning mist.

# CHAPTER XV

Working round Gildair's stubby southern cape, *Anfluga* began to pitch. When we reached the wide gap between Sandouin and Hamair and turned south-east across the swing of open water, she began to roll as well, and I looked anxiously at Therkon, who gave me a somewhat dry smile.

"I don't actually get 'sea-qualm'," he observed mildly. "Unless my stomach upsets first."

Calling up Two's record, I realized that it had never happened in the worst times aboard *Aspis*. Of course, in Dhasdein, he must have been on and off galleys most of his life. But what would his stomach make of *Anfluga*'s uncompromising dry rations?

I eyed him even more anxiously, and met a grin openly mischievous. "Rathi," he observed, "has been most exercised. I heard him interrogating Heillor over 'what tack a fussy stomach'd manage, aye?'"

"Oh." I felt only frank relief. Rathi had taken thought and care, despite his faintly disparaging attitude. If he could help it, Therkon at least would reach Kaastria in creditable shape.

Hamair appeared next morning, a high, ragged silhouette that grew into crag after crag of deeply indented cliffs, first grey, then honey-gold above a white-capped sea. "Aye," Rathi said when he came off-watch. "They call it Crag, an' it earns the name. There's ne'er a harbour, an' hardly a livin' soul down this side, nowadays, until ye round into Muirwick." I knew already this was the island's largest bay. "An' not much but sheep an' timber an' rabbits anywhere."

He tapped out his breakfast biscuit on a strake, and glanced swiftly back north. I did not need confirmation that the wind had been strengthening since the early hours, but my stomach twisted at his expression. Too well, too clearly, I remembered the wind hounding *Aspis*.

Therkon said, "Will it clear, do you think?" He spoke as he might to *Aspis*' captain, and I caught the surprise in Rathi's glance: respect was well enough, but what if he began wondering about the source for that air of command?

"So long," I said, "as it doesn't rain," and Rathi turned back, with a crinkle at his eye-corners that signaled ease, approval, perhaps the inclination of a smile.

"Rain it may not, lass. But if it clears, ye may get snow instead."

I groaned graphically, and he smiled outright. "Even with a norther, aye."

It had not snowed next morning, though it was far colder, with a sky more white than grey. But the wind was steady, and with it on her flank, *Anfluga* was fairly stable as well. As we stowed away breakfast, including Therkon's slightly stale but definitely white bread rolls, I suddenly realized that I need not sit idle on this passage. Therkon was here. It would help not to fret about this future, my ribs hardly came to mind any more, and I was direly in need of exercise.

I said, "Do you think you could work out with me?"

Deoren would have taught him drills, I was sure. Hand-to-hand moves, skirmish techniques, basic weapon-work were River troublecrew standard. He was steady enough now, and if the worst scathes were not completely settled, it would help him to move about. And restore his strength and balance and confidence too.

He gave me a dubious look. He would be remembering my sessions with Azo and Verrith. I said meekly, "Just the basics. Not too fast."

Ten repeats of step-in-and-engage had the furs and my weather-canvas off, but as I expected, Deoren had not neglected his charge. Therkon knew the drills, and as he warmed up a certain snap in his responses made me think he had used them on the field.

Five ground-shifting scrimmages taught us both to avoid dunnage and inconvenient strakes. When Therkon wiped his forehead I said, "I could use some weapons work."

The look on Rathi's face almost made me laugh. Therkon's expression was as daunted, if not so alarmed.

"Chaeris?"

I might not mean harm, but he knew my standard with weapons. Did I imagine he could equal that?

"You could use Hvestang." I forestalled the look of outright horror. "Tie the peace-strings, I'll keep my knives sheathed. No edge or point at all."

Hvestang had the orthodox ties to keep a sword in the scabbard, and my knife sheaths were made to slip off the straps. After a few nervous passes, Therkon began to accept that he would neither bruise nor behead nor even hit me unless I chose, and started to explore his own weapon. It was probably, I realized, the first time he had actually worked out with Hvestang.

When he started to slow and fumble I called a halt, and we wiped down, did a few muscle-easers, and hurried into our clothes before the chill undid it all. Settling against the side, Therkon observed ruefully, "I shall be stiffer than old fish tomorrow." But the tone said it had been worth the price.

"Heillor had some muscle-oil." Turning to rout among the baggage, I caught the faces of *Anfluga*'s crew in the shifting corner of an eye.

Carefully blank expressions. Aimed over my head, or aft into the wind, or at Segil, with the steering oar. All of them utterly quiet.

I glanced the other way. Therkon was watching me, and his face told me he understood. For most of them, it had been the first actual sight of what my knives could do.

I said under my breath, "I'm troublecrew. I *need* to know this. I *need* to work out." I could already feel muscle and sinew starved for exercise relaxing in relief.

Therkon nodded. He did not have to say, I understand. I lived with troublecrew. Predictably, it was Segil who spoke out one thing that would have been on the others' minds.

"I see," he observed, leaning with deceptive indolence on the steering oar, "why ye've no use for skirts."

* * * *

*Anfluga* ran eight days down the Hamair coast, and we worked out on every one. Therkon's scathes settled almost completely, and he had learnt enough about Hvestang to give me an actual tussle the morning of our third landfall, on the high, canted end of Hostack, the cape guarding the north side of Furshaven bay.

"Third point, aye," Rathi agreed, sounding relieved. "Across Hellir strait to Hamair head, then Muickhond, t'south side o' Muirwick bay. T'one more cast across Tankerness water, an' now we turn in for Rangar. It's been," with another of those uneasy glances behind us, "an uncommon clear run."

I had not wanted to think about that. The whole eight days had been a time as in Gildair, an enchanted, sanctuary pause in which it seemed nothing could touch us, nothing was dangerous, nothing could change. All I wanted was to sail on, chewing hard tack and tolerating the cold and sitting, talking, working out with Therkon, and never come to shore again.

Even with the nights.

The first time it was I who plunged sweating and gasping back to the windy ocean-dark, the light secure hand about my wrist. The solid warmth against my shoulder, and Therkon saying, as he had among the rocks of the Brettabreck, "It's all right. I'm here. It's all right, Chaeris."

And in the dark of *Anfluga*'s open deck, with all but Rathi and the watch-man asleep, it seemed beyond question that he should put an arm about me, and I should settle my head into his shoulder, and we should find a way to keep together as we slept.

The second night, it was he who woke with a huge gasp and jerk and then a strangled sound half-choke, half-snarl as his hands clawed the gunwale almost up to the second I caught his shoulder and hissed, "It's me, it's *Anfluga*, it's all right!"

We sat pressed together again, both no doubt wishing for that distraction of heating milk. His breathing was still rough and the heat of his cheek told me he had broken into a sweat. His arm shook a little, spasmodically, around me. I kept my hands from grasping his, and my questions quiet. The waking had betrayed him far enough.

*Anfluga* ran on, filling the night with the sounds, to me so reassuring, of a ship under sail: rope-creak, wave-hiss and slap. The muscle-shift of strake and bottom under us, the sway of Segil's head above the steering oar, against the starless dark. Presently, just audible, Therkon spoke.

"At the worst times. I used to tell myself: it was a recompense."

"For what?" Then I understood and was too shocked to fence. "For Ve Pool? For losing me? *No-one* would think, would expect you to pay for things like—not with *that!*"

He made a little sound that might almost have become a laugh. "Ah, Chaeris." Light as wind, his palm brushed my cheek. "My truest troublecrew." The lightness snuffed. He said flatly, "For Tanekhet."

It came too fittingly, too close to inner truth. Slavery, the horror voyages, even Angrir, he would have fought, for Dhasdein and Iskarda and the Isles as well as for me. But we did not weigh against that symmetry of suffering by which he, who had tortured his oldest idol, might die by torture himself.

I drew breath as carefully as if my ribs had still not knit.

"He forgave you," I said.

I did not have to add, You know that. You could not have forgotten. That morning we left Iskarda.

*Anfluga* heeled a little far and white foam kissed the gunwale. Therkon was silent, every muscle saying my anodyne had failed.

"Or perhaps," he answered, too softly, "for Keshaq."

Who had also been enslaved, but who had seen his country lost and his family destroyed atop it. A balance even death would not have redeemed.

"But . . . you didn't think—You didn't *want*—?"

He moved a little, his body firming. Not in his own security, but to reaffirm mine.

"No. I did not *want* to go like that. I did not want to think it, either. It was only, sometimes . . ."

Sometimes endurance must have seemed impossible. And the only alternative had been to justify surrender. To accept, to deem it just that he suffer pain, torture, death.

I said flatly, "They would not have wanted that. Neither of them would have wanted that. And *I* would not want it. Whatever you did," I heard the note warm, however I tried, "I would not want to lose you. Nor would anyone else in Iskarda. Nor," the king-stroke, "in Dhasdein."

Quite sharply he turned his head away. I bit my lip and kept my hands still, though my arms ached to reach for him, for comfort, for reassurance to us both. For more than comfort. *Shut up*, I ordered Two brutally. *This isn't the time, and like that it never will be. Shut **up**.*

*Anfluga* rolled, and Segil swayed. And gradually I felt the arm about me ease, begin to signal balance, composure reclaimed. In a moment, face still slightly averted, he spoke.

"Well," he said, "perhaps, not *everyone* in Dhasdein."

My eyes swam. It was neither wise nor safe, given how Two's impulse matched with mine, to lay a hand, as I so longed to do, against his cheek.

"Oh, someone you forced to bake a whole week of poppy rolls . . ."

And my reward, however bittersweet, was in the breath of a laugh, the brief almost hug before he gave the packs a little shove and murmured, "I suppose we should try again."

*He meant, to settle down,* I told Two fiercely. *To lie down, if not together, and try to sleep.*

He talked to me after that, more than he had ever done, and without the formality, the submerged wariness and sudden recollections of my human age that he had used on the River, or the baffling switches from warmth to brusquerie on Phaerea, or even the ruler's informality he might have used to Deoren. I wondered sometimes if he had ever talked to anyone like this. As to a friend, an equal, to the peer he could never have had.

In cooler moments I told Two ferociously that I *was* his peer, not just fighting partner or ally or sharer of dangers, but the heir to another nation. His equal in rank. At other times I shut both our eyes and clung to a moment where the future, in Kaastria or beyond it, did not exist.

\* \* \* \*

Like Yinstey, Rangar lay at the very depth of its bay, but Furshaven was not the Gnufe, however long its run, however precipitous and fir-lined its cliffs. And Rangar was no wretched hamlet but a good-sized town, once, Rathi said, a prosperous port for timber sales. "If there's one thing Hamair can grow, t'is pine."

But as we reached into the final cove, walls that should have been as brightly white-washed as Ve Pool's began to show dull, faded, stained, or even sheeted with dirt. Where walls remained. Almost every neatly aligned street showed open-doored, broken-windowed houses, or outright fallen rubble and orphaned chimneystacks, like decayed molars in a mouthful of once healthy teeth.

"T'is south Hamair, no' south Phaerea," Rathi said dourly, meeting my glance. "Too close." He did not finish, but I knew he meant, to Kaastria. To the spreading edge of ruin outright. "Folk or trade, there's no' a lot left."

The harbour held one disreputable freighter and a cluster of fishing boats. On the quay rubbish lay everywhere, from shreds of net to untidily splayed, over-weathered heaps of planks, and every third door along the shippers' row was boarded shut. Or beaten in. "Aye," Rathi said grimly, "there's always scum, when t'pond starts to rot."

His own shipper remained, a short, saturnine man with two empty stools in his counting room and a watchful wariness. But he paid for the cargo, and named a trustworthy inn. "Leave a watch aboard," he added, with a glance across to *Anfluga's* mast. "She's a weatherly craft, an' there's none so many left."

The Pine Man was close to the quay, which, I realized, would lessen the risk of changing watches. It also had a tub and would heat water, the shore luxury I had coveted most. But its servery offered one stringy mutton stew, its taproom was three quarters empty, and the beer was rationed. I watched the gaunt, terse serving-maid and wondered if the same fear that haunted Fiskri loomed over her.

Rathi and his men sat together, quiet and watchful, and carried belaying pins. Therkon looked as grim as I felt. I was logically as much as cravenly relieved that he had taken us a shared room, and without demur. Whatever danger the great enemy might have in mind, every sense told me that theft, banditry, and all the other pests of incipient lawlessness were already here.

It was a paradoxical relief to rise in another rainy dawn, nag a breakfast from surly kitchen-folk, and gather up our traps. Rathi was curt as well as anxious, because, I realized, after hearing an exchange with Segil, they had not been able to find any more "soft tack." Dry rations only, I thought, my heart sinking. How if Therkon's stomach rebelled?

The shipper had offered no cargo. Rathi had in fact been evasive about our next port, and when the little point began to occlude Rangar behind us, he glanced back with something near open relief. "Ye run nor'east out o' Rangar," he observed, "wherever ye're goin'."

Whether north or south, he meant, after clearing Furshaven. He had not wanted to let the shipper know we were headed for Kaastria.

The day was colder than ever, and grey as approaching dusk. When nothing lay beyond *Anfluga's* dragon prow but open sea, Rathi leant suddenly, decisively on the steering oar and brought her round to lie into the wind. Then he jerked his head for Segil to take over, and came to Therkon and me.

"Ye know where we are, lass?" He crouched before us, balanced easily to the swing of the ship. "Back there's Furshead. T'last cape o' Hamair. After this, there's naught but Hvalwrast reach. An' then . . ."

He had rehearsed it, over and over, in Gildair. One long last southern leg, and our next landfall would be Kaastria itself.

"So I ask ye, lass. Both o' ye." He glanced between us, brows deep-drawn in a frown. "What ye'd want now?"

"We're in open sea," he said, when both of us stared. "We can turn as we please. South. Or north. Back to Burayn, up in Muirwick. Or to Gildair. Or—wherever ye'd choose." His eyes locked on mine, dark and more than anxious. "We can take ye. Wherever it may be."

The sea and the wind spoke, and my heart thumped somewhere in my throat. Therkon looked at me, once. His lips tightened, and then, without my or Two's prompt, he spoke for us all.

"You know," he said to Rathi, "that we no longer have a choice."

The wind and sea sound sank into some vast invisible gulf where, for an instant, I heard only the beating of my heart. Then Rathi's eyes dropped. He got slowly up from his heels, said, just audibly, "Aye," and turned away.

\* \* \* \*

The change began almost the instant *Anfluga* turned fully south. It did not come so unnaturally as the squall outside Riversend, but the sky darkened visibly, the clouds dropped lower, and spatters of rain began, altering rapidly to shreds of sleet. Then the wind rose, not savagely but steadily, from a brisk blow to the verge of a gale and on toward outright storm.

By then I was crouched under the gunwale, struggling to retain even a hint of control. *Aspis*, my memories cried, over and over, replaying the hideous indelible images, it's going to come again like that, they're all going to die, this time we'll die with them, it's just like *Aspis, Aspis, Aspis* . . .

Therkon must have understood as well as I, but Therkon had been a commander, on whose composure others leant. I could feel his shoulder stiffen against mine, and see the tension knot his profile as he looked astern. But the first sleet had hardly scudded over us before he got up and crossed to Rathi and said, "Shorten sail."

Rathi gave him a more than startled look: it had been the crown prince's voice, undisguised.

"What d'ye say?" The look added: Who are you to order us, a man who threw hysterics on Yinstey beach?

"It blew like this," Therkon said precisely, "outside Riversend."

Rathi opened and shut his mouth. Then the stare became a glower. Under his breath he growled, "And what good did shortenin' do ye then?"

"If you were meant to wreck, it could have happened already. A dozen times. That time, the aim is still uncertain. This time—"

"This time?" Rathi snapped.

Therkon's mouth corner rose in a blade-edge of a smile. "This time, I think, Sthassamaer is also wanting haste."

Rathi recoiled, and half the men in earshot shrank with him. Then he snapped his head around and bawled at the ropemen, "Reef!"

\* \* \* \*

By the time Therkon came back Two had shamed me into silence, at least. Her own conclusions, finally heard, let me speak almost steadily as he sank down.

"You really think this time we won't—won't—"

He gave me a quick glance. Then he turned right round and took my hands. The light was dwindling momently, but I could still read his face.

"We have no weapons except logic, Chaeris. How this—thing—works, thinks—if it thinks—may not be logical. But logic says, if it wanted us destroyed . . ."

It had only to leave us on Skall. The steps we had already traced in Gildair. Two almost snorted impatience. *"But what if it miscalculates?"*

Another man might have said, *What?* Therkon only sucked in his breath and took a moment's recovery. Then he glanced mast-ward, where they were tying down reef-points on a bare half of the sail, and said, "This *is* a better ship."

I felt the strakes and bottom shift in yet another of the count-less adjustments *Anfluga* made with every touch of the sea. I remembered the rigid timbers of *Aspis*. I glanced round the seasoned, Isle men's faces, and Two agreed. However it might gall Therkon to admit, *Aspis* had not half these vantages. Even if the gale went right out of hand, *Anfluga* was likelier to survive.

I made a noise to signal Two's, Yes, and saw Therkon's jaw set. Before he added bleakly, "If it does misjudge the wind . . . at the worst, we could be better so."

The logic of that froze me where I sat: that drowning, in real black water, might be a better end than whatever awaited us alive.

\* \* \* \*

The light failed more quickly after that. By the time my undaunted stomach signaled, *Midday*, we could hardly see each other's faces. Along Hamair we had lain to at night, when the helmsman finally admitted guessing a course by wind and wave was too risky. But we could not lie to here.

When Segil came crouching down to the ship supplies for the tiny night lanterns, cursing well over his breath as he tried to get them alight, I nerved myself to ask, "Will we, can we lie to, in this?"

"Nay." He answered briefly but not curtly, intent on his task. "We'll use the glass to count watches, an' steer by the wind. T'is steady enough, for all its fuss. Unless it veers."

"If it veers?"

"Set a sea-anchor an' wait." A flint-flare showed the visible side of his mouth, curved in Segil's usual sardonic grin. "If this 'bogle's' so resty for ye, it'll haul its wind, fast enough."

Haul wind, far too literally. I clamped down images of the sea-anchor cable parting on *Aspis*. Memories of Therkon, and ancient Amberlight Heads' caution warned not to erode ignorant courage by telling Segil just what strength that wind could reach.

The lantern caught. He sat back on his heels and Two blurted, *"What if we arrive like this?"*

"Make landfall? We'll no' run up a cape-snout, lass. The wind flaws, well back. Ye can feel it, aye? An' the sea'll shift. T'will be a lee-shore, surely. But there's ways, with a sixer, even round that."

In this wind? In this night? I bit those queries down as well. He handed me a lantern and said, "Break out y'r stores. Dark

or no dark, ye've to eat, or ye'll both be legless as in Gildair."
Rising, agile and easy on the ship-shifts, he added over his shoulder. "Just ask the Mither no' to send a whale."

"A—!"

"Why d'ye think t'is called Whalewatch? They come through every spring." The lantern occluded behind his bulk. "An' that's the one thing we'll no' see. Or hear."

Whalewatch. Hvalwrast. The whale's road. Two had reclaimed it for that woman, dying in a Sea fort bed. That was what she had recognized: not poetry, but a landmark in her own lost world.

Well before actual night it was too dark for a view, too dark to move around, far too dark to work out. In any case, the seas had become huge, big as mountains to my appalled eyes. Even with half the sail reefed *Anfluga* hurtled over them, flying up, up, up to the crest, crashing over and plunging down like a runaway boulder till I was convinced she would shatter her prow at every chasm's foot.

But we were in almost open sea: however enormous, the waves were regular, and they were widely spaced. The only other danger, Rathi said when he came off watch, was if we had to reef so much sail we lost momentum below the crests. "An' if she won't steer, an' we broach to, down one o' those waterslides?" He made a brief, graphic gesture, read my face by the lantern and shook his head. "Nay, lass." His own half-smile twisted. "Trust y'r brither, then. If it wants ye, this bogle has to get ye there. In one piece."

The entire crew seemed buoyed by the same irrational belief. If they had made horn signs at Therkon when he first mentioned Sthassamaer, they had turned the idea to a mascot since.

* * * *

One day's passage, the ship's glass counted. One night I counted, sleepless as the watch. The dark had closed in, black, I heard someone mutter, "as mid-winter." Sleet flew, the wind howled and ropes shrieked, the sea roared and spouted gouts of phosphoric white, but *Anfluga* charged on, undeterred as the great ocean albatross, hurdling waves until my very terror numbed from repetition. And sometimes, in the dark where there was nothing to do but hone weapons and count time, and eat to order, and dare the limits of sense to relieve ourselves, I could not help falling into snatches of sleep.

Two days' passage. Two days and a night, Rathi informed us, coming off watch. He and Segil were hollow-eyed and stiff as puppets, but when I tried delicately to gauge their endurance, Segil merely shrugged. "T'is dark, aye, but a gale's a gale, an' ye learn to wait it out. A week of it, times, ye learn. Or," with Segil's flinty candour, "ye die."

With a fair wind, I heard Rathi telling Therkon when I woke once, *Anfluga* might cross Hvalwrast Reach in six full days and nights. "Wi' this winterblast? Who knows?" Seeing my opened eyes shine, perhaps, he bestowed a quick pat on my boot. "One thing ye can be sure. This'll no' take near so long."

And on the fourth morning, by the glass, I woke from a doze into light.

A bare and grudging illumination, diffusing palely over the tempest-heaped sea. Only the wind and the steersmen's conviction to say which way remained east. But light it was, coming so slowly that even my darkness-honed eyes could bear its growth.

Seas materialized, a spectrum-range of rolling, foam-flecked greys, but already, my storm-sharpened senses judged, lower than before. The dourly pressing belly of cloud-cover still hung over us, its unbroken murk shedding pale flecks of sleet, but gunwales showed, ropes, the mast's straight whipping length, the sail, battered more than a little but unbroken. Benches, rowlocks, human shapes. Hummocks of crumpled weather canvas, slowly acquiring heads. Identifiable, bristle-blurred faces, hollow, seeing eyes. Segil, upright once more at the steering oar, Rathi, a heap of blankets and canvas by us on the planks. Therkon at my side, his fur hood turning. Lifting his face, pushing the hood back. Raising eyes, sunken like the rest but watchful and warded in composure, toward the bow.

Before he asked Segil, "Can you see anything?"

From his minor vantage as the one man on his feet, Segil merely shook his head.

"Wind's no' breakin'," he answered after a moment, tilting his cheek. "Sea's droppin', but we're no' that close."

And if the sea were dropping, and the light returned, the conclusion was obvious to us all. We had crossed Hvalwrast. However long it took now, the unnatural voyage was near its end.

Before noon by the glass, Kaastria hove in sight.

\* \* \* \*

At first it was the merest horizon smudge, but by early afternoon Segil and Rathi were postulating landmarks and had begun, however dourly, to plume themselves. "Aye," Rathi conceded after half an hour's staring, "there's no mistakin' it. That's Haugar cape."

The easternmost point, I learned, of Kaastria's relatively short north shore. After four days in the dark we had made landfall at the optimal point to run either west to land's end, or south-east down the once more-populous eastern coast.

"Though whether we did it or the bogle did," Segil added saturninely, "t'is the Mither's own guess."

Another hour or so produced a coastline, almost as low and rolling as Phaerea's, though nearly colorless in the brooding light. Its single height was the cape itself, which earned its name of Mound.

Eyeing that rounded crest, Rathi glanced once, automatically, behind him. Then he laid *Anfluga* a point or two off the wind, and said, "Well, lass? Where now?"

"'Where'?" All my thoughts, fears, even Two's projections had held nothing but Kaastria. "But—we're *here*?"

"We're in sight o' Haugar, aye. But Kaastria's no' Skall. T'is big as Terrace, an' there's—there was—half a score o' ports, west-away," his hand waved, "clear t'the Fingerpoint. Or," another wave, "sou'east. Where d'ye, where does y'r brither, an y'r 'companion': which d'ye want?"

For once Two was as flabbergasted as I. I glanced wildly at Therkon, whose face told me he was floundering too. If I had not thought beyond reaching Kaastria, it was, I realized, partly in the tacit expectation that our way would be destined. "I thought *it* would—"

Rathi's expression retorted, *Well, "it" hasn't, so is it not time you did?*

The name came from nowhere. My own memory, perhaps, but not from Two.

"Hondeland." Veenn's words. "Someone said Hondeland was, was, inundated." Surely, if Kaaastria's name was insufficient guide, full ruin would fit this rendezvous?

Therkon's mouth was clipped shut, but his eye demanded, Where *is* it? Rathi answered, clearly including him even when he addressed me.

"Hondeland's down coast from here. Biggest east-side port, once. Like Jurrick on Phaerea, aye. Lost in a—lost, a year an' more ago." A little shiver went over him. I could almost see the other half-visible faces record the sensation of hair lifted on the neck. "Aye. That would be—"

He glanced ahead and laid *Anfluga* off again. And let all of us finish: for something that had blown us clear across Hvalwrast in the dark, surely, that would be signal enough?

The wind had eased, the seas were falling, we were still clear of what was no longer a lee shore. Segil handed the steering oar off to one of the ropemen, and he and Rathi sank down by the ship's stores with silent grunts of relief. A lull, I realized. One peril over, the next conveniently distanced ahead. The oarsmen had begun to arrange food, tend themselves or the ship, simply ease cramped muscles. My own eyelids drooped. Another precious little hiatus where the future need not be confronted, yet.

A blast of air and water slapped my bow-side cheek.

I yelped and shot half upright and sea-strung instinct spoke before I moved. Bow-side, an abrupt, unexpectedly rough blow of wind and sea. Bone and blood had no need for vision. The wind had changed.

Rathi lunged clean across to the steering oar and Segil shot after him. Therkon was on his feet. Oarsmen flung themselves benchward, biscuit, canteens, water dippers went everywhere. Sheer terror thrust my head above the gunwale to find what they had seen.

Darkness was my first thought: a blotch of near-true dark between cloud and sea rim, separate and conspicuous as a rising boil. Truly a boil, wind and water coalescing, thunderous black and deadly above, with an underbelly that touched the wave-backs with dense lethal white. A sudden, unpredicted squall.

On our starboard bow. Coming up out of the south-east, clean against the wind's way. Unexpected, unpredicted. Unnatural.

My tongue dried. My backbone froze. The din of preparation died around me like an extinguished lamp. There was nothing but the wind's scream, the squall's rising note. The onset of black water, rising, freezingly inevitable, in a leaking hold.

Around us, the wind died in a breath.

*Anfluga* died with it, steering way lost. An albatross unwinged. I heard Rathi swear like a madman and then bawl at the top of his lungs, "Out oars!"

Men grunted, oar-blades splashed. *Anfluga* heaved, shivered, picked up way. Rathi shouted again. The ropemen were already locked with the thrashing sail, Segil sprang to help. Rathi bellowed, "Put y'r backs in it!" Full in my face the stroke oar heaved, baring teeth. With a whistling hiss a volley of sleet and spray swept over us and the squall struck.

Two records that I did not cower under the gunwale with ears covered and eyes squeezed shut, but of the maelstrom I retain little enough. Spray, wave, water, patches of wood or weather-canvas amid cascades of streaming white. The frantic plunge of timber round me, the bruises on elbow, shoulder, hip, icy drenches swamping us. Too familiar sea and wind-thrash, the sound of tortured wood and rope, the broken human shouts. All too reminiscent of *Aspis*, that single ferocious over-riding crack.

I did hide my head then. Under the weather canvas, one arm still locked hopelessly in a belaying-pin tie. Anything not to see the lost sea anchor, the shattered side, the broken oars. The broken men.

It took a good minute to realize *Anfluga* was still bucking and plunging and rearing onward over the swells like an indignant horse, that men were yelling, cursing vitriolically, but with outrage, not in panic or fear. And nobody had begun to scream.

I let one eye out of the hood.

Canvas slapped me instantly over the head. Wood groaned and Segil swore as ferociously as Rathi had, before he roared, "Gone at t'hance!" And a voice I recognized as Rathi's roared back, "Cut the shicker loose!"

Every hidden oarsman cursed. Feet thumped, voices shouted, something thrashed and banged like a canvas beast in a trap. Over it came the vibrating thunks of an axe.

Abruptly the canvas beast fell quiet. The sea buffeted us, water beat round and over me, but *Anfluga* was plunging onward, unslowed, undeterred. Somebody stumbled over me and Therkon's voice rapped, "Give me that!" Belated troublecrew instinct yanked me from the hood in time to see him grab a bailer from somebody's hand.

Sea water, biscuits, dippers, loose dunnage sloshed in the bottom's deep innermost curve, but *Anfluga*'s sides were intact. The oarsmen were riding each onslaught of wave and wind as cannily and independently as Rathi with the steering oar. The dragon figurehead leapt upward, downward, hither and yon, but now it was limned against open if sunless sky.

And amidships the ropemen and Segil heaved at a tangle of wood and canvas that had once been the sail.

"Parted t'whore at the hances, easy as breakin' sticks." Rathi was near panting, with outrage, it seemed, as much as effort. "Even with a full half reef!"

Therkon's face beyond him answered, *No surprise. I* eyed the crushed heap of canvas as Two translated, Hances, parts of the yard nearest the mast. The yard is broken. We cannot use the sail.

"An' no' a chance o' fishin' it this side o'—" Rathi cut that short. Over the canvas-heap, he and Segil exchanged one long speaking glance.

Therkon put the bailer down and said, "We turn back."

* * * *

"If you cannot read that signal," he said, when the yelling dropped enough for them to hear his normal, if grim voice, "I can."

"Signal, what signal?" Segil shouted. "Read *what*?" But Rathi out-topped him. "Ye can't turn *back*!"

Therkon gave him one chilling stare. "The wind brought us to Kaastria. To the north of Kaastria. When we tried to sail further, the wind changed." He still sounded as blank as if he were reading out some disastrous imperial dispatch. "So we are not to go further south."

Rathi and Segil both stopped yelling at once. The faces of the oarsmen echoed the sag of their jaws.

"Gentlemen, think." He did not emphasise the noun, but the ice-voice held cut enough. "We have been signaled. Halted. Warned. We are not to go to Hondeland, but we were brought to Kaastria. So there must be some other destination. What ports are, were near here?"

The wind skreeled and *Anfluga* pitched, astray in the squall's wake, bereft of way from oar or sail. Therkon looked at Rathi as I had seen him look at Deoren. And Rathi's eyes seemed to hollow in his head as he looked back.

Then he sucked his lips in and tore a hand through his beard and said, "Hringstenn. Hringstenn's near to under our lee."

"And Hringstenn is?"

"A port, aye, t'is—was—t'chief northern port. Whalers' town. Port o' landing for the Reach. Boiling-down plant. Bone-strippers. We'd call at season's end, for t' whalebone, the oil."

"So the town is still there?"

"Nay.

"T'plague came." Rathi went on, at last. Too loud, in the sea's hush. "Two winters past. Bad curin', maybe, of a carcass. They'd share the meat out. Or somethin' in the water. The air. Hringstenn, Hringstenn was empty, before Hondeland."

Despite the wind, the air around us seemed empty too. Every face was turned into it. Away from everyone else. Then Therkon lifted his chin and looked at me.

Two said. *"Ruins. And the wind changed. Is that not clear enough?"*

\* \* \* \*

If Rangar was a shadow of Ve Pool, Hringstenn was Rangar's skeleton. With every oar-stroke taking us in under the roll of its hill, through a scatter of islets, across its bay's ample width, the qualms deepened in my belly. Rangar's port had been half-deserted, but not empty. People had walked, however sparsely, on Rangar's quay. Smoke had risen, despite the empty houses, above Rangar's streets. Hringstenn's harbour held only water. Even rubbish did not litter the quay. And the streets . . .

"Couple o' gales'll lift half a roof o' shingles off," Segil said quietly, while I stared. "Rain'll do the rest. Over a couple o' years."

And Hringstenn's roofs had had a couple of years. Wind and time had torn the centers out, opening houses like gutted beasts. Chimneys and solid Isle gable-ends stood pathetically isolate, their stone black with water and old soot, above the bleak mercy of the veiling snow.

"Aye," I heard Rathi mutter, in answer to some question from Therkon, "likely it's been fallin' a couple o' days."

Longer, something said inside me: the season has been turning backward, retreating toward winter, ever since we left Eithay. It is mid-winter, dead water, the desolation of the solstice, here.

In deathly silence *Anfluga* edged up to the wharf. Rowing in had taken most of the night, and just before dawn the wind dropped altogether, as abruptly and capriciously as it had turned for the squall. Or perhaps, something insisted with terrifying logic, it had not been caprice, but intent.

Whatever the source, the bleak grey water now was all but motionless, a mirror for the deserted shore. No wave-wash to break the silence, any more than any wheel squeaked or fowl cackled, doors banged, feet tramped. No human voice, not even a gull's voice called.

Gulls would leave, logic told me, when the flesh-refuse failed. But somewhere in this ruin, something was awake; aware and waiting, silent as black water, under the sporadically falling snow.

I shuddered uncontrollably and Segil grunted beside me, hefting the aft warp. *I know*, that sound answered. It was not only cold, unnaturally cold, but uncanny. Such silence, such stillness, in a place of human habitation, such absolute emptiness.

He tossed the warp with automatic skill around a snow-capped bollard, and *Anfluga* touched her side to stone.

Ahead of me, Hringstenn lay empty. Behind me, too, nothing moved. The whole crew, the whole ship, was waiting. For whatever waited for us. For a choice on our part, a decision. For me.

Then a step and a presence came beside me and Therkon asked quietly, "Do we go ashore?"

Never was I more grateful for the crown prince, let alone the imperial hatchet man. Because whatever he felt, his voice, like his face, was coolly blank.

Even if he had laid the onus on me. On me, reason insisted above the rising stress that had my fingers tight on wood, that shortened my breath as Two drew near sparking, on me as well as Two. And it's nothing to do with oracles, less with available facts. If you are what it wants, the decision is yours.

Go looking for the enemy? Or simply, cunningly, cravenly, wait?

If I went ashore, Therkon would go. Even if I asked, I would not be permitted to go alone.

But if we went ashore, all Azo's hackles rose at once, we would be in the open, vulnerable, isolable, in the deadliest of urban terrains: empty, hostile, ruined streets.

And searching, therefore open to attack and ambush. Losing the slight initiative of immobility and defense.

If I stayed, the enemy would have to come to us.

To me, and Therkon. With the crew behind us. Eighteen more strong, able men.

Eighteen more lives in jeopardy, if the enemy took the bait.

In a spasm of panic I jerked my eyes across the snow-swathed quay, into the mouth of an empty, ominously twisted street, up again over the broken roofs, and onto the crest of Hringstenn's hill.

Lower than the hill behind Yinstey, even lower than Haugar cape. Smoother than the rocky perimeter of Ve Pool, swelling treeless and seeming all but rockless under its sheath of snow.

With a crown upon its crest.

Stones, Two said in the hiatus of shock and recognition. Artificially placed, upright, standing stones.

Tall stones, broad stones, snow-thatched or snow-clothed stones, their own color lost against the snow-thick sky, but their variant bulks and heights and angles making an identifiable shape.

"Long Stone," a burred Isle voice said in my memory. "Sights come all of a piece to me. At the Giants' Dance."

Where Nouip had Seen, on another island, so now, here, might I?

I lifted a hand and said, "Up there."

# CHAPTER XVI

The quay was so quiet I could hear every crunch of snow under our boots. The fall itself had almost stopped: only scattered flakes drifted around us, white moving flecks in the frozen vista of blacks and greys and solid unsullied white. Without other sounds, the town's emptiness seemed to reach out to us, not merely a desolate but a deadly, listening hush. As if an ambush were already laid, and the ambushers crouching, poised to strike.

Rathi had disliked the idea of any sortie almost as much as would Azo. Two eventually overrode his protests with a brusque, *"Who gains more from time?"* The counter that would have moved Azo, if not for my reason. If she cared nothing for strangers' lives, she would never begin a waiting match that we, denied the sea, needing food and shelter eventually, could only lose.

The quay was not so very wide. Past a ruined cargo-hoist waited the mouth of the nearest street. Snow, water-stained stone, broken windows. A sudden jink shut all but half a bowshot from view. Therkon broke stride and looked at me.

Rathi said curtly, "Down here."

Bested over the sortie, he had campaigned hotly for the whole crew to go ashore. When Therkon pointed out why they should ward themselves, protect innocent lives, and most important, guard the ship that might take us all away, he had set his jaw. And after a seething pause, announced flatly, "Blades or no blades, the pair o' ye'll be toddlin' babes in there. *I'm* comin' with ye."

"That," he jerked his hand now at the closest street, "'ll go east-about. The one ye want's here."

Therkon gave him a measuring stare. Azo counseled coldly, *For good or ill, let the guide go first.* Two ruled that if Rathi knew the town well enough to reach the hill with the least chance of ambush, we would take his word.

The second street was half as narrow again, and twisted as rapidly the opposite way. Too well reminded of Amberlight slums and hair-crispingly swift ambushes, Two and Azo had the first knife almost in my hand. Therkon was treading on my heels. Before me, Rathi walked swiftly but steadily down the street center, a hand tucked under his weather-canvas, doubtless on the hilt of his own sword.

The street swung again: another vista of neglected or ruined house-fronts, shutters dangling, doors broken or ajar, site on site for ambush amid the mounded snow. The silence under our footsteps stretched my nerves like softened bowstrings. Two was on the verge of a spark.

Rathi glanced left and right and muttered, "Ye'd look, at least, for rats."

Therkon answered, coolly as on the *Aspis*, "Too long for them as well."

The street opened suddenly into a little space with a low broad snow-shape at its centre. Rathi skirted it with one brief mutter of "T'well." I thought how it would have looked once, the town's hub. Market stalls perhaps, people with loaves or vegetables, people fetching water, a cart or two jolting past. The busy racket of voices, of ongoing human life.

Rathi veered seaward. Down another street we found a cross-road, and a house-width later, the gate.

One wooden leaf still hung, but the other had rotted at the hinges, leaving shards as warning above the deceptive hump of snow. Sidestepping, Rathi heaved at the standing half. Its snow-muffled *Sskrrriiirrk* over the threshold stones almost scared Two into a spark again.

Open ground appeared, perhaps once a common pasture, now a mere sward of hummocky white under clumps of snow-spatched, leafless trees. A hundred yards away rose the foot of the hill.

Not Skall, I told my thundering heart. Nowhere near so high, and it's not raining, and no screaming seagulls, and up there is no Angrir.

What might, what must be somewhere here instead almost undid Two. I only got the better of her as we angled after Rathi into the open snow. "There's a path, somewheres, over here."

The path started behind the foothill's bulge, and followed an easy slant up the hill-crease beyond. A well-trodden path, it had been once. Its beaten depth, and the lines of verge-stones, showed even through the snow. Silent, trying to husband our breaths, we toiled up.

Probably the whole slope would once have carried grass, if nothing else. All that remained was irregular bumps in the blanket of pall-pure white. Except at our backs, it lay utterly pristine. No beast had marked it, not a single bird.

Rathi muttered, "Used to be rooks. A hare or two. Curlews, whaupin' over the tops. Springs, ye'd hear a wren. Or turnstanes, down t'shore, *tuck-tuck, tuck-tuck*."

The little echoing bird-call bounced eerily as a turned pebble itself. I was grateful when he fell quiet.

The crease narrowed. A last scramble through a gauntlet of boulders brought us to the crest.

Wholly treeless, it would have drawn wind at all times, if the merest breeze. Now the air hung immobile, pinned under swollen cloud-bellies. Not a breath slanted the noiseless sift of snow.

Rathi hesitated. Therkon glanced swiftly left, right, behind, before. Two's upset was blurring my vision. I could barely make out the stones.

At close quarters most stood tall and attenuated, though the shapes and angles of side and top were wildly different. The snow had thatched their salients, laying white patches amid the rust or dun blots of moss, but the rock beneath was all a muted cinnabar red.

I did not try to count them. The circle, I managed to guess, was perhaps half a bowshot across. The stones loomed higher than a man, silent, brooding, lost in their own reveries. Where perhaps not even the circle-makers had impinged.

Without knowing it I too had stopped. Therkon was a pace behind my left shoulder: assuming, I had one ironic moment of realization, the place of troublecrew. Rathi waited on my right. They had checked the surroundings, then, and found them empty. Only the circle remained.

The path, my second step showed me, was also the formal approach. We had come up on a slight northward curve, curling to find the circle's gate on the inland side. The circle itself would face outward, over the town, over the sea, into the north-east.

The gate was open, or perhaps had never been closed. Two massive stones, broader than they were high, made a porch for jambs set in the circle itself.

I stopped again. Snow lay between the stone quartet, thick untrampled snow, and shadow, it seemed, more than the scanted light would explain, lingered among those crowded blocks. A stillness came out of them that had nothing to do with the desolation of the town beneath.

The porch stones were marked. Carved, or at least grooved, with wide spiraling circles linked across each face. Their patterns crossed under the spatchings of snow and lichen, like ancient ditches in a half-grazed field.

The force of the stones' presence, the prickle of my neck-hairs warned, sacred. Consecrated. A place, like the lookout over Iskarda, perilous to outrage.

It would not, could not be the place that actually harbored Sthassamaer.

Two's tension eased, and my vision cleared. Beyond the portal the circle spread to the hill's brow, with a spar of three outliers running to either side. The hilltop itself fell left and right in long descending spurs, perhaps where the makers had hauled up their stones.

The evenness of the ground within betokened a clear place, even under the snow. Flattened, if not actually paved. Made for procession, dancing, ritual. A single, tallest menhir stood at its heart.

I did not know I had meant to move until the snow crunched again under my boots, but the men came with me, wordless as very stones. Now the portal's shadow received me willingly, welcomingly, I wanted to think, as would Iskarda's qherrique: a creature recognized, if not known. And the men with me, vouched for by me.

The central menhir was uncarved. Nothing about it said, Focal point. I walked past, carefully keeping to its right, sunward side.

The circle's farther rim opened before me, two tall slender standing stones flanking another enormous recumbent block. Over its back the fall of snow-cased earth, the spatched clutter of town, rimmed an immense shield of winter-grey sea.

In all that prospect, only snow-flecks moved.

The men were still wordless. Rathi, too, had fallen back a step, for he was no longer in the corner of my eye. I looked out into the emptiness and waited for Two to see, to extrapolate, to find and uncover Sthassamaer.

Two did nothing at all.

The men were waiting. They would expect an oracle. Or some insight, at the very least something noticed about the circle, the land beneath. Something to show I had not merely frozen where I stood.

"Well," I said stupidly, "we're here."

The sound seemed to shudder in the air, a blasphemy. Someone behind me gave a quick little sigh.

"So," Rathi's voice said, "ye are."

\* \* \* \*

I did not spin round and hurl the wrist-knife. I did not even try to control Two. I could only stand, feeling bone and blood and muscle congeal to the rigidity of the stones.

Not a place to harbour Sthassamaer. And that had been true. This place had not harboured Sthassamaer. I had brought Sthassamaer with me.

How long had this been planned? How long had it been waiting? How long had it traveled with us, seeking the perfect moment? How much had it known?

How much had Rathi known?

I turned then. Slowly as a circle's heel-stone, revolving on its pivot. Letting my eyes find the men.

Therkon's face was pallid, frozen as his limbs. He too had understood.

Rathi was looking at me. I actually saw it happen: a heartbeat's struggle, a flash of bewilderment. And the dark eyes that had shown such concern for me, for us, were gone.

Sthassamaer looked out at me, through eyes whose pupils, irises, retinas were unbroken black.

\* \* \* \*

I ought to have been running, screaming like a rabbit, terrified beyond thought. Two ought to have been paralyzed, or sparking out of control. But in that moment all I felt was red, molten rage.

"You took him," I said.

"Aye."

The word was right, the voice wrong. Rathi, but speaking as from the bottom of a well.

"You *took* him. An ordinary man. A good man. And you *took* him, like a castle piece, a dice-bone, a *toy*."

The face moved. A kind of writhe, that might have been meant for a smile.

"You stole him. And you cheated us. All this time. All this way."

It nodded its head, as if pleased.

"You got us to Skall. You made me kill people. You sank *Aspis*—" the air reddened to opacity—"*you* drowned them. Deoren, and Verrith, and Azo!"

It bobbed its head again, as at a compliment.

My hand leapt in Verrith's reflex, the knife whipped from its sheath and Two flamed like the smallest light gun charged by its handler's will as we hurled that white lance of light.

Rathi's body sprang back. The knife vanished in mid-flight. The black eyes widened, and then black spilled from them over the entire face.

Head, beard, shoulders melted into cascading black. Like water the flood poured down and out and rose again in an impossible tide, ankle, knee, waist-high, spreading, reaching out, engulfing me.

My feet clove to the snow-bound stones. Two froze with me, paralyzed as the rest.

And the water rose, rapid, silent, black as bilge-seep, cold on my legs and hips as very ice, waist-high, sucking, pulling me down into blackness that had already eaten Therkon, the stones, the hilltop, nothing was left around me, not Hringstenn, not Kaastria, not the Isles, not the rest of the vanishing world.

My eyes had failed already. The black grip was about my chest. In a moment my lungs would stop, and then my heart. Blackness would have it all.

But my ears still worked. Into them, blackness admitted one heavy swashing thud.

And the water stopped.

Blackness hung icy at the base of my throat, shutting down breath. I struggled by intent alone. But I could still breathe. I could still hear. Across my lungs' susurrus came another, lighter thump. A brief strangling noise. Then nothing at all.

But the water began to ebb.

My throat came free, my shoulders, my chest. My waist. My arms would move. Blackness thinned about me, sinking away to release the earth as well.

Reverse shadows coalesced first, tall standing darknesses on fading dark, then a variegated shadow-dark paling down to murky grey, and then that faded too, a zone of dusk above paling, purifying white.

Shadows assumed color and edge and shape, a tall single menhir, a further rank of snow-patched, earth-coloured stones. The gulf of the portal, the fall of the hilltop, other hillsides beyond. Earth and air reassembled, cold air blessedly clean, flakes of white falling across it into reaches of white untainted snow.

And at my feet, a great outflung swathe of red.

Brilliant living red, glistening like very water, spreading with the speed of water, but hot water, steaming into the frigid air. Red intense as heart's blood, and carrying the stench of heart's blood, brutal as the stink of an abattoir, eating out into the unarmoured snow.

With a strange tangled-starfish shape at its rim, a sprawl of dun and weathered grey, canvas, weather-canvas, with outliers of a limp hand. A sidelong fallen boot. A hideous gouting hole to mark the redness' source.

I looked across it into Therkon's face.

It was almost as pallid as the snow. His limbs were rigid, but his lips shook. His hands shook too, and the sword he grasped shook with them, scattering crimson drops down into the steaming red.

For a moment I could hear my heart beat. Could hear the blood, melting its way toward earth.

Therkon whispered, "You disappeared."

I could only stare.

"First the knife. Then you. There was nothing. A hole. A no place." His voice began trembling as well. "Not you. Not the stones. Not the snow. Not the—Nothing. Nothing was left.

"He," the sword wavered. Perhaps a gesture, perhaps not. "I could still see him. Fading. Going. I—I—"

He did move the sword that time. One shaky, travestied intimation of a sweep. But it spoke clearer than the words.

*I did the only thing I could.*

Time seemed to creep over me, slower than half-thawed water, slow as it must seem to the stones. Painfully, time seamed together past, present, sections of scene, comprehension. The heap was Rathi's body. The gory odd-shaped hummock over there, a good eight feet away, was Rathi's head.

I had taught Therkon to use Hvestang. Nouip had said, he would have use for it. A mere human, left with a human weapon, human knowledge, in the face of—whatever Sthassamaer did. In a time of more than human need.

I tried to make my lips move. I could not, yet, bear to look at Rathi—what was left of Rathi—but I was alive. Therkon was alive. He knew what he had done, in both its senses. For me, to me. His was the prior need.

I drew breath at last, consciously tasting the cold, clean air. Something inside me was starting to tremble, but I could still manage words.

"You did what you could."

The words might have been judgement, indictment, blame. Hatred. I managed to make them understanding. Acknowledgement. Nothing more.

But he was Therkon. He understood.

The white-knuckled clench on the sword-hilt eased. The blade stopped quaking. The eyes, far too big, far too dark, began to lose their distended rings of white. His lips steadied. He drew his own first full, careful breath.

And the eyes, the bronze-dark Quetzistani eyes I knew so well, emptied. No struggle this time. A smooth uncontested transition, from bronze-dark to fathomless black.

\* \* \* \*

I think my heart stopped. I know I could not breathe. Only vision, comprehension, seared through me, numbing as a lightning strike.

We had met Sthassamaer at last. And it had made one of my wards kill the second, and the second—I was the only one left. Alone. Alone to face the monster, and the monster's face . . .

I looked at Therkon, my dearest friend, my companion, I his troublecrew, he pledged to protect me with his own life. The hope and heart of Dhasdein, as he had become my heart.

Now I could not even drive the enemy from the world without his death.

Even if I succeeded, it would only hasten my own end.

I stared back into the blackness that pinioned me, that was watching, knowing what it had done. Savoring, in this waste of horror, what it would do next.

Perhaps it was the disbelief of trying to imagine anything that could conceive, let alone do such a thing, that brought the words. Or perhaps it was Two, fettered even beyond terror's spark, whose deepest, oldest impulse drew them up.

"Who are you? *What* are you? How could you ever . . ."

Neither Two nor I could manage any more. But it was enough. The thing smirked. Even yet, I can hardly bear to confront that memory. That look, on Therkon's face. Then, prolonging the savor, no doubt, it spoke.

"So *what* am I, madam oracle?"

No doubt it intended a mere fencing point. But the polar ice within me stirred. A feeble movement, action, then Two's own familiar blizzard whirl of white.

It had asked us a question, using Therkon's voice, wearing Therkon's face. The memory of such questions, from such a source, woke our oldest reflexes: to provide an answer. To assemble facts.

Image-snips flew past: Therkon in the Iskarda council room, speaking of storms and refugees. The woman in the Sea-fort bed, giving us a name. Whale road, swan's way. Carsia. Therkon on Evvamoor beach, saying, A child hearing sagas on a corner could think of it. Nouip by her fireside saying, Black water. Giving Therkon the sword, the cloak. Saying, with her Sight, You will have use for this.

Another clot of recollections then, the Grithsperry shipper saying, Sea-sark, saying, Where He comes ashore after the winter's storms, Skatir bellowing, They think you're Winter's King! Veenn talking of Hondeland, inundated, Fiskri of gales and lost fishing fleets. Rathi himself—the threads almost snapped—speaking of

Rangar, of Hondeland, of the edges of ruin. The images in the White Grebe's tap-room, dark with candle-wax and smoke. Skatir shouting, He's *of* the Isles! Veenn saying, there's the Mither, and the one who fights her, the Mither's opposite. The Winter Man.

Myself wearing Nouip's cloak, bearing Hvestang into a hall on Eithay, up a hill on Skall.

Therkon in the Winter Man's cloak, carrying the sword.

Then at last, as Nouip had once predicted, the streams of data merged. Two and I looked at the enemy together, and for the first time, we Saw.

We said, "**Tiran.**"

It blinked. Then it raised Therkon's brows. I had one stabbing moment to recall how he would have looked, hearing, with the joy of the philosopher, this riddle finally read.

It said, "Very good."

My heart might have broken then. But the Sight endured: and in its grasp the patterns began to coalesce, images balancing, connections meshing, projections dovetailing, the great mass of knowledge crystallizing from that heart-point out and out about us, making sense of everything.

Black water, rising. Darkness. Winter's fall.

Summer's ascent, dawn over Phaerea. The world opening to the sun.

A story pattern, a belief pattern, a world pattern. A pattern found and framed by storytellers, but not to please the imagination. Framed because it spoke humankind's understanding, human remembrance of the truth. The greatest pattern of all.

"**You are the Winter dark. The Mother's foe. In autumn, the one who prevails.**"

It raised Therkon's eyebrows, and looked obscenely pleased.

"**So you have brought winter. Not once, not in season, not in its rightful place, but out of time, beyond the Isles, over the world's bounds. You have not stopped with ice and snow. You have wrecked, and overthrown, and inundated, and destroyed.**"

It was preening. There is no other word. It did not shift the sword, it did not move Therkon's body. But the eyes glistened, and the ambient air conveyed it. The thing preened.

"**You have been bringing winter, out of season, these five years.**"

It nodded. Gravely, judicially, as Therkon might at a sensible, approved council proposal. And then I understood what Two and I were doing.

Our words were not flattery, not outrage. Not seeking to manipulate, nor recapitulation, either. We were laying down an indictment. Bringing it to judgement. Reciting its offence.

And it was accepting the guilt.

"**Why did you do this?**"

The way it gazed back at me wrung my heart. Because, so like Therkon, so heart-breakingly like Therkon, it looked, for a moment, slightly bemused.

Then it said, "I am winter. I can prevail."

It sounded exactly like Therkon too. Alone, I would have had to bite my tongue on pleas and protests and screams of, *Don't, don't do this, come back to me, come back!*

But Two and I were one, and as one we spoke.

**"This is spring."**

It glanced around the snow, and smiled.

**"Your place now is to retreat. To yield, and wait for autumn. To go."**

It looked at me in amusement and let that say, I am here, in the ascendant, and you have no way to alter that. All your talking may delay. It cannot change your fate.

But Two and I knew a way to do that too, and given time to rally, we had the power. I turned our vision inward upon one memory. A wall in Cataract, my mother's hands on a lighted, blazing, burning statuette.

*Make*, I said to Two, *light*.

I saw it on the snow first. The coalescing shadow, running outward from my feet. The distorted shape of my own body thrown in all directions round me, as light encircles the glowing lamp.

And then the second long blackness growing outward behind Therkon, the dark shapes coalescing, sharpening, behind the central menhir, behind the flanking stones. The air brightened round me as the light crescendoed, not merely clear but brilliant, dazzling, whiter, brighter, fiercer and more implacable than the heart of the midday sun.

Therkon's throat made a weird cawing noise. His hands dropped the sword hilt and tried to fly upward but the light pinned them and he almost screamed, cringing, clawing air, squeezing his eyes shut, trying to shrink and back away and run, mindless in the light's glare, unable to think beyond escape.

**"Be still."**

The flight stopped. Therkon—it—the creature tried to crouch and huddle, and when it could not do that it first screamed and then, helplessly, it wept.

And we stared at it, now seeing only Sthassamaer. Knowing beyond doubt that we could expel it, not merely from Therkon's body but from the living world.

We could excise Tiran as well. In the world that opened before us, there would be spring, and summer, and autumn. But there need never be winter again.

It was no longer any form of retribution, let alone revenge. We knew, as a god would know, that the world would be infinitely better, happier, kinder, without winter. Good was a simple choice.

Perpetual day. Perpetual light.

It dazzled and battered round us, fiery as summer, fiercer than a cloudless noon, pure, overwhelming light. The circle and the outlier stones were bathed in it, we could make it pour out to evaporate the clouds, melt the snow, revive the town, restore an azure summer sea.

Across that blinding vista ran a wisp of memory: my fathers, somewhere in a night I had never shared, talking about gods.

My father Alkhes, his black hair and troublecrew gear a shadow and voice in the darkness, saying, "Gods above—no, that's not right, is it? If there're no gods, is there an Above at all?"

After a moment my father Sarth replied. I could see his classic profile above some building's level, held in that familiar pause for thought.

He said, "There may be no gods as we think of them. And no Above, as we think of it. But there are patterns. Whoever or whatever made them, in everything, the patterns are there."

Black water, rising. Darkness. Winter's fall.

Spring's ascent, dawn over Phaerea. The world opening to the sun.

But that was not the pattern's end.

Summer was its consummation, yes: grainfields ripening, maturing fruit. But then came harvest. Apples falling. Leaves falling. The world closing, as the sun changed, so it could sleep.

Because it had to sleep.

Because alone, light was not enough.

The brilliance of our own light eased as we understood. It was possible to erase Sthassamaer, but we could not expunge Tiran. Veenn had said it, we ourselves had said it. In the autumn, he prevailed. This was spring.

And every spring was bedded in time, as we were, as Therkon was, as Rathi had been, as Tiran had been. As Tiran must be again.

**"You have broken the pattern,"** we said. **"You and the Mother are the two sides of the balance. You both have your part, but you must keep the whole. Winter rises. Winter must also fall."**

It was all so obvious, so clear beyond contention, that we were not surprised when, as the light subsided, Therkon's body began, gingerly, to uncoil from its cringe. To lower its hands, and relax its face, and dare to look at us with its eyes again.

To pick up the sword, that had fallen into the blood and snow at its feet.

Even then, the solution was so clear and perfect and right as a puzzle piece finally fitted, that we did not heed his movement. Did not invoke the councils of Azo. Did not think on the human, or even on the sagas' plane, at all.

Until Tiran smiled at us, and lifted the sword to guard, and purred, "But for the proper pattern, there must be a battle first."

\* \* \* \*

The light died. It was bleak midwinter noon, and we were trapped there, mute and paralyzed as a flesh and blood menhir, amid the bloodied but undispelled snow. Only the calamity had changed.

Its lips smiled, Therkon's less familiar winner's smile, and it moved the sword a little. The blade no longer dripped, but over its knuckles, where it had retrieved the fallen hilt, everything was smeared with red.

Battle, it had said. A proper part of the pattern, it claimed. And it was true. The pattern was the story, and the story said, Fight. Not merely transition, but struggle and supersession, a balance of opposing triumphs. Opposing defeats.

If Two and I were to bind it to the pattern, we must also bind ourselves.

So we must fight the same, the endless battle.

But was it expecting, this time, to win?

Horror choked my throat. I had one knife left. Therkon had the sword. How would the world fare, if the ultimate story went awry? If spring came, and Tiran won?

I shut my eyes and my soul cringed. *Oh*, my mind said numbly. *Oh, Mother, what am I to do?*

Silence came then, within me as without. The silence of the circle, of the standing stones, whose place had been defiled by death and violence, but could not be destroyed.

*Where*, a still small voice said into that quiet, *do you think the Mother is?*

My heart labored as if my blood had thickened. Dryness filled my throat. I could not have said it, but too, too clearly, I understood.

If this was the climactic battle, and we its human actants, who could, who must, Two and I be, if Therkon was Winter's King?

My hair crisped with more than awe. And then crisped again as Two formed the inevitable corollaries.

If we are the Mother, then somehow, however impossibly, story dictates that we must win.

But if Tiran wore Therkon's body, how could we inflict that defeat on him?

I opened my eyes and it smiled at me. It had Therkon's wits along with his flesh and blood. It had worked out the strategy and the inevitable conclusions. Whether the Mother won or not, Two and I could only lose.

"*Why?*" we said. We did not consciously plan delay, but there would only be so much time to ask our own questions. And now they were driven by rage, by the bursting denial of grief. "**How long**?"

We expected it to understand, and it did. Why had it sought me in particular, once I came within its ken, and how far back had that knowledge, that seeking run? To the squall that pushed *Aspis* from the River, to the wreck of the survivor's ship, to the expulsion of its crew from Kaastria, to the fall of Hondeland?

To the fall of Hringstenn, or further? Right back to the beginning? Even to my beginning? Had knowledge of me, yet greater disaster, first driven Tiran to break the pattern at all?

"**How long**?"

It shrugged a little. Not with indifference, or denial. This, we understood, in such leaps of thought as Tiran itself made, was a pattern beyond human understanding. And Two's as well.

"But why? *Why?*"

Why me, why us, I wanted to scream at it: what was so important that you, whatever you are, would overturn whole nations to get possession of a single, human girl?

Two's own logic answered. Because I was not simply human. Because I was Two, as well.

"Because of us?"

It narrowed its eyes and stared at me. It was not an expression of Therkon's. I had one fleeting wild impression that I had pushed it beyond Therkon's mental and physical repertoire. Now, in this unfamiliar body, Tiran, or Sthassamaer, was acting for itself.

The lids dropped over inhuman black. It looked down into the snow, and answered so softly I could barely hear.

"For the light."

And as if light had struck to the depths of my own heart's cavern, I understood.

It lived in, moved with, was itself darkness. It could pursue summer, and overthrow autumn, and best the Mother, for a season. But even if it ran wild, spreading its dominion over the year's length, what it worsted and hunted could never be held for good.

But Two and I, however anomalous, were merely part of the Mother's world. We bore, we could kindle light. And we, at least, might be engulfed, assimilated. Possessed.

But if we were not the Mother? Fresh vision of that struck like a literal spear of light.

In this battle, we stood for Her, but we did not become Her. So if we must fight in Her place, we could use our own weapons. We need not accept the adversary's challenge with a sword. Or even with a knife.

I took a step back as the vision blossomed in my mind like another qherrique statuette. I looked at Tiran, at Therkon, at the sword in his hand, and the Sight melded past and present and I knew what to do.

I stretched my right hand out, empty, not needing any other focus than the will. And I told Two: *Fire.*

At the gesture Therkon-Tiran blinked. Took in my weaponless hand, and smiled.

It stepped forward. I stepped backward. It raised Langlieve's sword.

I pointed and Two passed fire through my fingers so I never felt a flush of heat. The blaze streamed out between us without touching Therkon either, and its white spear struck just below Hvestang's hilt.

Two had recalled even more than I. The sword blade was triple-tempered, laminated, Isle-made steel. It could probably withstand even our fire. It could go into an iron-ore smelting furnace, and never melt.

But Therkon's hand was human flesh.

The heat blazed upward from steel to ivory and that flesh reacted as it had to the blinding light: Therkon screamed and jerked in pure reflex and hurled the sword away from him as far as it would fly.

Hvestang struck the foot of the recumbent stone's right jamb with a ringing clash. Therkon reeled back, Tiran spun his body round and tried to take a step in pursuit and we said, "*Stop.*"

It sounded like my voice, but the air shuddered. The very stones seemed to reverberate. Tiran managed one stride, and froze.

Perhaps the Mother spoke through us again, as when we commanded Tiran before. We had no time to consider. We said what the Sight showed us, with Her authority.

"*Battle has been offered. And won. Go now. Find your proper place.*"

It raised Therkon's face. The eyes were still wholly black, but now they glistened. Now, despite the black inhuman sentience, emotion was in them. Longing, perhaps. Unmistakably, grief.

"*You cannot possess the light. If you did, the world would die. There would be no light without the world.*"

Unspoken, impossible visions flooded through us, light as the product of air and earth and water and the sun's operation, on some scope both larger than the planet and tinier than its grains of dust. Without those necessities, light would not exist.

And in the dark, they could not exist.

What it loved, what it most desired, it would destroy.

The voice had grown gentle, when we spoke again.

"*But if you hold your place, the world will hold. You will not possess the light, but it will go and come again, and you will know of it. It will pass beside you. You will know that. As you could not have seen or known before.*"

I really did think my heart had stopped. Because Two and I knew what we were hearing now: not merely the restoration of balance, of the pattern, the ancient story, but the birth of change. We were the witnesses of a new bargain between gods.

Of a new way of being a god.

Tiran raised its—his—Therkon's face, and Tiran's eyes, and looked into ours, but this time I knew Who he was seeing.

Someone lifted my right hand, upright, fingers straight, palm out. Go, that gesture said. The pact is made. The pattern changed. Peace returns. It is time to leave.

Therkon's body joined its hands before its breast. Ours did the same. Tiran bowed its head. We bowed mine. It was not a reverence, on either side. It was a peer's acknowledgement.

\* \* \* \*

As my eyes rose again everything around us seemed to pause. In the edge of my vision, for one impossible moment, I saw snow-flakes halted in mid-air. Unable, unwilling, to fall.

Then the last flake sifted down to earth and stopped. My lungs filled on a long automatic breath. And Therkon raised his head.

Blinking, dazedly, at the bloody snow, the fallen sword. Turning his palm over, to find the great red scorch-mark that in a minute or so would begin to pain worse than any wound. Turning his face toward me.

Looking at me with Therkon's own bewildered, bronze-dark, human stare.

\* \* \* \*

I had to run about at once for snow to pack his palm and combat the worst of the pain, a purpose that helped swallow the tears and the convulsive shudders of aftermath, to curb the frantic need to scream like a lunatic and hurl us bodily into his arms. If I babbled throughout, I managed to get him, staggering himself now, to sit down on the recumbent stone. To upturn his snow-filled hand on a knee. To succor his body, before his eyes found the bloody wreckage on the snow.

And after that one blank moment, he understood.

Babble died in my throat. So I heard quite clearly, even though he had his good hand to his mouth as he whispered it, barely audible.

"Oh. Oh, Dhe."

I should have been frantic with relief. He understood. Tiran had begun to relinquish him, his wits, if not scathed like his body, might be intact. But all I could see was the look on his face.

The snow sifted, vertically, soundlessly, down through the frigid air, and I wanted to scream it at him: Not your fault, not your doing, not your blame, the Seer foretold it, *it wasn't you!*

Then he gave one great shudder and jerked his torso upright, and his bronze-dark eyes turned, as a drowning man's hand claws for succour, to my own.

I whispered, "How much do you—did you—know?"

Snow-flakes drifted, slightly out of vertical, one alighting, a white moth, on the shoulder of Nouip's furs. Imperceptibly, it began to melt. He shuddered again, and spoke.

"It was like—seeing through water." He was still whispering too. "Wavery. No . . . sound." He rubbed the back of the good hand across a cheek. "I was—there. I . . . felt. But . . . no words. No thoughts." He lifted the burned hand and stared at it. "No . . . Nothing would move. Not for me."

In his palm the snow had melted too. The great red weal showed slick and wet and my own body moved without conscious decision, scooping up another handful, fitting it tenderly among his fingers. Anything to avoid the expression on his face.

"You *had*," my own voice shook, but I could say it, "no choice."

He looked blankly at the snow-pack. His face was remote as the stones.

"And you did act. At the end." I tried not to shiver. "You threw away the sword."

"I don't—" He stopped, dazed again. "That wasn't—me."

That was your body, I told him silently. If not by conscious volition, it was the act of your flesh and blood.

And thank the Mother that flesh and blood had reacted before Tiran caught up, before it, he, understood and could make you hold on, and force me to yield. Or else to watch your hand burn, hear your pain, myself torture your flesh.

I sat down beside him with something near a thump and seized his good hand as substitute for hurling both arms round him and clutching hard enough to hurt. He let me take it. He was still staring, more dazed than before.

"Rathi." He swallowed, as if it hurt his throat. "I remember— Rathi. *That* was my choice. But the rest." He shook his head like a drunkard. "Chaeris, what was all the rest? What were we—*who* were we? What were we doing?"

He had been a conscious witness to it all. But how much, and in what form, did he retain?

"I remember—light." He had screwed his eyes up involuntarily. "I never saw light like that. Not just shining. It hurt. My eyes would not shut . . ."

I had inflicted that too. I gripped his hand hard enough to crush bones and tried not to haul him bodily into my lap.

"That was me, that was Two, that was the only way to stop it, once it had you." Even now I can hardly bear to remember that first glimpse of Tiran in his face. "I'm so sorry, I never meant to hurt you, I didn't even know . . ."

If you were still alive, let alone conscious. If anything of you remained.

The snow had begun to thin atop the great recumbent stone. Dark bumps and hollows shadowed the white blanket, hard stone pressed up under my flesh. Against my shoulder, Therkon shook his head again.

"That was you? Like the qherrique?"

For all that Tiran, all that I had done to him, he had kept his wits.

"That was Two and me. Yes."

He drew in his breath. And more than his wits had survived.

"*You* shone? Not like on Skall? Not the knife or, or something else?"

"Not this time. No."

Oh Mother, I was thinking as the tears pricked, tears of sheer gratitude, I know now why they light You candles across the Isles. The philosopher has survived. Next time, I'll light a dozen myself.

Beyond my feet the blood no longer steamed. The great red pool glistened though, starkly aberrant, ringed now by slick brown stone.

"The light stopped it?" He hunched suddenly and it came almost in a moan. "I need never have, should never have touched Rathi? You and Two could have—?" He tried to put the wounded hand over his face.

"*No.*" I snatched it down. The snow in his palm had melted. I scooped up more. "With Rathi, it, Tiran, Sthassamaer had taken me. You said it. You saw. It was the water. The black water." Could I, did I have to rehearse for him the inner terrors of that too often told dream? "I couldn't stop it. If you hadn't. If Rathi hadn't been . . ." I did not want to say, I know you felt what you had done then, to me as well as Rathi. But if Tiran had taken me, what else might it have won?

"**If Tiran had won then, all would now be lost.**"

We spoke no exaggeration, the Sight affirmed. From Two and me to Therkon, on to *Anfluga*, to the rest of Kaastria, the Isles, Dhasdein, the River. Beyond the River. Tiran would have had the world.

I shuddered. Therkon turned his head and stared at me. More than stared.

"Chaeris." Then he half withdrew his hand. His muscles began to contract. "Chaeris, is that—you?"

"It's us." Suddenly there was no more room for alarm or affront or that ancient fear of being rejected, being different. I pushed the hood back on his shoulders. Then I leant in and actually kissed his cheek in pure exuberance. "It's me and Two both. Nouip Saw truly. Now, so do we."

"Oh." He breathed it, a rising note of comprehension, wonder. Actual joy. For the first time, I suddenly realized in how long, his haggard, bristly face opened in a smile. "Oh, Chaeris!"

His hand turned, grasping mine. He would have used the wounded one as well, had I not caught his wrist. "That is—" It was pure imagination that the light itself had changed, brightening the mid-winter murk. "That is—"

He kissed the back of my grasping hand as impulsively as I had kissed his cheek. He even straightened a little. Though the frown revived, it held a shadow of philosopher's eagerness.

"Was that when you talked? I could see that. Not hear. Not what anyone said."

I opened my mouth to say, *Yes,* and stopped. Someone had spoken, yes. But how could I presume, suppose, suggest, let alone attempt to explain Who?

Did he even know the truth about the Winter Man?

"Do you remember Grithsperry?"

He nodded, looking puzzled.

"They, the shippers, talked about the Winter Man."

He nodded again.

"Veenn told me. Outside Ve Pool. The Winter Man is the Mother's adversary. They fight in autumn, and in spring. In spring, the Mother wins. In autumn, it's the Winter Man. It—His name is Tiran."

He blinked. "The name you said?" His brows creased. "Then what is—was—Sthassamaer?"

I wanted to kiss him, this time, in pure relief at the speed of his wits.

"Sthassamaer *was* Tiran. Tiran gone mad. Trying to make Winter last forever. Trying to take," I swallowed, "the light."

He had not spoken to Veenn, but he had heard sagas. I could have expected the world pattern to be spelt out more than once.

"To stop the seasons? But. But that would stop the world."

I could not help but smile at him, however lunatic it might appear. "Oh, yes."

He frowned again. And made the next, for him predictable leap.

"So you had to beat Tiran, to stop Sthassamaer?"

I could only nod.

His face had gone blank as the stones. But then his eyes dilated, almost as widely as when he looked at Rathi.

"But if you fought Tiran . . . Chaeris, that's the story. If you fought Tiran—who were *you*?"

I swallowed, hard. "If, if Tiran had taken you. And it really was the story. Who could I, who would I have to be?"

He actually pulled back along the stone. Drops cascaded from the furs and water scattered round him as naked rock appeared between us, under our feet.

"You mean *we* were—?"

Gods?

"I think—we took Their places. Or They took ours. Or They spoke through us. Or They used us, or—I don't know how it worked. I don't think we can know. At least, I don't think we can explain."

He licked his lips and then he said it with conscious quotation. "Your words do not work, do not work, do not work."

"Yes. I think, Yes."

He shivered as if back in *Aspis'* gale. I remembered those moments when I had felt, known another voice speaking through me, and shivered myself.

"But the story." We were not finished. "Putting that right wasn't all."

"What?"

I steeled myself. "At the end, I think. I think She did speak. For Herself. She told Tiran that the way things were would change. The light could not be part of the dark, but, now, the dark could know the light was there. Beside it. And that was something the dark could never have before."

His eyes shot up to mine. His mouth opened, and nothing came out. Only his expression spoke.

Before he lowered his eyes again, and very carefully, made, left-handed, a gesture that might have been a salute, and might only have mimed taking up a handful of water and letting it slip away.

The gesture he had made with real water, I recalled, when he remembered his dead.

I did not have to say, Do you understand? I did not need, I realized with boundless relief, to say anything. He too had caught the greatest wonder. That we had enacted not merely pattern, but change.

On the heels of that came another, differently appalling thought.

"Oh, heavens, what will my father say?"

"What?"

"My father Sarth." Consternation pulled me to my feet. "My mother says he's a philosopher. He reasons that there's no such thing as a god."

Therkon's mouth sagged open like an emptied purse.

"If I have to go back and tell him they exist, that I know they do, firsthand, I've felt it, I might even have *been* one. Oh, how will he deal with that?"

My father's whole thought-edifice, his world-view, assembled with such pain and struggle in the teeth of others' easier, pre-scribed beliefs, the scaffolding of his new life, dismantled. By first-hand experience, the one argument he could never overthrow.

Therkon was laughing. I realized it with disbelief, with out-rage that burnt out the shock. "How can you sit there and just, just—! Stop it! Blight and blast it, stop!"

"My lady. My . . . Chaeris." He was still laughing, shaking with it, tears had streamed unheeded down his cheeks. But he got himself on his feet, and reached his good hand to clamp over mine.

"We are stuck here in the snow, in the furthest reach of the Isles, uncounted voyages from anywhere. And we have still to get down this hill, let alone reach the one small ship. Your father is upRiver. Beyond even Iskarda. Do you not think his answer might be—a matter for some other day?"

I stared at him, as stupidly as he had looked at me. But Two agreed. Yes. We remained in the heart of desolation, we had still to reach Hringstenn, let alone *Anfluga*, let alone Hamair, Sand-ouin, all the countless other islands northward. Dhasdein, let be Iskarda, was beyond the limits of our ken.

And if he laughed, perhaps it had been the release of tension, close kin to if not pure hysteria itself.

This truly was here and now. The gods had departed. All that remained was us.

A strand of hair touched my cheek. Fallen from a plait at some point in the upheavals, dropping loose.

And dry. Softly fanning across my cheekbone. Carried by a breath of air.

Therkon's head came up almost as quickly as mine. He half-turned on a heel. As he moved, wind breathed across us, a tan-gible drift.

"The snow's stopped."

I heard myself say it, stupid with disbelief. Because it had not only stopped, it had been melting. The recumbent stone's top, the circle-stone salients were all darkly wet and glistening, their white thatches gone.

And the light, that I had thought pure imagination at Therkon's joy, really was brightening. Illuminating more vividly, more terribly, the great pool at our feet.

* * * *

Therkon was staring at it too, face speaking all that I felt. Loss. Regret. Rage. Protest. Grief. Abiding guilt.

I did not repeat what Azo had told me on the Sea-fort tower, or Two had argued on the way into Gildair. Whatever prizes death bought, they could not mitigate the price.

I shut my eyes a moment, letting Two carry me through the passages of memory, Eithay, Skall, Gildair, Rangar, the long spaces of ocean, the kaleidoscope of images. What use to ask wh ere or when Sthassamaer had found him, if there had been influence, or knowledge, or how much knowledge, before the end? Perhaps it had already been happening on the way to Gildair, when I had seen that contradictory flash of greed in Rathi's face. Who, using the words of humans to trace the path of—gods— through time, could possibly say?

Therkon's arm came round me. Very softly, Therkon's voice spoke in my ear.

"We will come back. With the others. With a bier. We will not demean him. Nor will we leave him. Not like this."

He moved away from me. The furs swirled and stooped. Steady-handed, he lifted Rathi's head from the muck of blood and water, brought it to the body. Suddenly knowing what he intended, I hurried in turn to help re-arrange the corpse. To draw the weather-canvas over all.

To make my own invocation as Therkon made his strewn-water reverence. *We will come for you. You will be cared for. We will not forget.*

When we turned, at last, for the circle's entrance, the blood had already diminished. It was seeping away into the earth, I realized, as rain or snow might, between the faces of small resurfacing stones.

* * * *

Beyond the portal we met the first actual gust, blowing up out of the south-west in a rush very nearly warm. Instinctively I unfastened my weather-canvas, and Therkon put back Nouip's cloak. As he shifted Hvestang's harness to his other shoulder, I saw that the hilt had been scorched brown, but remained intact.

By the time we reached the hill foot the snow was melting like a mirage, bedraggled grass and bushes swimming up through the mid-winter white, sterile purity dissolving into earth ochres, reds, browns. And suddenly, green. A bud sat on the lowest bush on the open sward. A single dot of color upon naked brown twigs. But beneath, incredibly, impossibly on the still-dark earth . . .

Therkon and I broke stride together, exclaiming in chorus, "Crocuses!"

They were only buds, but already the colors announced themselves, brilliant little sheath-rims of purple and gold. They would open in a few days, in a day or two. Perhaps, in this sudden enchanted termination of winter, this very day.

Already grass stems, old, bedraggled, but shot with dull, faint green, showed between the town cobbles. Water was running down a street center, and sound rose everywhere, the tinkle and rattle and burble of water freed in thaw. However unlovely the wreckage that thaw released.

And as we came out at the quay-end, a bow-shot from where *Anfluga* lay, half a dozen plump, short-legged brown-mottled birds suddenly materialized among the headland stones.

We both stopped: it was impossible not to stop, not to absorb the first moving life in Hringstenn, to stare, no longer with disbelief, but irresistibly, with joy.

The birds scuttled and scurried amid the beach pebbles. One of them began calling as we looked. *Tuck-tuck*, it cried, sharp as a rock-hammer. *Tuck-tuck, tuck-tuck*

"Turnstanes, down on the beach, *tuck-tuck, tuck-tuck . . .*"

For the first time I began to weep.

# CHAPTER XVII

I cried again when they carried Rathi's bier of oars and spare canvas out onto the now muddy waste of quay. But after the bearers had set him down, and slowly withdrawn to join work on the yard, Segil came over with a roll of spare canvas and the sailmaker's awl and palm. As he began to measure the bundled shape, I said, startled, "What are you doing?"

We had come back without their captain, with a story beyond incredible: yet they had accepted our attempts to tell it with what seemed miraculous quiet. Perhaps they had seen or sensed more than any would admit. Perhaps it was Therkon's wounded hand, or my unstoppable tears. But when we had stumbled to silence, there had been a long, dead pause. Before Segil, massive and silent in the midst, cleared his throat.

And after another teetering hush, rumbled, "Yfar, Vanri, we'll fetch t'skipper. Ruilf, get started on t' yard. Gylf," his eyes moved, and I realised they were on Therkon's hand, nursed in his other elbow crook. "Fettle that. Lass, ye come wi' me."

At that moment we had all accepted his leadership without question. Now he looked up, in mild surprise, to resolve my fresh puzzlement.

"Too far to bear him home." To burial back in Munen, I understood. And we had none of the ingredients for a rough-and-ready sea-preservation, even a firkin of rum. "We'll take him out in t'Hvalwrast."

And return him, in death, to the place where he had most truly lived. The sea.

To its black nether depths, the reality of the nightmare that had haunted me. To the killing water that had swallowed Deoren, and Verrith, and Azo.

"Make him a pyre," I said, too sharply. "We can take the, we can take home his ashes, can't we?"

Segil's hands stopped. In a moment he said, "Aye. We could. But. Lass, what could we burn?"

In a derelict town, snowbound, its remaining timber now sodden as the surrounding fields? Where would they find kindling, let alone sufficient wood? And how long before it dried enough to light?

But suddenly it was vital that Rathi's earthly husk should pass amid light and warmth, not in the black waters of Tiran's realm.

"**Find the fuel**," we said. "**There will be flame**."

Segil's eyes actually grew almost round. Then he said, just above a whisper, "Aye." I could hear the bitten-off "m'lady." He set the sailmaker's gear down and nearly hurried away.

\* \* \* \*

And there was fire, roaring, leaping into the lampless twilight, fast and vehement as if it burned in summer-parched grass. As Two and I had Seen, with past glimpses of broken doors and shattered shutters and rotting planks matched to the extrapolation of a day's scavenging amid Hringstenn's debris, and then added to the scope of our present powers: we had fire enough to kindle even sodden wood, and fuel sufficient for the task.

We all watched from anchor off-shore. Segil had informed me firmly that the coals would ward Rathi till dawn: if two seals had appeared in the harbor, and all of us had heard sporadic but joyful bird-song, by dusk the rapid scuttle of vermin was all too visible in the debris-ridden streets. "I'll stay for m'skipper," Segil decreed, "but I'll no' take off Hringstenn's rats."

Thankfully, Therkon's burn proved wide and horrific in appearance, but he had reacted so fast it was not deep. Moreover, the snow poultice seemed to have limited much of the actual damage. That afternoon Gylf, *Anfluga*'s second starboard oar and closest approach to a healer, had anointed Therkon's palm with something he called "burn potion," a clear fluid from some plant I never heard of, bandaged the hand lightly, forbidden Therkon to use it, and turned him loose. Indeed, remembering back over the day, worrying about both him and Rathi, I took far longer going to sleep.

I woke to gulls crying, the high, clear whistle and mew that was the essence of the Isles. But there was something strange about the rest.

I sat up, by the gunwale as usual. Except I had kicked off the blankets, tossed away my weather-canvas, even shed my Iskardan cloak. And before my eyes were truly open, the shadows of my boots, of Hvestang propped against the side, of Therkon's sleeping head, stood sharp as cutouts in a brilliant light.

The clouds had broken. Overhead hung mighty towers of gold and alexandrite and grape-shadowed smoke. Between them, over the stones above Hringstenn, up into the zenith's indigo and amethyst abyss, far out to the invisible east, light spread like a great golden-rayed wheel: the sun was coming up.

I leant by Segil in the stern, watching the gulls swoop and plane like light-stained snowflakes as the day opened round us, till even Hringstenn glowed like amber in its decay. As morning widened, as the world accepted the ransom that we, that all of us had bought.

Then a gull shrieked by under our very noses and Segil gave an indignant grunt. "Away wi' ye, ye brazen sweep. We've naught to give t'ye, an' ye'll give naught tae us but feathers an' shit."

At which I laughed so hard the whole crew woke.

* * * *

The gulls had fish guts by midday, tossed by the volunteer cook who took a line around the cape, while everyone else worked on the yard. Scavenging for the pyre had unearthed half of another broken spar, fit, the sailmen judged, to protect our own break. "Nay, lass," Segil corrected me almost indignantly, "*no'* a splint. That's for human beings."

And by the time the fish cooked, the pyre had cooled enough to approach.

"A flotskyll, aye. He'd like that," Segil observed, fetching another handful of ash and charcoal and things I did not want to identify, and tipping it carefully into the wide-mouthed canvas bag. Round the drawstring was embroidered a neat running-feather pattern in red, and on the side, less skillfully, something that bore *Anfluga's* name. "A seaman's carry. An' Ruilf's at that." He glanced at the port stroke, still busy round the yard. "Mither's brither-son, ye ken."

Kinfolk, then, close kin as they count it in the Isles. That, at least, was fitting enough.

And with both the yard and Rathi salved, by late afternoon Segil was ready to sail.

"There'll be naught in Hringstenn worth eatin' till summer. We've hard-tack'll get us to Hamair, an' this time, we can fish. That is," he glanced from me to Therkon and back, "if ye can thole the rations. An' ye're no' in haste."

The slower the better, I desperately did not want to say. While I tried to keep my face noncommittal, Segil looked at Therkon again.

And Therkon moved his bandaged hand and inclined his head and said, "At the best speed you choose. I can deal with the hard tack. I think," with that slight, consciously charming smile, "I can manage the fish."

If not, we still had the vial of imperial spice. I thought that Segil had caught more than a little of the crown prince, from the way his brow cocked before he nodded and said, "I've a mind to make for Sule. That's north o' Rangar, mind ye, an' we'll have no bogle speedin' us now. But t'will save a mort o' questions, aye? We can provision there. An' the Mither smile, we'll make one more long leg to Munen, east-about Sandouin." When he glanced at me I caught the old, sardonic glint. "I take it ye've no mind to pass by Skall."

When I shuddered, he nodded too. "Well, then," he was hesitating perhaps between "lass" and "lady," and perhaps some title for Therkon. "If ye're willing, we'd as well go now."

So we cast off, hoisted sail gently to test the yard, and slid away from Hringstenn on the warm, strong south-westerly. I watched till the last as the ruined streets, the gulls and seals in the harbour, the great black burn mark on the empty quay, and eventually, the coronet of stones on the hilltop, with the other great stain that I knew lay beneath them, dwindled into the cobalt evening sea.

* * * *

I woke inside a huge, fathomless bowl of dark: but this bowl was lit from rim to rim with the splendour of a moonless ocean night.

For a while sight was enough. I traced the glitter of familiar constellations in their unfamiliar places, Winejar and Sickle, Hunter and River's Queen. Then, through the equally familiar swash of water and rope-creak, voices began to impinge.

Segil, I realized. And Therkon. A hot spurt of jealousy rode atop the concern. Did the hand pain him, had his stomach started to misbehave, was it another bad dream? And how had I not woken too?

But the voices were quiet as the note was contemplative. Two men, acquainted but just coming to know each other, changing thoughts in a ship-deck night.

". . . not remember much," Therkon was saying, "myself. Chaeris was—there—the most."

"But ye'd remember something?" Segil pondered. "A man'd remember something, after bein' tangled so, eh? Wi' the likes o' the Mither. An' Tiran."

The word he had not used hung in the starlit air between them. With the gods.

When Therkon answered he sounded remoter than the very stars.

"I do not think what we call the Mother, or in my country, the River-lord—is more than our picture of them. Our hopes, perhaps. Our fears, yes. But what They are," I could hear the capital this time, "I doubt we can ever comprehend."

"Ye're sayin' they're a lie?"

"No." It came flatly as the blade of a sword. "They exist. Something exists. Chaeris' father must change his thoughts on that. But what it is . . . I think, what we—see—or wish, or propose about Them—is only a tip of the reality. A guess. Even a distortion. What They truly are . . ."

Segil let that lie a very long moment before he spoke again. "Nothin' like what we'd expect?"

Therkon made a sudden little puffing noise that might have been a laugh.

"If I had to use words at all, I would have to speak like the people we call philosophers. No. What we call the Mother is nothing like our images. They are much, much more. And much less. Nothing we could pray to, and expect an answer. Nor even something that will judge us, let alone watch over us. A, a force of nature, perhaps. More than wind or fire. They have some kind of, of sentience. But one that must—comprehend—the world, reality—in ways we cannot imagine. That might perceive one of us for a moment. Pick us up, perhaps. Even, maybe, do something like, work through us. But not, not like a puppet. Or even a tool. Not in any way I can put into words."

He stopped. The wind hushed. Segil was silent. When he spoke again Therkon sounded bleak as winter itself.

"It is not in their nature to feel or to think like humans. In our way—They do not care."

I could make out the line of his profile now, very still and very distant, against a flower spray of stars. He did not look round. But presently Segil said, "D'ye think t'was just that one? Tiran?"

An angle of Therkon's shoulder lifted. "Or Sthassamaer? If there was a difference, between them, or from the Mother, I cannot tell. Or remember. Nothing It—whatever inhabited my body did—was my own."

When Segil did not speak, he added curtly, "Except with Rathi."

His conscience again, I thought. Still. Under all this philosophy, over all this bleak retrospect. I ached to rise and intervene, but something warned, *This is between them. Let be.*

But I waited through a very long pause, before Segil spoke.

"He'd have thanked ye."

"What?"

"If the—if Sthassamaer took him. Tried to work ill through him. Tried to harm the lass. He'd have thanked ye to stop it. To be set free."

Therkon said half a word and stopped himself.

"He liked her," Segil was almost murmuring, shielded in the starry dark. "Called her a brave, canny lass." A flick of his own humour surfaced. "Aye, well, he'd no' call her 'wee'."

"She liked him too."

Therkon's voice was so raw it would have silenced me.

"An' ye like her fine, y'rself." When he did speak, Segil's voice had changed. Now he sounded almost unnaturally casual. "That's no' always certain, among kin."

Waves swashed and the salvaged yard creaked. I caught the lift of Segil's head against occluded stars. He had relaxed again before Therkon replied.

"You surely know otherwise."

Segil's pause was almost as long. "Aye," he said at last. "Some's been thinkin' it. But, kin or no kin, seems ye like her still."

"Chaeris is . . . Chaeris." I could feel Therkon swallow. "Brave, and loyal, and, and, 'canny,' yes: clever, cunning. Wise. And I owe her my life, and—I swore I would protect her with mine." And with a bitter twist. "That I have not done so well."

"Ye're alive," Segil said. "Ye never saw her when she thought it might be otherwise. If ye like her well enough, t'is more than sure she likes ye."

Therkon's shadow froze. Before he could answer, Segil went on.

"An' here in the Isles, we like her more than fine. Canny, aye. Bountiful as the Mither. An' kind. Paid our passages, bought Ve Pool herrin'. An' stood for us, before—Sthassamaer. Before Tiran.

Whatever ye feel or think about Them, t'is those names we know. In Munen, my mam's a Teller. When we come ashore, if the lass wills, if she'll bear to say it out, mam'll make it a tale. An' we'll remember. The lass'll no' have to speak it again."

Therkon's body language had glossed throughout: wariness, some pleasure at the compliments to me, harsh memories. Concern and doubt, and at the last, relief. Telling *Anfluga*'s folk had been hard enough. He knew how I dreaded having to rehearse it all again.

"An'," Segil's voice was still soft, but the note had changed once more, "always, we'll keep watch an' ward for her. Wherever she might be."

Therkon drew one sharp breath that became an equally sharp involuntary cough of a laugh. But he did not say, You have no idea of who we are, of where we come from, let alone how to get there. You are an unlettered South Isles fisherman. And you think to protect her? You think you can threaten *me*?

What he said was, "Chaeris. I think the Isles' kindness will mean much to her. Very much indeed."

"What does it mean to ye?"

Therkon stopped short. The undernote in that soft question had my own hand on a sheath.

"I guess well, in y'r own land ye're more than a merchant man. Or even a lord, mebbe. At least, as we count Lord, in the Isles. So I'll ask again, wi' us both mindful o' that. What does our kindness mean to ye?"

To the man, I was ciphering desperately, or to the lord, the figure of power? How much does Segil guess? What is he trying to do?

Water hushed and rose, and passed. One wave, two, three.

"I have already sworn to guard Chaeris, with my life. To her own folk. To those even closer than . . . the Isles. However grateful to the Isles . . . we, both of us, will always be."

Amid the pauses, the careful threading of word-choices, I caught more than a hint of imperial affront. *Do not*, I prayed, *poker up and invoke your rank here. Not with Segil.*

"Y'r life, aye." As I expected, Segil was not impressed. "An' no doubt ye'd lay it down for her. But what about the rest?"

"What rest?"

"The harm," Segil said very softly, "ye y'rself might do."

When Therkon spoke this time it held a menace I never heard even from the hatchet man.

"Are you suggesting that I—"

"Ye'd ne'er debauch her, nay. Ye've too much thought for that. An' honor. Separate beds, separate rooms. Ye tender her like a brither. But d'ye see? She's but a lass, an' a young lass. A maid, I'm fair sure. An' whatever *ye* are, she's a lovin' heart. Already ye've the most of it. D'ye ken what harm ye can do, if she fixes it all on ye?"

*Anfluga* slapped a wave, but I saw Therkon's recoil. And the endless moment while they faced each other, two starlit silhouettes. Both rigid, down to the out-thrust jaw.

Then Therkon half drew away. All but propped himself on the gunwale. When he spoke his voice cracked.

"Gods, man. Do you think I haven't *seen*?"

Water rose and fell beyond them, its facets catching the starlight to glints of foam. I wondered if my heart had stopped, before Segil spoke.

"What, then, d'ye mean to do?"

Therkon should have pokered up in earnest. If he could not wax indignant at anyone taxing him in what should have been my fathers' place, it ought to have been enough that Segil dared question a future emperor.

But Therkon only turned his head and stared away past the dragontail sternpost where the foam glinted, brief as flowers, along *Anfluga*'s trail. When he spoke, it sounded empty as the receding sea.

"I will do—what must be done."

He put both hands on the stern-rail and bowed his head and the rest reached me in the barest whisper, less heard than imagined through the sounds of wind and wave.

"Whatever that means to me."

\* \* \* \*

Segil's "mam" was almost as massive as he was, with his dark eyes and skin, but something in her facial bones that said, distant white blood. She met us on the wharf, after *Anfluga* worked in through the plentiful traffic under Munen's sun-white terraces, vivid above a laughing blue and white sea. Someone had recognized the sail a long way out, and word had run through the town. One of their own, coming home.

And with Segil's mother, Rathi's widow came.

Of all the voyage it was the moment, I had dreaded most. Segil had told us, almost in passing, "T'was fixed, long ago. When t'skipper went, I'd take her on." *Anfluga*, he meant. Smoothing a palm over the hand-worn, sweat-stained tiller bar. "Split the difference, costs an' pay, wi' Druath. She's a canny woman. An' sea-born, herself."

Small, going grey, but upright and composed, even when Segil brought ashore the "flotskyll" and gave her the news that mattered most to her.

"Ye'll hear the tale," he told her, "from my mam. But we'll sing him this eve." They had been working on the songs all up Hamair's coast, across Hellir Strait, even round the sunlit, green-glinting lands of Sandouin. "Aye, me mam'll do the tale," he said to me, "but we'll wake Rathi. We're his crew."

That plan had been the most constant pattern of the voyage, after the weather, which produced showers and spring squalls but always cleared to sunshine, to blue skies that Segil snorted were "t'bogle's amends," and that spoke, clear as the scent of woken earth on the wind, of spring.

As constant as the slight, impalpable, unmistakable resumption of Therkon's courtesy to me.

He let me change the bandages and keep close ward over his healing hand, he still smiled and called me "Chaeris" without hesitating over "my lady," and spoke to me, at times, like his friend. But always, afterwards, the constraint would fall again. Transparent as a veil of glass, and as unbreakable.

Because I could not even ask what had gone wrong between us. Because of how I already knew.

When I tried to speak to Druath, the platitudes drew on my own past and present grief. But though she listened somberly, it was without tears.

"He was flotna," she said. "Like my own pa. Seafarers. Ye ne'er know when they're comin' home. An' ye ne'er know when they'll go."

She had a brief contest with Segil's mother over housing Therkon and me, before we spent four days in Segil's family house on its upper terrace, a wholly fascinating, deceptively narrow-fronted pile of gables and shingle roofs. The three floors climbed like terraces too, a single stair up the middle, curtains for walls, and a hearth at either end. Therkon and I were bestowed, apologetically, on the "weens' floor": boys' room to the right, girls' to the left, snug under the topmost ceiling. On the second floor Segil's parents, his aunt, his two sisters and their husbands lived. Segil had space there, but he never slept in it. "Away to Haggar's daughter, down t'road," his elder sister told me amusedly. The ground floor was common-space and kitchen, where Segil's father held sway. He had broken a thigh at sea and come home to stay, Segil said, adding, ironic as ever, "He's more time for it than mam. An' he's a better cook."

The first was certainly true. Skalr was a true Teller. What that meant in the Isles I had not yet understood.

After a professed healer had seen Therkon's hand, judged it healing beyond need for extra help, and supplied a new salve "to ease in the scar," we spent the days exploring the house, or investigating passages from Munen. Neither of us had wanted to draw *Anfluga* further astray. Segil argued at first that they would take us right home, but then he stopped short, and said abruptly, "Aye, lass. Ye deserve at least one trip wi' a proper necessary."

It did not stop him exhaustively criticizing every possible vessel, captain or crew. But for the most time, we slept. I had not realized how much I had needed a true, safe, stable bed until I woke the first morning only a little before noon.

Each day, though, people came to see Skalr with what seemed trivial news, even gossip, births and marriages and ships out or in. Between times she moved about the house, or ran minor errands, or occasionally joined conversations, all with an absent air of listening. After the rest went upstairs the first night, she had sat me down at the left ground-floor hearth, the common space. I had been unsure how much to tell, of our origins, our identities. But when I said, "Where shall I start?" She said, "Begin at the beginning, and go on to the end." And Two took her at her word.

The third afternoon she appeared as we were shaking off a shower's wet from a harbor trip. Segil took one look and went alert. Skalr nodded to him and said, "I've told Thengir." Thengir had no title, and lived in an ordinary house, but he seemed the nearest Munen had to a lord. "He'll call Gather tonight."

The rain had cleared by sunset, and the moon rose exquisitely, four days from full. Its lop-sided golden globe lit the rain-limpid air, the distant horizons I could never get enough of, the panorama of harbor and streets and the steady stream of people filling the space behind the quay. In a more formal town it might have had a fountain, and been called a square. Here it was just the gather-ground. People sat on steps, on native boulders, on long kitchen stools. And the gods sat with them, Tiran and the Mother, in a little thicket of candles that helped lamps and lanterns and open windows eke out the moon.

There was very little noise. It stopped completely when Skalr emerged on the back step of the quayside inn, crossed hands on her breast, and bowed her head to the Mother, briefly as to an old friend.

Then she raised her low, casual voice that now carried like a honey-toned trumpet, and said, "Hear the tale of the Winter Dark. The deed of Therkon Burnt-Hand and Chaeris, the Seer of Iskarda."

Therkon was perched beside me on a convenient step. I felt rather than heard the quick intake of his breath. I could imagine his rapt, dazzled look. We were about to become legend. He had told me sagas. Now we would enter a saga ourselves.

> Cold lay the Isles
> in desolate winter,
> Dark as the grave,
> in Sthassamaer's hold.
> Stark snow blighted
> Kaldr's fishermen.
> Cruel wind struck
> at Ve Pool's fleet,
> Wrath of the sea
> punished brave Hondeland,
> Plague broke the dream
> of Hringstenn's stones.
> Hard rock at Cuwen
> lies bare and lone.

She half sang, half chanted, low-pitched but resonant. There were towns and islands I never heard of in that list, and as the roll-call extended I began to understand what "Teller" meant.

Two can reclaim them all. I have telescoped that part to moon and lamplit shadow, the audience's absolute quiet. Until Skalr paused, not for breath, but for emphasis.

> Then from northward
>    came the heroes,
> Cast by waves
>    on Sickle's beach,
> Their sea toll paid.
>    The Winter Man claimed
> White-sailed *Aspis*,
>    her sixty rowers.
> Sailmen and captain,
>    Avergil, Crespis, Suris, Deoren . . .

A list of names that I had never known, but I knew who they were. Ten Imperial guards. The captain. Deoren's troublecrew. She had talked to Therkon too.

> And of Iskarda,
>    Verrith, Azo.

My eyes filled as I fully understood. A Teller in the Isles told more than story, or even saga. This was history. Record, honor, epitaph. Memorial.
And they would not honor even outland heroes alone.

> The Seer found them
>    come to Evvamoor,
> Quieted sorrow and
>    Saw their way.
> Then said Therkon
>    the far-planner,
> 'Farther southward
>    I will to go,
> Wherever fate takes us,
>    whatever the cost.'
> 'Where you go, I go,'
>    the lady said.

Suddenly I was blinking away my own tears of awe and wonder at apotheosis. I could not, yet, hear the capital "L" for "lady," but I knew that it would come.

We reached Grithsperry. If a talespinner was meticulous in listing the dead, so was she with less savory events. Hvestang caused tumult, Skatir imprisoned us, we fired the tower and fled. *Tolla* took us south with

> Frotha the ship-wife, Colne the master,
>> to Jurrick they sailed.

Where, scrupulously not awarding blame where neither Two nor I had certainty, we lost Nouip's brooch, and Therkon sold his ring.

> What is a treasure,
>> said Therkon Burnt-hand,
> So it be not spent
>> in the hour's need?

In the quiet around us I could almost hear *Anfluga*'s men adding passage costs and herring sales, and finding the real source of my bountifulness.

We fled Jurrick, I fell on the cliff, less, I was grateful to hear, from rashness than haste. Veenn and her kin salvaged me, while my "true companion" ran for help.

A Teller names evil-doers along with the good and the dead. "Stokka, Lord of Ve Pool" was as unsparingly described as the Ve Pool thieves, as "*Aerful* of Ve Pool," and Fiskri, Halri and Sheinn.

When we moved to Eithay I stopped listening: not for the embarrassment of the herring sale. Meeting Rathi, the first traumatic voyage with *Anfluga*, was bad enough. But I could not bear to think about Skall again.

> By the ceat, on the hillside,
>> strong-hearted Chaeris
> Struck for her way-mate,
>> waking light,
> Wiping out sea-kites.
>> Nine at a blow.
> Never again,
>> will the flotnar fear Skall.

A teller's, a historian's, a justice's verdict. Two retrieves it. I was only trying to escape the rain and mist, the dead men lying round me in the raw wind and seabirds' cries.

Nor can I bear, even now, to retrieve the rest of that journey into winter. Even those last minutes among Hringstenn's stones.

I opened my eyes again when Skalr's tone announced conclusion. The gather-space was utterly still. All the faces were lifted, blurs in the half-light. Not a few of them, to my appalled realization, were turned to Therkon and me.

> Go now, bade the Mother,
>> your grievance settled.
> Yield the day.
>> The Seer has spoken,
> Seeing for Me.

The heroes have fought.
Hvestang has brought the
    end of dispute. Dawn will waken,
Dayspring return.
    The comfort of grief
Comes from remembrance
    in honor, in truth.
Now the Isles will remember
    *Aspis, Aerful, Anfluga,*
Iskarda's Seer,
    and Therkon Burnt-Hand,
So long as sails move
    out to sea.

\* \* \* \*

I would have liked to stay in Munen, not only to watch the Isles' summer succeed their tardy spring, but because, lacking lords, Munen seemed a town both odder and far easier than any other we had seen. But Therkon, I knew, would be worrying about Dhasdein. And though Skalr's tale had met only the deepest, most respectful silence, followed by a steady surge of candle-lighting before the images, next day people were already following me, calling me Lady, trying to touch me, to ask for Sights in the street.

I had lit a candle too. It was less thanks than invocation, though I could not decide what I really sought. That we stay in the Isles? That we find swift passage home? That Therkon treat me as before? That I could ignore his last words to Segil? Certainly, I did not expect Segil himself to thump in the third-next noonday and burst out, "There's a schooner in! *Skthoja,* out of Inganess!"

"First souther o' the season," he added in satisfaction, as he and Therkon and I and half the household began tumbling down the hill. "She'll have the pick o' the lading, such as it is. An' she's a fine weatherly hull as well as fast, an'," on a note of triumph, "there's a necessary!"

Skalr caught my eye behind his back. I tried to smother my own laugh. To remember Dhasdein and Iskarda. To silence my divided heart that cried one instant, *I want to go home,* and the next, *I want things as they were.*

*Skthoja*'s tall, laconic captain knew Munen, and Segil. And some of the tale had already traveled, for when he heard whose passage Segil wanted, I felt him half-check to stare. Before he nodded across the tap-room table to Segil, and then inclined his head to me. "Aye, m'lady. Where is it ye'd go?"

Segil opened his mouth to say, Inganess. Therkon's eye amended, Phaerea. I spared one wistful thought for Ve Pool. When I had asked if Stokka might avenge her tale on Fiskri's folk, Skalr had shaken her head with a curt smile. "Wi' every Isle eye upon him? He'd never dare." But prudence warned to avoid provocation, all the same.

I opened my own mouth to suggest, Jurrick? Two's extrapolation meshed with memory, clear back, clear forward to Sickle, and we Saw.

"**Hranhaven**," we said.

\* \* \* \*

We farewelled Munen on the wharf, as we had farewelled so many towns, though seldom in a crisp wind, under full sun, and with what seemed like the whole populace out to see us off. It made parting from those we knew more difficult. Especially from *Anfluga*'s crew.

Looking up at Segil as Two added time, I realized that I had known him longest of anyone in the Isles. Had traveled further with him. Shared greater perils and distresses with him than with anyone except Therkon. A tale is a saga, a record of heroes. How does one list, let alone mourn, the threads of tiny everyday events that weave lives together, that we were about to sever for good?

He was looking almost wooden. There was a lump in my throat: I wanted to put out my hand, but though courteous it seemed inadequate. No doubt he would hesitate about offering his. Then feelings overran caution and courtesy too, I put both arms round him as far as they would go and hugged.

"Thank you," I said, when we did let go. "For everything."

He nodded once. "A fair wind," he said. The traditional Isles' sea-farewell. "An'," he blinked, once, twice. "Remember us. As we'll be rememberin' ye."

"We'll remember." And suddenly we Saw, past my own life-span, past even a saga's memorial. Two would remember him, as humans never could. And Two would pass her memories to the qherrique, into the record we had inherited. The record that had preserved seven hundred years of Amberlight.

"**You will never be forgotten**," we said.

His face told me he understood. At least, that it was a Sight. He bowed his head as to the Mother. Then he lifted it, Segil again.

"A brave, canny lass," he said, straight-faced. "An' fast wi' a blade. But none'll ever call ye 'wee'."

So I could pull a face and threaten mayhem as for once in a roar of friendly laughter Therkon and I climbed a gangplank, and prepared to wave goodbye.

\* \* \* \*

*Skthoja* was as fast as promised, and the weather stayed fair. West about Terrace to Inganess, west and north for a brief call at Mirkadin, then east about the tip of Phaerea, north again, a long leg to avoid Grithsperry, a harrowing wide cast about Rack Head, then a last south-east run into the bight of the Sickle, to Hranhaven itself: for all that long but easy passage I ate, and slept, in a tiny passenger's cabin, and worked out with Therkon daily. Hand to hand. Neither of us wanted to use a blade. And all the way I struggled not to feel that thin tether of constraint, not to wonder what his last words to Segil might come to mean.

It was relief beyond expression when *Skthoja* worked in under summer-bright hills to Hranhaven, and my eyes beheld what we had Seen in Munen: the tall, grey-haired, pale-skinned woman waiting on the quay.

"Aye," she said, when I stopped laughing and weeping and crying into the shoulder of her homespun cloak, "I Saw you! I Saw you here! Nouip, I can See!" There was a smile for once on that reticent face, equal parts amusement, joy and pride. "And I knew you had. Two months gone, when the season changed. I knew ye'd prevailed. I Saw ye, on a dockside. An' third yestermorn, when I let the dogs out, the wind said, *Hranhaven*."

She held me a little away from her. "There's been rags o' the tale, with every keel in." The Sickle accent seemed almost Outland after the thicker voices of the southern Isles. "Come ye now to my sister-daughter's house, up the way here, and give me it all."

Nouip's niece was almost as grey-haired as she, and as taciturn. We sat behind what seemed, after Skalr's house, a scrupulously tidy but almost mundane cottage, and drank Sickle ale with new bread and home-gathered eggs, under the first tiny fruit setting on her apple-tree. Since Two had Skalr's tale word-perfect, I let her begin.

"A canny spinner," Nouip said, when the final silence had gone long enough. "To honor ye, and pass matters outbye her bailiwick. 'From northward.'" She smiled slightly. "Aye."

"Oh! I see." It had not occurred to me, among the dazzle and embarrassment of being hailed a hero, the careful accounting of everything within the Isles, how masterfully Skalr had excluded so much outside. I had to laugh myself. Even after retelling that tale, nowadays laughter came easily. "I wonder what the other sagas had to leave out?"

"Such as," Nouip observed, "that you've grown an inch since ye saw me last?"

"Oh, Nouip! You too? Segil *said*, I'll never be called 'wee'!"

Therkon had laughed with us. Now he said, "Especially, the sagas forget things about how tired, and cold, and hungry, and frightened the heroes were." He glanced across to Nouip. "But one thing they never omit is the thanks." He rose and turned to our packs.

"My lady Nouip." Formally, he laid the seal-furs out on the simple plank table. "We have no gift that would suffice. We do not even have all we were given." I knew he had never forgotten the loss of the cloak-brooch in Jurrick. "But what we have, we can return."

He lifted Hvestang from where it had leaned on the bench beside him, and laid it atop the cloak. "Even if it—bears marks of the journey, too."

The furs looked no different, though the scent of cedar had become human sweat, and salt, and I always fancied, the after-memory of snow. Hvestang's sheath was clean and polished to match the blade within. Only the hilt, scorched now to the color of dark honey, had changed.

Nouip examined both in silence. Then she shifted Hvestang carefully and gathered the cloak to her side of the table, as formally as Therkon had laid it down.

"This," she said, "is of and from Evvamoor. It belongs to the Winter Man. T'was lent for the enterprise, and were it lost, that would be within the gift. Now I will keep it in trust once more."

"But this," she took up Hvestang by mid-sheath, "is of my own house, my own line. This I can bestow as I will." She rose, and held it out, formally, across both hands. "Take this with you, Dhasdein."

Therkon very nearly gulped. He did back a step. "My lady Nouip, this is a, an heirloom. A treasure of the Isles. It belongs here, it should not—"

"T'is of the Isles, aye. And ye've seen for y'rselves, t'would be better *out* of the Isles. For longer than I shall live."

Therkon looked up sharply, but he did not try to argue. We had indeed seen for ourselves, at Grithsperry.

Nouip shifted the sword a little. "Take it for your sake, as well as ours. For the memory. Of who you are. Of what you did."

Therkon turned his face away. In a constricted voice he said, "My lady, I have no great desire—nor, indeed, any great claim—to remember what I did."

"Think twice, then," Nouip said flatly. "Why d'you think Skalr named the deed for both o' ye? And gave you a talename? Spare me false modesty, Dhasdein. Without ye both, we would ne'er have prevailed."

We. We, the Isles, we, the Seers, Two extrapolated. We, the inhabitants of the earth, the Isles and Outsea with them.

And, as resonance invoked the Seeing eye, We, also. We, the gods.

Therkon was looking at his hands. Less abashed than silenced perhaps, despite the tiny flush that did not signal shame.

Nouip's voice changed. "Keep it, too, for memory of what you are. T'was you, at the sticking point, that had the nerve, and the hardihood, and the skill to swing this blade."

Therkon's head came up with a jerk. Nouip looked him straight in the eye and went on in her Seer's voice, "To see, and to do what must be done."

To override companionship and compassion and conscience and give me, the gods, the world, a second chance. To strike down Rathi.

To play the role he had warned me of. The imperial hatchet man.

They stared at each other, while Therkon's face spoke for him. Yes. She had seen truly. She knew what, as well as who he was.

Then Nouip's face softened a fraction. She set the sword down, came round the table, and took his right hand, turning it up to show the broad, healed but still angry red mark across the palm.

"But keep it too, for who else you are. For who, now, you will always be."

Therkon Burnt-hand. Companion, helper, hero. Whose deed and cost and right to honor were printed in his own flesh.

She let his hand go. Then she added very softly, "Take it, most of all, so you'll not forget the Isles. When your day comes."

\* \* \* \*

I will not forget, I thought, two mornings later when the freighter cast off, and hoisted sail, and stood out northward, and Nouip and her niece dwindled to doll figures on the quay. I may go back to Dhasdein, I may go all the way home, but whatever Therkon does, I will never forget the Isles. The faces, the places, the names. Sunlight on whitewash, blue tiles dark with rain. The smell of salt and tar and sea-kelp and labouring, unwashed men, the creak of rope and oar, the swash of waves and the thud and crackle of a sail. The rise of cliff and headland, a mere smudge or great towers of rock rising from the sea, and the cry of birds. Plovers, curlews, hawks, gulls. Turnstanes, cracking pebbles on a beach. I will hear them, always, in my dreams.

# CHAPTER XVIII

Therkon leant so long on the stern rail beside me that I nerved myself to ask the question which had plagued my own mind. "Are you thinking—worrying about Dhasdein?"

He looked round. Met my eyes. Started to shake his head. Then suddenly grimaced and said almost roughly, "I cannot help but think about Dhasdein."

And I knew what he had not said: I cannot bring myself to ask you, yet again, even now you have your Sight, to tell me what is happening or might have happened there.

"I'd tell you, if we knew." It was my turn to be abrupt. "There just isn't enough news. I know that's what we've always said, but I don't think our Sight works like Nouip's. Ours has to have information. However much or little that is."

"Sights are different?" I had roused the philosopher's unquenchable interest. "Where does Nouip's come from, then?"

I could only shrug. "She thinks, perhaps from dreams?"

"But if you and Two only have enough information, then a Sight is different to a, a forecast? As you could do before?"

"Different, yes." I felt again that indescribable sensation as all the facts and images and memories and projections coalesced and the universe gave me a single unassailable answer, back among Hringstenn's stones. "It's far, far—bigger. Far more—certain. It—" I fell back, trying to smile, on the qherrique's own slogan. "Our words do not work, do not work, do not work."

"I can believe that."

He said it quite simply, but I saw in his eyes the memory of those moments when, however passively, he had known, felt, been Tiran.

He leant back over the rail. And the companionship was there, as it had been across half the Isles, while we watched Sickle's ling-green hills grow blue and indeterminate beyond the sparkling sea.

Presently he said, "Can Seers See for themselves?"

The simplest, most obvious question. The one I had an answer for, having asked it myself.

"Nouip says, her Sights can show what she'll see or do or meet, the way she met us. But they come as they please. And she can't ask directly about herself. She says, no Seer can."

"Do yours come as they please?"

"It seems so." I could not help sounding wry. "At least, I never know exactly when there'll be enough of, of whatever it takes, to make one happen."

"You have not yet asked anything? Specifically?

I had asked. It was what brought Nouip's explanation, because the question now nearest my heart had not produced even Two's usual white turmoil. Just a perfect blank.

Nouip had sought an answer for me, so far as any Seer could. Two had no need to engrave those words on my mind.

'You've a road ahead, aye, a fair and clear one, but t'is long too, and twisty as a skein of wool. And t'will end where you wish, but not where you expect that wish to be.'

I had delayed too long. I could feel Therkon's eye, and knew it had already read more than I wanted, while past experience told me his wits would not be far behind.

"I did ask, yes. About how—when—I'd get home. When nothing happened, I asked Nouip."

"Oh."

He might justifiably have been disappointed, had I said I failed to See anything about Dhasdein. But there was something here a little more crestfallen, more despondent than I might have expected. Something that might have reached past even the crown prince, into the truly personal.

Then he stepped back from the rail and said, "It's early yet. And this deck," running his eye along it, "has plenty of room. Perhaps you would care to work out, Chaeris?"

And the restraint was back, courteous, thoughtful, delicate as spider's silk. Impossible to query. Impossible to undo.

* * * *

I could not breach that wall. Nor could I stop it widening, inexplicably but inevitably, from courtesy to quiet, to something darker and more worrying, however speedily we headed north.

*Seony* was faster than anything we had sailed in before, including *Aspis*. The weather's lift had brought her south from Doubleface, the Far North Isles as they counted them in Sickle, bringing grain and timber in hopes that expensive small-goods like whale oil and ivory might already have percolated north. Since little had, they were highly relieved when we used another of Therkon's azians to pay passage clear to her home port of Prospect. So highly relieved that they never questioned how a pair of shipwrecked Dhasdeini merchant siblings might have either gems to barter, or a sword like Hvestang.

Two insists the journey proceeded at normal speed: calling at Sprite for water, passing South Island and the barren Groans, swinging west from Whale Island round Doubleface to the wide, foliate inlet of Prospect Port. Even with a usually brisk southwesterly, it took nearly three weeks. And this, Therkon estimated, from names of islands Dhasdein and Two had at least heard of, was barely half the way *Aspis* had been driven in six days and nights. Considered rationally, I could not believe she had held together to reach Sickle at all.

But irrationally, three weeks to Prospect passed like the fall of an eyelash in the time of my now protesting heart.

After the South Isles Prospect was a busy, kempt, half-alien town: no red-sailed fishing fleets, no sixers like *Anfluga* at sea, no white-washed domes or brechs ashore. A council of lords ruled, merchant warehouses lined the harbour, freighters of every size berthed beside *Seony*, busy with the North Isles' own staples of grain, timber, fruit. And wine.

Prospect was also a town where we might expect not merely ex-Navy Isle men but true Dhasdeinis. We lodged discreetly in what passed for a small backstreet inn, and to his chagrin, Therkon had to concede Two was right. Safer to leave the hunt for an ongoing passage to me.

Overnight my prepared excuse became a reality: something at dinner, perhaps the local crayfish we had been coaxed to try, upset Therkon's stomach as *Anfluga*'s rations never had, so I set out after breakfast, laden with cautions and injunctions, but alone.

After Ve Pool and Eithay, let be Skall, such an expedition did not daunt me overmuch, but by early afternoon I had to give in. Despite the truly formidable array of shipper's offices, not to mention the multitude of actual ships, the best I could find was not direct passage to Dhasdein, but a next morning passage north-west to the island of Summertree.

Leg-weary and hungry, I headed back. At this setback I expected Therkon to grumble, fret at his own limits, then say, Wait, try again. When I tapped at his door, I did not expect to be answered by a groan. Nor, when I shot inside, wrist-knife loose, to meet a heartfelt, "Oh, Chaeris. Thank the Lord it's you."

The landlady's brother had left the Imperial Navy with a very different view to Skatir's. A fine-looking Dhasdeini merchant suffering a mild belly-ache had amplified the Isles' off-hand kindness with distressed strangers to the point of three visits to offer possets, query about calling a healer, and, "I cannot think what she wanted last time. Or at least, I can. I could shake court leeches in my cradle, but this . . . A passage to Summertree, tomorrow? Take it. Take it! And don't dare leave me alone again!"

\* \* \* \*

Pointing out the contradiction in these orders ruffled him anew. Worse, next morning, the Summertree skipper proved a Navy man of Skatir's ilk. We were hardly aboard when his barbed comments on Dhasdeini seamanship and idle merchants' wealth had me wound tight enough either to try Azo's intimidation mode, or drag Therkon bodily below.

He did limit himself to a deal of imperial frost, and lasting selective deafness. A single round of *Wavewalker*'s deck, Therkon with Hvestang and me with both my knives, silenced most of the crew. But I was not in the least surprised when an almost-storm caught us north of Greenhill, the timber in ballast shifted, and when we limped into Grey Island's tiny harbor, the skipper informed us with vindictive zeal that he could not justifiably hinder our journey further. "Here's the half of y'r passage money. There'll be keels headed north, far sooner than us."

*Not*, Therkon furiously did not retort, *from this sketch of a port!* But he took the money with frigid displeasure and stalked off down the wharf.

Five mornings after the actual storm, it was a bright day, white clouds puffed up like argosies overhead. Grey Island's bony hills smiled down on us, fawn, gold or brown, its select few vine-yards dark with fruit. The warm, salt-flavored air was leaning toward heat and dust. Summer, I realized with something near amazement, would already be past its zenith in Dhasdein, let alone Iskarda.

Therkon glanced longingly up to the white block of pillars and walls that signaled an Imperial governor's ex-residence, probably still a Dhasdeini consulate. But it would break our incognito to ask official help. Azo, let alone my own instincts, vetoed it instantly. We were still too far from home.

*Wavewalker* was the biggest hull among the scatter of vessels in port. I did not have to hear the growl rising in Therkon's throat. Without official help, we would be crawling the last leg in another *Tolla*, or even a simple fishing boat.

The best we found was in fact a fishing boat, headed away off our line, north-east to the last islet in the Tail, the string hanging like beads south from Wave Island. Even if we island-hopped from there to Wave, we would still be a good ten days from Dhasdein.

Despite his previous huff I had expected Therkon to sigh, finally change his mood and accept the next best choice. With a face of thunder, he simply demanded, "How soon can you leave?"

We were four days snailing to the Tailbone. The weather was average, the three-man crew polite but wary, and Therkon stayed in what, from a man of lesser courtesy or status, could only have been termed a sulk.

He did not improve over the week it took to reach Southwater, Wave's nearest port. When we actually had to go overland to Wineweigh in the north, I rode two days in virtual silence over the spine of the island, through ripening vineyards that made the Riverworld's most famous wine, over dusty terraces and enchant-ing vignettes of distant sea, in company with a terse, brooding creature I hardly recognized as the hatchet man. Let alone the philosopher.

He was fretting over Dhasdein, I thought. With no other distraction, that would grow more and more imperative. I could not give him a Sight, far less solider news. Gossip was rare, we could not ask outright, at least, not the sort of questions he would want. He had been too long away, on this irresponsible quest. It had succeeded, and we were heroes, yes. But now he had to forget Therkon Burnt-Hand, who had met adversity with courage and endurance, and given me kindness, friendship, laughter, even at the bitter worst. The time I had had him to myself, when nothing had mattered more to him, was almost over. Now, he only wanted to become the crown prince again.

It helped neither of our spirits that the only freighter at Wineweigh even half interested in sailing north before vintage was small and fairly slow. Finally, in sheer exasperation, Therkon actually bought half a holdful of Redrock hemp and tar, plausibly re-saleable to the Riversend shipyards, and the *Puffin* at last put to sea.

From Wineweigh to the Delta, Therkon fumed in a more accessible moment, would, for a big Dhasdeini freighter, "be no more than ten days!" Our ship would probably have taken a fortnight. Even had we not run afoul of pirates almost in sight of the Washes, the eastern Delta isles.

They came running briskly up from south-westward, between us and Riversend: a vessel hardly larger than a sloop, but with low lean lines and a two-masted spread of sail that spelt, Trouble, long before we caught the sheen of steel on board. At the first definite word from his look-out, the *Puffin*'s master winced and swung the tiller. "All hands!" he bellowed. "Make sail!"

"She's got the weather-gauge," he snapped when Therkon began to protest. "Wind from her to us an' we're tryin' to cross her stem. She can tack as she likes and we've not a quarter her speed. Or her fighting load." He snorted at Therkon's glare. "I've seven men and a pair o' cutlasses. That kite'll carry thirty or more. With bows. The Washes is our only hope. We're flat as a scow, we can sweep through the channels. They'll not risk that keel in there."

At Therkon's expression I thought he would demand we turn and try to fight, whatever the odds. His hand did go to Hvestang, conspicuous at his shoulder blade. When he discovered the pirate was probably Dhasdeini—"the coast boats'll do it, 'specially out of Quetzistan—" I feared the long-threatened explosion would finally break. Culminating outrage of a journey replete with insults to his imperial rank, that the last and most ignominious threat should come in his home waters, from a source his galleys must have worked and suffered to control. From within Dhasdein, and from folk of his own blood.

We managed to dive into a channel among the spatter of reedy islets, and I hoped a turn on the sweeps would calm him in weariness, if not relief. But once the pirate turned away, and we crept with sweep, pole and sounding-lead to something with a few trees, a clutter of reed-thatched huts, and an actual timber landing stage, his expression at the news that we had to stay overnight made me literally shiver in my boots.

"T'is not so very bad, sir." Escaping the pirate had left the shipmaster almost placatory with relief. "There's an inn of sorts, if ye'd rather sleep ashore. Ye'll eat well, they bake the marsh ducks hereabouts in mud. Very tasty. We've been to Grinsey two-three times before." He became a little too casual. Smuggling, I thought suddenly. "An' we've freight for the inn, if ye'd wish to sample it. A special order, our own yard's wine."

Smuggling, I thought, for a certainty. Therkon's glare had all but combusted. Driven, the master actually dared pat him on the arm. "An' the morn, ye'll not even need to work out to sea with us. There's a ferry ashore. Rise betimes, ye'll see the night in Rivers-end!"

A ferry. And then, doubtless, flea-bitten hired horses to get the Crown Prince and his gear and his embarrassing encumbrance into the Imperial capital. Like a peddler, arriving rough and dusty at the gate.

I thought Therkon might actually choke. The man I remembered in the Isles would have summoned, at the very least, a few words of thanks. This one glowered like a perfect Skall boor. Before he almost snarled, "Fetch our gear," and stamped off up the landing stage.

\* \* \* \*

I followed, feeling lower than ever in my life, except under the Brettabreck cliff. I had seen Therkon stressed, distressed to incoherency, grieving, affronted to freezing point. I had never expected someone so basically even-tempered, at the very least someone with the crown prince's monumental composure, to fray like this.

He was quieter, if no less dour, by the time we ate. The ducks were excellent. The inn's single storey was mostly wattle and daub and reed-thatch, but the two sleeping rooms were clean, the inn-keeper, thoroughly intimidated by a princely tantrum, swore to me that they never had fleas, and the wine was all Wave Island reds are claimed to be.

Perhaps I drank more than I thought. Perhaps the wine was stronger than I knew. Or perhaps it was simply the catalyst for long weeks of diminished friendship, and now bewilderment, and guilt, and misery. Whatever it was, when Therkon walked me to my door, the one routine no amount of ill humor ever broke, I set the candlestick inside, and turned with something more like pain than reluctance, to attempt a formal goodnight.

In the half-light past my elbow his jawbone showed the stubble of days at sea. Strands of hair hung from their tie, the circles under his eyes had returned, and deep brackets showed around his mouth. He looked as tired and dispirited and wretched as I felt, and suddenly I could bear no more.

Before I had time to reconsider I took the two steps in arms-length, wrapped both arms round him, went on tiptoe to reach his cheek and said impulsively, "Goodnight, my—goodnight, Therkon."

At least, I meant to kiss his cheek. He flinched or pulled his head somehow, and my lips landed squarely on his.

He jerked as if it had been an arrowhead. I tried to spring back in an anguish of embarrassment. He made one hoarse wordless sound, threw his own candle on the floor and grabbed for me.

A grown trained man in an access of—something I took for rage. He was too fast even for Two. Arms like steel pythons punched out my breath and almost bent my ribs, one hand came up and caught my chin in a blacksmith's vice. Then he was kissing me.

I had never kissed in passion. Two had seven hundred years' vicarious experience. Therkon had been a lover more than half his life, and every fraction of that knowledge he used. But skill was a mere egg-shell on the torrent of feeling that impelled it, a convulsion too long pent, and now impossible to control.

He lifted his mouth at last. I was bruised and breathless, he was breathless too. I never had time to ask questions either. He made another too clearly despairing noise and tried to push me away.

"No," I said through my teeth and locked both fists in his coat. If I was neither a man nor full-grown, I had strength enough, and I was maddened too. "First explain this."

"Explain what?" It cracked in his throat. "Gods, was that not clear—!"

"Not this, blight and blast it!" Now I had my breath back that kiss seemed to have fired the wine in my veins. Anger jetted like true fire in the wake of a sudden vast relief.

"Not that! This other thing, this whole—ever since Hringstenn! You were my friend! My companion, my shield-man—you were *warm*! But after Hringstenn you went polite, and kind, and you shut me out as if polite was something you *had* to do. Now you're so angry you won't talk at all. Just tell me, what is it? What have I done?"

The pause went so deep I heard his breathing, irregular and fast as my own. *Puffin*'s crew chattering in the taproom sounded loud as drums. Then he made another noise in his throat and tore both hands through his hair.

"Chaeris—I have a trust. I made a promise. I swore to ward you from harm. With my *life*."

"And you did! You have! So why are you behaving like this?"

"Oh, gods above!" He actually stamped on the beaten earth of the passageway. "Because I have failed! Because I cannot do it any more!"

The fallen candle flared between us. Automatically, he tamped it out with the toe of a boot.

"Because," he went on, almost coldly, "Segil said, I would never debauch you. And that is not—I cannot—" his voice wave red. "That is no longer true."

I reached for my own candle. The guilt had evaporated. The bewilderment was gone. We could See, and what we Saw set my heart fluttering like the wrens above Hringstenn, freed into spring.

"**You love us**," we said.

He made another inarticulate noise and swung half away. I caught his coat and pulled him back.

"You love me." The wrens were flying now, upward in a great singing cloud. "It isn't Dhasdein that's upset you, it's me. You started by liking me, I know you did, and you swore to look after me, and the journey, the road, all the trouble made us friends, and then more than friends. And now you love me." And with love had come desire. Strong as my own, but strangled in honor and obligation, so while I had longed to stop time he had been frantic to hurry it, because our proximity had become a rack on which every delay added another turn of the screw. "So you can't go on being a holy virtuous guardian and pretending I'm just a parcel or a gem to ward. Nothing's my fault, it's nothing I've done. You want me." Light and sound rained down from heaven. "Nothing's wrong at all."

"Oh, gods—!"

I hung onto his coat. "You want me. And I want you."

He went absolutely still. Then he turned round, and his face said anything but joy.

"Chaeris." It was pure pain. "No."

"What do you mean, No? You swore to protect me. You did it. We're almost back to Riversend. I'm safe. And since when did 'protect' include 'not debauch'? If it's my choice, especially?"

"Chaeris." It came with a grunt as if I had put a knife-hilt in his ribs.

"What?" I shifted my grip to his coat front. "You don't want me at all?"

He hissed and grabbed my hand so hard it hurt. "You can think that *now*?"

Two still had not offered a spark. I looked up in his eyes, so tired and pained and angry, but not angry as they had been the last few days, and I almost drowned in the contradictory joy.

"What, then? Your honor? Your mother—?"

"No, *your* mother. Your family! Gods, Chaeris, have you lost all your wits? Let be the shame, if I were to—when they trusted me—if I—your father would murder me!"

Two showed me which father he meant. And good cause to mean it literally.

"Dhasdein." I put the candle on a handy wall-niche. I was having to breathe for calm myself. "You think it matters what my family, my menfolk, my fathers say? *I* am not one of your Outland chattels, to trade about like a cow. I am a woman of Iskarda. I am of age. My body is mine. I will bestow it where I choose, and I choose you."

We stared at each other in the flickering candleglow. Joy was a light under my breastbone. He just looked haggard and distraught and unhappier than ever. My one hope was that he did not walk away.

"Well?" I braved it out. "What now?"

He shoved a hand back through his hair. The tie had almost given up, and locks hung disheveled everywhere. He looked this way and that, up the tiny colonnade.

"Chaeris. I am thirty-five years old. I have—I have—you *know* my reputation. Every word of it is true."

The Dragonfly Lover to half the great ladies of the Empire: I could hear Tanekhet warning me. A superlative lover who would break your heart in the end, because of the headlong generosity with which he gave his own. Before he walked away.

I did not say, What do I care for great ladies, let alone the past? Nor did I retort, If you're older, if you're so experienced, from my view, so much the better for me.

What I did say was, "And so?"

He gave a snort like a baited bull. I stared and waited. He looked back to me. Clenched his jaw. Looked away, as if his nerve had failed, and said it brusquely, to the kitchen door.

"You are too young."

Only troublecrew reflexes stopped me slapping his face. I did grab his coat again, two-handed, and manage to shake him where he stood.

"Too *young*? In human time, I'm twelve, yes. Thirteen!" Summer would be my year-turn. "What does human time have to do with me? I'm almost as tall as you: when we met, you thought I was sixteen or seventeen, and I've grown since. I'm of age. I have my Craft, tried and proved. I've trained as troublecrew. I've traveled the Isles alone. I've fought for you. I've *killed* for you!" Hringstenn's stones rose before my inner eye. "I've met gods—I've *been* a god! How much more grown do I have to be?"

He was shaking his head to and fro, a man beset by words as by a swarm of bees. I pulled him toward me, suddenly as furious as he had been in the last weeks, recalling troublecrew hand-to-hand moves and Zuri, who had once beaten a young husband to the point of suicide.

"Chaeris—Chaeris—stop."

"You stop! You want me, you can't even deny that, you just bent me almost in two! Your stupid honor's no use to you and it means nothing to me. Tell me then why you can't do this. Why *we* can't do this. Here and now. The last chance we'll have, before we're back in Dhasdein and everybody knows us and we can't ever," suddenly the joy had all melted and the anger was collapsing into tears. "If that Riversrun daughter has to get you, I'm going to have you first!"

"What? What daughter? Why Riversrun . . . What are you talking about?"

"Tanekhet said it." I was past caring what else this might reveal. "You're betrothed to Dhasdein, you said, and you are, even without the ring. And Tanekhet said, you have to marry, for the throne. And it will be some Riversrun lord's daughter—" the tears were beginning to run—"because you'd never marry outside the Empire, and I—and I—"

I could not go on, any more than I had with Tanekhet. But his face said he more than understood.

"Chaeris. Chaeris. Dhe behold me, can you possibly think I would, would—without *marrying* you?"

Dhasdeini customs, Dhasdeini thought: that a woman's body was not her own possession, or her honor kept anywhere but between her legs, and only marriage could sanctify a use of that body for herself.

We had traveled half a year together, and he had learnt to tolerate but never to comprehend. However he tried, his idea of honor, and treating me with honor, would diametrically oppose mine.

I blinked the tears away. He had forgotten to back off. He was all but nose to nose with me, his face almost as pale as after he killed Rathi.

"Chaeris, you *cannot* think that of me?"

He did not see both sides, and I did. He could not understand, but he would try to honor me, and put that honor before happiness, even if he loved me, perhaps more because he loved me, and honor behoved me to be understanding and accept his scruples, and doom us both to loss.

But I had Two, and Two cared nothing for Dhasdeini honor. Two gave me truth to use, however brutal it might be.

"But you can't marry me, can you?"

I heard my own heart beat. A whiff of wind brought food smells from the inn, twenty feet, a continent away.

And after an aeon he averted his face and let silence reply.

It should have been the final body blow. But Two had a stake in this struggle. Two wanted him as much as I did, always had done, and had shown it even more blatantly. Two filled my mind with the past of Amberlight, other women who had met this stick-fork, and the choices that our customs, our thinking, offered them.

I lifted my chin, and used those memories to shore the resolution that backed my choice.

"You can't marry me, no. But I can have you, all the same. It's no stain on *me*. Not in Iskarda. Even if it's just this one night. Two will remember. So I'll always have that." I could not quite control my voice's wobble. "I'll have the memories."

He leant his forehead against the door-post and stood quite, quite still. His shoulders had rounded, like a man weighed down under a heavier and heavier load, yet wholly unable to break free.

I took in one sip of breath. Then I spoke, deliberately keeping the tone cool.

"So?"

He drew breath in turn, a deep breath; then he lifted his head. Tears glittered faintly, in the candlelight, on his cheeks, but he took my hand with all the ceremony of a courtier, bowing over it with perfect grace. Then he straightened and brought it to his lips with passion displacing courtesy, and met my eyes. Though he sounded husky, the words were perfectly clear.

"My lady. Chaeris. My dearest lady. I—am honored beyond—I—" He drew a single steadying breath. "Yes."

\* \* \* \*

"Chaeris." Someone was murmuring, whispering, in my ear. "Chaeris . . . my sweet oracle. My darling troublecrew. My heart's helm. The gulls are waking. I have to leave."

My head was on something warmer, firmer than a pillow, yet with an unchancy fall and swell. Hair was tangled all over my shoulder, my face. My lips felt swollen. My nipples were almost sore, far more tender than before a course began, and there was a definite bruise at the top of my right breast. My belly felt chafed, so did my inner thighs, and elsewhere . . .

Elsewhere my body spoke with a proper function's satisfaction. With the aftermath of exertion that had been more than pleasure. That had been release, and comfort. And joy.

I shifted my cheek on my lover's chest and let my fingers explore. Nipples that flinched a little under my touch. They were tender too. A lovebite—I could feel the teeth-marks—at the base of his neck. I slid the hand downward, over his chest, over that satin belly skin, to velvety softness beneath. Flaccid now, but still bringing a murmur as I touched him, provoking fierce satisfaction as Two retrieved for us how he had groaned and arched into my fingers the first time I took him in hand. Familiar now, like every inch of him. Mine, I thought with fierce satisfaction. All of you, touched, known, possessed.

I turned my face a little against his jaw. Stubble, that had chafed my cheek like my belly skin. I opened my lips and licked, slowly, savoring, along the line of the bone.

"Stop that."

Husky, the merest whisper. Sleepy to the point of languor. Drained of tension and anger and all stress until it sounded faintly indulgent. Very nearly amused.

I drew my thigh a little higher over his. Found the outside of a knee, and stroked it with my toes. His breath caught. I hugged him till he gasped and whispered in his ear.

"You'd be in a tower, if this was Amberlight. I'd keep you in an upstairs room. All alone. I'd feed you on gold, and house you in furs, and dress you in silk and velvet and jewels, and then make you take it all off. While I watched." He tried to move. I pinned him down. Clenched him to me, letting bone and muscle repeat fiercely, Mine. Forget the Empire, the Riversrun daughter. Mine.

"I'd make up your eyes, and put your hair in lovelocks." Our hair was mingled in wild disorder, but I found a strand at his temple and drew my fingers through it, silky despite the accumulated sweat and dirt. "And keep you, secret, where no-one could find you. A prince in a tower. For the rest of your life."

His breath had quickened. His heart beat harder under my cheek. The words came soft and thick.

"And I would wait for you. Dress in silk and velvet, and make up my face, and wait, every evening. Until you came."

I held him so tightly neither of us could move. But in the silence, the gulls still called.

The sound of morning, the sound of time. Repeating, inexorably, But this is not a tower in Amberlight. Time cannot turn back.

Time cannot stop. The dawn is coming. The time when we must leave this bubble of happiness, and you must become the Seer of Iskarda. And he will be a crown prince again.

I eased my grasp. He reached his own hand to turn my face. His mouth parted at my touch, in the intent if not the completion of a kiss, and his fingers curved, shaping my cheek. As he had done in the night with every inch of me, first tentatively, fearfully, then delicately, almost incredulously, the whole thundercloud of rage and denial dispelled, leaving only tenderness.

I could hear him smiling when he spoke, against my mouth.

"My precious tyrant. It grieves me to rebel." The amusement faltered. "But this is not Amberlight. And it would grieve me more to leave you, in this place—open to—to—"

"Dishonor?" I could not help but sigh.

"Especially when you are—were—"

"A virgin? Who's been 'deflowered'? Such peculiar words your people use. Do you think a woman's a sort of rosetree? What about the thorns?"

He laughed. Smothered for silence, but the chest-deep outbreak I had heard first among Iskarda's rocks. "Oh, Chaeris—! What does Iskarda call it, then?"

"A woman's first passage with a man? We say, moon-free, if we say anything. What matters is when your courses begin. You're a woman, then. Come of age. You can use your body as you please."

I slid my arm further over him, and rolled a fraction closer, all my senses recording for Two to keep: the firm warmth of muscle and bone, the shape of that deep narrow chest and haunches, the mixed scent of dust and some half-eroded spice that spoke from his skin and hair, his alone. The night's common residue: human heat and contact and passion. Sweat. Salt. Sex.

Then I drew my hand slowly up his spine, and let my arm go loose, so the motion spoke for me. *You are right. Time is undefeatable. It is time to go.*

He kissed me once more, cupping my face double-handed, leaning over me, still too spent and sated from the night's joy to do more than acknowledge the coming grief. Then he slid carefully out of the bed, and left me alone.

* * * *

Assessing matters by daylight, I had to admit he was right. I had heard him order cans of hot water, since there was no bath, but though he had left his lovebite discreetly on my breast, even after washing my hair was a rat's nest, my lips felt bee-stung, and I was convinced the beard chafe showed on my cheeks. Worse still, I could picture the expression, smug and wholly indelible, on my face.

Therkon himself was worse. "Scowl," I muttered as we met in the tap-room door. There was no time for embarrassment. "Scowl now and then. Otherwise everybody'll know what you've been doing."

He raised a princely eyebrow. His lovebite lay behind a buttoned shirt collar, his hair had been combed out, and he was shaved. But the thunderous aura of yesterday had vanished, and if the night's release, the passion, when he thought I was ready for it, the outright abandon, were no longer visible, the ease and serenity and unconscious almost-smile remained.

"What," he murmured, "have I been doing?"

"Segil called it, getting your rocks off. That's just how you look!"

The supercilious expression collapsed. He managed not to clap a hand to his mouth, but I nearly fell apart myself at the strangled whoop.

But the tap-room was already public, forcing us toward decorum, however counterfeit. Making us suppress memory, and forego all the silly lovers' behaviour, the compulsion to link hands, rub shoulders, lock eyes, even touch boots under the table. Let alone the foolish escape of euphoria in stupid grins and involuntary jests.

By the time we lugged our gear down the landing stage to join three women with market greens and a man with a basket of fish, the social blankness was less and less counterfeit. Balancing on the raft-cum-punt that shuttled us to another untidy landing, hunting halfway decent mounts among the four or five dejected horses by a thatched shelter, haggling with the hireman . . . Setting foot to stirrup, I already ached. With the memory of love, and the need to touch, caress, re-affirm it, and the understanding, colder and colder, that it could not happen. I had demanded one night, and only one night. Whatever it built between us, that night was gone.

Raised a crown prince, Therkon had learnt to mask every feeling in the hardest of schools. Whatever he felt now, he gave me courtesy immaculate and cool as spring water, and as chilling. As if the Isles, let alone the night, had never happened at all.

* * * *

Though technically within the Delta, the ferry landed well east of Riversend. Our sluggish mounts plodded half the morning over plashy tracks, then wagon-muddy roadways, then something like a thoroughfare, before we ever reached the city's penumbra of tumbledown shacks and the actual eastern gates. By then we were in a stream of riders, carts, wagons, pedestrians, people, eyes everywhere. The man with fish had hired a mount at the landing, and tagged within earshot from the start. We had never been able to drop the masks. We had never again been alone.

The gates were just a towering set of pylons and a pair of decorative city guards, between which the traffic stream constricted and then spread unimpeded onto half-cobbled streets. The outer slums. We rode together, we exchanged words when needed, for direction, or warning. Nothing else.

Next came the merchants' quarter, where our dusty clothes looked more out of place. And then the lords' part, the streets of great mansions and expensive shops and exclusive eating places, that would give on the imperial quarter proper. At that gate Therkon would finally be recognized. It would be the end of incognitos. The true end of the Isles. Dhasdein would take us back, swallow us, whole.

I had made a bargain, for what seemed the best I could get. Even if I sued to renege, even if his own resolution crumbled, the best it could bring would be a half-life, secluded in the palace, furtive assignations, worse and worse deceit. And when he married in truth . . .

Like Therkon, I had made my own trap. Unlike Therkon, I had no-one to break me out.

But if I held to the bargain it was worse. We Saw the full horror before us then, recognition for Therkon, for us both, comprehension of our success. Welcome, growing more and more ecstatic and more public, not merely family greetings but proclamations, celebrations, ceremonies, probably thanksgiving to the Dhasdein gods. I would not be merely a foreign asset, but a hero, the Seer of Iskarda.

And with every piling acknowledgement of our glory, Therkon would become more wholly the crown prince. Locked in an ever-broadening wall of witnesses, servants, ceremony, officials, urgent imperial business. When he eluded that, I would have to ride, sit, talk, go to banquets and ceremonies, eat, drink, do everything but sleep beside him. The very force of public gratitude would compel it. I would have to share it all. Even while I could never be as much to him as troublecrew. Forget assignations. I could never kiss, touch, even speak to him informally, let alone show love or make love with him, ever again.

When the Imperial wall emerged above the latest clean, tree-lined, lightly trafficked avenue, I could bear no more. I reined in. Therkon noticed at once. As he drew his horse near I spoke hastily, muffled for his ear alone.

"I have to go."

"What is it?" His eye raked me for overt signs of illness, pallor, a fever sweat. "Is it your courses? Early?" Six months with a female way-friend had inured him to knowledge most Outland men would sooner die than admit. "Cramp . . .?"

"Not cramp. Not courses. I just have to go." I shut my eyes and tried to breathe. To put it all in words would have been worse than a knife in the heart. "I can't go any further. I have to go . . . home."

"But . . ."

He stopped in mid-breath. His public face was perfect, but he was still Therkon. He had shared the night, and the weeks before, and the Isles, and all that our journey meant. And he had kept his wits, his intuition, as well.

The elegant traffic moved around us, ladies or courtesans in carriages or palanquins, lords and courtiers ahorse or on wheels. At any moment someone really would recognize him, there would be a blaze of question and exclamation, and then the ordeal would be beyond escape.

He put one hand out. The barest motion, toward my wrist. And withdrawn. His eyes shut a moment. Then he set a heel to his horse and finished, just audible.

"I will take you to the wharf."

The upRiver wharves, he meant. Where we would find freshwater freighters. Where I might buy a passage to Marbleport.

All through the tumbling, crowded city, we never spoke. Only, somehow, we managed to keep the horses together. So we were near, even if we never touched.

We dismounted at the inner fringe of shipping offices, such a familiar ambience now, that faced the River itself. Therkon tied the horses, I hefted my belongings. We walked together, out onto the wide, bustling quay, with the grey waters beyond.

The third office offered passages, "UpRiver, all destinations, domestic and foreign." Even, when we enquired of the clerk behind the modest marble counter, beyond Verrain.

Therkon drew out the gem pouch, with the last money he had changed for a finghend in Prospect. Dhasdein silver, Archipelago coinage. When I realized I had thought "Archipelago" and not "Isles," it was a stab all of its own.

Used to motley currencies, the clerk counted and sorted and asked, hardly looking up, "Both parties? UpRiver, or up and back?"

Therkon said, "One person. UpRiver." He sounded almost normal. But I saw the muscles move in his throat.

If we had been ordinary people I could still have touched his hand, we could have exchanged concerns and injunctions, have hugged if not kissed. I swallowed the boulder that had suddenly filled my own throat. All the concentration, all the courage I had was bent on bearing this to the end. On parting, saying farewell, without breaking down. Without clutching him, or begging for impossibilities. Or just starting to weep.

"You're in luck," the clerk was telling the counter-top. "*Dhanissa*'s just loading deck cargo. They're set to catch the midday tide."

Because of course the River would be tidal, almost to the outskirts of Riversend.

Distantly I heard Therkon, still deploying his Dhasdeini merchant mask, making arrangements for baggage, provisions, asking about cabins, a necessary, days estimated for the trip. The ship-line or owner. The clerk answering, "Consort line. They work out of Marbleport."

Final, cruelest good fortune. The ship was one of Tanekhet's.

Therkon turned from the counter, out toward the fringe of masts and gunwales and mooring ropes, the hustle of seamen, officers, agents, stevedores, the racket of wheels and orders and voices in every accent along the River's length. He was saying something, but he seemed to be speaking underwater. I could hardly hear.

He heaved my pack off the floor. Slid his free hand under my elbow. The touch burnt like fire, but I could not let it show. We paced over the functional tiling to the outer door.

*Dhanissa* lay four berths along. She still had traffic up the gangplank, but the hatches were drawn, and they were taking ties off the sails.

Someone came down to us: I dimly heard Therkon explaining, doubtless the story of a female relative, cousin or sister, traveling upRiver. The pack changed hands, the person vanished. Therkon turned to me.

Our eyes met. A vast weight suffocated my whole chest. And if it had not, what was there to say?

He looked down at me, the presence so dear, familiar, learnt from so many days' journey, so many trials and perils, so many ports of strife or sanctuary. The silky hair, the bronze-dark eyes, the flamboyant bones, the features were all the same. Except they seemed to have hardened, shrinking inward. So what looked down at me, severe, graven, beautiful and empty-faced, was not my friend and lover and way companion. It was the hatchet man.

Nouip had Seen right. It was the core of his nature. To see, and to do what must be done.

Except he had to clear his throat, twice, before he spoke. "Chaeris."

I let my eyes answer, *Therkon*. The other words, clythx, caissyl, beloved, life's core, I spoke in my heart alone.

"I—"

He stopped. Took a tiny breath.

Then he said, sounding just a little breathless, "I wish you good journey. A safe coming. A welcome home."

I managed to nod. I did not speak. I did not dare. Nor did he dare any formal gesture of farewell. Only the look that broke the mask in those eyes for a fleeting moment, as he lifted his hand to me, once.

Then he turned, and I watched him walk away.

# CHAPTER XIX

It was fortunate, I know now, that *Skthoja* and *Seony* gave us such a fast passage as far as Prospect, because however slow the rest proved, we were still ahead of anything but speculation when we reached Riversend. Perhaps it was more than fortune, though neither Two nor the Sight can tell me, that brought me to go on so soon. And that *Dhanissa* was there, and ready too.

So whatever public hubbub burst upon my heels, for all that long blur when I must have eaten, slept, worked out, however sketchily, in the roomy passenger cabin, to everyone else I was just one more anonymous woman in Iskardan cloak and leggings, with a bearing that hinted troublecrew. A no-one, with only the past to haunt me, till the journey's end.

When *Dhanissa* moored after that three weeks' hiatus, and still feeling half a sleepwalker, I came down the gangplank into the familiar, utterly different waterfront of Marbleport. And the first person I saw was Tanekhet.

He would come down on occasion, to meet his ships. Either by turn in his consort, or of his own choice. Or for some particular reason, but my flinch at that thought died unborn at the look on his face.

"Chaeris!"

With such a heart-stabbing Dhasdeini accent that every scar ripped away together and I fell headlong in his arms and wept.

When I came to he was rubbing my back: gently, expertly, a slow light circle below my shoulderblades, the touch of a man long accustomed to lovers, to women, to assuaging grief. In a way he had never dared touch me before.

I lifted my head and tried to sniffle. The shoulder of his coat was soaked. I had almost had to lean down to it, though we had been of a height when I left. I made to rub my streaming nose with a wrist and he put a handkerchief in the fingers. And went on holding me, lightly, one arm about my waist, while I tried to re-assemble myself.

At some time he must have made arrangements, offered makeshift explanations. Got us indoors. It was an office, small and cramped with an overloaded desk. Dust motes turned in sunlight through a dirty window, though the room itself was clean. Outside voices spoke and hooves and wheels clattered. On the River, waterbirds called. Not gulls, at least. Inside, it was quite still. And empty, apart from us.

Then Tanekhet tightened his arm a fraction and said, "Therkon?" on a note of such compassion, such understanding, that I broke down all over again.

Someone came in. The fluctuation of light and air, the door's click half-spun me round, but the newcomer already had both arms tight round the pair of us, a smell familiar long before Therkon's. Identified before she said, "Chaeris."

Tez.

I cried a little longer, in the common sanctuary of their arms. About the time I was ready to lift my head and wipe my nose yet again, Tez said, "We had the letter. From Hranhaven."

Tez to her backbone: not exclamations or sympathies or pity, but information. Telling me how much they knew. What I could now omit.

When I only nodded, she said very softly, "Verrith? Azo?"

I could not speak, but I turned my left arm to show the wrist-knife, and felt her grasp go slack as she understood.

Then she re-braced herself. And asked, too calmly, "Therkon?"

Tanekhet said, "He is safe."

I was too grateful for the chance to bury my face again. So I only had to listen to his over-cool response at what must have been a dagger stare.

"He was with her after the wreck. If he had not come back now, neither would Chaeris."

*It's true*, I thought, *but how did you know?* While I sniffled and tried to find words, Tanekhet lightly, tenderly, brushed my hair.

"She is wearing Verrith's knives. When you came in, she moved like troublecrew. And if she has been troublecrew, it could only be for Therkon."

And Iskardan, Amberlight troublecrew might die in place of their charges, but come back without them, never. Not alive.

I could feel Tez's stare myself. A heated dagger point, in the small of my back.

Presently, just above a whisper, she said, in Tez's steel-cool disaster voice, "Did you fail?"

"No! Then neither of us would have come back!"

I had been too passionate. I felt her tension sharpen, but still she put the great matters first.

"You found what it was? You could, still, do something?"

"We fixed it. Him. Sthassamaer." I had put that name in the letter, a priority. If we had not come back, Iskarda and Dhasdein would need whatever information they could get. "Skalr—in the Isles, they made a tale. Two can tell you," I let the inflection add, *Not now.* Suddenly I was exhausted beyond a mere weeping bout. It was over. All over. The details could wait.

Tez's arm loosed in relief. And then drew carefully tight. As carefully she said, "Then what has made you weep, Chaeris?"

When I did not answer, minutely, her voice hardened. "And why are you here alone?"

"I came upRiver. It was nothing, I stayed in the cabin mostly, they knew I was Iskardan, there was never trouble—"

"Why alone?"

"Therkon," Tanekhet said.

In quite another tone this time, so soft and lethal I grabbed him as if he intended murder on the spot.

"He didn't do it, I did! The fuss, the uproar, the, the celebrations, and, and—we were in Riversend, I couldn't face it. I said, I have to go. He helped me find a ship . . ."

The silence was a thunder-hush.

Then Tanekhet said even more softly, "Did you heed my warning, Chaeris?"

When I could only hang my head he moved. He would have gone straight out the door and I did not need the Sight to picture where and why, horror-images filled my inner sight, *Dhanissa* dispatched straight back downRiver on a killing mission, trouble-crew, Tanekhet's own men, Tanekhet himself landing in Riversend, getting into the palace, finding . . . "No! No!"

I grabbed him in earnest, with every ounce of trained trouble-crew's strength. "It wasn't his fault!"

They were both staring. The same look was on both faces: understanding, misunderstanding, quiet but lethal, all but uncontrollable homicidal rage.

"We were lovers, yes. Only once! He didn't want to, he tried not to, he kept saying, his honor, my honor, the family, my fathers would kill him, he was too old, I was too young. He would never have done it, but I made him! It was the last chance. I made a bargain, I said, I know you have to marry the Riversrun daughter, but I want you first. I want this one night."

Tanekhet had both hands in his hair. His sole vulnerable point was that he thought it unlovely, and he never, ever, disarranged it in public view. He groaned, and I knew what he was thinking. He himself had done this, with a well-intentioned warning, trying to avoid the selfsame thing.

Tez's eyes were daggers and she was very nearly white. Then she moved, and the words slid out thin as a dagger point.

"I'll kill him," she said.

"*No!*" I grabbed her too. "I made the bargain, I got what I wanted. I just couldn't. Couldn't—"

Keep the terms. Bear the consequences to their full, public end.

She tried to detach me. I hung on. I actually glared at her, and Two reacted before I thought. White fire danced at my sleeve-cuff, sharp-tongued, ready to spark.

"Let him alone!"

She stared down at our hands, then, with the strangest expression, up at my face.

Then the look changed. Wryly as if she bit into a lemon, but deliberately, she said, "You are of Iskarda. You are a woman. Of age. And I think," suddenly, she was using her own Sight, "you have come into your Craft."

She did not mean Two's spark. When I nodded, I felt both her and Tanekhet's muscles ease with paradoxical relief.

"So," Tez went on after a moment, even more quietly, "you are entitled to your choice."

"Yes." Suddenly I could not bear any more. The voyage was done. The night was over. Everything was over, between Therkon and me. The Isles were behind us. Dhasdein was behind me. Now I only had to deal with the rest of my life.

"Can we," suddenly the tears rose again, recurring showers after a deluge, blood from a re-opened wound. "Can we just—go home?"

\* \* \* \*

They gave me the same mule I had ridden down from Iskarda. After horses in the Isles, it no longer seemed daunting, any more than Two or I had to strain to check every hillside as they passed. The spaces at my side still echoed the absence of Verrith and Azo, but though Tanekhet and Tez rode with me, they hardly spoke. Mirror signals had already sent the vital news: I was back, we had succeeded. The rest could wait.

On the Iskans autumn was well in train, silver-tawny grass that ruffled the hillsides like folded silk at the wind's every dust-and-wood-smoke breath. The few deciduous trees had taken on a lemon tint, so conifers and helliens stood out dark, or unmoved silver-grey, green, blue. The morning air already had a hill country sting. In Iskarda the fields would be stubble, bleached stalks over darker earth, the plums all eaten, the few appletrees ready for harvest. The roses, all the flowers of summer, the great festivals of Spring Thanks and Midsummer, would be long gone.

When we came round the quarry-head it all looked the same, yet irreparably different. The named, known, remembered house fronts, the vistas of crest and hillside beyond, the traffic of homing hunters and water-carriers, quarry folk dribbling out the gate. The Market chimneys, higher than the rest, dark stacks against golden cloud-shapes, emitting their evening cloud of smoke.

At my elbow Tez said, "We told them, No fuss."

I felt my shoulders and even my mule-braced legs relax. The lookouts would have signaled our approach, but there would be no general welcome, such as Iskarda must have been panting to give. Their youngest, most sensational daughter, safe home, bringing success. And no salt in the wounds, either. No voices calling, openly, for Verrith and Azo. Nobody needing me to wave, smile, hug, behave as for a victorious hero's return.

I need only tell the story, the full story, in council. They would do the rest.

\* \* \* \*

Nor did I have to do it that night. Tez decreed that Chaeris was weary from the ride, the voyage upRiver, all the prior labour and stress. I did not even have to face supper in the kitchen with the House, the explosive cries of Darr and Saarieq and Aretho, long since back from Amberlight, who would certainly demand the whole story with piercing queries and absolutely no abridgement if they were let in earshot of me.

I heard their clamor outside, the thumping rushes of feet. I myself had been slid indoors, deposited with my gear in my old room, left to unpack. Later, I had supper, with the consort: Tez, Keshaq, Asaskian and Tanekhet. With equally rigid care, nobody said a word about my trip. It was all news of Iskarda.

I did not have to ask my most important question, the one that had burned like a coal under my breastbone all the way UpRiver. Tez had told me, before we ever left that Marbleport office, at my own just-steady, "Are the others back?" Quietly, knowing my desperate need to fly like a veritable child to my mother's embrace, my fathers' comfort, she had answered, "Not yet."

Nor had there been letters from upRiver. It was a long way, they reminded me over the supper dishes, the familiar, estranged food of home, new season plum jam, barley bread, the dish of harvest-plump quail. Nobody could reasonably expect a letter yet. Even if all had gone optimally well.

"We did send," Tez added, her nearest approach to my own affairs, "a copy of yours."

So they might already know, I realized as Two added weeks, about the wreck, about the deadlier second enterprise. Another anxiety amid their own dangers. My mother, both my fathers, would burn with it: their dearling, their daughter in peril, and they elsewhere.

Despite it all I slept fairly well, in the peculiarly safe yet limiting confines of my own bed, and what should have been my own room. Now it felt only like some new, slightly cramped casing for a person who had never actually been here before.

And directly after breakfast came the chief ordeal. My official report, as the daughter, but also the emissary, an agent sent on a mission, of Iskarda.

I let Two begin, with Skalr's tale. At its end, as I blinked my own eyes back into focus, the faces round the council table wore the same expressions as Skalr's hearers. Quiet, assimilation, respect. Wonder. A tinge of naked awe.

Then Asaskian's cool, clear voice enquired, "How many islands *are* down there?" Just as Duitho leant past Eria and began with eagerness verging on open rapacity, "Chaeris, with the dagger: how far could the light reach?"

I started to laugh. I could not help myself. *Oh, Mother,* I did not have to cry aloud, *I'm home.* There would be no candle-lighting here. Awe, perhaps, assuredly sympathy: but first and foremost would come the politics, the strategy, the weapon-potential. The import for Iskarda.

Then Iatha snapped over the hubbub, "What will Dhasdein do now?"

The noise stopped. The floor lurched under me. I could feel all the eyes turn. The eager or anxious or simply concerned eyes of the unenlightened, the too carefully blank eyes of the consort, who already knew the rest.

And I could not tell it. At the mere thought my throat tightened, my eyes burned, if Two did not spark or throw a tantrum, in a moment I would burst into tears.

Tez said in her Head's voice, "We should ask, what will the River do, now Chaeris has her Sight?"

Uproar broke instantly, Iatha among the rest. As usual, like my mother, Tez let them burn the first of it off. So they were ready to listen when she broke in, again in that carrying Head's voice.

"Sight or no Sight, our concerns are little changed. We must still find a way to protect Chaeris from oracle-chasers. And to keep the overflow, the chaos they would cause, from Iskarda."

Several people began an exclamation or suggestion or query, and stopped. Tez's expression said she had already prepared a proposal, at the very least.

"Chaeris deserves to keep her home, and her life, intact." She did not look at me. I did not have to look as if such a thing might be possible. "But her Sight is known, and that cannot be either repressed or denied. Nor," carefully blank now, "do we have the right to deny the River her resources. Or Chaeris her true Craft."

Now I knew where she was going I could as easily have kissed as strangled her. She meant, on the one hand, to protect both me and Iskarda. On the other, I had claimed amnesty for Therkon, and she had granted it, as my choice. As a woman, a Crafter, whose decisions about her body, at least, were hers alone.

But as a Crafter, I was expected to work for the House. I had claimed Crafter's right, and she was calling my bluff. Making it the basis of House strategy. Planning, demanding, that I use my Sight. For real.

It was Iatha who asked for me, wary to gruffness if not yet belligerent.

"What do you suggest?"

Now Tez looked at me, with more concern, compassion, outright love than her first words had implied. "Firstly," she said, "we double-garrison both roads. From this new moon."

New moon was barely two days ahead. Blood and old custom told me without need for thought. And Tez had already estimated that no desperate oracle-seeker would reach us before then.

Iatha frowned. *The hills*, she did not have to say. Iskarda had no walls, no outer defenses, no force to defend them if we did. What would blocking roads do?

"And the blockade guards," Tez said evenly, "will say the same thing as the customs and quay-watch at Marbleport, as the customs at Amberlight. As the Notes we will send to Verrain, and Dhasdein, and Cataract. Our Seer is returned from the Isles," already hardly anyone was saying Archipelago, "and she has her Sight. And she will See for those who ask. But only for five days every moon. Only for those who seek a proper audience. And only at Marbleport."

No wonder, I was thinking among the hubbub, that my mother named her Head. She has the wits, the speed in planning, the grasp of resource and strategy. She hardly needs a Sight.

It was bearable, as well as practicable. I could feel Two calm, even as my own muscles eased. Five days a moon, five covenanted, ordered, rigidly arranged days. No need to ensure that I would have protection, an escort down, my own troublecrew, other people to meet the seekers, to sieve their demands, to allot waiting places—I struggled to keep my face straight.

Because of course, while this protected Iskarda, it would bring the flow of custom and demand and wealth straight into Marbleport.

The council were already past that. Suggestions and questions and projections flew like hail, where I would stay in Marbleport, what new buildings would be needed, stables, another inn, perhaps a hostel of some sort, a quay-watch, customs craft to catch the River inflow, provisions, suppliers, stipulations for those who came.

"We must expect to deal with the first comers here." Tez was making another general announcement. "This autumn. We have perhaps another two months, before winter shuts the River. We can use that time to spread the word and organize Marbleport. By spring, we will need everything in place."

Because spring would see the arrivals in full flood. None of us doubted it. Twelve years the River had been waiting to call on my gift. Everyone who had a concern or a problem or a dilemma or simply a question about the present or future would come. Everyone from farmers to emperors.

Iatha said it, sharply, again, into the resuming flood. "And Dhasdein? What will Dhasdein do?"

Tez did not look at me. Iatha knew the story by now, no doubt of it. She had not asked to pain me, but because the question had to be voiced. Tez's answer was flattened with the charge of what she herself knew. The tension of speaking, with different nuances, to us both.

"Dhasdein will do nothing," she said.

\* \* \* \*

And she was right. As autumn lengthened we garrisoned both roads, though only two or three would-be supplicants got beyond Marbleport or Amberlight. At Applegather, the last harvest feast, both House and village held a ceremony for Verrith and Azo, who had gone to the Mother, not through fire and water in the old Amberlight way, but through water alone.

In earliest autumn I had faced the journey's last trial: telling the news to Herar, Azo's husband. He had married her as a youth, he had gone with her upRiver to the Source, he had shared her, always, with Verrith. But the hole her loss would leave in his heart, I knew even the story of her going could not close.

I said and did what I could, with fellow feeling deliberately smothered under the sympathy. Nothing would heal him, except time. If he ever healed.

Then, whatever griefs endured, routine resumed. I worked out with troublecrew, took my turns, anonymous in shirt and cloak and leggings, on the mirror-signal lookouts, on the guard-posts, in the household work. What they told Darr and Saarieq and Aretho I cannot imagine, but when they were at last let near, they treated me like something made of cut-crystal. Not dangerous, like qherrique, just too fragile for common touch.

I used my Sight in earnest at a trial of the Marbleport arrangements, the first day of the first winter moon.

We rode down to the biggest inn the night before. I had not wanted to seem an oracle—in a Marbleport inn parlor? But they insisted on some adornment. "If we don't seem to prize you, neither will they." So I sat between my advisers, retinue, troublecrew, leaning on the arms of an austerely ornamented, cushioned chair.

The questioners had been rigorously selected too. There were only three, already warned that they were not guaranteed a reply. One was a Verraini farmer whose father had died leaving the household treasure lost, buried during the Families' overthrow. One was a woman of Amberlight, desperate to know if she could conceive a child. And one was the kinglet, once a Dhasdeini puppet, now genuine ruler, of Mel'eth.

"I think," Tez said reluctantly, as we discussed the choices, "that we must allow this one. He's a slaver, he probably raids the River trade, but . . . He wants to ask, can Mel'eth live without selling slaves."

Two was already whiting out our vision. I myself could see past the surface question, past the deeper calculations based on current income, known resources, history, to the projections of possibility. And where those outcomes might lead.

"Yes," I said. "You're right."

In the event, it was far simpler than my over-keyed nerves let me expect. For the woman, fidgeting and white-faced, the answer came as much from her skin and shape as Caitha's lore, accumulated long past. A posset to drink, a regime to observe. And the answer would be, *Yes*.

For the farmer, a handful of questions on his father and his farm let us See, clearly as if we stood in the caissyn field among the tall, rustling, purple-skinned stems ourselves.

For the kinglet there were questions too. I tried to be diplomatic, but Two was more than half in charge by then, and some queries pressed harder than I feared he would bear. But though he had entered already pale under his gorgeously brocaded cap, and there were times when his sweat reeked, however impassive he kept his face, he answered, if with due thought, every time.

So we could store the harvest of new information atop the old, and answer, with the full confidence of the Sight.

**"Mel'eth can live without selling slaves. To balance the extra people, improve the western waters. Dig deeper wells. Look into River aqueducts. Or covered channels. Consider exports: dates from the oases, your spun goat-hair. Wall**

hangings. To the River, and also to the Isles. Seek finance, to begin. Expect to find it, for the price of peace and an alliance, in Dhasdein."

\* \* \* \*

When he had gone, after copious obeisances and a cascade of thanks, wonder, eagerness, even an offer, which my trouble-crew thankfully discouraged, to kiss my hands, Tez let out a long, long sigh.

At my other elbow, Iatha said, very softly, "Mother be praised."

I found myself shaking. Now it was over, the tension, anxiety, relief were uncontrollable. In the act there had been no time for self-consideration. We had been one entity, one vision, no more than a faculty of perfected Sight.

Tez touched my elbow and handed me a half-cup of watered wine. As I sipped, she said softly, "I cannot imagine what it must be like."

"Like . . . It *is* a Sight. But it's more than place. It's time. The, the threads run forward, and back, and through the present, as it spreads. Then it all connects, it's all the one thing, ahead and behind and out to the edges of the world."

Iatha too drew a wondering, very nearly awed breath.

"It won't always w-work." Now I could not keep the quaver at bay. "There'll be times—questions—too little information, things we just can't see. Things, maybe, we can't say."

Tez's arm shut round my shoulders, warm and firm as a human shield. "But to have you do it, at last. To watch it happen." She hugged me. "Chaeris, that was worth everything."

Then suddenly she laughed aloud and called past me to Iatha, "Imagine the faces, in Riversend!"

Iatha let out a grunt. "They'd best be happy, any road. If Shothen does as he was told, we've pulled half Dhasdein's thorns overnight."

Half Dhasdein's thorns. The ramifications were opening wider and wider now. The woman, the farmer's questions might change their lives, but if Shothen tried the half of what we had Seen . . .

It would not simply change Mel'eth. One trial, one Sight, and we could already have begun to transform the River world.

For a vertiginous instant I wanted to cower and squeak, *This is too much, I can't do this!* No matter what we Saw, I could not bear the responsibility.

Then I shot upright at a new thought, horrific as a lightning bolt.

"What if he thinks it was *for* Dhasdein? If he thinks it was a—a—!" A partiality, a favor, a personal signal to the crown prince? A reward? Or, Mother spare me, some sort of lure, some new overture?

"I never meant it to—! It was real! It was a Sight!"

"Of course it was, dearling." Iatha patted me, too elated to think. Even if she far too clearly understood who "he" must be. "We could tell that. Neither fear nor favor. To anyone."

Tez, more perceptive, touched my wrist and said, "Let Dhasdein think what it likes. If there is favor, it's also for Iskarda and Amberlight."

Because if Mel'eth made peace with Dhasdein they would have to stop raiding the River trade, maybe even lower their punitive tolls. And from better River trade, we would benefit too.

I started to laugh. I could not help it, that Tez intended comfort not from the thought that I would do no favors, but that I would distribute them for us and Dhasdein both.

She gave me a glinting smile. "So long as you See truly, and speak with no knowing fear or favor," she said, "someone will always find fault, because you do not favor them." She anticipated me. "As, sooner or later, any Sight must do."

I groaned. Tez stood up.

"Let troubles hatch in their own time," she said. "For now, let's go home."

\* \* \* \*

We rode into Iskarda just ahead of the first winter storm. And on its heels, couriered up from Amberlight, the letters came.

I had been up the mountain, hunting hares: another of those tiny remembering stabs, that this time it had been with Duitho and a troublecrew recruit. At midday a new fall drove us home, laughing and shivering and shaking off snowflakes in the wine-sharp air that had greyed abruptly over threadbare patchwork of dark and light trees, silvered grass, fallen snow. So different from the clammy cold of Kaastria. But as I came up our own house steps, Ashar popped up at my elbow, troublecrew on watch, and said, "Tez wants you. In the council room."

"Oh." Nothing in her face or look. That alone made my belly drop. I shucked outer boots and cloak in the damp-floored hall. When I came into the council room, the brazier was lit as for a meeting, but Tez was alone.

She looked up. Our eyes met. We did not have to say, *There you are,* or, *You wanted me?* Or, *What is it?* Or, *There is news, but not what you might expect.* Or hope. I drew up a chair, and she passed me a sheet of papyrus that had lain before her on the tabletop.

It had been the enclosure in a double packet. The outer leaf lay there as well: slightly crumpled, stained, perhaps with mud. It still held a faint, elusive scent that I had never smelt before.

But Two knew it. The tang of reed-beds. Of the great upRiver swamp, labyrinthine windings of reeds and strange beasts and mud.

"Dearling," it began. My mother's so familiar, instantly recognisable, bold Amberlight hand.

A gap followed. The papyrus had a peculiar texture, as if it had been spattered with water, and dried.

"We have your letter from the Isles. This last quarter moon, we asked Rion, the folk's Seer. She dreamed that she saw you leave a ship in Marbleport. She says, You are safe home."

There was another gap.

"From what she says, you have grown."

Already my own heart had constricted in my chest. I could feel her longing, yearning to be here, to touch, hug, experience the full dear reality of flesh and blood. To see for herself how her child had changed.

"And I think, you may truly have come of age."

My own heart was bursting with the need to see and hold her, shout out the whole story for myself. How had she guessed? How did she know? Sheer mother's wish, some described, deciphered detail of the seer's dream?

Some resonance from the past, carried further than I could imagine? Something from the qherrique?

"So we have talked it over, all of us. We are," something crossed out there, black and so decisive not even a letter remained. "We reached here before middle summer. We are all safe and well. We arrived in time."

I did not have to wonder where they were. At Thilliansar, the place whose name she would not even write. Past the Source, with the mysterious people of her own partner, her dearly beloved Errisal. Who had written for help before last spring, and whatever the crisis, had that request fulfilled. Their quest had been successful too.

*So why*, my selfish heart was crying, *are you not already headed home?*

"And we have decided it is time. You are of age. You have your Craft. Tez and her consort will be settled in Iskarda. You should have the House to yourselves."

My vision greyed as my heart gave one great jerk. My mind, like my body, was shocked to incoherence. Someone, somewhere, was repeating silently, *No. No. No.*

"You will watch over and help each other. You will have counsel, from Iatha, from Tanekhet." The writing actually wobbled a little there. "You will miss us, but you will manage very well. We," there was another blot, "will never cease missing you. But we all know the choice is right. The folk from Marbleport, and Ahio, Keraz and Quiran, and Esrafal, will return when spring comes. They have ties, places that they still need to fill. But your fathers, and Zuri and Varris, and I, are not coming back."

The writing itself wavered, on its creamy background, as well as swimming through my tears. Errisal, I glimpsed, and 'dearly beloved,' too long apart, more about arrangements in the community, a new place chosen, a house built, where they would all live together. Why, not even Two could tell me, would they not do that as a matter of course? And one day, perhaps next spring, an excursion even further, over the mountains beyond the River's Source.

"It is time for new blood in Iskarda. But it is also time for us to move, to live differently. Perhaps to be someone else.

"It grieves Sarth the most that he must break our promise, to tell and show you everything. But we will always love you. Letters will come. Letters, I hope, will return. And one day, I so hope, you will make another journey. We will look up the track for travelers and find none so welcome, my dearling. You, and whoever you may bring. We will always hope, look, long to meet again."

They had signed it underneath. The letters were blotched in two or three places, but the hands were perfectly identifable. I had seen all three many times. "Your mother," first, and, below that, "Your father," twice.

Silently, Tez pushed the outer cover over. Now it was inner side up. "My ever-beloved daughter," the writing began. It was not my mother's hand, but I knew it all the same.

If I had lost all three parents, Tez had lost a blood mother, then an adopted foster-mother, and a blood father. Unlike me, she had only had those last for twelve years of her grown life.

I looked up. Her eyes were swimming too. We fell in each other's arms then, and wept as only sisters could.

* * * *

Pass over the House's consternation, lamentation, protest, grief. Pass over too, the surprising number who tried, tactfully or clumsily, to comfort me. Even those who did not know the full story of my journey considered my lot the worst in the House. Of all the commiserations, I remember Saarieq best.

The consort's eldest child, she was ten now to my human thirteen, while Darr was eight and Aretho only seven. I had known them as well as children may, who live fifty miles and three or more years apart. We only shared a house for the few weeks before Asaskian took them off to Amberlight, and now we seemed divided by the universe between children and adults. But the fourth day after the letters came, when I was all but raw from well-meaning attempts at sympathy, I fled Iskarda for the sanctuary of the lookout. Alone, I thought, until I came into the little rock-bay to find Saarieq standing, silent, motionless, before the qherrique.

It was not a rapport. She turned too quickly, and the qherrique, almost indivisible from the mealy grey of snow-littered rock and weeping white-grey mist, had not kindled for her. But her small pointed face in its frame of pale fur and damp brown hood was quite composed.

"I never came," she said, "up here before."

"*But you found the way,*" Two said.

She looked startled. Though I doubt she ever heard Two speak, she knew who it was. I had been startled myself. I waited to see what either of them would say next.

Her skin was perfect Amberlight, though it was expression rather than features that bespoke Tez. Her hair, straggling brown and almost straight, and her eyes, not yet hooded but dark green in this light as shadowed forest pools, were pure Tanekhet. As were her composure, and, I already knew, her wits.

"Shall I go away?" she said.

Raw from my parents' loss and the other grief that I could not share with anyone, my heart shouted, *Yes! This is my place. My own!* I would not let it add, *This is where I met him first.*

"It won't speak to me, will it?"

I did not need willed compassion, let alone rational thought to reply. Two and I had already Seen.

We said, "**Not yet.**"

Her eyes went wide. She knew what she had heard, but she did not exclaim, either in fear or delight. Only that look asked, *Truly?* with all the vulnerable ardor of a child.

"You're bound to have a Craft." At least I could manage manners about this. "After all, your mother was a light-gunner. And her parents had—have—some of the best ears in Amberlight."

The sun came out, briefly but composedly, in her face. Then she tucked her head down and dug a little in the snow with the toe of a boot. I had just enough intelligence left to find an out for us both.

"Let's try the lookout," I said.

We swept snow off the time-polished boulders and settled ourselves, looking out as generations of Iskardans had looked, through gelidly bleached old hellien leaves, over the spatchcocked white and brown hillside, the building blocks of Iskarda, the huge dun and silver-grey and dark-mottled vista beyond. In the wake of the first storm, the winds had almost subsided. Nothing stirred the air but our breaths.

And presently, like generations of Iskardans, I found in that indifferent, enduring landscape a modicum of my own peace.

Saarieq had her father's sense of timing as well. I hardly noticed her move on the boulder beside me, though Two said she had drawn up a knee and laid her chin on it, not looking directly at me. Her voice was very small, and quiet.

"If you wanted, you could share my mother," she said.

Whatever our other divergences, we had been raised as girls of Iskarda. We both stared steadfastly out toward the River, letting silence speak the rest. Her compassion, her sense of the loss. The scope of the offer, not in the least childish. My struggle to avoid the worst reaction to a seeing heart's sympathy, and not, in equally un-Iskardan fashion, to burst into tears.

Presently I managed to swallow, and say in a fairly normal voice, "Thank you. I think—in a way—I already do."

Her mother. My sister, my House-head, who had never wanted me to leave Iskarda; who had foreseen a shadow of the grief it would bring.

Saarieq slid neatly down from her boulder and scrambled up on mine. She squeezed in beside me and then she set a hand on my knee. Half a diversion, the skill of the people-handlers who had bred her, half the trust of a child who, as I had, burned to know new things. She said, "Tell me about the Isles, Chaeris."

A bitter wind breathed round us, warning of more snow on the way, but stirring my heart from its own winter loss and apathy.

"Come down to the House, then," I said. "To the kitchen, where we won't freeze."

She asked again that evening, almost straight after supper, the time when tales and songs would go round the kitchen. And music, once, from my father Sarth's flute, and from Esrafal the House musician's drum. Now, in the first lull, Saarieq repeated in that small solemn voice, "Tell us about the Isles, Chaeris."

I could not have spoken long. But it was easier than I had thought, in some way a letting of grief, to answer, knowing Two could bring out the information, "Which Isle would you choose?"

* * * *

After that they would ask almost every night, just for a few minutes of description and anecdote: the houses at Ve Pool, the ships of the Isles. Veenn and Dath and Skeag, Fiskri and his family. Most of all, Nouip: the dark house at Evvamoor never failed to keep the whole kitchen enthralled. It became a qualified joy, to forget the absences round the hearth, and gift others with the treasures of my voyage.

Early the next moon, Saarieq brought me a message from Tanekhet.

"Fa says, he has a 'streaming nose'." She gazed up at me with her usual solemnity, but I was learning to read her now. Tanekhet's own irony was in the quote, not to mention the glint. "He says, as a favor, will you work out today with Keshaq?"

"I can do that." I always seemed to fall into her propriety. Even when experience, let alone Azo's training, demanded, what is that conniver up to now?

I worked out with Keshaq the next day as well. It was painful at first, the way a half-resemblance to a lost beloved can be, as it was when a gesture or voice-turn of Tez's brought back my father Sarth. When Tanekhet reclaimed his partner, Duitho asked me, just a little too casually, "Chaeris, can you fill in today with Nethor?"

Nethor was the recruit who had gone hunting with us. Our first Iskardan troublecrew, and only the third of a more revolutionary kind, for Nethor was a man.

Or at least, a youth, an inch shorter than me, swarthy as most Iskardans, with straight black hair that spoke of Dhasdeini or Cataract blood, springy as a tree-snare, wiry and tireless. True to his outlying hunter mother, who had dispatched him to us as casually as she would have lent a bow.

"You'd be the best," Duitho was saying cheerfully. "You've worked out with men before."

I just contained Two's spark. Never mind working out with Keshaq. Never mind my fathers' training either. They had guessed about Therkon and the Isles, or they had actual intelligence from Dhasdein. And they meant either to burn out the memories' sting, or to "draw me out of myself." Fussing about the shadow I could still feel round me, as transparently and well-meaningly as Saarieq.

Luckily, I had my back to Nethor himself. I kept my voice quite easy as I answered, "Whatever you say, Duitho."

Nethor and I worked well together, even hand-to-hand. At least he did not remind me so piercingly of Therkon as did Keshaq. We fell in the habit of hunting and doing troublecrew work together. He had a sharp mind and a fierce thirst for troublecrew lore, and once he realized how much Two could tell him, he began to seek me out in the kitchen as well. Politely, never encroaching. But insensibly, we drifted into comradeship.

Mid-winter came. We put out the fires and waited for dawn, while up by the village's holy stone the Mother's Chosen offered his wrist to the sacrificial knife, and the token of his life for Iskarda. Two knew how it had been done in the old days, but she thankfully spared me the worst of those memories.

And when the sun topped the mountains in a well-omened brilliantly white morning, I bit back tears as I saw light lifting far south in the Isles, on another mid-winter morning, by another stone slaked with blood.

In all those days, weeks, months, there was no word from Dhasdein.

Our intelligencers did not need to gather word of Therkon's welcome, it reverberated from one to the other River's end. They did report with cruel clarity the official explanation for my absence: the lady Chaeris had wanted, needed, to go straight home. But after the fuss, reports became mere routine. Dhasdein was setting its Outsea trade in order. Building merchant ships. Haggling, as ever, with Mel'eth and Shirran. I bit my nails in private until Tez observed with careful casualness that if Shothen had made overtures for finance before winter, it would have been at a level far beyond our reach.

It hurt more than I wanted to admit that Dhasdein sent nothing, official or private, to Iskarda. But the news I truly feared, dreaded, could not bear to think about, never came.

And after mid-winter Nethor's company was gradually augmented by other young, unattached men, first of the House, then of Iskarda.

They would stop to watch a workout. Or to talk at a guard-post, in the kitchen, passing on the street. Three or four would gather instantly, if I had errands to Iskarda itself. In the close quarters of winter, immersed in training, busied with spring plans for Marbleport, trying so hard to ignore the silent questions eating my own heart, I hardly thought about it. Until the morning I came upon Duitho, Tez and Iatha outside the council room, and heard Iatha answer some question with a brisk, "Like bees to a honeypot. It'll still take some time. Give him his chance. Let her alone."

My feet, silent in indoor moccasins, clove to the floor. I had just wits to draw back, muscle by muscle, to the shelter of a doorway, and slip inside before I had to explode.

I had thought Duitho's plot to yoke me with Nethor a devious attempt to distract me, perhaps ease my loss. Now, as Two's projections flew by lightning leaps, I decoded with outrage another, more nefarious cause. Oh, they had connived to match me, and Nethor had wanted companionship, and perhaps he too had wanted more. Hero-worship, status as the Seer's friend and sparring partner, at the least. But my consent had sent a signal elsewhere.

And they had answered it, all the unattached young men. Bees to a honeypot. They had swarmed around me, as they had once, Two remembered, with Asaskian. She for her beauty, I as the highest ranking single woman in Iskarda. What a coup, to be the man who attracted, won, married or just partnered me?

Two almost burnt a hole in the door-curtain as another memory blazed past: Tanekhet writing a report. Asking my mother, *Am I here to build a new world only as a man buys a stallion, for his breeding stock?*

I, too, had new, precious blood. In kindness, with my parents gone, Therkon only a disastrous memory, they might wish, even mildly scheme to find my heart a substitute. But this was a House from Amberlight. There would be no more children like me. They would want—the whole room swam in fury—to hand down my heritage.

How did I manage not to rip that curtain apart, storm down the passage and rend Iatha, at least, limb from limb? Not that Tez was innocent. My sister, my surrogate mother, she was still the House-head. She would be complicit too.

I did find myself soundlessly and suddenly at Iatha's elbow, asking, with a hiss Two remembered as my father Alkhes' edge-of-killing voice, "Which bee should I take first?"

# CHAPTER XX

Iatha yelped and stumbled into incoherency. Tez, sharper as well as more candid, said only, "Oh, dear."

"Oh, dear, yes." I was still hissing. Two trembled at my very fingertips. "Do you have no favorites? Or did you just hope I'd breed, no matter who?"

They both yelled, "No!" And Iatha cried, "Chaeris, we never meant that!" with pain that needed no verifying. But Tez spoke with the lethal softness of her most deadly ripostes.

"Are you not of age, Chaeris?"

I stared back into her familiar, beloved, ruthless eyes. We both knew what she meant. I had claimed I was of age: I had used it, to shield Therkon. And a woman of age in an Amberlight House, especially a woman of Craft, might, would, if she had any sense of her importance, be looking, however leisurely, for a lover. A partner, perhaps a marriage alliance, but certainly, at some point, a child.

I gritted my teeth and answered, "Yes."

Iatha started to say something. Tez lifted a hand and she fell quiet.

"And do you have a woman in your eye?"

Around us the house smelt of people and food and woodsmoke, the prolonged winter froust. Someone, perhaps Ashar, who had a good ear, went whistling liquidly toward the outer door. Tez and I looked at each other, and it needed no words to reply.

Tez dropped her voice a little and asked almost gently, "Then what harm can it do to look?"

At the young men, she meant. The ones who were begging to be seen.

"If you wanted, had thought of a partner, we would thank the Mother. We would be grateful if you chose to stay alone." It was a choice even in the Crafts of Amberlight. "If," her brows knotted in a look of pain, "you were only happy in that choice."

"Oh, my dearling," Iatha broke in suddenly, sounding choked, and put both arms round me, "we don't care about children. We only want you to be *happy*. We just thought, if you had a choice . . ."

That if every bee thronged round me, I might forget the one I had already accepted. And agreed to give away.

"You're still so quiet. So sad."

My throat had shut. I hugged her back, convulsively, the smell and shape and presence old as memory. Impossible to wound further, when all they had wanted was my good.

"All right," I said, and tried not to sigh. "I'll look."

* * * *

For the rest of winter I dutifully walked, talked, ate, worked, played with young men, bore every version from crass to subtle of the attempts to impress, cajole, outright seduce me, or simply make themselves visible. I could have snubbed the eligibles, the mature young men who already had a trade, or even a Craft. I did not have the heart to rebuff the third sons of Iskardan families, or the Craftless House youths who knew their cause lost before it was begun. I could not bring myself to rank them all like horses in a market. But nor could I bear to manufacture passion from a spark of momentary pity, or of liking only well-enough.

And however I looked, not a spark of deeper feeling woke for any of them.

Nethor brought it to a head. We were riding back from Marbleport, the day before Spring Thanks, the festival my mother founded, in the first spring moon. It is really too early for a festival: the snow is just gone, the deciduous trees bare, ploughing just begun. Food is short and motley, and hardly any flowers are out except the crocuses. Nor do I know why it has to be exactly at the end of first quarter, but there it is.

Spring had suffered a change of heart as well, so we rode amid biting wind and showers if not actual snow. I told myself the greyness was purely the weather. That the leaden weariness that seemed to overhang me was just winter's usual tail. That the festival would raise my spirits, as it was designed to do.

Nethor was quiet too, though it was natural with him. Or so I thought, until we rode away from the last signal-station. In the temporary lee of the next hill, he said, "You all right, Chaeris?"

He was troublecrew. Companion, fighting partner, friend. I could tell the truth for once. I answered with one quick shrug. *No.*

He let the mules take another five paces. Then he asked, "Anything I can do?"

He was always calm, often he seemed almost casual. But this was too consciously easy. It rang in my ear, attuned to his inflections, like a cracked bell.

A signal, an appeal. An overture, of the most subtle, careful, precious sort. Nethor had never courted me, never shown the slightest sign of partiality. Now I knew otherwise.

And if it cracked both our hearts, still the most honorable response I could give him was the truth.

I looked at the muddied, raveled snow between the mule's ears, and sighed. And let him hear me sigh. He deserved the truth of that, more than anyone else in Iskarda.

"I don't think," I said, "there's anything anyone can do."

The mules leant into the next slope. We stood in the stirrups to help. As they grunted over the crest and he settled back in the saddle, Nethor answered quietly, "If there ever is, just let me know."

I had not cried for weeks, it seemed. The tears had finally dried and withered, lost, like almost all feeling, in this overmastering grey. But I did blink tears back before I could answer, almost whispering, "Thank you, Nethor."

\* \* \* \*

I was scrubbing saddle-oil from my riding trousers next morning when Asaskian came into the washing bay, Saarieq at her heels. Between them they sorted a load of children's gear, filled a boiling-copper, found wood and set it alight. You hardly noticed Asaskian's missing arm, except when she did such work. We exchanged day-greetings. But then Asaskian waved Saarieq upstairs, and settled herself like any lazing urchin on the steps.

"How are the bees?" she asked.

My every trouble-sense came alert. Iatha's hasty simile had become a private joke, but Asaskian rarely made jokes. I knew her best in council, a piercing critic if not a source of strategies, I was coming to know her in the House. Iatha might be Steward, but Asaskian actually ran our household, so smoothly you hardly noticed trouble's lack. And where Tez treated Tanekhet as a lover, House-mate, fellow strategist, Asaskian was the one who noticed, and took steps, when he had a cold or over-tired himself.

I thumped the current trouser leg harder and found a smile. "Oh—much the same."

In a moment she said, "Not going well?"

She had to be scouting, for the consort, for the House. I decided not to prevaricate.

"No."

She said nothing. I thumped harder at the trouser leg, until her sheer silence forced me to go on.

"Iatha—and Eria—even Tez—all hope I'll find someone. Like someone. But I can't." The silence impelled me on. "You can't *make* yourself like anyone! It doesn't work like that!"

Asaskian looked down at her remaining fingers, still slender and shapely as the rest of her. Still, despite the rise of a new generation, the beauty of Iskarda.

The memory of her own past nerved me to go further. "What did *you* do?"

She looked up. A glimpse of topaz Amberlight eyes in that perfect face. Acknowledging that she too had been courted, pressed, pestered to take a husband or partner. Then she answered, however cryptically, the question I had really asked.

"When it comes to the point," she said, "you must listen to your heart. No-one else."

"Oh!" I let the trousers slip back in the tub and just bit down a curse. *Don't feed me such pap*, I wanted to shout. I did manage to get out, "Don't mock me," not quite between my teeth.

She had weathered far worse tantrums than mine. Unflustered. "I listened," she said, "too."

Two gave me what history I did not already know. When with Iskarda at her feet she had chosen to love, and love without waver or substitute the most unsuitable man available, even in his own estimation. When she had fixed her choice on Tanekhet.

I fished the trousers out and muttered something that might have been apology.

"At whatever cost," Asaskian said.

I looked up, startled. She held my eyes and let me remember the rest. That she had wanted Tanekhet alone, and Tanekhet had wanted Tez alone. And then become involved with Keshaq when he despaired of winning Tez. Asaskian had only joined the consort afterward. She had never had Tanekhet wholly, completely, on her terms. But she had taken him on what terms she could get.

For an instant hope shifted my heart, as a fledgling rocks a hatching egg. Then I thought of Dhasdein. Of Tanekhet's warning. Even if I chose to be Therkon's mistress, Iskarda would never stand for it. It would be his death. Therkon himself had admitted he could not marry me. I saw the dark, elegant deer again, turning and turning in a net it could not, did not want, could not bring itself to break.

"For you, perhaps," I said. "Not for me."

Asaskian was quiet a moment. Then she said in her strategist's voice, "Are you quite, quite sure, this is the one? The only one?"

Two did not have to answer, I did not have to think. It was printed like flesh's map in every drop of my blood.

"It's impossible," I said.

I rolled the trousers over and slapped them on the tub-side. Water trickled down the drain. The copper fire muttered, and above it rose the first wisps of steam. I looked at the splattered floor, the dripping clothes, and the greyness seemed to close down as if it would swallow the rest of my life.

Asaskian got abruptly to her feet. "Then if there can be no other," she said, "and you cannot live without him, you should stop thinking why it cannot happen, and begin thinking how it could."

And she walked briskly up the stairs.

* * * *

I fumed at her smug certainty, her own successful vantage atop a love achieved. I spat her words out like bitter aloes twenty times a day. Loving Tanekhet had been a matter for compromise, a choice within her power. Loving Therkon was not an option, and winning him was a field where I could not prevail.

I fumed clear through Spring Thanks, and the horde of 'bees' who besieged me to dance, talk, eat supper with them. I was still fuming when moon-end came. And with it, the first of the covenanted five days in Marbleport.

Tez claimed, afterward, that it was better than she had feared. Most of the arrangements did work: the outer seines of customs and quay-watch, set this time to siphon off all but the most urgent petitioners, the people delegated to organize food and beds and latrines, the influx of outland night-watchmen and cooks and even apprentice troublecrew of sorts, who had already cost half Iskarda's yearly building funds. People surged into Marbleport from upRiver, downRiver, from both Riversides, and miraculously, the system channeled them where they had to go.

All I had to do was sit five days in an inn parlor, and bear the voracity of their need.

The very sieve that made the numbers manageable also ensured only the most desperate reached me. And the questions hardest on us both: what's wrong with my daughter, has my husband been drowned at sea, is my wife dying? Is there a remedy, an answer, a cure?

And sometimes, Two and I had to answer, No.

Worse were the ones to whom I could only say, "There is not enough data. We cannot See."

And then the reactions, the grief, the break-downs, simply watching the impact of the blow. Or, when I could not answer, the pleas, the demands. Sometimes, before troublecrew dragged them out, the actual abuse.

Worse again were the physical pleas: My children are starving, I can't redeem my debts. Can you give me money? Can you help? I need a place to live, my boat was sunk in a storm, I fell under a log in a timber-yard and lost my leg . . . Until I thought, listening to them, that my heart would break.

Because we could See possibilities and offer suggestions, but money, work, a place to live, the concrete help I ached to give, was impossible. Iskarda simply could not save them all. And I would not, could not bear to help some, but not all.

Was the worst the three barefaced swindlers who tried to cozen money out of me?

There, Caitha had to risk her own life and grab me because Two got out of hand. Not merely in disappointment at their cheapness, but in fury that they could so befoul our gift, I had let her wake the fire. And we would have struck the last one where he stood.

Of course that threw all Iskarda into consternation, not least because the whole River would now hear of my other gift. But on the fifth afternoon, when Duitho reported with grim pleasure that there had been a sudden decline in late petitioners, Tez grinned like a veritable wolf.

"Makes 'em think twice," she said, "that the Sight reads true for more than questions. And that the Seer bites."

I was too fraught and exhausted to think, let alone dispute. All I wanted was to get on a mule and flee, fast as hooves could carry me, from the din and the crowds and the guards, the tension, the threat of some mad or maddened attacker. And with every day, the accumulating memories. The faces. The questions. The answers. The hideous, unanticipated ordeal of the Sight.

When we were away at last, Marbleport and its compendium of distresses dwindling amid a prospect of unpeopled hills and remembered trees, the wide rampart of the Iskans rising like sanctuary ahead, I said it first to Tez, riding close beside me.

"I don't think," I said, mostly to my saddlebow, "I can bear to do that again."

I felt her shoot me one stabbing Head's glance. But she did not burst out in the obvious, callous protests, I had a gift, I had contracted to use it, I could not deny people who knew about it and needed it. Or, far more compellingly, that I had opened the box of horrors. They would not stop coming. Whether I could bear it or not.

Or clinching closure, *You have to go on. To protect Iskarda.*

What she did say, as quietly as I, was, "There'll be no more liars."

Then, before I could react, "This will have been the worst. Because we had to favor the really bad ones, and there will have been a build-up. And because you've made your own protection. Before they come asking now, a lot of people will think twice."

Hard, Head's consolation. Taking the unarguable premise, that I had to go on, as read.

I leant both hands on the mule's neck. Her hand came out to clasp on mine.

"We'll cut the days back. Four, at most." Five days had literally drained me. That, too, she knew. "And filter tighter. Troublecrew right in with you." To silence protest or abuse at the start. "Make it clear that if you *can* See, what you See is the truth. Not for negotiation. Not your fault. If they're not prepared to accept that, they don't get in at all."

I could hear the strain in her voice now, too. She had overseen the entire operation, as complicated and stressful as any war initiative. And had to watch what it did to her sister, her surrogate daughter, the core, for the last twelve years, of every concern for Iskarda.

"For the rest, we'll set up some kind of, hmm, assistance." A snort. "We'll levy the River." The River's rulers, she meant. "They'll all be here next round: Verrain, Mel'eth, Shirran. Cataract. The assembly." Of Amberlight. "Half the land-mayors in Verrain, half the tribe-leaders in Quetzistan." She did not add, Dhasdein's own overlords. "Half the Isles after them, I shouldn't wonder. You don't work for pay. But if they want your Sight, from now on, they put in for their own people. Let the ones on top pay back to the ones underneath."

Oh, Mother, I thought, as Two's seven hundred years of illusionless memory unrolled before me. Did she have any idea of the corruption, the deceit, the outright swindling, on both sides, that such a charity would breed? Of the monstrous size to which it might grow? How could Iskarda, which all but exhausted itself organizing this one month's convulsion, sustain such a thing?

Iskarda would not have to: Two told me that, a moment before the Sight. If we chose to help the ones the Sight could not aid, we could draw people from the same place as the money. From the River nations. From another, handier, less corruptible source.

"Maybe, some of the people who need help could stay. Could work?"

Tez's hand jumped on mine. I heard her splutter, and then she hugged me, yanking our mounts together for a moment, laughing it in my ear.

"Mother's eyes, Chaeris, you don't *need* a Sight!"

\* \* \* \*

I took that gratitude and delight and belief to bed with me. I told myself, as thought faded in sleep, that after this it would be all right. When Duitho flatly ordered me to rest a day before I tried another workout, I slouched off to breakfast, telling myself food would right matters. Before I drained the first cup of coffee, I knew that as a lie.

In my heart I could feel, as perhaps a sufferer identifies incurable illness, that this greyness leaching the world was no simple exhaustion, of body or of spirit. You have not been well, my own insight told me piercingly, since you left Grinsey. It would take more than sleep or food to exorcise this.

I set the cup down and said, "I'm going to the lookout." Iatha, Tez, Tanekhet looked up with quick anxiety. But it was a traditional remedy, after all. Asaskian gave me one brief scrutiny and waved her hand. *Go.*

The trees were leafing out at last, hillsides brilliant above little pink legumes and the last spidery white cluster-lilies in the reviving grass. The air played round me, crisp with morning as well as the season, blending flower-scents into a breathtaking waft of new-turned soil. In the upper field, they were working the plough-team. I waved and scooted impenitently by. My turn would come soon enough.

The lookout boulders sat dappled cream and silver beneath the chartreuse and lime of new-leafed helliens. And at the qherrique's feet the grape-blue mountain hyacinths were again in flower.

The qherrique had grown too. The boss was now wider than my arms would reach. Already it had wakened, was beginning to glow. I came as to a mother's embrace, laying both hands on the stone.

However long after, I detached myself, tenderly as a lover, and stood back. There had been rapport, and welcome, and healing comfort. The greyness had lifted a little. But now I was back in the world.

And however long I stood here, or dallied in the lookout, eventually I would have to go back down to Iskarda. To the rest of the day.

I looked into the pearl-depths of the qherrique, and the question looked out at me: *Is this how you want to spend the rest of your life?*

An endless dwindling vista of obligation, labor, duty. Using the Sight. Working with whatever enormity came into being at Marbleport. Taking a lover, a husband, a partner, perhaps. Having children. Pretending there was love. All of it hollow as an ant-eaten tree. At the core, emptiness.

*I can't do it,* I said. *I can't do it like this.*

Logic and duty answered remorselessly. *You have been given a gift. You cannot refuse to use it. You cannot give it back.*

I put my elbows down on the qherrique and rested my forehead between them. *I can't do it,* I insisted wearily, *like this.*

But what could I do otherwise?

I opened my eyes into the grey shadows of the qherrique and knew with a certainty that came not from the Sight, but from the heart.

I wanted Therkon. I *needed* Therkon. Not just for pleasure, or even love, but the way trees need water or cattle need grass. No matter the barriers or the problems or the costs. I had to have him. If I had Therkon, I could deal with the rest of this. For the rest of my life.

Logic repeated, stupid, stubborn, obdurate. *You can't have Therkon. It's impossible.*

*Then stop thinking why it cannot happen, and begin thinking how it could.*

\* \* \* \*

Two rapped it at me, almost as tartly as Asaskian. I actually jerked upright from the shock.

Then I stood gaping at the rocks while solid matter parted, windows opened, vision and resolution pouring themselves like lava into the gap.

Nothing but death is impossible to change. You only have to change how you see.

I turned my eyes inward, and answered Two. I said, *Show me how.*

Seven hundred years of history, all the past of Amberlight. Every possible variation on every possible love-tie, every possible impossibility, and how it had been solved. Two had stored them all. We had the present too, all the data for that present, and the function of extrapolation. Put them together, and you have the Sight.

And now it was a matter of How, no longer a query on what I wanted or needed, we Saw.

I sat down on the hyacinths, plump. My back came up against the qherrique, thump, as vision drove every vestige of breath from my lungs.

Before I lurched to my feet like a newborn foal and just managed not to dance round the qherrique whooping and skirling and waving both arms in the air, howling at the top of my voice, "Yes! *Yes!* YES!"

The sun was in the rock-bay, dazzling as the light over Hringstenn's stones. The qherrique was glowing like a lighthouse, but it was nothing to the brilliance in my heart. I could have lifted off the ground on it, spread my arms like wings and sailed over the Iskans, weightless with joy.

I stopped at last and stood puffing, grinning all over my face. It was all so easy, so obvious, there would be obstacles but nothing unsurmountable. Nothing was impossible now. I had only to walk back down into Iskarda and begin.

I patted the qherrique as if it were a friend's shoulder, a beloved child. Turned toward the bay's entry. And stopped.

Someone was coming through the rocks.

Troublecrew reflex froze my feet. My right hand slid to the wrist-sheath. Half my mind chortled that nobody could harm me now, I was invincible. The other half was firing Azo's drills at me, trying to identify the step.

Not a woman's stride. Not a child's, like Saarieq. Not a man's I knew, of the two or three who would dare, want, have the right to come in here. Not . . .

He stepped out from among the stones.

He was wearing his clothes from the Isles: the boots were scuffed and dusty, the trousers crumpled, the shirt had not been washed for a week. The coat-arms were tied scruffily round his neck. His cloak had been bundled over the pack straps, and he had just pulled off a disreputable straw Korite hat. He had not shaved for a week, either. The stubble made him look a veritable Quezistani bandit, and his hair had been yanked summarily back, showing his face drawn, tired as it had been in Grinsey, the mouth tight, brows clenched in a frown. Over all lay the wariness of a man who travels alone, who has encountered trouble. And has learnt he must deal with it for himself.

But if the groomed gaudy Dragonfly had vanished, the striking bones remained, the eyes, the narrow, graceful body. Stepping out into my sunlight, nervous, wary, tentative. Yet still elegant and cautious as some dark, beautiful deer.

Then he must have made out my features against the glow of the qherrique. His eyes flew wide open. The mask shattered and joy burst like a sun-shower all over his face.

"Chaeris!"

He dropped the hat and rushed and I flew straight into his arms.

We stopped kissing, eventually. Eventually, I could let him draw back an inch or so, so I could look up in his face. Move beyond the tangible reality, the dear recovered shape of him, and doubtless return a stare as besotted as the one he was giving me.

"But what, what, *what* are you doing here?"

He laughed down at me. Not aloud, but in a way I had never seen before. This silent mirth was the visible sign of irrepressible joy. Of something else, that might have been mischief. Even a hint of wickedness.

He said, "I ran away."

"You did *what?*"

"I found these," he glanced down at his sleeve, "in some chest. Put them in the pack. Wrapped the pack in the cloak . . . I couldn't bring Hvestang." He sounded almost apologetic. He was also, I realized, talking like some dock-worker out of Riversrun. "It wouldn't fit. Then I sent a message to—my mother. Told my secretary I was going to the Sea-forts. Told Hurid, my troublecrew leader, to carry the bundle for me. To the Mel'ethi."

"The—the—"

"The delegation. Shoshen's envoys . . . You didn't know?" He gripped me suddenly by the shoulders and I went dizzy at the brilliance of that smile. "My sweet oracle, you mean you sent those Mel'ethi all that way downRiver to me, and your intelligencers didn't. Even. Know?"

He was kissing me between words as if he could not help himself. I kissed him back, breathless, laughing, until we both managed to regain sense.

"No, I didn't know! *I* didn't send them, either, don't plume yourself! The Sight told them." But he would know that. "I wasn't even sure they'd go. I only hoped. But. I see why the clothes, the message, the messages—but why the Mel'ethi?"

"Because, adorable damis, I needed dates."

"Dates?"

"I've baffled Two," he said with immense satisfaction. "At last."

"D . . . d . . . Huh! They were strangers so they wouldn't give you away and nobody could blame them afterwards. And you could make what's-his-name stop outside their suite, and I bet—I bet they had some sort of outside door."

He winded me with a hug of approval. "But the dates?"

"I don't—we don't—blight and blast, that isn't fair! Wait: you were coming upRiver and you still had the last finghend, didn't you? So you could buy passage but you needed an excuse. A reason to travel. No, wait, not just travel, to get ashore at Marbleport without being headed off as a questioner, and reach Iskarda—oh! Oh, Mother! You've been peddling *dates?*"

He beat my back heartily until I recovered breath. "I see nothing funny," he announced, in well counterfeited huff. "I noticed their samples. The closest, most expensive wares I could find. And I learnt how to chaffer," he actually smirked, "watching you."

I hiccupped, and leant back in his grasp. Then I remembered. "I *told* them dates would be good trade!"

That time he had to lean on me. It isn't so very funny, I told myself, it's just that I'm so delirious, so happy, I can't stop laughing. We can't stop.

"So you got clear out of Riversend—"

"They smuggled me," he said with satisfaction. "I told them it was a secret mission I could trust to nobody else. Then I dressed, and packed the dates, and they paid a visit to their consulate. Just adding another ruffian to Sitha's train."

"And of course we've heard nothing. Oh, Mother, the palace—Riversend must be going crazy. And your mother." I stopped laughing, though I still had to keep good hold of him. "Therkon, what will your mother say?"

"I don't know yet." He had half-sobered too. "I told her I was going away. Not to worry, no matter what happened. That she was perfectly capable of managing without me, as she had for the, the last six months. In any case, it's her own fault."

"What's her own—?"

I stopped laughing altogether. I even reached up and pulled his head forward by the rascally loose tail of hair. Suddenly the bliss was qualified.

"Therkon. *What* are you doing here?"

His joy had vanished too. He looked tired, harassed, and dispirited as on that night in Grinsey.

"I tried to do my—duty, Chaeris. I did try. I thought I could manage, once you, you were safe. At home. Beginning to use your Sight." He hugged me suddenly, almost convulsively. "I did, I did think, at first, with Mel'eth . . . No. At first, I did *hope*." That it had been a signal, as I feared. He looked down at me, his face suddenly naked. "But I knew, in my heart, it was not so. And then. I knew too, you would remember—everything. But I, no matter how I tried . . . I was beginning to forget."

It was my turn to hug him to strangling point. The one thing I had not, did not, should have remembered. Two's memory, that had come at times to seem almost a curse. But I had told him about it, and he was only human. Which is worse, to remember when you wish otherwise, or to have no choice when you forget?

He leant his face lightly into my hair.

"I told myself, it was impossible. I could never marry you. I would never make you my mistress. Even if you ever would." Oh, that Dhasdeini honor. I tried not to sigh. "And now I, you, we were both chained in responsibilities. I told myself that I had to forget."

He broke off and took a sharp little breath. Then he reburied his face. "So," he said into my hair, "when the council began hinting, suggesting, saying—"

"That you ought to marry," I supplied.

He made a muffled sound. Then, more strongly, "When they said you were gathering young men. When I knew you had begun to look."

"Oh, clythx." I could say that aloud now. "None of them ever mattered. I told the House so. Didn't your intelligencers pick up *that*?"

He made another noise. *No.* And, *Would it have mattered?* When, I could extrapolate the rest all too well, the blade of possibility was already in his heart?

"If you knew how I used to cringe, every time we got down-River intelligence."

"Did you?" He kissed me, a sunflower revived. "Did you truly?" He beamed at me, fatuously as I was undoubtedly beaming at him.

Then he sighed, the brilliance snuffed. Shut his eyes, and leant his cheek to mine, like a man come from bitter cold to the sanctuary of temporary, impermanent fire.

"So." I cleared my throat. "They found her, didn't they? The lord's daughter? Out of Riversrun?"

He lifted his face, and stared past me at the qherrique.

"They found her," he answered bleakly, "and she was perfectly groomed, perfectly trained, perfectly—amiable. An ideal empress."

"Amiable." I wanted to hate her, but pity was expelling all else. "Therkon, did you—how—" but there was no tactful way to say it. "How far did it go?"

He took my face in both hands and looked carefully in my eyes. Satisfied, apparently, that this was not jealousy, he gave a little nod. "I never slept with her. I never, I tried never to, to attach her. You know what I mean?"

"To court her, honestly? Not just for show?"

"Yes. That. I never did that. But. I kept telling myself, it had to be done. I couldn't have you, that was impossible. I had to do my duty, and remember Dhasdein."

I shuddered. How had we escaped, when we had both been so mindful of our shackles, when disaster had been a day, a breath away?

I said, "Asaskian told me, If the one I wanted was the only one, I should stop thinking why it couldn't happen, and start thinking how it might."

At his startled half-laugh I understood. I said, "Who did it for you?"

He put both hands on my shoulders, looking down, grave now, into my face.

"I might really have done it," he said, slowly. "I might have deluded myself so far. But one night when we dined together, my mother said to me, 'Are you sure? Is this really what you want?'"

His mother. The Empress, who had served the qherrique. Who loved him, I knew with bone-deep certainty, far more for himself than for whatever role he might fill for Dhasdein.

"I went back to my rooms, and the moon was coming up." He glanced back down at me, again almost smiling. "Second winter moon. Two days past full."

I had taught him to keep moon-time. In the Isles.

"The next night, it was intended—it had been planned—that I should—propose."

I felt a shiver go through me from head to foot. He nodded, and himself took a firmer grip.

"But the moon looked at me through the window, and something, someone said, *Your own life is your business. But will you ruin two others as well?*"

I leant my forehead into his throat, and said silently, *Mother, I owe you a mule-load of candles. Whether that was You or not.*

His hands drew my face up again. He gazed unsmiling into my eyes.

"It made me think of Tanekhet. Whose real love—died. Who married twice after and was never happy. The moon said, *His love died. Yours has not.*"

I caught my breath. He gave me a short unsmiling nod.

"I knew then, yes. That I could not go on with the . . . other. And I understood. Not what I wanted: what I had to have. What I truly could not live without."

He smiled a little, with one side of his mouth.

"So, like you," he was trying for lightness, "I forgot about saying why not, and began thinking how."

"Yes. Oh, yes." The plan of escape, the trip upRiver, how he had not only passed Marbleport but come all the way to me. "But. Wait one moment. How did you get *into* Iskarda? We are supposed to have *some* guard posts. And how did you know to come up here?"

"Ah." I felt him shift his weight. The way he had, the very first time we met. "The road-guards were simple." He dropped into a thicker River accent. "I gotta commission, I'm on hire! I brung these poxy fruit all the way from Riversend 'cos the paymaster says, There's a mark'll buy every spoonful you can haul. Up there. Sunset, Tankard, something. I've drug 'em three weeks upRiver, lady. Have a heart, don't stop me now!"

"Oh, you—fox! Just like Jurrick." He pretended to preen himself. "But how did you get up here?"

The foolery dropped away. "I was in the street. By the fountain. Trying to think which would be the, the House. And this woman came past. The most beautiful woman I ever saw in my life."

My breath stuck. I could just whisper, "Go on."

"She took one look at me and stopped dead. Then she said, 'You're from Riversend'."

He pulled a face. "I thought it was all over. I tried whining, talking harder. When I got to 'Sunset' she held up her hand. I think—really, I think she was trying not to laugh. She said, 'You don't need him.' She pointed up the hill. 'Up there is the one you want'."

I was trying not to gasp like a fish. "Oh, my—oh, Mother. She—what did you say?"

He looked rueful. "I never had to say anything. Someone was coming past. I think, maybe, troublecrew. She gave her this, look. And said, 'Set our guest on his way to the look-out, Duitho'."

Somebody seemed to have punched me under the ribs. I managed to exhale an, "And—?"

"And Duitho showed me the hill track, and I tried not to let her see I knew it. And she never said a word."

"Oh. Oh." The earth was wobbling under me. He had been intercepted, recognized beyond all doubt, and passed. Sent straight to me. By Iskarda's Trouble-head, and . . .

"Who *was* she, Chaeris?" He had me by both elbows. "The beautiful one. Why did she—how could she—"

"Because she knows all about it. Because she's the one who," I managed a steadying breath. "That was Asaskian."

And how was she so opportunely in the street, who hardly ever left the house, and how did Duitho happen to be there as well? Wheels within wheels turned before me, how and what had either of them known or guessed, and who, who, or was it Who, had concatenated all this timing so finely, down to the very hour, the very minute?

Two answered silently, *Not me.*

Therkon's own jaw had dropped. "That was Asaskian?"

"They know." I tried frenziedly not to blush. "She knows who you are."

"They know who I am? They—!"

"If they'd meant to stop you, it would have happened. No. I think. I think they know. They all know. What's happening up here." I held onto him as my head spun out of all control. "I think—"

It was he who said the rest for me. He sounded almost as winded as I felt.

"You think, they *want* this?"

"Asaskian said, think how to make it happen. Iatha said, we just want you to be happy." I did not need Two. The logic was inescapable. "I think. I think . . . Yes."

There was a moment of almost complete quiet. Then he said, hushed to awe, "Merciful Dhe."

We must have stood a good half minute, staring, like a pair of moonstruck sheep. But then he physically shook himself, and blinked, and managed a sort of laugh, before he reached for me as if he needed a prop to hold him up.

"Oh, Chaeris." He breathed it against my cheek. "If that's so . . . really so . . ."

I opened my eyes and rocks came into focus. The qherrique, still glowing brighter than a lamp. Hyacinths, crushed or intact, purple-black in the qherrique's shade. Time re-assembled too. Coherent again, chaining moments together. Back to what his own words had implied before this earthquake intervened. Forward into the future I had Seen.

My breath stopped. I could hardly get out the words.

"You said. You started thinking, How."

It took him only a second to catch up. Then he nodded, watching my face. Now the solemnity lightened, hinting a first glimmer of smile.

"Coming upRiver, there was time to think. Too much time to think. To wonder if—I was already too late."

I nodded. I had known that feeling far too well.

"And in one of the Quetzistani towns, a storyman, a saga teller, was performing. On the wharf." The smile had brightened, a little conscious, ever so slightly tentative, but now his whole face lit. "Chaeris, do you know what he sang?"

I did not even have to think. "Skalr's Tale."

He laughed aloud. "Skalr's Tale. I was listening to a saga, in a saga-pattern: the tale told before the hidden hero. And I was in the saga myself."

I hugged him like a best beloved child. I was so happy to hear that candid, philosopher's delight.

"It really is like the sagas. The prince who ran away."

"Ah." He looked down, and cleared his throat. "To be truthful, beloved. Not quite."

He looked back to me. Therkon's bronze-dark eyes, softer, warmer than I had ever seen them. And now all but fearful, lest, at the last, I blight his culminating hope.

"After the storyman, I was still thinking. About the tale. The Mother, and Tiran. What it means. That everything has to be balance. Alternation. And I suddenly thought . . ."

I could not breathe at all.

"Neither of us can go only one way. To Iskarda, or to Dhasdein. But we *can* be together. I don't care how we do it, we can be married or not, partners or a consort or whatever they have here. But we can be the Seer, and the emperor. We just have to balance. Six months of the year here. And six months in Dhasdein."

"Oh—!" I flung both arms round his neck and jumped right off the ground, if it had not been imperative to hold him so tight I would have turned cartwheels like novice troublecrew showing off. "Oh, yes! It works, it works!"

He staggered and grabbed to hold me up. He had gasped at the impact, but now he hissed in my ear, wickedly, "If you just put those legs round my waist . . ." I squeaked mock-horror, remembering Grinsey for myself.

Then I set foot to earth again, and he let me stand on my own feet. He was looking more like a peacock than a peddler. Or even a crown prince.

"I did think," he remarked complacently, "it was quite a good idea. Dhasdein will raise all sorts of objections, I cannot be away another six months, let alone yearly, there must be a legitimate heir—"

I cupped his face in both hands and kissed him and said, "Clythx. Caissyl. Heart's heart. Shut up."

"What do you mean, shut—"

"Just before you came out of those rocks, do you know what we Saw?"

He stared at me, but my face was signal enough. He raised his brows.

"The Mother." Laughter was bubbling up in me, the way joy had outside that Grinsey room. "We Saw the Mother, and Tiran. Balance. Alternation. Half the year for each."

For an instant I saw the expression with which he heard me say we had been the vessels of gods. Then he whispered, "Oh, Dhe."

I knew what had stunned him: not the solution, but the correlation. That we had both seen the selfsame thing. That our connection had worked.

He grabbed me up again then and spun me round and round with my feet flying out like a child's. He was laughing. We were both laughing, until we ran out of breath. The sun shone on us, even in the shadow of the rocks.

"Oh, Chaeris . . . ."

"We can. We really can." I was dizzy with joy to the point of insanity. It was not impossible. We could love each other, we could be together, for the rest of our lives.

"*And the children.*" Two had suddenly begun projecting too. "*Girls come here. If there are boys, they go to Dhasdein.*"

His mouth fell half-open. Sounding abruptly stifled, he said, "Chaeris, you are not—?"

"Not yet, no. In Grinsey, I was past the moon-time—but you knew that. You asked if it was my courses, next day." Sudden understanding almost winded me. "*You* were keeping count!"

"It isn't that hard." He looked embarrassed, but not for any reason that would apply with other men. "It was, was something I could do."

Be aware of a woman's cycle, and try to help with its difficult parts, in any way he could. And if I actually had conceived . . .

He had tightened his grip again, now sounding almost dour. "If you *had* conceived, I would have been here before winter. And I would have married you. Then and there. Whatever anyone said."

Dhasdein honor. Dhasdein morality. Always, Dhasdein intelligencers.

"I see." I tried very hard to sound affronted. "Whatever *I* said, either?"

"You've had your say." He was smiling at me, no longer in the exuberance of joy, but from a deep, deep well of tenderness. "The pair of you. Now we just have to decide exactly how—"

"Wait. Wait." I held him back, both hands on his chest. Warm, solid bone and muscle, reality, no longer impossible, no longer only to be yearned for. But suddenly the full sense of that "exactly" loomed, daunting as another five days in Marbleport.

"Therkon, have you really thought? Do you understand? About the Sight? I have to go on with it. I won't be able to stop. There are so many people. But it's so big, so hard to manage, so—"

He drew me close this time with fierce protectiveness. "We'll deal with that. Dhasdein has the funds, the people, we can make the space. In Riversend," his arms tightened, "nobody will ever trouble you more than they need. Ever again."

He had come through Marbleport. He had picked up for himself the wake of those five days' pain and grief, disappointment, deceit, abuse. He would see, with more than altruistic interest, that it was never so bad again.

I leant my head against him and let myself sigh. No quibbles, no conditions: he would accept my obligations as he had his own. And no more fear of draining Iskarda's resources. Whatever could be done for me, and for those who needed me, Dhasdein would do.

But for those who needed more?

"What is it, beloved?"

My body had transmitted far too much. But I could not hedge with him, ever. Least of all now.

"Tez. Tez said. Blight it, I feel like a dowry-hunter—"

That brought his full-chested laugh. "Gods, how I've missed you, Chaeris! But what about Tez?"

"I'm pleased to amuse you. But, in Marbleport, there were people who needed more than a Sight. People with a boat sunk, or hurt too badly to work. Debts they couldn't meet. Maybe they'll have to sell children." We both shuddered. "All I could say was, *I can give you advice.*"

His hands tightened again. He felt for me, at least. "And Tez?"

"Tez said, So you don't charge for Sights. We'll levy the River instead. We'll make the lords and rulers help their own people. Pay for them. Pay them back."

He went absolutely still. Then he let out a long, long sigh.

"Chaeris. My lady." He took both my hands and kissed them, one by one. "Tanekhet called your mother a world-shaper. I see it runs in the blood."

I stared up at him, still too nervous to ask aloud.

"I thought, once, you wanted me to make a revolution to match Verrain's. I could not do that. But Tez. Tez thinks the same way. And this." He drew in a long, long breath. "*This*, we can do."

"Truly?" I hardly dared to ask. "We can? You will?"

"*We* will." The warmth in those bronze-dark eyes was dizzying, but the joy reached beyond my relief. He was looking into his own future. His own chance to be a revolutionary.

"Dhasdein will pay. Dhasdein will make others pay. And we will try not to let it founder between officials and bribery on one side and swindlers and lies on the other. This one time, perhaps . . ."

He might not have seven hundred years' memory, but he had grown up with Riversend officialdom.

"I thought," I hazarded, "we could use the people who come asking for help." He began to nod. "They'd be willing. And less likely to cheat."

"And then there is you." He took the words out of my mouth. "Perhaps you cannot test them all, but knowing that you might. That could be enough."

"Yes. Yes!" I won't mind Seeing, I thought, if it's Seeing like this, if it can end in physical help. If I have you beside me, perhaps I can even bear the ones I can't help at all. "Oh, clythx!" I threw both arms round his neck. "I can do that. Yes! Oh, Mother, yes! Come on, let's go!"

I caught his hand to pull him with me and he snatched my wrist. "One moment, damis!" His mouth was smiling but his eyes had gone suddenly serious.

"What then?" I was dancing to be away.

"Chaeris." The smile went altogether. "Chaeris," he said abruptly. "Are you sure?"

"Sure?"

"I'm thirty-five. Twice, more than twice your age. It may not matter now. But when you're a woman in your prime, and I am— an old man. When you're left with a husband tied to a sick-room, only fit to swallow possets, and, and hobble round on a stick. Will it matter then?"

"Oh. Caissyl." My throat shut in my own turn for fierce protectiveness. A vision flashed before me, Asaskian, warding, watching over Tanekhet. Then Two showed me the other side of the coin.

"Are *you* sure?" I said.

He looked blank.

"I'm thirteen now, and I look seventeen. The qherrique, I think the qherrique made me grow so fast. But how if it doesn't stop? We don't know anything about—people like me. There is no-one else like me. I could keep on growing, living, at this pace. Always. And if I do . . ."

Then who was to say my lifespan would not be half of his? That I might even die before him?

He had gone almost white. Now he hauled me to him and clenched both arms round me as if he could stop time and possibility with mere human flesh. "Chaeris. Oh, gods, Chaeris."

His grip eased eventually. I leant back far enough to see his face, to meet his eyes.

"So are *you* sure, clythx?"

He swallowed hard. Then he said hoarsely but fiercely, "Yes."

He shut his hands to frame my face and said the rest even more fiercely, full into my eyes. "I've missed too much already. I'll have whatever there is to have. As much as there is. Whatever it costs."

I looked into his face and saw the new world, our world, beginning. As for a Sight, Two merged it with words out of the past.

"Ye've a road ahead, aye, a fair and clear one, but t'is long and twisty, too, as a skein of wool. And t'will end where you wish, but not where you expect that wish to be."

Therkon looked his, What? I said, "That was what Nouip told me. When I asked her to See. About us."

As always, he understood. His eyes lit. "*That* was what you meant, when—"

"On *Seony*, yes." On the stern deck, when I had wondered at his being crestfallen, after I claimed to have asked and had no answer about my road home.

He leant back a little, as if to see me better, and then he smiled. Not a just description, of that look. "I think she Saw true. Or should I ask again?"

I opened my mouth, and we did it. We too Saw.

"Chaeris?"

A long road, yes, but not one that ended here, or even in transforming the River, or with children. Or with being a Seer. Or an emperor.

"You know about, about my mother and fathers. Don't you?"

His face sobered again. He gave a silent nod. DownRiver, how must he have longed to receive, welcomed, dwelt over every morsel of his Dhasdein intelligence?

I twined my fingers in the fastening of his shirt. "And what . . . the letter said?"

He did not deny it. Just asked softly, "Which part?"

Two naturally had it pat. *"One day, I so hope, you will make another journey. We will look up the track for travelers and find none so welcome, my dearling. You, and whoever you may bring."*

My voice died away and the rock bay, the hillside, all of the Iskans was suddenly lapped in total hush. Then Therkon lifted his hand and closed it over mine.

"Chaeris?" I could feel his heart quicken under my knuckles. When he spoke again he sounded almost like a little boy. "You mean me? As well?"

"Oh, caissyl." I stood on tiptoe and kissed his mouth. "Would I go anywhere, any more, without you?"

He drew in a long, almost trembling breath. His eyes glowed, gazing at me, through me, at a vista he must have longed for, dreamed of, and silently, uncomplainingly renounced. Not merely of leaving the Empire, of undoing the shackles of rulership. Or even of seeing as far as, perhaps, beyond the Source.

I saw the dark beautiful deer lift its head and stop its turning. And then step, delicately, decisively, through, out, beyond the nets.

Then he pressed my fingers fiercely to his lips and caught my other hand between us. "Then, if even *they* say, Yes . . ."

We were close again, close enough to feel his warmth in the shadow, to smell dust and his own body odor and sweat and dirty clothes. His eyes were locked with mine, holding me tighter than his hands. I felt the air change, purpose informing it, as thunder charges the air before a lightning strike.

Before I had even started to respond, Two said, *"Yes."*

"Oh—!" I caught up then. "Two, shut up! Shut *up!*"

Therkon had looked momentarily startled, but it was already past. I could feel the blush, foolish, uncontrollable, but he ignored that too. He let my hands go, but he did not step back. His face, so close to mine, was utterly serious.

"Two says, Yes. Iskarda. It seems Iskarda says, Yes. The moon, whichever way it matters, says, Yes. *They* say, Yes . . ." I knew the slight tremble in that familiar, that beloved voice. "What do *you* say, Chaeris?"

I, in myself, for myself, sole and separate. Not Two's other, or the hope of Iskarda, or the Seer or my parents' daughter or maybe, someday, the empress of Dhasdein. Not even his beloved. I, as he had seen me, as no-one else had ever seen me, the first time we met. Chaeris, nothing and no-one more.

The joy swelled up like its own form of thunder, and I knew its reply. I, I wanted him as fiercely, as passionately as I had that night on Grinsey. Mine, my heart said, but no longer just storing memories. Emperor, hero, hatchet man, philosopher, any or all of them, no matter. Mine.

"Keep Two," I said, "out of this." I held out my hands. "This is *my* answer. And *I* say, Yes."

He took a deep breath, and looked full in my face, and I could read his thoughts. Then he made a little snort through his teeth and pulled me into him and kissed me, full on the mouth.

I wrapped both arms around him, fiercely tight. Then I pressed up in his grasp and kissed him back, and felt our flesh, our blood, our wills and vision fuse, past, present, future, all in harmony, now and here, at last.

And for a long time after that, none of us talked at all.